Dear Reader:

We were delighted that the folks at Waldenbooks asked us to participate in their Romance Club membership drive by preparing four special books, each containing two previously published *LOVESWEPT* romances from favorite authors. Of course, we are pleased to be reissuing these marvelous love stories ... but we are especially pleased to be doing so because of the wonderful support you and the people behind the scenes at the Romance Club have given to our authors in particular and to our *LOVESWEPT* line in general.

Why not use these special editions with their twin tales to introduce a friend to the *LOVESWEPT* line and to the Waldenbooks Romance Club? Everyone would benefit ... and I can assure you that we would be most grateful!

We certainly hope you enjoy these old favorites.

Warm regards from everyone at *LOVESWEPT*,

Sincerely,

Carolyn Nichols

Carolyn Nichols

Bantam Books by Iris Johansen
Ask your bookseller for the titles you have missed.

WHAT ARE *LOVESWEPT* ROMANCES?

They are stories of true romance and touching emotion. We believe those two very important ingredients are constants in our highly sensual and very believable stories in the *LOVESWEPT* line. Our goal is to give you, the reader, stories of consistently high quality that may sometimes make you laugh, sometimes make you cry, but are always fresh and creative and contain many delightful surprises within their pages.

Most romance fans read an enormous number of books. Those they truly love, they keep. Others may be traded with friends and soon forgotten. We hope that each *LOVESWEPT* romance will be a treasure—a "keeper." We will always try to publish

*LOVE STORIES YOU'LL NEVER FORGET
BY AUTHORS YOU'LL ALWAYS REMEMBER*

The Editors

LOVESWEPT SPECIAL

TWO GREAT ROMANCES IN ONE VOLUME

Iris Johansen

The Golden Valkyrie
- **previously published as Loveswept #31**

The Trustworthy Redhead
- **previously published as Loveswept #35**

BANTAM BOOKS
TORONTO • NEW YORK • LONDON • SYDNEY • AUCKLAND

THE GOLDEN VALKYRIE
THE TRUSTWORTHY REDHEAD
A Bantam Book / September 1986

The Golden Valkyrie *was first published in February 1984.*
The Trustworthy Redhead *was first published in March 1984.*

LOVESWEPT and the wave device are registered
*trademarks of Bantam Books, Inc. Registered in U.S. Patent
and Trademark Office and elsewhere.*

ISBN 0-553-21803-4

*Bantam Books are published by Bantam Books, Inc. Its
trademark, consisting of the words "Bantam Books" and
the portrayal of a rooster, is Registered in U.S. Patent and
Trademark Office and in other countries. Marca Registrada.
Bantam Books, Inc., 666 Fifth Avenue, New York, New
York 10103.*

PRINTED IN THE UNITED STATES OF AMERICA

O   0 9 8 7 6 5 4 3 2 1

The Golden Valkyrie

(Previously published as Loveswept #31)

One

"Raphael will be waiting for you in the alley behind the hotel," Nancy Rodriguez said briskly as she deftly maneuvered the Toyota through Houston's heavy early-evening traffic. "If the coast is clear, he'll take you right up to the suite and let you in with a passkey." She grimaced. "If not, you're on your own, Honey."

"Fine," Honey Winston said absently, anchoring a strand of white-gold hair firmly back away from her face with a hairpin.

"Fine!" Nancy exclaimed, shooting her a glance of intense exasperation. "*Caramba!* You're crazy, do you know that? If they catch you, the least they'll do is take away your license. They might even throw you in jail." She tapped the folded newspaper lying between them on the seat. "The mayor is really rolling out the red carpet for Prince Rubinoff and his cousin. He's not going to be at all pleased if you provoke any unpleasant publicity."

A frown creased Honey's brow. "Even royalty has no right to behave as unscrupulously and heartlessly as he has," Honey said indignantly. "That poor woman was almost beside herself."

"That 'poor' woman is heiress to a coffee plantation the approximate size of Ecuador," Nancy said dryly. "And if you ask me, Señora Gomez appeared just a little *too* upset."

"How can you say that?" Honey asked with a frown, "She was crying as if her heart were breaking."

"And you melted, as usual." Nancy sighed, her dark eyes affectionate. "Didn't anyone ever tell you that private detectives are supposed to be hard-boiled?"

"My secretary is at me constantly about that very thing." Honey grinned teasingly, her blue eyes twinkling. "But how can I believe her, when she's such a marshmallow herself?"

"Marshmallow!" Nancy squeaked. "Me?"

"You," Honey affirmed. "You wouldn't even take a salary if I didn't practically force it on you."

"I get along," Nancy said crossly. "Which is better than you do. When I was over at your apartment last week, there wasn't anything in the cupboard but peanut butter. No wonder you've lost weight lately."

"Peanut butter is very nourishing," Honey said defensively. "All the nutritionists say so."

"Not as a sole diet, darn it," Nancy argued. "Do you know how it makes me feel to take money from you, when I know that you barely have enough to survive? Why can't you be sensible?"

"We agreed that the week I couldn't afford to pay your salary was the week you'd look for another job," Honey said, a stubborn set to her chin. "It's bad enough being poor as a church mouse. I won't accept charity."

"It wouldn't be charity, blast it," Nancy argued. "I'd be a fool if I didn't realize by now how independent you are. It would be a loan." She made a face. "Knowing you, you'll probably even insist on paying me interest."

"We've gone through all this before," Honey said gently, her eyes warmly affectionate. "The answer is still no."

"Madre de Dios!" Nancy exclaimed in exasperation.

Watching her, Honey hid a smile of amusement. If Nancy's hands had not gripped the steering wheel, she would have thrown them in the air with her usual Latin expressiveness. "Why do you have to be so damned dedicated and idealistic? It wouldn't hurt you to accept a little help. Why do you have to be a private investigator anyway? With your looks you could be anything you wanted. Why the hell can't you want what normal women want?"

Honey's lips twitched. "And what do 'normal' women want?" she asked solemnly, her eyes dancing.

Nancy cast her a glance of extreme irritation. "Fame, riches, and multiple O's," she pronounced impressively, then looked greatly insulted when Honey burst into giggles. "It's not funny." Then her own lips curved in a reluctant grin. "Well, maybe it is to a little Puritan like you."

"Wrong on both counts," Honey protested, still chuckling. "No one in her right mind would call me little, and I'm not a Puritan, merely discriminating."

"A virgin at twenty-four is not a Puritan?" Nancy lifted her eyebrows skeptically. "You've got to be kidding."

"Why did I let you ply me with those margaritas and encourage me to tell you my life story?" Honey asked gloomily. "You've been throwing that up to me ever since."

"If I remember correctly, you needed all the comfort you could get that night," Nancy said dryly.

"How was I to know you were practically a teeto-taler? You forgot to mention that when you were mooning about the injustice of a system that allowed the sexual harassment of dedicated young sleuths like one Honey Winston."

"I guess I *was* pretty maudlin that night," Honey confessed sheepishly. Even now, thinking back on that day, she felt a twinge of anger. "I simply couldn't believe that a reputable investigator like Ben Lackland would fire me just because I wouldn't go to bed with him."

"That's because you're green as grass, Little Nell," Nancy said cynically. She shook her head wonderingly. "It constantly amazes me how a girl who was first in her class at the Police Academy and spent two years on the force could still be so blasted naive. Everyone in Houston knows Ben Lackland is a chaser as well as a king-sized rat, but you thought he was being fatherly toward you!"

"But he had such a sweet wife," Honey protested. "And he never actually tried anything until that last night in the office."

"They all have very sweet wives," Nancy said, her tone ironic. "It's an excellent insurance policy. Remind me to tell you about my ex-husband sometime. He was a great one for insurance."

"He was also crazy as a loon to ever let you get away." Honey spoke fiercely. "Some men don't know their luck."

Nancy gave her an impish grin. "Don't worry. I've made sure that every man since knows what a prize I am." She made a left turn into Fannin and then a right into the alley that ran alongside the towering white hotel that was their destination. She brought the Toyota to a halt a little distance from a wide double door, obviously used for deliveries. She flicked off the headlights and then reached up to turn on the dome light.

"Honey," she said, her face suddenly serious, "forget about this. You don't need the money badly enough to take a risk like this. There will be other jobs."

"I haven't noticed anyone beating down our door," Honey said dryly.

"It's only been six months since you opened your own agency," Nancy said persuasively. "Give them a chance. You're good, really good. The only reason Lackland didn't try anything before was that you were the best agent he had. You'd be there now if his ego weren't bigger than that pea brain of his."

"And we'd both be eating better," Honey replied ruefully. She shook her head. "You know that we need this job, no matter what the risks, Nancy. I won't even be able to pay the rent next month without this fee." She tried to smile reassuringly, despite her own apprehensions regarding this night's task. "It's not all that dangerous. It will probably be only thirty minutes' work once I'm in Prince Rubinoff's suite. All I have to do is to locate Señora Gomez's letters and be on my way." Her lips curled scornfully. "A man like that probably keeps them under his pillow, so he can bring them out and gloat over them."

Nancy chuckled. "I doubt that. With as many women as 'Lusty Lance' is reputed to have—and have had—that could prove a trifle inconvenient." She picked up the newspaper and looked at the picture critically. "Heavens, he's a handsome stud. Just look at that face. Adonis . . . with a little touch of the devil."

"More than a little, according to the gossip columns," Honey said caustically, glancing at the picture.

Grudgingly, she had to admit that Nancy was right. That face, with its strong, regular features and beautifully shaped mouth, was arrestingly attractive, and the mischievous grin and dancing eyes saved it from being too handsome. "I'm sure that Señora Gomez would agree with them."

Nevertheless, she reached over and took the paper from Nancy, fascinated in spite of herself by that compelling face. Not that she was alone in that fascination, she assured herself quickly. Prince Anton Sergei Lancelot Rubinoff exerted a powerful charisma that was acknowledged worldwide. The younger son of the royal house of the Balkan state of Tamrovia, he had been a godsend to the media since he was a college student at Oxford. They had dubbed him 'Lusty Lance,' and that nickname had not only pertained to his formidable bedroom activities. Lance Rubinoff also had a boundless lust for adventure and life itself. In his early thirties, he had been in more scrapes than Honey could remember.

It was rumored that their Majesties were less than approving of their errant son, as was the Crown Prince Stefan. That they exerted little control over his activities was principally due to the partiality of his Uncle Nicholas, another black sheep, who unexpectedly had had the surprising good sense to marry the only daughter of Sheik Karim Ben Raschid. Young Lance had spent much of his childhood with his uncle in Sedikhan, and the sheik, ruler of a staggeringly oil-rich sheikdom, had developed a fondness for young Lance. He had deeded him a few choice acres on his twenty-first birthday, which produced enough oil yearly to buy Tamrovia outright. The cousin mentioned accompanying Rubinoff on his visit to Houston must be Nicholas's son, Alex Ben Raschid, Honey thought idly.

"Can it be that Lusty Lance is stirring a little fire under that cool facade?" Nancy asked archly, her eyes on Honey's absorbed face.

Honey quickly closed the paper and dropped it

back on the seat. "Nonsense," she said briskly. "I was checking to see what time the party the mayor's giving him begins. It's at nine, and they'll undoubtedly be dining with the mayor before the party." She checked her watch. "It's eight-ten now. It should be safe to go up to the suite. You're sure that this Raphael can be trusted?"

Nancy nodded. "He's a friend of my younger brother's. The only thing you have to worry about is Raphael's luring you into a vacant hotel suite and trying to make a pass. He's got a thing for big, beautiful blondes."

Honey made a face. "Haven't most men?" she asked wryly. "I've been fighting that particular problem since I left the orphanage when I was sixteen. They all think just because I look like some damn fertility goddess that my sole role in life is destined to be flat on my back in bed, preferably their bed."

"I should be so lucky," Nancy said teasingly, gazing enviously at Honey as she opened the door and got out of the car. "I'd almost give up sex to look like you." Her brown eyes twinkled. "Of course, if I gave up sex, I wouldn't need to look like you."

In a black leotard and sheer lycra tights, Honey Winston did resemble the fertility goddess she'd derided so scornfully. Standing five feet nine in her stockinged feet, she was built along voluptuous, queenly lines, with full, high breasts, a slim waist, and long, shapely legs that most women would have given their false eyelashes to possess. Even her face had a certain sensual earthiness, owing to the passionate curve of her lower lip and the slightly slanted deep violet eyes that gave her a curiously smoldering look. Her hair was a shimmering white-gold, and she tried to detract from its rather spectacular effect by wearing its luxurious length swathed severely about her head. She'd tried cutting it once, but she'd found that when it was short, it persisted in curling riotously about her head and only augmented that provocative sensuality.

"I hadn't noticed that you're having any problem attracting admirers," Honey retorted.

"I'm not bad," Nancy admitted with a wink. In her late twenties, Nancy Rodriguez was attractive rather than pretty, with the smooth olive skin and big, dark, flashing eyes that revealed her Mexican heritage. Her medium-length brown hair was permed into a riot of gypsy curls, and was very becoming to her piquant features. "Are you sure you don't want me to wait for you?" she asked.

Honey shook her head. "After I get the letters, I'll grab a taxi back to the apartment." She smiled soothingly. "I'll call you as soon as I get home."

"You'd better," Nancy said grimly. "Or I just may come knocking on Prince Rubinoff's door." She pulled a face. "Though I'd probably have to take a number."

Honey chuckled. "Kama Sutra twenty-two?" she asked teasingly.

"Something like that," Nancy agreed absently, her expression suddenly very sober. "Be careful, Honey."

"Always," Honey said lightly. She slammed the car door and waved reassuringly before turning and walking briskly toward the wide double doors.

The portable dining table moved smoothly over the plush hunter-green carpet of the hall, despite the added weight of the passenger occupying the bottom storage shelf. Why couldn't she have been one of those petite five-foot-nothing types? Honey wondered gloomily, trying to keep her long legs curled under the sheltering confines of the overhanging white damask tablecloth.

"Okay?" Raphael called down to her cheerfully.

"We're almost there, Miss Winston. It's just down the next corridor."

"I'm fine," Honey lied, knowing she'd scarcely be able to walk when she was able finally to uncurl from this pretzel-like position and get off this blasted shelf. There wasn't any use complaining to Raphael. He had done the best he could under the circumstances.

When she had met the young Latin bellhop inside the delivery doors forty minutes ago, she had been deluged by bad news. Security for the hotel's famous guests had been tightened unexpectedly, with the locks changed on the VIP suite, and only the security officers had been given passkeys. In addition, Prince Rubinoff had canceled his plans to dine with the mayor this evening, and he and his cousin were having dinner in their suite before leaving for River Oaks to attend the party.

Honey had scarcely had time for the disappointment to sink in when Raphael had come up with an alternate plan. He had persuaded the usual waiter from the dining room to let him substitute, and he was going to smuggle Honey into the suite on the shelf under the dining table. She could hide there while Prince Rubinoff and Alex Ben Raschid dined. Once they'd left the suite, she would be able to slip off the trolley and go about her business. He had clearly thought his solution a stroke of pure genius, and Honey had fallen in with the plan out of sheer desperation. It might not be foolproof, but it was the only plan in town.

The trolley had halted now, and she heard Raphael knock softly on the door. Then there was a murmur of voices and the table was once more in motion. This time the carpet was even plusher, and of a rich russet shade, she noticed before the trolley once more came to a halt. There was a murmur of voices once again. Raphael's and two others', and then the soft closing of a door.

She was on her own. Now all she had to do was to keep absolutely still for perhaps another forty-five minutes and she would be home free. It might not be all that easy, she thought ruefully. She was already getting a cramp in her left thigh. Why didn't they sit down and eat their dinner, damn it?

The gentlemen were obviously not willing to oblige her, for she heard the soft clink of crystal across the room. Marvelous. They were going to have a cozy predinner drink. They must have carried their drinks across the room, for though their footsteps were silent on the thick carpet, their voices were suddenly clearly audible.

"You know that his honor the mayor isn't going to be pleased about this, Lance," a deep voice drawled casually. "He's not a man who's used to being stood up."

"Too damn bad." He was answered coolly. "I've put up with this bureaucratic folderol for three days now, Alex. You told me this was going to be a vacation."

"Be patient," Ben Raschid urged lazily. "A few more social duties and we'll be free to play a little. It doesn't hurt to strengthen diplomatic ties with a city as rich in technology as Houston."

"I should have known that you'd squeeze a few business shenanigans into this trip." Rubinoff's voice had an underlying note of amusement, despite its exasperation. "If I recall, you persuaded me to come with you on the pretext that it would be your last spree before you took over control of the business from your grandfather. Yet here you are, wheeling and dealing. I might just as well have stayed in Zurich."

It was odd how much you noticed about voices when you couldn't see the people involved, Honey mused. Both men were speaking in English, which wasn't unusual, considering that they'd attended

Oxford together. But neither had the upper-class, public-school accent that she would have expected. Ben Raschid had a trace of a British accent, but Lance Rubinoff sounded almost aggressively American.

"You were getting bored with painting all that snow anyway," Ben Raschid replied. There was the abrasive sound of a match being struck, a short pause, and then Ben Raschid continued, "You said yourself that you were ready for a change."

Oh, my Lord, she hadn't considered the possibility that one of the men might smoke! Oh, please, let Ben Raschid be sitting far away from the table, or let it just be a cigarette. She was violently allergic to cigar smoke, and its effect on her soon escalated from violent sneezing fits to actual nausea.

"You caught me in a weak moment," Rubinoff said lightly. "I was finding that red-haired Olympic figure skater a trifle boring. She kept nagging me."

"Nagging?" Ben Raschid asked, puzzled. "The woman appeared to be completely crazy about you. She couldn't keep her hands off you."

Oh, Lord, it *was* cigar smoke, and Ben Raschid must be practically right next to her. Honey could feel that first tingle in her nostrils that was the ominous harbinger of things to come.

"Oh, I couldn't fault her eagerness," Rubinoff was saying gloomily. "It was her kinkiness that was the problem. She wanted to do it on the ice."

There was a short silence, and then Ben Raschid asked carefully, "It?"

Rubinoff tersely supplied an obscene Anglo-Saxon noun that caused Honey's eyes to widen in shock.

Ben Raschid exploded in laughter. "My Lord, you do know how to pick them. Nude?"

Rubinoff was chuckling now too. "Of course.

She seemed to think it would be the ultimate experience," he said ruefully. "I must be getting old. Ten years ago I would probably have done it."

"Ten *weeks* ago you probably would have done it," Ben Raschid corrected dryly. "She must have caught you in an unusually sedate mood."

The tickle in her nose was getting almost unbearable. Why couldn't Ben Raschid be a pipe smoker? Hadn't anyone ever told him that Middle Eastern potentates were supposed to be addicted to the hookah?

"Perhaps," Rubinoff admitted. "I might have been more amenable if she'd settled for an indoor rink, but she was continually raving about the magnificence of nature in the raw. It's below freezing in Switzerland at this time of year!"

It was coming. Why did this have to happen? Why couldn't everything have gone as smoothly as she'd planned? It just wasn't fair, damn it!

"I can see how you could have found that a bit dampening to your enthusiasm," Ben Rachid said solemnly. "Perhaps you could have worn—"

He broke off abruptly as Honey sneezed explosively. The sneeze was followed by two more of equal violence. They couldn't have helped but hear, Honey thought morosely. That sudden silence in the room was very expressive. Bracing herself for the coming confrontation, she waited resignedly.

The damask tablecloth was abruptly flipped back, and she was suddenly practically nose to nose with that face Nancy had rightly described as full of the devil. The bright blue eyes so close to her own were certainly dancing with satanic mischief at the moment. His gaze traveled leisurely over her contorted figure before returning to her face.

"Are you supposed to be the hors d'oeuvres or do we save you for dessert?" Rubinoff asked politely, squatting down so that they were on the same level.

Honey gazed at him hopefully. "Would you believe that I'm a quality-control agent for the hotel, checking on the dining service?"

He cocked his head consideringly. "No, I don't think I'd believe that," he said slowly.

"I didn't think you would," Honey said gloomily. "I guess you might as well help me out of here."

"Delighted," the prince said solemnly, offering his hand and helping her solicitously from her metal nest. As she unwound to her full five feet nine, he pursed his lips in a soundless whistle of appreciation. "I underestimated you. You're not a dessert; you're a blooming smorgasbord."

But she was in no mood for clever metaphors. No wonder the smoke had affected her so quickly, she thought crossly. Ben Raschid was lounging lazily on the couch not six feet from the elegantly appointed dinner trolley, and he still had the slender brown cigarette in his hand that had been her downfall. Despite its thinness, it must have been exceptionally strong, for now that she was no longer protected by the filter of the tablecloth, it was overpowering. Her stomach lurched, and she experienced a dizzying nausea. She was going to be sick. "Oh, no," she moaned miserably, and turned and flew toward the silk-curtained window at the end of the room.

"My God, she's going to jump!" Rubinoff cried, startled, as she tore the beige drapes aside and worked frantically at the window. "You little fool, we're twenty stories up!"

Honey had the window up now and was leaning out, breathing in the brisk, invigorating coolness, when she felt two strong arms forcefully grab her from behind.

"Are you crazy?" Rubinoff asked angrily. "You could have been killed. What the hell is wrong with you?"

The fresh air was blessedly relieving her of that

horrible queasiness, but she took a few more deep breaths before she risked an answer. "I wasn't trying to jump," she gasped, "I just felt sick and needed some air."

"I see," Lance Rubinoff said slowly, his arms tightening around her. "You weren't thinking about escaping, then?"

She shook her head, still breathing deeply.

He moved closer, his hands sliding up and around her rib cage to just below her breasts. "You're not even a little suicidal?" he asked softly.

"Of course not," Honey said. "You can let me go now."

"Perhaps that wouldn't be a very good idea," he said silkily, his hands moving up a fraction so that he was lightly cupping the fullness of her breasts. "You said that you were ill. What if you got dizzy and fell out the window?"

"I'm not dizzy anymore," she told him breathlessly. That wasn't quite true. She was feeling oddly light-headed, and those strong, gentle hands seemed to burn through the cotton of her leotard.

"You're sure?" Rubinoff murmured wistfully. "We wouldn't want an international incident, you know. Can't you see the headlines? Lascivious prince throws beautiful trespasser out the window."

She giggled helplessly. The man was completely mad. "I'm quite sure," she said firmly.

"Pity," he said, and his arms dropped reluctantly away from her. He stepped back, and she turned to face him. His blue eyes were twinkling. "No one in his right mind would believe that I'd toss a luscious thing like you away under any circumstance." He raised an eyebrow mockingly. "If you get so violently claustrophobic, don't you think you could have tried to meet me some other way than hiding under that little cart?"

"I'm not claustrophobic," she said indignantly. "It was the smoke. I'm allergic to it." She pointed accusingly to Ben Raschid, who was regarding them both with quizzical amusement. "Tell him to put out the cigar."

"Put out your cigar, Alex," Rubinoff ordered obediently, his lips twitching.

"Certainly," Ben Raschid said politely, leaning forward to crush out the cigar in the crystal ashtray on the coffee table. "Anything else?"

Rubinoff turned to Honey. "Anything else?" he asked gravely.

Honey shook her head.

"That will be all, Alex," Rubinoff said grandly. "We'll let you know if she changes her mind."

"Good," Ben Raschid drawled. "Now, bring her over here and let's get a better look at her."

Rubinoff gestured mockingly. "Milady?" Taking her by the elbow he propelled her gently across the room until she stood before Ben Raschid. Then he strolled over to half lean, half sit on the arm of the couch beside his cousin.

Honey felt rather like a slave on an auction block as they appraised her admiringly and intimately from her ballet-slippered feet to the top of her white-gold head. In sheer self-defense she stared back just as blatantly.

Both men were tanned, dressed in dark evening clothes, and were well over six feet, and there the similarities ended. Cousins they were, but they bore practically no resemblance to each other. Prince Rubinoff's dark-auburn hair and brilliant blue eyes shone like restless burning flames in contrast to the raven-dark hair and piercing black eyes of Alex Ben Raschid. Though the contrast in coloring was extraordinary, it was their expressions that truly set them apart.

Lance Rubinoff's countenance was so boldly, joyously alive that Honey found herself gazing at him in helpless fascination despite herself. It was as if he were lit from within by that flame to which she had mentally compared him. Ben Raschid's expression, on the other hand, was guarded and faintly cynical, and if there was passion behind that dark, saturnine face, it would be released only at Ben Raschid's will.

"Very nice," Ben Raschid said casually, leaning back on the couch, his gaze narrowing on Honey's lower anatomy speculatively. "Gorgeous legs. I'll flip you for her."

"No way!" Rubinoff said softly, his eyes not leaving Honey. "This one's mine. She's got me hot as a firecracker just looking at her. I think you'll have to make my excuses to the mayor. I plan on being very busy this evening."

Honey frowned fiercely. "If you're through gloating over me as if I were a piece of prime sirloin—"

"Very prime, indeed," Rubinoff murmured outrageously, and as she glared at him indignantly, he said solemnly, "Sorry. Please continue. You were saying?"

"I was about to ask what you intend to do with me," she asked tautly.

"But I've just been telling you, love," Rubinoff protested gently. "Such ingenuity deserves a reward. I'm going to skip the party and we're going to spend the evening in bed." He grinned mischievously. "Perhaps tomorrow, too." He shook his head admiringly. "God, you're a clever little puss. Cleopatra could have taken lessons from you."

"Cleopatra?" Honey asked.

"She had herself wrapped in a carpet and smuggled into Caesar's audience chamber," he explained patiently. "I'm sure she did the best she could with the materials at hand. I doubt that they had portable dining trolleys in ancient Egypt."

"From what I hear, she did exceptionally well with what she had 'on hand,'" Ben Raschid commented, his lips quirking. "A girl after your own persuasion, Miss . . ." He trailed off inquiringly.

"Honey Winston," she supplied.

The men exchanged amused glances.

"An actress?" Rubinoff asked.

"No," Honey answered crossly. She had always hated her name with a passion. "It's my real name. I was told that my mother thought my hair looked like honey when I was born."

"It must have lightened considerably since then," Rubinoff said softly. "It looks like snow in the moonlight now. How long is it when you take it down?"

"Almost to the middle of my back," she answered automatically, gazing hypnotically into those soft, glowing eyes. Then she shook her head as if to clear it. "What earthly difference does it make how long my hair is?" she demanded, almost stamping her foot in exasperation.

"I like long hair," he explained with utmost reasonableness. "It's virtually a fetish with me."

"I'm sure a man of your experience has quite a few of those," she said crossly. "I'm surprised you didn't give in to your little figure-skater's demands."

He looked momentarily surprised. "That's right! You did overhear that, didn't you?" He smiled so warmly that it took her breath away. "Did the idea appeal to you? I wouldn't mind doing it with you, sweetheart. I don't think I'd even notice the cold."

Honey mentally counted to ten before she said quite slowly, enunciating every word precisely, "No, it does not appeal to me. I do not want to make love with you on the ice, or in a bed, or on top of Mount Everest. I do not want to make love with you at all. Is that clear?"

"I didn't offer Mount Everest," Rubinoff said, his lips curving in an impish grin. "But it's not a bad idea. The thin air could make it quite an erotic experience. Perhaps we'd better think about that." He turned to Ben Raschid and asked interestedly, "You do a lot of mountain climbing, Alex. Is this a good time of the year for scaling Mount Everest?"

Ben Raschid cocked his head thoughtfully. "I shouldn't think so," he said lazily. "I'd wait a month or so, until the weather is less uncertain."

"Why don't you listen to me?" Honey wailed. "I didn't come here to go to bed with you. I came to get Señora Gomez's letters." She ran her hand frustratedly through her carefully coiffed hair, scattering pins in all directions. "If you hadn't been such an egotistical monster and insisted on keeping them, none of this would have happened."

"Letters?" Ben Raschid asked, raising an eyebrow quizzically. "Have you started collecting mementos, Lance?"

"Of course not," Rubinoff said, still gazing at Honey with that molten, glowing warmth. She wished he wouldn't do that. It had a very peculiar effect on her. "Manuela Gomez? I don't even recall receiving any letters from Manuela. Are you a friend of hers, sweetheart?"

"She hired me to get back the letters," Honey said. She was a bit relieved that at least they were beginning to listen to her. "I'm a private investigator." She glared at Rubinoff accusingly. "She was very upset. She said she'd begged you to return her letters but you just laughed at her."

"A private investigator?" Lance Rubinoff asked softly. He shook his head firmly. "That's not a job for a lovely thing like you. You could get into all kinds of trouble, smuggling yourself into strange men's hotel suites."

His eyes traveled admiringly over her curves and long, shapely legs in the black tights. "I thought private detectives all wore trenchcoats and deerstalker hats. I must admit that I much prefer your outfit, sweetheart. Is it your usual garb or do you save it for burgling hotel suites?"

"Of course it's not my usual outfit," she said in exasperation. "I didn't know what I'd find when I arrived here. I thought I might possibly have to get in by way of an air-conditioning vent or something."

Rubinoff cocked his head consideringly as his eyes went to the twelve-inch-square opening of the vent across the room. His eyes returned to linger on the voluptuous swell of her breasts. "You'd never have made it, love," he said solemnly.

"I know that now," she said. "Will you or will you not give me those letters to return to Señora Gomez?"

"I don't have the slightest idea what you're talking about," Rubinoff said, as he lazily rose to his feet. "But I have every intention of finding out. I'll just give Manuela a call and see what she's up to." He took a step closer to Honey. "We might as well take the rest of those pins out; it's falling down anyway," he added softly, his gaze holding hers. She was scarcely aware of his deft hands plucking at the remaining pins, until her hair tumbled into a heavy white-gold glory about her shoulders.

"God, that's fantastic," he breathed hoarsely. "Isn't that beautiful, Alex?"

"Beautiful," Alex agreed lightly, but his voice served to break the spell Rubinoff seemed to weave about her so effortlessly.

She took a deep breath and stepped back. "I am not a *thing*," she said firmly. "I'm an intelligent professional, not some pretty little sex object for your amusement."

"And spirit, too," Rubinoff said. "Damn, she's a sweet little th—woman," he corrected smoothly. He turned and strode swiftly toward a door on the far side of the room. "I'll call Manuela on the bedroom extension," he continued briskly. "Don't let our guest leave before I get back, Alex." He turned at the door, his blue eyes twinkling. "And don't let her put her hair back up!"

Little? She'd never felt little or lacking in strength in her whole life until she'd encountered one Prince Rubinoff, she mused bewilderedly. Why did the man have such a weird effect on her?

"Is he always like that?" she asked dazedly, gazing blankly at the closed bedroom door.

"Most of the time," Ben Raschid said with a shrug. "Won't you sit down, Miss Winston? Lance may be some time. As I remember, Manuela Gomez can be voluble."

Honey crossed to the couch and dropped down on its cushioned surface, her eyes still fixed on the room into which Rubinoff had disappeared. "He's totally and certifiably insane," she said positively.

Ben Raschid shook his head, his dark eyes thoughtfully following her own. "No," he denied quietly. "He's quite brilliant, really. Don't be fooled by that flippant facade. Have you ever read Rafael Sabatini?" At Honey's questioning nod, he went on. "There's an opening line in *Scaramouche* that always makes me think of Lance." He quoted softly: " 'He was born with the gift of laughter and a sense of the world gone mad.' " His lips twisted mockingly. "You'll note the distinction. If a man believes the world is mad, how can you expect him to take it seriously?"

"It must be a trifle uncomfortable for those around him who don't view life so lightly," Honey said, frowning disapprovingly.

"I don't think he's had any complaints so far." There was a suspicion of a twinkle in the dark eyes. "Certainly not from any of the women of his acquaintance."

That went without saying. Honey had just had a potent demonstration of that dizzying charm and overpowering virility. Yet she still felt called upon to protest acidly. "Evidently Señora Gomez is the exception to the rule."

"I suggest that we wait and see," Ben Raschid answered cynically. "I rather suspect that Manuela is playing a little game. If Lance says there were no letters, then they just don't exist. I've never known Lance to lie about anything. He has a positive passion for honesty." He grimaced wryly. "Which is why we try to keep him away from the company director's meetings."

"He's no businessman, I gather."

"No one expects him to be. His interests lie in other areas," Ben Raschid said carelessly. "When Grandfather deeded him his property, his only stipulation was that he cast his vote in the board meetings with mine. He knew he could trust Lance to keep his promise. He's completely loyal to those he cares about."

"Like Señora Gomez?" Honey asked caustically. "He doesn't appear to have been too trustworthy in her case. She was absolutely terrified when she couldn't persuade him to either destroy or return those letters. She was sure that her husband would discover that she'd had an affair with Prince Rubinoff."

Ben Raschid frowned. "That doesn't fit the picture either. Alonzo Gomez is usually very tolerant of Manuela's affairs as long as she's discreet. Why should she be in such a tizzy at this late date?"

"Since when are Prince Rubinoff's affairs ever discreet?" Honey asked dryly.

A smile lit up Ben Raschid's dark, guarded face with surprising warmth. "You have a point there," he admitted. "So I suppose we'll just have to wait and see what Manuela has to say, won't we?"

Whatever Manuela had to say seemed to take an inconceivably long time, for it was another ten minutes at least before Rubinoff came back into the room. It was clear that the conversation had not pleased him, for there was a dark frown on his face.

"The woman has the brain of a flea," he said disgustedly as he strolled over to the couch to stand before Honey. "And the ethical standards of the commandant of a concentration camp. I'm sorry, Honey."

"Sorry?" Honey asked slowly, sitting up straighter on the couch.

"It was Manuela's idea of a joke," Rubinoff explained, his expression grave. "I haven't called her since we flew into town, and she thought it would be a clever way of getting my attention." His scowl darkened. "Dear heaven, how I hate kittenish women!"

"But you weren't even supposed to be here," Honey said blankly, trying to comprehend what he was telling her.

"She was going to make an anonymous phone call at the dinner party tonight and have me summoned back to the suite." He grimaced. "She thought finding a luscious blonde in my suite who was supposedly sent by her would intrigue me. Like I said, she's not very bright. It never occurred to her that the blonde would make me forget that Manuela ever existed."

"Oh, I don't know. I think she's quite clever," Honey said slowly. At first she had been stunned and disbelieving, but now she felt a slow-burning anger that was greater than any she had known. "She was certainly clever enough to fool me. Your mistress must have been very pleased with herself. I was completely taken in."

It only increased her fury when he shrugged and failed to deny the accusation. "I told you she was a fool," he said gruffly. "And she's not my mistress. Not anymore."

Honey jumped to her feet and faced him, her hands knotted into fists at her sides. "Do you mean that her charming little ploy didn't earn her a place back in your affections?" she asked caustically. "I'd have thought it would have amused you enormously, Your Highness. You're quite a one for pranks yourself, I understand. No wonder she thought that making a fool out of an innocent bystander would intrigue you."

There was an answering flicker of anger in Rubinoff's eyes. "I don't believe I've ever been accused of any real maliciousness in any of the mischief I've perpetrated," he said curtly. "And I'll be damned if I'll accept the responsibility for Manuela's little tricks." He drew a deep breath and said more quietly, "I said I was sorry. If you'll just calm down, we can discuss how I can make it up to you."

Honey was pacing up and down like an enraged lioness, her hair floating about her in a shimmering white-gold veil, her face taut with fury. "And what do you intend to do to recompense me, *Your Highness*?" she asked furiously. "Perhaps you could write me a check for my trouble. Isn't that the usual method of handling the hoi polloi? Write the lady a check and she'll forget she'd been humiliated and manipulated. After all, it was just a joke!"

"Don't you think you're being a bit unfair, Miss Winston?" Ben Raschid asked quietly. "Lance has already explained that this wasn't a part of his game plan."

"Game plan," Honey repeated bitterly. "Yes, that's really the right name for it. It's all a game to people like you, isn't it? You think that you can use people and then just throw them away like tissues. Well, I don't like being considered disposable. I may not be a member of your precious jet set, but I have more integrity than the whole kit and kaboodle of you, despite the fact that I have to work for my living!" She paused in her pacing to stand before Rubinoff, her breasts heaving, her cheeks flaming with bright flags of color. "You should try it sometime. It's a great character builder, a quality you're obviously lacking. Perhaps if you had something to occupy you besides bedding malicious little coffee heiresses and nympho ice skaters, you might develop a little."

"I agree," Rubinoff said solemnly, his lips twitching. "I think bedding a dedicated private detective would be much more inspiring."

Honey gritted her teeth to keep from shouting at him. Couldn't the man stay serious for two consecutive minutes? "I'm glad you finding this amusing," she said fiercely. "But then, what else could I expect from a dilettante like you?"

She wheeled and strode swiftly across the room, toward the door, her back rigid with fury. "Good night, gentlemen. It's been an experience to remember, but not one I'd care to repeat." The door slammed sharply behind her.

"Somehow I don't think you managed to soothe her ruffled feelings," Ben Raschid said mockingly, taking a sip of his drink. "She still appears a trifle perturbed with you."

"Can you blame her?" Rubinoff asked tersely, frowning at the closed door moodily. "Damn Manuela Gomez!"

Ben Raschid finished his drink in one swallow and rose lithely to his feet. "As entertaining as I found it to see you under fire, I'm glad your gorgeous Valkyrie decided to put an end to the scene. We're going to be late for the party as it is. I suggest that we grab a quick bite and get on our way."

"You go ahead. I'm not hungry," Rubinoff told him absently, still staring at the door. "With all that shining silvery hair floating about her and those great blazing eyes, she *was* rather like a Valkyrie, wasn't she?"

Ben Raschid's gaze narrowed thoughtfully on his cousin's absorbed face. "It's natural that she should capture your imagination," he said slowly. "But may I remind you that the Valkyries were reputed to be very dangerous ladies?"

"But not boring," Rubinoff murmured. "Definitely not boring." He turned away abruptly and strode toward the telephone on the graceful Sheraton desk in the corner of the room. "Do you still have the card that fellow from the State Department gave you? What was his name?"

"Josh Davies," Ben Raschid answered. "I think I tossed it in the top desk drawer." He watched curiously as Rubinoff riffled through the drawer impatiently until he found the business card and picked up the phone. "He'll probably be at the party this evening. Why not wait and speak to him there?"

Rubinoff shook his head, his hair glowing flame-like under the overhead light. "This will only take a minute," he said crisply, "and I want him to get started on it right away."

Two

"You know, of course, that I'm not going to let you get away without furnishing me with all the gory details," Nancy Rodriguez warned sternly the moment that Honey walked into the office the next morning.

"I told you on the phone last night." Honey shrugged and strolled over to the oval mirror on the wall that Nancy had insisted was an essential office expenditure. She smoothed a few errant strands of her hair back into its sleek coil while carefully avoiding Nancy's bright, curious eyes. "Señora Gomez turned out to be a lady rat on the same scale as Ben Lackland. I think under the circumstances we're justified in keeping the retainer."

"You're damn right we are," Nancy replied emphatically. "But that's not what I want to hear about, and you know it, Honey Winston." She sighed. "You're the only woman on the face of the earth who could be closeted with two of the sexiest men in the world for almost an hour and come out talking coolly about retainers. What was Prince Rubinoff like? Was he as handsome as his pictures? Did he make a pass at you? Talk to me!"

Somehow she didn't want to talk about that strange, exasperating meeting with Lance Rubinoff, even with Nancy. After she had cooled down a bit she'd realized that she probably owed Lance Rubinoff an apology for the insults she had hurled at him before she'd stalked out the door. He hadn't been directly responsible for his former mistress's misdeeds and had even apologized most sincerely and offered to recompense her. He had really acted with surprising generosity, when she considered that she had tried to burgle his suite. If she hadn't felt so manipulated and betrayed, she would never have been so unjust as to blame the prince for the woman's crimes. Perhaps she'd send him a note of explanation and apology before he left Houston.

She smiled ruefully at her reflection in the mirror. Lance Rubinoff would probably not even remember her name, much less the events of the last evening, in a few weeks' time. She'd skip the note.

"Do you really think it likely that he would be interested in making advances to a trespasser?" Honey asked evasively.

"If the trespasser looked like you and the trespassee was Lusty Lance," Nancy answered promptly. Her lips curled in disgust. "You're not going to tell me anything, are you?"

"There's nothing to tell," Honey said lightly. She turned away from the mirror, crossed back to her secretary's desk, and perched on the corner. "I'm sure that, given the same set of circumstances, you'd have a much more interesting tale to disclose. But then, you're always telling me how dull I am," she said with an affectionate grin.

"Well, you've really outdone yourself this time,"

Nancy said morosely. "You're a disgrace to woman-hood." She sighed resignedly. "I guess it's just as well; Rubinoff would be pretty strong stuff for a novice."

"I'm glad that you've seen fit to forgive me," Honey commented dryly, she stood up and strolled toward her office. "I don't suppose there have been any messages? Why should today be any different?"

"Oh, *madre de Dios!* I forget to tell you. There's a man waiting for you in your office. He's been here about thirty minutes."

"A client?" Honey asked hopefully, her face brightening. She could use a little good news, after that debacle last night.

"Could be," Nancy replied cheerfully. "He wouldn't confide his business to a lowly secretary like me. But he's fairly well dressed and has that solid-citizen look. His name is Josh Davies."

Honey crossed her fingers and held them up in a farewell salute before disappearing into her office. She could see immediately why Nancy referred to the man who rose politely from the visitor's chair at her entrance as a solid-citizen type. In his mid-fifties, his stocky body was clad in a dark-blue suit that was beautifully tailored, and his crisp white shirt was a discreet contrast. His gray-streaked hair was neither too long nor too short, but just right, and meticulously styled into smooth waves. Even his expression was smooth and bland, though his gray eyes were surprisingly keen.

"I'm sorry to have kept you waiting, Mr. Davies," Honey said briskly, coming forward with her hand outstretched. "How may I help you?"

Josh Davies's handshake was firm, and his glance discreetly appreciative as it traveled over her full graceful curves in the pearl-gray pants suit.

"I'm afraid that I'm guilty of being a little

overeager, Miss Winston," Davies said with a rueful smile. "I wanted to be sure to catch you before you took on any other assignments today. It's extremely important that you start working for us right away."

"Us?" Honey asked, her brows arched in enquiry as she strolled behind her desk and dropped into the leather executive chair. "Please sit down, Mr. Davies. I admit to being very intrigued by your urgency."

"I'm with the Department of State, Miss Winston," Davies said in a low tone. "And I assure you that I'm not exaggerating the importance of the job that I have for you, or its extreme urgency. We want you to assume the duty of personal bodyguard to a foreign dignitary visiting in this country, whom we believe is marked for assassination." He pulled out a notebook from his pocket and flipped it open. "According to your dossier, you've twice acted in that capacity while you worked for the Houston Police Department—first, protecting a material witness while awaiting trial; second, guarding a television anchorwoman who received a death threat."

"Dossier?" Honey asked blankly. "You have a dossier on me?"

Davies closed the notebook and smiled soothingly at her. "We felt it was necessary when your name was suggested for the assignment. We had to be sure of both your personal integrity and your competence before entrusting you with Prince Rubinoff's safety."

"Prince Rubinoff?" Honey sat bolt upright in her chair, and her eyes widened in surprise. "You want me to protect Prince Rubinoff?"

"Actually, the job would involve the safety of both Prince Rubinoff and his cousin, Alex Ben Raschid, but naturally you would be Prince Rubinoff's official bodyguard," Davies said briskly. "The job would be essentially the same as the ones you've worked before. You'd live on the premises and accompany the prince everywhere he goes. If you feel the situation calls for backup, you need only phone me or one of my assistants and we'll see that you have the additional manpower."

"Wait a minute," Honey said slowly. "You're going a little too fast for me. Since when has the United States government contracted out its security assignments? What happened to the FBI or the CIA?"

Davies looked a little uncomfortable. "It seems that Prince Rubinoff won't permit the usual security arrangements. It's either you or nothing. He was quite adamant on that point when he called me last night and—"

"He called you last night?" Honey interrupted, her lips tightening. "I think I'm beginning to see the light." And she had actually been feeling guilty for her verbal attack on him! Her physical appeal for him had been obvious, but she hadn't thought that he'd go to these lengths to maneuver her into a vulnerable position. She felt a tiny stirring of disappointment that he'd used his position and clout to advance his pursuit of her. Somehow she'd thought better of him than that.

"I don't think you need to worry about an assassination attempt on Prince Rubinoff. After you investigate his little ploy, I believe you'll find that this threat comes straight from his imagination." She rose to her feet. "In any case, I'm not interested in this particular assignment, Mr. Davies. You'll have to find someone else to hold Prince Rubinoff's hand. I'm sure he can supply you with a lengthy list of substitutes. Good day."

"Sit down, Miss Winston." Josh Davies's voice was as courteous and well modulated as before, but there was a trace of steel in it now, which was echoed in the sharpness of his keen gray eyes.

"We haven't finished our discussion, and I have no intention of permitting you to refuse me. The stakes are far too high."

"This is my office, Mr. Davies," Honey said belligerently, "and I have no intention of—"

"Sit down, Miss Winston," Davies repeated, and this time the steel was sharpened into razorlike menace. "I wanted our arrangement to be an amicable one, but it seems you're going to require some 'persuasion.' You realize that your action last night in entering Prince Rubinoff's suite for purposes of theft was not only unorthodox but actually criminal?"

Honey sat down again. "He told you about that?" she asked, moistening her lips nervously.

Davies nodded. "He told me not to use it as a lever unless I was unable to obtain your services in any other way." His lips curved cynically. "It appears that he read your character very well, considering you have such a short acquaintance. You do know that a telephone call to City Hall from either myself or Prince Rubinoff would result in immediate revocation of your license?"

"Yes, I'd be a fool not to be aware of that," Honey replied faintly. "It was the risk I took." What an incredibly stupid risk it had been, to put her entire career on the line because she was tempted by a large fee and conned by a malicious little schemer.

Davies evidently agreed with her. "It was extremely foolish of you, Miss Winston," he said disapprovingly. He glanced at the notebook in his hand. "Understandable, perhaps, considering your present financial circumstances, but still very foolish. You're very fortunate that Prince Rubinoff is willing to forego pressing charges."

"Provided that I move into his suite," Honey said caustically. "I had no idea that the State

Department was providing that type of service for visiting dignitaries."

Davies's expression soured. "I'm not acting as a pimp for His Highness, Miss Winston," he said tautly. "The position I've offered you is a legitimate one in every way. It's an opportunity that any of your colleagues would snap up in a minute. I might add that a good deal of prestige and publicity always accompanies the protection of royalty."

"I don't doubt that there would be publicity, but not the type that I'd relish," Honey said bitterly. She leaned forward, her expression earnestly appealing. "Look, Mr. Davies, if your department looks upon this as legitimate employment, surely you can see that it's totally unnecessary. Lance Rubinoff doesn't need protection." Her lips curved in a mocking smile. "Except perhaps from his ex-mistress. It's all just a trick, a huge practical joke at my expense. Prince Rubinoff obviously has a rather bizarre sense of humor."

Davies shook his head. "You seem to be suffering from a misapprehension, Miss Winston. Prince Rubinoff didn't come to us with a threat on his life. We went to him. I can assure you that the danger is quite real and that the informant is most reliable. Unfortunately, we haven't been able to convince either His Highness or his cousin to accept a live-in bodyguard. Consequently, we've had to limit our surveillance. Naturally, when Prince Rubinoff called and offered to let us have an agent on the premises, we jumped at it."

"Naturally," Honey echoed dazedly. This information put an entirely different slant on the situation. No wonder security had been tightened at the hotel last night. Not tight enough, however, she thought with a little shiver. She'd managed to breach that security herself with ridiculous ease. "Why would anyone want to assassinate Prince

Rubinoff?" she asked wonderingly. "He's not even heir to the throne."

He shrugged. "It has nothing to do with the politics of Tamrovia. The assassination plot also involves Alex Ben Raschid. Ben Raschid is the heir to one of the richest oil sheikdoms in the world, and Rubinoff, too, controls a sizeable portion of those oil fields. A double assassination would throw Ben Raschid's country into a turmoil and might instigate an overthrow of the old sheik."

"I see," Honey said thoughtfully. An oil-rich sheikdom in political chaos would be ideal strategically for any number of petroleum-hungry countries. "Then, why wouldn't they accept your help when you told them of the danger?"

"They're two very independent and self-willed men. They insisted that they could handle any problem that might come up themselves. Their refusal wouldn't lessen this country's responsibility if anything happened to them, however. Sheik Ben Raschid is inordinately fond of both his grandson and Prince Rubinoff. It would be sure to trigger an international furor."

"I can see how you'd want an agent actually occupying the suite," Honey said soberly. "But I still don't see why it has to be me. I'm sure it wasn't protection that Lance Rubinoff had in mind when he arranged for you to contact me."

"So am I, Miss Winston," Davies said dryly. "You're a very attractive woman, and, considering His Highness's reputation, I'd be a fool if I didn't realize where his true interests rest." He hesitated for a moment before adding deliberately, "It doesn't matter."

"It matters to me," Honey said indignantly, her face flushing angrily. "I have no desire to spend the next few weeks dodging passes from one of the most disreputable playboys in the world."

"I'm afraid that's your problem, Miss Winston,"

Davies said coolly. "You're being hired for certain specific duties, and how you accomplish them is your own business. That also goes for any impediments you might encounter along the way. This is too important to us to allow you the option of refusing. Play along with us and we'll not only throw other choice plums in your direction, but we'll also make sure the media are aware that you're a government agent and not Rubinoff's latest mistress. I don't think we need to discuss the results of a possible refusal."

"No, I don't think we do," Honey said silkily. "Blackmail threats are so distasteful."

"Exactly." Davies allowed himself a small smile. "I assume that we're in agreement, then?"

Honey nodded. "It appears that I have little choice."

"None at all," Davies agreed blandly, rising to his feet. He slipped his notebook into his vest pocket, extracted a card, and handed it to her. "This number will reach me any time, day or night. Don't hesitate to use it at even a hint of trouble. I want you moved into Prince Rubinoff's suite by three this afternoon. I hope that will be satisfactory."

He didn't give a damn whether it was satisfactory, Honey thought cynically. Beneath that smooth, conventional facade Josh Davies was obviously one very tough gentleman. "I'll be there, Mr. Davies," Honey replied. "I'm sure you'd know about it if I weren't."

"Yes, of course," he said composedly. "Though it's remote at the moment, our surveillance is quite thorough. Good day, Miss Winston."

"Good day, Mr. Davies," Honey said, and sighed in resignation.

Honey knocked briskly on the door to the VIP

suite and then waited impatiently for an answer to her summons. A frown of annoyance creased her forehead as the delay lengthened. After the elaborate rigmarole that had taken place downstairs at the reception desk, surely it wasn't too much to ask that she not be kept waiting in the hall like an overeager chambermaid. The reception clerk had taken care to phone the suite to check that she was welcome.

The door was flung open at last, and she was confronted by a grinning Lance Rubinoff, dressed only in a rich brown velvet robe that made his auburn hair burn even more brightly in contrast. "Welcome, Honey," he said mockingly, stepping aside to let her enter. "I've been waiting for you."

She stared pointedly at the bare muscular chest, with its thatch of springy russet hair, which was revealed by the loosely belted robe. "Yes, I can see that you're dressed for the occasion," she said caustically, her chin lifting scornfully. She sailed regally past him into the living room and dropped her cream shoulder bag on the elegant mocha damask couch. "I think we have a few things to clarify, Your Highness," Honey said briskly. "Under the circumstances we must maintain a businesslike attitude toward each other. I'm here for only one reason, and that's to protect you. I'm not here to amuse you or entertain you—either in bed or out of it! I hope we understand each other."

"Of course we understand each other," Rubinoff said smoothly, his lips twitching. "You're going to do your best to protect me, and I'm going to do my best to get you into the sack. It's all very clear."

Honey's eyes widened in shock. Had the man no shame? He obviously felt no guilt at all for blackmailing her into this position. "You're not going to succeed," she said tersely. "You may think you're irresistible, Your Highness, but I have an odd fondness for an element of integrity in my men."

"Lance," he corrected, a frown wiping the amusement from his face. He straightened slowly and strolled toward her, his bare feet silent on the thick carpet. "I didn't want to bludgeon you into taking the job, damn it. I told Davies to try everything else first."

"But you used the whip when you had to, didn't you?" she charged scornfully, her eyes blazing. "When serfs get out of line, what other course is left to the aristocracy?"

"I used it," he admitted tightly, his blue eyes flickering. "Hell, yes, I used it." He stopped only a foot away from where she stood, and she could feel the vibrant heat emanating from his body and smell the heady scent of clean soap mixed with a tantalizing, faintly musky odor. "And I'd use it again without a qualm. Would you like to know why?"

"I already know," Honey said stormily, trying to ignore the effect his virile closeness was having on her breathing. "You've already expressed yourself very explicitly on the subject, and with such *delicacy*, too!"

"I was joking, for heaven's sake," Rubinoff said roughly. "Does everything have to be real and earnest with you?"

"It's better than never taking anything seriously," she retorted, stung. "Am I to assume, then, that you don't want to take me to bed? That it's all been a complete misunderstanding?"

"Of course I want to go to bed with you," he said impatiently. "That's what this is all about. But I had no intention of yanking you struggling and screaming into the nearest bedroom. I was going to give you time to get used to the idea."

"How very considerate, Your Highness," Honey snapped. "And what if I have no intention of getting used to the idea? Would you still be so lenient with your humble subject?"

"If you call me that one more time . . ." Rubinoff began, talking between his teeth. Then he took a deep, steadying breath. "Look, I can see that you could be a little annoyed at the way you were forced into agreeing, but if you'd just listen—"

"Didn't anyone ever tell you that royalty doesn't have to make explanations?" Honey interrupted caustically, ignoring the storm signals in Rubinoff's eyes. "They just wave their scepters and we lowly plebians fall meekly to our knees."

"Meekly!" Rubinoff exclaimed, running his fingers through his hair in exasperation. "You're about as meek as a hydrogen bomb." Suddenly he stepped forward with lightning swiftness, enfolding her in his arms and bending her back in a Valentino-style embrace. Looking soulfully into her eyes he crooned tenderly, "I give up, sweetheart; you're much too clever for me. I was only waiting for you to walk through that door to pounce on you. As soon as they called up from reception, I dashed into the bedroom and threw off all my clothes so that I could ravish your senses with glimpses of my strong, virile body. If that didn't do the job, I was going to ply you with liquor and cocaine, until you were completely in my power, and then quench my insatiable hunger with your voluptuous form. Now that you've found me out, I can confess it all."

Honey was staring up at him wide-eyed, her eyes fixed in helpless fascination on the intense face so close to her own. "I beg your pardon," she said belligerently.

Rubinoff stared at her in blank disbelief, then closed his eyes and shook his head wonderingly. "Dear Lord, you're utterly incredible." He groaned softly. "You've got to be an imposter. How could a private detective be so damn naive?" He opened his eyes and looked down at her, his lips twisting in a wry smile. "I was joking again," he said patiently, as if to a slightly retarded child.

"Well, how was I to know that?" she asked defensively. "You did take an awfully long time to open the door, and when you did answer it, you weren't exactly formally dressed." Her gaze dropped down to his hair-roughened chest, which was now pressed closely to her own. Too closely, she thought breathlessly, because his warmth seemed to pierce the material that separated them and cause a hot, melting sensation in her limbs. She knew she should move away from this travesty of a torrid embrace, but for some reason she felt oddly weak and languid.

"The clerk got me out of the shower when he called to announce you," Rubinoff said resignedly. "I had to dry off and slip on a robe."

"Oh," Honey said weakly. His auburn hair did look slightly damp. "Well, you did say that the only reason you wanted me here was to try to seduce me."

"No." He shook his head firmly. "That's what you said. Naturally I want to seduce you. You turn me on more than any woman I've ever met. But that's not the only reason I wanted you here." His eyes twinkled roguishly. "The principle one, but not the only one. I wanted to make amends for Manuela's idiotic practical joke."

"By blackmailing me?" Honey asked doubtfully.

"I knew that you probably wouldn't be persuaded to come any other way," he said absently, his gaze fixed disapprovingly on her hair. "You've bundled up your hair again. Why the hell do you do that, when it's so gorgeous floating all around you like a silver cape?"

"It's more professional like this," she said, feeling ridiculously guilty at his disappointment.

She suddenly realized that she was still being

held over his arm in that dramatic Valentino embrace. "Hadn't you better let me go?" she asked breathlessly.

"If you insist." He sighed as he pulled her upright, then reluctantly released her and stepped back. Tightening the belt of his robe, he asked, "Would you like a drink?"

"I'll have a ginger ale, if you have it," Honey answered as she followed him across the room to the mirrored bar. What was it about the man that kept her constantly in a state of uncertainty? she mused as she perched on a maroon-velvet-cushioned barstool and watched Rubinoff behind the bar deftly pouring her drink. When she had marched into the apartment a short time ago, she'd been determined that she was going to establish barriers even Houdini couldn't overcome. Yet here she was, accepting a drink and gazing bemusedly at Rubinoff's intent face as he concentrated on mixing his own bourbon and water. His lashes were ridiculously long for a man's, she noticed idly. Their russet color was sun-streaked gold at the tips.

Those lashes swept up swiftly as his head lifted, and he handed her a tall frosted glass. "Now," he said firmly, leaning his elbows on the bar and gazing at her with surprising gravity, "we talk."

"I believe we've been doing that for some time," Honey said dryly, taking a sip of her ginger ale. "We've just not been communicating."

His lips quirked impishly. "Oh, we've been communicating. Perhaps not verbally, but we've definitely been communicating." He held up his hand as she started to protest. "All right, I'll be as solemn and boringly sincere as even you could wish, sweetheart." He took a drink of his bourbon and water before setting his glass on the counter. "Let's enumerate the reasons why you should take the job Davies offered you, shall we?" He held up a long, graceful finger. "One, according to Davies's report, you need the money." He held up another finger. "Two, being my bodyguard would be an intelligent career move. Three . . ." A third finger joined the others. "It's your patriotic duty as an American citizen to prevent a possible international incident." He arched an eyebrow inquiringly. "Shall I go on? I've got plenty of fingers left if you're not convinced."

"I think you'd really be in a quandary by the time you reached that last digit," Honey said, her lips curving in a reluctant smile. "I think you've almost exhausted your stock of arguments now."

"I've left out two of the most important ones," he said softly as he lowered his hand and covered her own. "It'll allow me to rid myself of this damn guilt I've been feeling ever since I talked to Manuela last night."

"I don't have to ask what the last one is," Honey said dryly.

He frowned. "No, I guess you don't," he said tersely. "I've been fairly open on that score. Too damn open. I should have tried seduction." He picked up his glass and took another drink. His eyes met hers as he slowly lowered the glass. "I didn't want to seduce you, damn it," he said tautly. "You're not a woman to enjoy games. There's not much honesty in the world today, but I think you're an exception, Honey Winston. You deserve better than that." His hand tightened on hers, and his gaze was as direct as his tone. "I want you, Honey; I'm going to do everything in my power to make you want me, too. But that doesn't mean that I'm going to try to bulldoze you into anything." His lips twisted. "Sexual harassment isn't my style. I'm no Ben Lackland, Honey."

"You know about that?" Honey's eyes widened in surprise.

"Davies's dossier was fairly detailed." Rubinoff

shrugged. "I can see why you'd be wary after such an experience, but I can't say that I'm flattered at being compared to him." He grimaced. "I hope that I'm a bit more subtle in my approach than that bastard."

"I'm sure you are," Honey said soothingly, amused in spite of herself at the indignation in his face. He looked very much like a cross little boy.

"My reputation may not be exactly pure as driven snow." His scowl became even darker as Honey choked on her drink at that gross understatement. "But I do not *pounce*."

He wouldn't have to, Honey thought ruefully. That impish and almost overpowering charismatic virility would be potent enough.

"I'd let you set the pace," Rubinoff went on briskly. "I don't enjoy unwilling women."

Had he ever known any? Honey wondered. She hadn't the slightest doubt that he was supremely confident that he could overcome her resistance in short order. "And what if I remain unwilling?" she asked thoughtfully.

His smile lit the darkness of his face with heart-catching warmth. "Then I have a new experience in store," he said lightly. "I don't believe I've ever had a woman for a friend." His husky voice was coaxing, the blue eyes wistful and appealing. "Will you be my friend, Honey Winston?"

Honey felt a melting sensation in her breast that had no resemblance to the desire he had formerly inspired in her. "And if I still don't agree with your proposal?" Honey asked quietly.

He sighed resignedly. "Then I guess I'll just have to resume the blackmail tactics." His blue eyes twinkled. "For your own good, of course."

"Of course," Honey echoed, shaking her head in rueful amusement. The man was utterly impossible. She was beginning to realize that there was a layer of diamond-hard steel beneath that careless exterior. Yet she felt an odd sense of trust in the man beneath that mask. "Then I'd better give in gracefully, hadn't I?" she asked lightly.

She was rewarded by a smile so blindingly brilliant that she felt strangely dizzy. "Good girl," he said briskly, setting down his glass on the counter and coming around from behind the bar to stand before her. "I'm sure that I'll feel much safer with you in the next room." He gave her a wistful look. "Of course, I'd feel *really* secure with you in my bed." She chuckled and shook her head. "No?" He shrugged resignedly. "I didn't think so."

"I'm afraid that wouldn't be very practical in this case," Honey said lightly. "I've never heard that you were fond of *ménages à trois*, and my duties include the protection of your cousin."

"Alex?" Rubinoff looked decidedly uneasy. "Now, that might present a few problems."

"Problems?" Honey asked warily, her gaze narrowed on his face.

He put his hands on her slim waist and lifted her lightly off the stool. "Alex refuses to accept you as his bodyguard," he said ruefully, then continued hurriedly as she started to protest. "It's not you personally whom he objects to, you understand. He'd reject anyone hired for the same position." He turned her gently, his hand at her waist, and began to propel her across the living room, toward a door on the opposite side of the room. "He has no objection to you acting as my bodyguard, however. He thought you were quite charming."

"How very kind of him," Honey said ironically, wondering how she was supposed to guard someone when he wouldn't even acknowledge her as his protector. "I thought men in your position were accustomed to having bodyguards and security men buzzing around you. Why are you and your cousin so adamantly against it?"

"We value our privacy," Rubinoff said simply. He smiled at her grimly. "And Alex and I were brought up rather differently from what most people would expect. Remind me to tell you about it sometime."

They'd reached the bedroom door, and he opened it with a little flourish. "This is your room," he said, leaning lazily against the doorjamb. "There's an adjoining bath. I think you'll be fairly comfortable." His eyes twinkled mischievously. "I'm right next door, so if you need anything, just call."

"I'm the one who's supposed to be able to hear *you* if you need me," she said unthinkingly, and then could have bitten her tongue.

It was too much to expect him to let that pass. His face took on an expression of cherubic innocence. "Does that mean you'll come if I want you to?" he asked, gazing limpidly into her eyes. "Perhaps we'd better have them put in a connecting door. It would save considerable wear and tear on the carpet from the traffic back and forth."

"You know I meant that you were to call if you were in danger," she said sternly, trying to frown disapprovingly into that mischievous face.

"Unfortunately, I did," he said morosely. "We'll be dining at eight and then going somewhere later to dance. Since this is your territory, Alex and I will let you choose." He made a face. "Just don't make it any place where we might run into one of Alex's business chums or any political bureaucrats. He's promised me that the party last night was the final little social duty we'd have to suffer through, but I don't want to put temptation in his path."

Honey frowned. "Don't you think that it would be safer to have dinner in the suite? It will be difficult maintaining any degree of security in a crowd."

"But I can see that you're a woman who thrives on challenges," Rubinoff said lightly. "I feel completely safe in your capable hands." He turned away, and then looked over his shoulder to say, "Wear your hair down. We wouldn't want you to look too businesslike, would we? It might remind Alex that you're here to guard, not entertain, us."

He was gone before she could reply, and there was still a lingering smile on her face as she slowly closed the door and leaned against it bemusedly. Then she gave herself a little shake and straightened slowly. What was the matter with her? She was as languid and dreamy-eyed as a teenager who'd been asked to her first prom by the captain of the football team. Where was the cool insouciance that had been her shield and buckler for so long? It had taken less than an hour for Lance Rubinoff to raise in her a bewildering mixture of emotions. The physical magnetism she could recognize and understand, but what of that odd melting tenderness? He was as stimulating and intoxicating as those margaritas that Nancy had offered her as liquid comfort.

Just when she became convinced that the slightly mad, impish dilettante was the true Prince Rubinoff, he allowed her a fleeting glimpse beneath the glittering facade to the personality beneath. It was like trying to unravel the clues in a complicated and masterly crafted mystery thriller. And she'd always had a passion for mysteries. It was the primary reason she'd entered her profession. Well, this particular mystery might be more addictive and dangerous than any she had solved to date. She would have to guard her own emotions as assiduously as she would guard Rubinoff and Alex Ben Raschid.

She strode briskly toward the bathroom door

Rubinoff had indicated. She had left her suit-cases downstairs at the reception desk, in the last-ditch hope that she could convince Rubinoff to abandon his blackmail ploy. She would have to call down and have them sent up. But first she'd shower and wash her hair. She cast a cursory glance about the bedroom.

She supposed it could be considered as lux-uriously elegant as the rest of the suite, but it was definitely not to her taste. The cool-looking blue carpet contrasted perfectly with the rich cream taf-feta spread on the king-sized bed. The Louis XIV chair in the corner of the room was cushioned in the same patterned cream taffeta. It was all very fastidious, expensive, and icily impersonal. Evi-dently this stiff, aloof beauty was what the hotel management considered suitable for its most au-gust guests. Personally, she preferred a little more informality and color in her surroundings, and she had an idea that Lance Rubinoff did too.

As Honey entered the spacious blue-and-white bathroom and began to strip off her pants suit, she firmly dismissed Rubinoff from her con-sciousness. He had been occupying her thoughts far too much lately. She pulled the pins from her hair and let it tumble down her back in wild silky profusion. There was certainly no possibility of her leaving her hair loose just because that wild, impossible man liked it that way. No possibility at all.

Three

"Did I tell you how beautiful you are this evening?" Lance Rubinoff murmured in her ear as he took her black velvet wrap and seated her with graceful panache at the small table. "Your hair shines like silver against that black velvet. I'm glad you wore it down."

Honey fingered a long tress almost guiltily. "It had nothing to do with you. I just decided that there was no use antagonizing Alex unnecessarily." She touched the skirt of the simple black velvet sheath she was wearing. "And my intention was not to be beautiful, just discreet."

Rubinoff's lips quirked and one eyebrow arched mockingly as his gaze ran over her lingeringly. The dress in question may have been modest in cut, with its bateau neckline and long tight sleeves, which ended at her wrists, but on Honey's full, graceful figure it took on a tactile sensuality that was causing every man in the crowded smoky room to stare at her with distinct lasciviousness.

"Sorry, sweetheart, you didn't succeed," he

drawled as he dropped into a chair next to her. "There's no way you could fade into the background no matter what you wore." His gaze ran around the room appraisingly. "This is quite an unusual place. Do you come here often?"

Honey shook her head, her own eyes following his about the room. "It's not my kind of scene," she answered. "But I thought you might find it amusing." She smiled impishly. "And you certainly won't run into the governor or the mayor here."

"No?" Rubinoff asked quizzically, and looked about him with renewed interest. "Have you brought us to a den of iniquity? It appears fairly innocuous."

The Starburst was a disco whose decor and loud, pulsating music fully lived up to its name. The only illumination in the large room was provided by the elaborate pyrotechnics beneath the clear plastic panels of the dance floor. The brilliant center ball of scarlet was constantly exploding into starlike fragments and then reforming once again into its shimmering, pulsing core. When combined with the throbbing music and intimate darkness, the atmosphere was curiously erotic.

"It's not that bad," Honey said absently. "It's just a meat market." A frown clouded her face as her gaze anxiously circled the room. "Where is Alex? I thought he was right behind us."

"He stopped in the lobby to make a phone call. Don't worry, no one's kidnapping him from beneath your eagle eye. What's a meat market?"

Honey felt the tension gripping her relax, and she leaned back in her chair with a little sigh of relief. "You haven't heard that particular bit of slang before?" she asked. "It refers to a bar or disco whose patrons are a trifle overly aggressive in their pursuit of the opposite sex."

"Very descriptive," Rubinoff said idly, watching

the gyrating couples. "I gather that there are more moves on the sidelines than on the dance floor?"

"Exactly," Honey said with a grin. "I thought you'd feel right at home here." She tilted her head and gazed at him curiously. "That's the first time you've asked me to explain the meaning of any colloquialism. Your grasp of the vernacular is really exceptional. Both you and Alex sound like born and bred Americans."

"Alex and I were practically raised by a Texas oil roughneck by the name of Clancy Donahue," Rubinoff explained with a reminiscent smile. "And his colloquialisms were often a good deal bluer than yours, sweetheart."

"Wasn't that a rather unusual choice of tutor for a royal prince and the heir-apparent to a sheik-dom?" Honey asked, leaning forward, her face alight with interest.

"Not if you knew Karim Ben Raschid, Alex's grandfather," Rubinoff said dryly. "He's a wily old cutthroat with a healthy respect for American know-how and a fierce determination to keep what's his. Not an easy task, when the plum's as rich as Sedikhan. There have been border skirmishes there as long as I can remember, and the diplomatic maneuverings can be more dangerous than the battles themselves. Clancy was a mercenary, a smuggler, and God knows what else, before he turned up in one of Karim's oil fields twenty years ago. Karim turned us over to his tender mercies when Alex was twelve and I was ten, with instructions to do whatever was necessary to turn us from boys into men." His eyes were dancing. "Clancy's methods were a trifle unorthodox for princely training, but that suited Karim. He taught us everything from guerrilla warfare to the art of bringing in a gusher. I went on my first full-fledged border battle when I was fourteen. Clancy certainly made things interesting."

"Didn't your own parents have anything to say about that?" Honey asked. "I would have thought that they would object to Karim's putting you in danger."

His lips curled in a cynical smile. "Tamrovia needed oil, like every other country. Karim knew just how to pull the right strings to get what he wanted, and what he wanted was a companion for Alex of equal birth and status to temper that Ben Raschid arrogance." He shrugged. "It was the wisest arrangement for everyone concerned. I was a thorn in my parents' serene, conventional lives from the moment I was born. I was always more at home in Sedikhan than Tamrovia, and Alex and I grew up as close as brothers."

"And what of Clancy Donahue? Is he still in Sedikhan?" Honey asked, her gaze on Rubinoff's face in the flickering lights, which illuminated his face, only to return it to shadow in the next instant. Had there been a touch of bitterness behind the cynicism in his expression?

"Clancy?" There was no question of the affection in his face, even in the dimness of the room. "Oh, yes, Clancy's a permanent member of Alex's household now. He generally accompanies him everywhere. He was mad as hell when Alex made him stay behind on this trip." He chuckled. "He tends to get a little overprotective and has a tendency to cramp Alex's style."

"I think he should have brought him along this time," Honey said, frowning. "If he won't accept my protection, there may come a time when he'll need all the help he can get."

"We're doing very well without him," Rubinoff said lightly. "And Alex was very receptive to you at dinner. Perhaps he'll even allow you eventually to instigate some minor security measures on his behalf."

Honey shook her head skeptically. "Charming

as your cousin was to me, I don't think he's about
to tolerate me in any capacity but as a dinner
companion."

The evening thus far had proved to be surprisingly pleasant, and she had found herself amazingly at ease with both Rubinoff and Ben Raschid
by the time they'd finished dinner. It had been a
fascinating exercise just to observe the cheerful
badinage between the men and attempt to detect
the subtle undercurrents that ran beneath the
surface of the mocking raillery. She could well
believe Rubinoff's claim that Alex was like a brother
to him. It was all there to see once you peered
beneath the masks they wore—respect, humor,
tolerance, and genuine affection.

The bonds that had forged their relationship
were so strong and long-standing that one would
have expected Honey to feel like an outsider.
Strangely, this was not the case. Rubinoff had
gently drawn her into the magic circle, and Ben
Raschid had followed his lead with the mocking
arrogance she was beginning to associate with
him. By the time they'd left the restaurant, she
was on a first-name basis with both men and felt
a camaraderie that she would never have believed
possible a few hours before. She was vaguely conscious that Lance was deliberately dampening
down that vibrant sensuality and giving her the
time and breathing space he'd promised her, and
the knowledge filled her with an odd breathless
warmth.

"You thought Alex was charming?" Lance asked
with a black scowl. "I wanted you to like him, but
you weren't supposed to find him charming, damn
it. I was the one who was supposed to dazzle you
with my rapier wit and virile attractiveness. It's
clear that I'll have to apply myself more assiduously to the project." He hitched his chair closer
to her own, until his hard muscular thigh was

pressed intimately against her own, and put his hand on her knee. "*Now* do I have your complete attention?"

Honey firmly removed his hand and placed it back on the table with a tolerant little pat. It was impossible to be angry with him when he was gazing at her with those wistful blue eyes that still held a glint of little-boy devilishness in their depths. "I have an idea that you've had a great deal too much attention from women in your career, Lance," she said lightly. "I wonder if you even remember their names."

"Not many of their names," he admitted frankly. "They're all a bit of a blur after a while." Then, as he saw the frown beginning to cloud her face, he covered her hand with his and said gently, "They didn't mean anything to me. How could I be expected to remember them, Honey? What I feel for you is entirely different."

She lowered her eyes to their joined hands, her lashes hiding the sudden jolt of pain at his callous remark. "I'd be something of a fool to believe that, wouldn't I?" she asked huskily. "Next month you'll probably be saying that to some other woman."

There was a flicker of anger in the blue eyes looking into hers. "I don't lie, Honey," he said curtly. "I don't know why or just how the way I feel for you is different as yet. I'm still a little confused on that score, but I do know that I've never felt anything quite like this before. When I lifted that tablecloth and found you curled up like a luscious kitten, staring up at me with those big violet eyes, it was as if someone had hit me in the stomach."

"Chemistry," Honey said firmly, still not looking at him. "What else could it be?"

"How the hell do I know?" he asked moodily. "If it was chemistry, why did it feel so right to have you with us tonight? It was as if you'd always been there across from me and always would be."

Her eyes flew up, and for a moment she forgot to breathe as she met the hot intensity of his. So she hadn't been the only one to feel that strange sense of belonging.

"Would you like me to go make another phone call?" Ben Raschid asked politely. Neither of them had seen him approach, but he was suddenly standing at their side, with an expression of amused resignation on his face and a distinctly sardonic smile on his lips.

Honey could feel the color rush to her face, and she tried to withdraw her hand from Lance's. "No, of course not," she said a little hurriedly. "We were beginning to be a little concerned for you. You've been gone a long time."

Lance firmly foiled her attempts at removing her hand from his by possessively tightening his clasp. "Yes, we've missed you," he said absently, not taking his eyes from Honey's face. "Why don't you leave, so that we can miss you again?"

"Lance!" Honey exclaimed, shocked at his rudeness.

Ben Raschid only chuckled, his dark eyes twinkling as he shook his head reprovingly at Rubinoff before dropping into the chair opposite them. "Presently," he drawled. "At the moment I have the urge to sample the delights of this unique establishment Honey has seen fit to bring us to. On my trip from the foyer to the table, I was accosted by three women, two of whom offered to buy me a drink. The third wanted me to dance. Are most Houston women this aggressive, Honey?"

"Only at meat markets," Rubinoff answered for her, reluctantly looking away from Honey to glance at Alex with a wry smile. "I don't think he needs a definition of the term after his recent experience, Honey. I'm surprised you didn't accept one of the invitations, Alex. Didn't any of them look good to you?"

"There was a rather ravishing little redhead," Ben Raschid said. "But I decided to look the field over before deciding."

"A redhead." Lance shook his head ruefully. "I should have known. Why bother to even browse, Alex? You know that you'll choose the redhead anyway." He turned to Honey and explained. "Alex has had a passion for redheads since we were boys."

"It won't hurt to make her wait a bit," Alex said lazily, and he imperiously signaled a passing waiter. "She was a little overeager. What will you have to drink?"

Honey had finally managed to wrest her hand from Lance's grasp, and she unobtrusively scooted her chair a few inches away from his. She was finding that hard muscular thigh so close to her own very distracting. "Just ginger ale for me," she answered.

While Ben Raschid gave the orders to the waiter, Lance lifted a brow inquiringly. "Don't you ever drink anything stronger?"

She shook her head with a wry grimace. "Not since I discovered the peculiar effect it has on my tongue. It causes it to waggle excessively."

"Fascinating," he murmured. "I must remember that. A few drinks and I'll know all your secrets."

Suddenly, a well-manicured hand cut through the space between them and slapped down a fifty-dollar bill. They both looked up, startled, at the woman standing beside the table.

"That's for you, darlin'," the woman slurred, swaying slightly and smiling at Rubinoff with a smug alcoholic leer. "And there's more where that came from. No one can say that Joanie Jessup's not willing to pay generously for what she wants."

"I beg your pardon?" Lance said blankly. "Were you speaking to me?"

"You bet your boots," Joanie Jessup said, laying one unsteady hand on his shoulder and beaming at him. "You're the lucky man tonight, Red. I've had my eye on you since you came into the place. Damn, you're a handsome brute."

"Thank you," Lance said warily. "That's very kind of you. Now, if you'll excuse us?"

Honey had first been so taken by surprise that she could only stare open-mouthed at the boldness of the woman. Joanie Jessup was in her early fifties, on the plump side, and sported an elaborate bouffant blond coiffure. She was expensively if a trifle garishly dressed in a pink décolleté cocktail gown. She was also very obviously under the influence. Then, as Honey gazed from Lance's stunned, wary face to the woman's drunken leer, she suddenly giggled helplessly. Lance shot her a glance of extreme displeasure.

"It's not enough?" The woman reached into her purse and drew out another fifty and slapped it down on top of the first. "I should have known you'd be expensive, you big gorgeous devil." She bent lurchingly, and nibbled seductively at his ear. "But you'll be worth it, sweetie. Redheads are always such passionate lovers."

"My premise exactly," Ben Raschid murmured, leaning back in his chair and observing his cousin's discomfort with every evidence of enjoyment.

"Very funny," Lance said caustically, trying to detach the woman's hold from about his neck and glaring at both Ben Raschid and Honey's grinning faces with profound disgust. "Miss Winston, I believe you're supposed to be my bodyguard," he said icily. "Well, guard my *body*, damn it!"

Honey hastily smothered her smile, but her eyes were still dancing as she said solemnly, "Right away, sir." She quickly got to her feet and leaned forward to whisper in Joanie Jessup's ear.

The plump blonde slowly straightened, her expression ludicrously disappointed. "You've got to be kidding," she pleaded almost tearfully, reluctantly releasing Lance's shoulder and gazing gloomily from him to Ben Raschid and then back again.

Honey shook her head silently, her expression equally mournful.

Joanie Jessup slowly picked up the two fifty-dollar bills and stuffed them back into her evening bag. "You're sure?" she asked despondently, gazing yearningly at Rubinoff.

"Positive," Honey said firmly.

"What a God-awful waste," the woman murmured. "But, then, all the best-looking ones are." She turned and lurched uncertainly away.

"Are what?" Lance asked, his eyes narrowed suspiciously on Honey's face.

"Gay," Honey said simply. "I told her that you and Alex were lovers."

"You told her what?" Lance asked explosively, and Ben Raschid muttered a brief, explicit obscenity.

"Well, you told me to get rid of her," Honey said defensively, trying to hide the giggles that persisted in welling up despite her efforts to stifle them. "I knew that would be the quickest way. Alex's remark about passionate redheads gave me the perfect lead-in."

"Oh my Lord," Alex groaned, burying his face in his hands. "If you don't murder her, I will, Lance."

"It's my privilege," Lance said grimly, standing up and pushing back his chair with barely restrained violence. He leaned over, grasping Honey by the wrist, and pulled her to her feet. "Come along, Honey."

"Where are we going?" Honey asked, startled, as he pulled her along behind him and crossed the room.

"I've got to expend my irritation by either shaking the living daylights out of you or channeling it into some other outlet." They had reached the dance floor, and he spun her onto the glowing, ever-changing plastic surface. "Dance with me, damn it!"

She danced with him, and it was like no dance she'd ever known. The music was loud and raucous, and the moves were as ritualistic and sensual as those in a primitive mating ceremony. The shifting colors and exploding pyrotechnics beneath their feet offered their own excitement, and Lance's face in the flaring crimson glow had a look of hungry sexuality that awoke an answering response in Honey. Then the music suddenly changed its wild tempo to a slow, mellow melody that was as sensual in its own fashion as the former wailing cacophony. Honey and Lance were both breathing hard, their emotions and senses as glowingly alive as the exhilarating adrenaline pounding through their bodies. They stood looking at each other for a moment and then, in silent agreement, they flowed together once again.

Lance wrapped his arms around her, cradling her in a close embrace, and her own arms slid almost instinctively under his suit coat and around his waist. Her head rested contentedly on his shoulder as they moved slowly around the dance floor. Honey was dreamily conscious only of the soft throbbing music and the strong beat of Lance's heart beneath her ear. His arms tightened around her, bringing her closer to the hard column of his thighs, and she felt a sudden weakening in her own limbs. How strange that the touch of warm hard sinews should make her feel so soft and weak in contrast. Strange and rather wonderful.

"Honey." Lance's voice was husky and velvet-soft in her ear.

"Hmmm?" she answered, snuggling closer to him.

"I'm definitely not gay."

"I know." Honey sighed dreamily. Nothing could be clearer than that fact at this moment. "Isn't it wonderful?"

His deep chuckle held a note of surprise. "I think so," he said, "but I'm glad you agree." His lips brushed her temple in a caress as gentle as a summer breeze. "You know what you're doing to me, don't you?"

She nodded, her arms tightening around him possessively. She was vaguely aware that her conduct was totally inconsistent with her usual behavior. Her cool serenity and pragmatic approach to life seemed to be completely banished by the potent combination of the music, lights, and the physical magic exerted by the man holding her so closely it was as if there were one entity.

"Let's get back to the hotel," Lance said huskily, stopping in the middle of the dance floor. His arms were still holding her so close to his body as he turned and propelled her gently back toward the table that their hips brushed at every step. It was almost as if they were still dancing, Honey thought hazily. She was momentarily jolted from her state of euphoria by the realization that Alex was gone from the table.

"Where's Alex?" she asked, her eyes searching the room in sudden panic as she realized just how derelict in her duty she'd been in the last hour. She had let Lance beguile her into completely forgetting her purpose in being here tonight, and now Alex was nowhere to be seen!

"I'm getting a little annoyed with your constant preoccupation with Alex's whereabouts," Lance drawled, his lips quirking. "I assure you that Alex can take exceptionally good care of himself. It's me you should be concerned about." He draped her black velvet wrap about her shoulders and threw a few bills down on the table. "Haven't I demonstrated sufficiently just how much I need you? What if another Joanie Jessup appears on the scene lusting after my irresistible physique?"

"But we can't just leave," Honey protested as he took her elbow. "He's my responsibility, too. I have to find him."

"Honey, I told you that . . ." Lance started when his eye fell on a piece of folded paper in the center of the table. He picked up the note and perused it swiftly. An amused smile was on his lips as he looked up to say, "It's from Alex. It seems that after you cast aspersions on his masculinity he felt the need for a little active reinforcement. He's gone after the redhead. He says he'll see us back at the suite." He lifted a mocking eyebrow. "Tomorrow morning."

"But where did he go?" Honey wailed. "How can I protect him if I don't know where he is?"

"You can't," Lance said cheerfully as he guided her swiftly through the nightclub to the front entrance. "So why don't you stop worrying about him? Alex will turn up early tomorrow morning, just as he promised. He knows that I've ordered the helicopter to take us to the Folly at ten o'clock."

"The Folly?"

Lance flagged down a passing taxi with an imperious hand, and the cab pulled to a smooth stop at the curb before them.

"Sedikhan Petroleum recently acquired an estate on a private island in the Gulf of Mexico about ninety miles off the coast of Galveston," Lance explained, opening the passenger door and helping Honey into the cab. He sank down in the vinyl seat beside her. After giving the driver the address, he continued. "It was formerly owned by an Englishman named Thomas Londale and became known as Londale's Folly."

"Why?" Honey asked curiously as Lance slid an arm about her shoulders and pulled her close to his side.

"Who knows? Perhaps because the island is located in the hurricane belt and Londale had all the buildings on the island built of stone. It probably cost him a small fortune just to import the building materials." His hand was playing idly with the silky hair tumbling about her shoulders. "Alex and I leased the property two years ago when we were here last, and found that it met our needs. It's close enough for Alex to keep in touch with his beloved power-play games, but private enough to allow him total relaxation if he wants it."

"And you?" Honey asked softly. "What does Londale's Folly offer you, Lance?"

His face became oddly guarded. "It gives me what I need too," he murmured, and before she could question the statement, his hand closed tightly in her hair and tilted her head back. He looked into her eyes, his own glowing with a warm intensity that made her feel oddly light-headed. "Do you know that I haven't even kissed you yet?"

It seemed incredible to her, too. The intimacy of the moments they'd shared tonight had bound them together with golden cords of passion. How strange to realize that they'd only touched each other in the most conventional ways.

"I can't wait any longer," Lance whispered huskily. "I sure as hell didn't want it to be in the back of a taxi, but I need you now, Honey."

Her eyes were wide and wondering as they gazed at the dark intent face slowly lowering to her own. The first touch of his lips was so light as to be almost tentative, a light, brushing caress that teased with a provocative gentleness, then wooed and persuaded, until her own lips were clinging to his in an exchange that was dizzyingly sweet.

Lance's hands framed her face with hands that

were as gentle as his lips. "Lord, that was good," he said softly when their lips finally parted. "God, you're a sweet little thing." Then he was kissing her again, and it was just as magical as before.

"I'm not little," she protested dazedly, while his lips moved to the sensitive hollow of her throat.

"You're not?" he asked. "No, I suppose you're not. Somehow I think of you as being small and cuddly." His lips closed on hers again, and they were both breathing in little gasps when Lance spoke again. "You may not be little, but you're definitely cuddly," he muttered. His hands left her face to slip beneath her black velvet wrap and cup the fullness of her breasts. "You're so soft and round and cushiony."

Her chuckle was a trifle breathless. "You make me sound like Grandma's feather bed," she said faintly, and then gasped as his thumbs lightly grazed her sensitive nipples through the soft velvet.

"I'd like to use you as a bed," he murmured hoarsely. He lowered his head to rest it on her breast, while his thumbs rhythmically caressed her nipples. "I'd like to have these lovely mounds cradle me like fleecy pillows, and bury myself in the softness of your body." She could feel the warmth of his mouth through the velvet as he rubbed his face back and forth across her swelling fullness with a sensual, almost catlike contentment. "Dear heaven, I want that."

No more than she did, Honey thought feverishly. The muscles of her throat and chest were so taut that it almost hurt to breathe, and every touch of Lance's hands or lips seemed to leave a trail of molten fire in its wake. The words that he was whispering were as evocatively passionate as his gentle, stroking hands.

Then his hands were sliding around the back of her dress and deftly undoing the zipper. At first she was so lost in the hot sensual haze that it seemed perfectly natural to feel the warm eager fingers on the naked flesh of her back. Then, as her black velvet wrap was pushed impatiently away from her shoulders, she abruptly came to her senses. What were they doing?

"No," she whispered, putting her hands on her chest. "We can't, Lance. Let me go."

He looked up, his face as flushed and dazed as her own. "Let you go?" he asked, as if the idea were totally incomprehensible. "You know I can't do that." His lips covered her own in a kiss as bruisingly fierce as the others had been gentle, parting her lips to invade the moist sweetness with his tongue and explore it with an erotic skill that almost made her forget why she was protesting. "You see?" he gasped, coming up for air, his heart beating like a trip-hammer against her breast. "How the hell can we stop?"

"The driver," she said faintly, nodding to the silent, discreet figure in the front seat of the cab. She was so aroused that for a moment she was tempted to ignore their audience and melt once more into Lance's arms and forget everything.

Lance muttered a shocking obscenity, and his arms tightened possessively around her for a brief instant. Then he drew a deep, shuddering breath, and his embrace loosened fractionally. "Okay," he growled raggedly. "Just give me a minute."

It was a bit longer than that before he slowly released her and drew away a scant few inches. "Sorry," he said gruffly, while his shaking hands reluctantly zipped up the back of her dress. "I guess you noticed that you have a fairly explosive effect on me. I don't usually attempt seduction in the back seat of a taxi cab." He shook his head disbelievingly. "If you hadn't stopped me, I think I would have taken you without a second thought." He tucked her wrap securely around her shoulders once more, and pulled her into the sheltering curve of his arm. "Now, be still, and I just may withstand temptation until we get back to the hotel."

She was obediently still, her head tucked contentedly into the hollow of his shoulder while he stared impatiently out the window at the slow-moving traffic. "My God, it's just like rush hour even at this time of the night," he said disgustedly. "It will take us forever to get anywhere."

"Houston has a growth problem," Honey said dreamily, thinking how beautifully sculptured were the bones of his cheek and jaw.

He glanced down at her languid clouded eyes and bruised swollen mouth, and for a moment there was a flicker of amusement warring with the desire in his eyes. "At the moment I can sympathize, no, *empathize* perfectly," he said thickly. "Oh, what the hell!" His lips swooped down, and once again she felt his teeth and tongue working with erotic expertise. "We might as well do something while we're waiting." His hands slipped once more beneath her wrap and began to knead and tease her swollen breasts. "I wouldn't want you to cool down and change your mind, would I?"

There was no danger of that, Honey thought ruefully. Her body responded like a Stradivarius in the hands of a master violinist in the wild, heated moments that followed, and she wasn't even conscious of when the cab drew up in front of the hotel.

Lance was, however, and he drew quickly away from her as the cab came to a halt before the brightly lit front entrance. "Thank God," he said fervently, withdrawing a bill from his wallet and handing it to the grinning cab driver without even looking at it. Ignoring the driver's dazed murmur of appreciation, he opened the cab door. "Come on, let's go," he said curtly, getting out of the taxi and pulling her after him. "Another five minutes and I wouldn't have made it."

And neither would she, Honey thought with a profound feeling of relief. In those last few minutes in the cab she had begun to feel that it wouldn't have mattered if they'd had an audience as large as one at the Astrodome. She came eagerly into the possessive curve of his arm as he propelled her swiftly through the front entrance into the sleekly luxurious foyer.

"One moment, please, Your Highness!"

They both looked up in surprise, and there was a sudden brilliant flash. "That's great . . . just one more!"

Honey heard Lance mutter a violent oath, and his arm tightened protectively about her waist. He increased his pace, until they were almost running toward the bank of elevators across the foyer.

The sharp-faced photographer who had taken their picture was right on their heels. "Is Miss Winston to accompany you on your entire tour, Your Highness?" he asked with machine-gun rapidity. "Did you know each other before you arrived in Houston? What do their Majesties have to say—" He tried to follow them into the elevator, but Lance placed a hand on his chest and gave him a rough shove while punching the button for the penthouse with the other hand. The doors closed on the photographer's frowning, frustrated face.

"I should have told the cab driver to go around to the service entrance," Lance said with a scowl. "I didn't think there would be any reporters persistent enough to be haunting the lobby this late at night." His glance was suddenly concerned as he noticed Honey's pale, set face. "Are you all right?"

"I'm fine," Honey said numbly, brushing the hair from her eyes with a shaking hand. "How did he know who I was?"

Lance shrugged. "I suppose Davies must have issued a press release. There was bound to be speculation when the news hounds snooped out the fact that you were occupying a room in our suite. It was probably the most discreet way of handling the affair." The doors of the elevator slid soundlessly open, and Honey preceded him dazedly from the cubicle and down the hall to the elegantly carved teak door of the suite.

Discreet. A discreet way of handling the affair. The words were so casually said. Well, why shouldn't they be? Lance probably hadn't noticed the double entendre that had struck her like a blow—for she *had* come within a breath of being one of Lance's "affairs." If that flashbulb had not rocked her to her senses, she would have crawled as eagerly into the prince's bed as any of his other playmates.

Lance unlocked the door and flicked on the wall switch, flooding the room with light before turning to face her. His narrowed eyes flickered warily. "Okay, let's have it," he said flatly. "What's wrong?"

"I think you know," she said huskily, not looking at him as she closed the door and moved slowly forward into the room, her gaze fixed desperately on the Corot lithograph on the wall across the room.

"The hell I do," Lance said roughly. "All I know is that in the taxi you wanted me as much as I wanted you, and now you're a million miles away from me. What happened?"

"I came to my senses," she said softly. "You're quite a man, Lance. You made me pretty dizzy for a while."

"Past tense?" he asked caustically. "I can't have a very lingering appeal. You seemed to have completely recovered your equilibrium." His voice was rough with frustration. "Look at me, damn it.

That blasted picture can't hold such a degree of fascination for you."

Her gaze moved reluctantly to his taut, angry face. She felt that familiar melting sensation even now, as her gaze lingered on the strong male beauty of that face, with its cap of shining auburn, burnished by the overhead lights. A man had no right to be so beautiful, she thought desperately, wanting to close her eyes and shut out the sheer virile magnetism of him. "I just don't consider the game worth the candle, Lance," she said, steadying her voice with no little effort. "I don't want to be one of your one-night stands; nor do I want to figure in the tabloids as your latest mistress." Her eyes darkened stormily. "I don't particularly relish the company I'd be in. Wasn't it only six months ago that you were squiring that extremely pricey call girl about the Riviera?"

"For God's sake, that has nothing to do with us," he said indignantly. "I told you—"

"I'm sure you tell all of us just the pretty lies that we crave to hear," Honey interrupted, her eyes flashing. She turned and stalked toward her room with regal dignity. "Well, I've heard all I want to hear tonight."

"Damn it, Honey, I don't lie," Lance grated cut behind her. "I know what happened downstairs came as a shock to you, but if you were thinking clearly, you'd realize that it has nothing to do with what we feel for each other. And don't try to tell me that what we shared in that taxi was one-sided."

She turned at the door, her eyes bright with tears. "I didn't say that," she said huskily, her lips trembling slightly. "I wanted you. I'd be a terrible hypocrite not to admit it. I just can't tolerate being Prince Rubinoff's latest. I wouldn't know how to cope with it." She shrugged helplessly. "I'm just not that tough."

His expression softened, the anger dissipating. He shook his head slowly. "You're not tough at all. You're a sweet, loving woman, and I want every single bit of you." He smiled ruefully. "But I guess I can wait a little longer. Run along and hide your head in the sand, sweetheart. You'll have to surface sometime, and when you do, I'll be here waiting."

"I mean it, Lance," Honey said gravely, her face troubled. "I don't want this type of relationship. I have no use for it in my life."

"I know you mean it." Lance smiled lovingly at her, his blue eyes twinkling. "But that doesn't mean you won't change your mind. I'm told that I can be a very persuasive fellow."

The door was closing behind her when he called softly. "Honey?"

She paused.

"I'll order breakfast for nine," he said. "If you have any packing to do, do it tonight. We'll be leaving for the island promptly at ten."

Four

Londale's Folly proved to be a tiny tropical island set like a glittering emerald in the azure waters of the Gulf. From the air it appeared to be scarcely two miles across, with the only habitation a large stone house on the crest of the hill overlooking a sheltered cove. When the orange-and-cream heli-copter was secured on the concrete landing pad in that same sheltered cove, Honey found that the notion there was only that one house on the is-land wasn't precisely correct.

Ben Raschid turned to Lance, one dark eyebrow arched inquiringly, as he picked up his small duf-fel bag from the pad. "Shall I tell Justine that you'll be up to the house for dinner?" he asked.

Lance shook his head. "Not tonight," he said absently, picking up his own small case as well as Honey's much larger one. "I have some work I want to do while the light is good. We'll rummage in the kitchen for something to snack on. Justine usually stocks the refrigerator pretty well."

His eyes flicked with sudden amusement to Ben

Raschid's face. "Besides, I don't think you'd be very entertaining company this evening, Alex—you're looking a bit on the frayed side. I imagine that you'll opt for an early night. Was your redhead worth it?"

"Inventive. Very inventive," Ben Raschid replied with a distinctly Mephistophelian grin. "But she wasn't a real redhead. I'd say she was originally a Scandinavian blonde, like our Honey, here." He gave a mocking bow in Honey's direction. "Though not as beautiful, of course."

"How disappointing for you," Lance said, his lips quirking as he took Honey's arm. "I'm glad that she made up in talent what she lacked in fire."

He turned Honey and gently propelled her forward, away from the helicopter. He looked over his shoulder to say, "We'll be up at the main house for brunch tomorrow at ten. I trust you'll be recovered enough to act the proper host. I know what a churlish bastard you can be, but we wouldn't want to disillusion Honey so early in your acquaintance."

Honey heard Ben Raschid's amused chuckle behind them, but Lance had accelerated his pace, and she hadn't time to glance behind as he hurried her from the landing pad down a gently sloping gravel path to the beach that she'd noticed from the air.

"Where are we going?" she asked breathlessly, trying to keep up with him. "And why isn't Alex going with us?" Then, when he didn't answer but continued to gaze at the horizon, she skidded to a stop and jerked her arm from his grasp. "Will you answer me, Lance?" she demanded in exasperation.

"What?" he asked absently, then apologized a trifle sheepishly. "Sorry, Honey. I was just admiring the play of the sun's rays on the water. The light is absolutely incredible here, isn't it? The only place that might possibly equal it is in Greece. There are times when Delphi appears to be bathed in liquid gold." His gaze went back to the horizon. "This island is much more arresting during a storm, though."

"That's utterly fascinating," Honey said caustically. "Now will you please tell me where you're taking me?"

Lance took her arm again. "We're almost there." He nodded to the curve in the beach ahead. "I have a small cottage on the beach, which I use when I'm here."

"You mean that you two don't even stay in the same house while you're on the island?" she asked. At his gentle nudge she once again fell into step with him, her eyes on his urbane face. "And may I ask how I'm supposed to maintain any kind of security if you're on opposite sides of the island?"

"We're not on opposite sides of the island," he said patiently. "The main house is only a five-minute walk from the cottage, and as for security, we couldn't be safer. The only permanent residents are Nate and Justine Sonders, who take care of the big house. Justine is cook and housekeeper, and her husband acts as general handyman." He darted her a mischievous glance. "They're both in their late sixties, so I think Alex and I may be able to handle them if they become *too* obstreperous."

"Very amusing," Honey said crossly. "They may be the only residents, but no island is totally inaccessible."

"This one comes pretty close. This is the only cove that's not too rocky to permit access by boat, and if a helicopter tried to land anywhere on the island, we'd hear it." He frowned at her impatiently. "Relax. We're both a hell of a lot safer than we were in Houston. Your only problem is going to be how to avoid getting a sunburn while you're playing on the beach. I hope you brought a bikini."

She shook her head. "I never wear one." She felt a sudden relief as she realized that Lance was probably right. If the island was as inaccessible as he'd said, then it would be fairly easy to keep an eye out for trespassers.

"Never?" Lance raised an eyebrow. "I don't know if I like the idea of your appearing in the altogether before anyone but me. The cove is fairly private, but it's visible from the big house. Perhaps you'd better wait until after dark to go skinny-dipping."

Honey's eyes had been searching the terrain for possible landing spots, but as the last words sank in, her eyes flew back to his face. "Skinny di—" she exclaimed. "What on earth are you talking about?" Then, as she met the dancing blue devils in Rubinoff's eyes, her own lips curved in a reluctant smile. "I meant I wear a very respectable maillot," she told him sternly. "A bikini on a woman of my proportions has a tendency to look a bit skimpy."

"An effect much to be desired," Lance murmured, his glance moving over her with a lingering intimacy that caused that hot, glowing warmth to kindle in the pit of her stomach. "All that lovely skin must be well-nigh mind-boggling. You're sure you won't go skinny-dipping with me?"

"I'm quite sure," she said firmly, frowning at him.

"Pity," he said morosely, shooting her a sly sidelong glance. "I guess we'll just have to confine it to the bathtub. Oh, well, it'll be cozier there anyway."

Honey shook her head ruefully. The man was totally incorrigible. Trying to distract him, she asked quickly, "The main house seems to be quite large. Why don't you stay there?"

He shrugged. "We both like to have our own space. It would take considerably more rooms than the Folly possesses to reconcile our two life-styles. I'd probably drive Alex up the wall in a matter of hours. My clutter would grate on that high-powered computer he calls a brain like the sound of nails on a chalkboard."

"Clutter?" Honey asked.

His expression became oddly guarded. "I paint a little," he said casually. "I'm afraid I have the usual artistic disregard for order." He made a face. "To be less euphemistic, I'm a complete slob."

"I don't remember reading anything in the papers about your being an artist," Honey said slowly. Actually, though, now that she thought about it, hadn't Alex mentioned something about Lance's painting when she had been crammed beneath that trolley? "Have you ever had a show?"

Rubinoff shook his head, his expression closed and tight. "I'm strictly an amateur," he said curtly. "And the gossip columns don't have access to *every* facet of my life." They had rounded the headland and come upon a white stone cottage with surprising suddenness. "Here we are, such as it is."

When Lance threw open the door and allowed her to precede him into the cottage, Honey realized what he meant. The interior seemed smaller than she had thought at first glance. Evidently the former owner had not wasted much of his extravagance on this tiny place. They entered directly into the principal living area, which consisted of a combination lounge/kitchen that was surprisingly stark and ascetic. There was no furniture at all in the room, with the exception of a black leather couch, a teak coffee table, and a scarlet leather breakfast booth in one corner of the room, opposite an ancient kerosene stove. Instead of carpet or tile, the floor consisted of polished flagstones in a dull slate blue. Two doors opened off the central area, and it was toward the farthest of these that Rubinoff headed.

"There's only one bedroom, with an adjoining bath," he said briskly as he threw open the door. "I've converted the other one into a studio. The light is better from the north." Then, as she started to protest, he waved her impatiently to silence. "Don't worry; there's a couch in the studio that I can bunk down on." He arched an eyebrow inquiringly. "That is, if you insist on being so selfish about sharing your bed."

"I insist," Honey said softly, glancing into the bedroom. It was as sparsely furnished as the other room, containing only one double bed, covered in a durable forest-green denim spread, and a strictly utilitarian night table. "I suppose the flagstone flooring is very practical in this climate," she commented. "It's probably cool no matter what the temperature."

"More practical than you'd imagine." Lance's tone was dry. "It was Londale's only sop to conventional practicality when he built the cottage. Located on an open beach, with nothing to shelter it, on an island that's smack dab in the hurricane belt?" He shook his head ruefully. "Every time the island is hit by a tropical storm, the cottage is completely flooded."

"So that's why it's furnished so meagerly," Honey said thoughtfully. "Don't you find it inconvenient to have to move to the main house whenever there's a storm?"

"It doesn't happen that often," he said casually, crossing the room to put her suitcase on the bed. "We'll probably only use the island a few months a year, and the chances of a really bad storm's hitting while we're here are minimal."

"Not if you plan on using it in September," Honey replied lightly, following him into the room and dropping her purse on the bed beside the suitcase. "Didn't anyone ever tell you that this is definitely not the season for island hopping?"

"I think I'll get to work," Lance said, and there was a barely restrained eagerness in his face that was oddly intriguing. "I'll see you later. Why don't you slip into that depressingly sensible swimsuit and go play on the beach? There should be something in the refrigerator if you get hungry later."

The door closed behind him, leaving Honey to stare at it in rueful bewilderment. So much for the trepidation she'd had about staving off Lance's amorous advances. He might just as well have told her to run along and not bother him. Not exactly uplifting to the ego. After those tempestuous moments in the taxi last night and his blunt threat before she'd left the room, she'd been distinctly wary. It appeared she'd definitely overestimated her attraction for Rubinoff.

Though both Lance and Alex had been charming to her on the trip from Houston, she didn't fool herself that either man had been pursuing her. She might almost have been a younger sister, for all the sexual awareness Alex had shown, and except for a few teasing remarks, Lance had displayed the same platonic affection.

In fact, Lance had been a little more abstracted than Alex. There had been that curious leashed eagerness, a charged restlessness that had seemed to electrify him from the moment they'd met in the living room of the suite for breakfast this morning. He'd been rather endearingly like a little boy anticipating a special treat. Well, the little boy had gone off to play with his paints, and she'd been sent off to the beach with her pail and shovel to amuse herself.

She didn't ask herself why she was experiencing this weird sense of betrayal, as she turned and briskly unstrapped her suitcase. She withdrew the maligned maillot and looked at it critically.

It wasn't all that stodgy, she thought defensively. Though not cut exceptionally low in the bodice, it had the popular French cut that made her legs look deliciously long and shapely, and its nude color was provocative in itself. Not that there would be anyone to provoke, with Lance locked in that room with his precious canvases.

He hadn't even made mention of her hairstyle, coiled in the usual businesslike style this morning. Not that it mattered to her, she assured herself. The less he noticed about her, the more pleased she would be. She was glad to be left alone to enjoy herself without masculine interference. She'd take a swim and explore the island and then come back to fix them a bite to eat. No, she'd fix herself a bite to eat. Lance could just shift for himself—if he decided to come out and grace her with his royal presence, she decided, and she began to unbutton her blouse. The less she saw of that impossible man, the happier it would make her.

Honey was frowning with annoyance, and her violet eyes were stormy as she traversed the last few yards to the front entrance of the Folly the next morning and knocked peremptorily on the brass-bracketed oak door. She knew that she was in no fit temper for a social breakfast, but there was no way she was going to remain by herself any longer in this so-called island paradise.

The door was opened by a small, plump woman dressed in a dark dress and a pretty flowered smock.

"How do you do. You must be Justine," Honey said, forcing a polite smile. "I'm Honey Winston. I believe Alex Ben Raschid is expecting me."

The woman smiled with quiet friendliness. "Mr. Ben Raschid is breakfasting on the terrace, Miss Winston," she said. She gestured toward an arched doorway on her left. "If you'll go right through, I can get back to my kitchen."

She turned and bustled away, and Honey obediently made her way through the arch into the spacious room, which was as different as chalk and cheese from the barren cottage she'd just left. She cast a glowering look at the gleaming white terazzo floor, covered with glowingly colorful scatter rugs, and the graceful cushioned white rattan furniture as she made her way toward the French doors. The room was full of lush green plants and bouquets of flowers, and everything about it was polished and well maintained. This aspect, more than any other, served to aggravate Honey's annoyance. If there was one thing that she wasn't feeling at the moment, it was cosseted and lovingly cared for.

Her displeasure must have been mirrored in her expression, for Alex's dark brows lifted in mock surprise as he slowly got to his feet when she strode out on the flagstone terrace.

"Don't say anything," he said, motioning to a graceful white wrought-iron chair at the elegantly appointed glass table. "Just sit down and have a cup of coffee. I gather Lance has gotten himself into your bad books. I rather thought he would." He poured a cup of hot fragrant coffee from the carafe on the table into an exquisite china cup. "He's not showing up for breakfast, I gather?"

"I really wouldn't know," Honey said shortly, plopping down in the chair he'd indicated. "I haven't seen him since yesterday afternoon." She glared at him crossly. "And I have no need to cool off. I'm not in the least annoyed. I just thought that someone should have the courtesy to show up and make an explanation."

A little smile tugged at his lips, and his dark eyes glinted with amusement. "I see," he said slowly. He refilled his own cup and set the carafe back on the table before resuming his seat and leaning lazily back in his chair. "Naturally, I appreciate your courtesy as well as your charming company," he drawled with an enigmatic smile as he stretched his jean-clad legs before him. "Drink your coffee," he urged quietly. "Justine is serving strawberry crepes this morning, and you won't even know what you're eating if you don't calm down."

"I am calm," she retorted indignantly. "I'm not in the least upset." Then, as she met the cool derision in the dark eyes opposite her, she admitted reluctantly, "Well, perhaps I'm a *little* upset." She rushed on hurriedly. "But it has nothing to do with Lance. It's this blasted island. I'm a city girl. I don't know what to do with all this fresh air and glorious nature in the raw."

"And you had no wild Scaramouche to keep you entertained," Alex added softly, taking a sip of his coffee.

"I told you that he had nothing to do with it," Honey said, frowning at him fiercely. "My relationship with Prince Rubinoff is strictly business, and I certainly have no right to expect him to treat me as anything but his bodyguard." She bit her lip vexedly. "I'm just not used to not having anything to do." She looked up hopefully. "Lance said this was going to be a working holiday for you. I'm pretty good at hunting and pecking on the typewriter—perhaps I could help."

Alex shook his head immediately. "No way," he said definitely. "Lance made it very clear that you're out of bounds for me in any capacity. I've no desire to provoke that redheaded temper of his by trespassing on his property." He held up his hand as she started to protest. "I know, you're just his bodyguard." He lifted his cup and took another sip of coffee. "But we both realize that Lance is aiming for another type of relationship entirely. If

I gave you something to do that would take you out of his immediate orbit, he'd raise the roof."

"He doesn't even know I'm on the same island," Honey said tartly. "He didn't come out of that studio all night, and when I knocked on the door this morning, he didn't even bother to answer." She pouted mutinously. "I don't think you need to worry about purloining my services."

"It's not unusual for Lance to get caught up in his work and labor through the night," Alex said quietly. "Particularly when he just gets back to it after an absence. Give him a day or so, and he'll surface to the point of being moderately civilized again." His lips quirked indulgently. "He's always just like a kid let out of school at first."

Honey took a drink of her coffee, not really tasting it, her gaze fixed unhappily on the delicate floral design on her cup. "I noticed," she said. "Are you as enthusiastic about your hobbies, Alex?"

"Hobby?" His dark eyes narrowed on her face. "Painting isn't a hobby with Lance; it's a full-scale passion. Didn't you see any of his work before he shut himself into his studio?"

She shook her head. "He couldn't be bothered to do anything but pat me on the head and send me off to play," she said. She looked up, a flicker of curiosity piercing the hurt. "If painting is such a passion for him, why haven't I read about it in the tabloids? He certainly makes no effort to avoid publicity. His life's an open book."

"Is it?" Alex asked mockingly. "I think you'll find when you get to know Lance a little better that he's an intensely private person concerning the things he cares about. If an item appears in the gossip column, you'll know that Lance doesn't give a damn about it. I doubt if more than five people in the world know that he's an artist." He lifted his cup in a little salute. "You should be honored, Honey."

"Is he any good?" Honey asked.

"Good?" A curious smile lifted the corners of his lips. "Yes, I think you might say he's good. Would you like to see one of his paintings?"

"You have one here?"

"In the library," Alex said, rising to his feet. "It's a portrait of my grandfather. Lance gave it to me for my birthday last year." His dark eyes were veiled. "I believe you might find it quite interesting."

Honey's first impression as she entered the book-lined library was how small the room was. Then she realized with a sense of shock that the room was quite spacious; it was the large portrait on the wall over the desk that was dwarfing and dominating the room and producing that curious shrinking effect. Karim Ben Raschid was dressed in the traditional robes of his desert people, but that was the only conventional aspect of the portrait. His booted feet were crossed and propped insolently on a massive desk, which was as sleekly modern as he was roughly barbaric. "A wily old cutthroat," Lance had called him, and it was all there in the strong, sensual face and gleaming dark eyes that were so like Alex's own.

But there was more, too. There was determination in the set of that bearded chin and a certain tenderness in the curve of his lips. Or was it mockery? She moved forward in compulsive fascination. No, she was sure it was tenderness. She shook her head in bewilderment as she noticed a fugitive devil in the depths of those ebony eyes, which had at first not been apparent. The more she looked, the more that was revealed to her.

"Well?" Alex's voice was amused, and she could feel his eyes on her from where he leaned indolently against the doorjamb.

"Is it as good as I think it is?" Honey asked in a hushed voice, not taking her eyes from the painting. "It's the most powerful portrait I've ever seen!"

"It's great," Alex agreed quietly. "And it's not even his best work. Lance prefers not to paint anyone he has a personal attachment to. He says that it ruins his perspective."

"But why hasn't he had a show? Any gallery in the world would be proud to display paintings of this caliber." She tilted her head, trying to determine what masterly technique Lance had used to make that barbaric figure in the frame come alive.

"You'll have to ask Lance about that," Alex said. "I just thought you ought to know that Lance isn't simply a dabbler amusing himself. It may help you to accept a few of his eccentricities." There was a thread of amusement running through his voice. "Like completely ignoring you for days at a time."

She reluctantly turned away from the painting, and faced him. "Thank you," she said thoughtfully. "I do understand better now."

"Good," Alex said with a grin that illuminated his dark, cynical face with surprising warmth. "Then Lance owes me one." His brow arched mockingly. "And believe me, I always collect."

She just bet he did, Honey thought, looking at that face that was as forcefully enigmatic as the one in the portrait above her. "Do you have to make excuses for your cousin very often?" she asked lightly.

He shook his head. "I don't usually bother. If Lance doesn't give a damn, why should I?" The mockery faded from his face. "But this time I think the situation's a little different."

"Different?" Honey asked.

"His reactions regarding anything concerning you have been a bit unusual, to say the least. I have an idea that he'll mind very much that he's made you upset with him."

"Not enough to interrupt his work, evidently.

Not that I'd expect him to, of course," she added quickly.

"Of course not," he said solemnly, his lips quirking. "As you say, it's strictly business between you two." He gestured for her to precede him from the library. "And since you're so adamant on that score, I don't feel in the least guilty about enjoying your exclusive company at breakfast. Come on along and try Justine's strawberry crepes. Perhaps you're in a better humor to enjoy them now."

The strawberry crepes were delicious, and Alex's conversation over breakfast was fascinating and carefully impersonal. He had little chance to enjoy his own breakfast, however. He was interrupted twice with business calls from Houston and once with an urgent call from Sedikhan.

When he returned to the table after the third call, he shook his head ruefully. "Sorry about that. I've told Justine to hold my calls until after breakfast."

"And this is a vacation for you?" Honey asked lightly as she sipped her coffee. "Lance said you were something of a workaholic."

"The pot calling the kettle black," he replied, refilling his cup. "He's as bad as I am. He just refuses to acknowledge that what he does is work. He calls it an enjoyable pastime and completely different from my dull, stuffy business affairs."

"But you don't look at it the same way, do you?" Honey asked thoughtfully, her eyes on his face.

"Very perceptive of you," he said softly, looking up. There was a flicker in the depth of his eyes. "No, I think we're both artists. I just use a different brush and a wider canvas." His eyes narrowed. "And I can assure you that the colors I select are just as carefully considered."

"But not always subdued," Honey said with an

impish grin. "I noticed that you have a distinct preference for red."

"Everyone has his little quirks," he said, grimacing. "And Lance makes damn sure that everyone is conversant with mine."

"Have you always had this passion for redheads?" Honey asked lightly.

"As long as I can remember." His expression was ruminative. "I've often wondered if it had something to do with Lance."

Honey's eyes grew round. "You mean that you . . . ?"

"No, I do *not* mean that," he rapped sharply, scowling at her with extreme displeasure. "And I'd appreciate it if you'd refrain from giving out tales to that effect even in the performance of your blasted duty."

"Sorry," Honey said, trying to hide a smile.

Evidently she didn't succeed, for Alex continued to frown at her fiercely. "I should hope so," he said emphatically. Then he sighed resignedly. "What I meant was that it might have some psychological connection to my relationship with Lance," he explained patiently. "I'm a very cynical person. My grandfather made sure of that, for sheer self-protection. Lance has been the only person in my life whom I've ever trusted totally. There's a possibility that I may be attracted by women of similar coloring because I feel safer with them."

"Not because they're more passionate, as you implied?" Honey asked, her eyes twinkling.

"Well, that, too," he replied, with an answering grin. Then, as if remembering his annoyance with her, he said belligerently, "And I'd like to state categorically that I've never been attracted to a member of the same sex, redheaded or not. Is that clear?"

Honey nodded meekly. "Very clear."

"Good," he said, relaxing. "Now that we've got

that settled, why don't we go back to the library, and you can choose a few books to read? They may come in handy when Lance opts out of the human race again."

When Honey opened the door to the cottage two hours later, it was as silent as when she'd left. She cast a speculative glance at the closed door of the studio on the way to her bedroom but resisted the temptation to knock. Surely the man couldn't still be painting. That would be carrying his artistic marathon into the realms of the ridiculous. No, she must just assume that he wanted to be left alone, and indulge his whims. She was a mature woman, and certainly didn't need anyone to amuse her, as Alex had suggested.

She dropped the armload of books she was carrying on the bed in her room and swiftly changed into her nude-colored maillot. It was still a little damp from her swim yesterday afternoon, she noticed, and felt clammy against her skin despite the noonday warmth. She supposed she really should have brought another suit with her. This island living was going to be very hard on her meager wardrobe, and how was she going to keep her clothing clean, when there wasn't even an automatic washer in the cottage? She'd just have to go up the hill to the big house and ask Justine if she could use the one at the Folly.

The door of the studio was still stubbornly closed when she left the cottage, and she determinedly looked away from it as she passed. If he was still in there when she returned from her swim, she would have to breach his privacy even if it did annoy him. She had to be certain that he was all right, didn't she? She'd be derelict in her duty if she let a full twenty-four hours go by without setting eyes on the man. There was a satisfied smile on her face as she ran lightheartedly down to the beach.

• • •

"Don't you have any sense at all? You're going to burn to a crisp, staying out this long."

Honey felt her heart leap in her breast at the sound of the familiar voice, but she didn't open her eyes. She was much too content just lying here on the beach with only the blanket between her and the soft cushiony sand.

"I have sunscreen on," she said composedly. "I haven't been out nearly as long as I was yesterday, and I didn't get even a little sunburned then."

"It was late afternoon when you went out yesterday," he said grimly. "The sun was a good deal lower." When she didn't answer, he let out an impatient imprecation. "For heaven's sake, will you open your eyes? I feel like I'm talking to a corpse."

She reluctantly did as he asked, and then wished she hadn't. He was standing only a few feet from where she was lying, and he looked much too disturbing. The tight faded jeans he wore, hung low on his hips and molded the powerful column of his thighs with loving detail. He was shirtless, and her eyes were drawn compulsively to the beautifully sculptured muscles of his shoulders and chest. He was almost copper-colored, she noticed dreamily, and the thick russet thatch of hair on his chest was burnished by the sun to a shimmering vitality. He was unfolding a white sheet that he was carrying, and the muscles of his arms and shoulders rippled with a supple beauty as he shook out the material and dropped it over her.

"I'll smother under this," she protested, pushing the fabric aside impatiently as he dropped to his knees beside her.

"Too bad," he said coolly, drawing the sheet up to her chin again. "It's better than second-degree burns. Perhaps it's wiser that you don't wear a bikini. The more of you that's covered, the better, if you're always so criminally careless on the beach."

"Aren't you overreacting?" she asked crossly, sitting up and brushing her hair away from her face. The movement caused the sheet to fall to her waist, and she brushed his hand aside as he attempted to pull it up again. "And this suit isn't all that staid," she said huffily.

"So I noticed," he said dryly, his eyes on the lush swell of her cleavage. "When I glanced out of the studio window, I thought you'd decided to go skinny-dipping after all. It was quite a shock to my nervous system. That color is as erotic as hell."

"I wouldn't have thought you'd even notice," she snapped, and then could have bitten her tongue. She had meant to be cool and completely uncaring and not even refer to the past twenty-four hours of loneliness. She rushed on brightly, trying to mend the break. "Alex said he would send Nate down later this afternoon to see if you'd be free for dinner this evening."

He sighed gloomily, running his hand restlessly through the fiery darkness of his hair. "I really blew it, didn't I?" he asked ruefully. "I suppose it's too late to apologize. Will it help if I promise you that it won't happen again?"

"According to Alex, it isn't a promise that you're likely to keep," Honey said huskily, not looking at him. "And you certainly don't have to make me any extravagant promises. You don't owe me that courtesy; I just work for you."

"Ouch!" he said, making a face. "If that particular prevarication didn't annoy the hell out of me, it would really hurt." His blue eyes were serious as he continued quietly, "Look, you have every right to be upset, because I give you that right. I'd be bloody well furious if you went off and forgot about me for that long." He shrugged wearily. "I don't even have a reasonable excuse. I just got involved and worked through the night. I only meant to take a catnap this morning, but I guess I must have passed out." His voice was curiously grave. "Will you forgive me?"

She looked up, about to deny the necessity for the apology, when she encountered the seriousness in the blue eyes. "Yes, I forgive you," she said instead. Then, with a reluctant honesty, she admitted, "I was lonely."

"God, I'm sorry, Honey," he said, drawing a little closer to her so that they were only inches away. He reached out and took her shoulders in his hands, holding her with a careful gentleness that gave her a richly treasured feeling. "I should have realized that I'd get carried away." His lips curved ruefully. "I guess I couldn't believe that I'd fall into my usual bad habits with you only a few yards away. I sure as hell couldn't think of anything else the night before."

"But then I had no competition," she said lightly. "How could I expect to rate your attention when genius was burning and the muse whispering in your ear?"

"I'd rather have you whispering in my ear," he said with a twinkle. "And I don't lay claim to any special talent; it's just a pleasant hobby."

"Not according to Alex," Honey said slowly, gazing at him earnestly. "And not if that painting in Alex's study is an example. You're absolutely fantastic, Lance."

"Alex must have been in a very talkative mood this morning. And it's not my artistic talent that I want you to appreciate. Would you like to know what else I'm fantastic at?"

"No," she said promptly, frowning at him reprovingly. "That particular talent is a matter of public record. I'm more interested in your unpublicized talent. Why haven't you had a show? It's not fair to hide a gift like that from the world. A talent of that magnitude carries a certain responsibility."

He sighed and shook his head resignedly. "I should have known you'd fasten those gorgeous white teeth on the subject and worry it until you pried it out of me." His expression sobered. "The truth is, I can't exhibit. It would blow the whole caper."

Honey's eyes widened. "Caper?" she asked.

He nodded unhappily. "One of those art experts would be bound to recognize my technique, and neither Alex nor I have a fondness for jail cells."

"What on earth are you talking about?"

"Sedikhan Petroleum went broke two years ago," Lance said, not looking at her. "It's only the money Alex and I have been able to pour into it from our scam that's kept it from becoming public knowledge. We couldn't let old Karim lose face with his people."

"Scam?" Honey asked, subdued.

"I do the painting, and Alex takes care of passing it discreetly into the right hands to set up the miraculous discovery of another lost masterpiece. You know the Rembrandt they found buried in that cellar in Munich eighteen months ago?"

She nodded.

"That was one of mine," he said sadly. "One of my best works. I hated to let it go."

"A forgery?" Honey squeaked. "You're a forger?"

"You needn't put it so crudely," Lance said, flinching. "It takes a great deal of work and a certain flair to imitate another artist's techniques. I spent more time and effort on *my* Vermeer than he ever did on his."

"Vermeer?" Honey repeated dazedly, feeling as if she were going mad.

"*Woman at the Mirror*," Lance supplied tersely. "Discovered last summer in Antwerp."

"Oh, my God," Honey breathed. All that incredible talent wasted on a shoddy confidence game. It made her physically ill. "That one too?"

He nodded slowly, still not looking at her, but she could see that his eyes were suspiciously bright. This confession was evidently not easy for him.

He said thoughtfully, "I suppose my greatest challenge was the Mona Lisa. The subtle shading for that one required great . . ." He glanced down at her shocked face and gaping lips and couldn't go on. He burst into great whoops of laughter, bent almost double with the force of the convulsions that shook him. "Oh, Lord, it's like taking candy from a baby," he gasped, wiping the tears from his eyes. "You're totally unbelievable, Honey. Tell me, have you ever bought the Brooklyn Bridge?"

"It was all a joke?" Honey asked blankly, and when he nodded, she felt a surge of hurt and anger of stunning strength. To think that she'd actually felt sorry for him. "You must have thought me very stupid, Your Highness."

The laughter was quickly wiped from his face and replaced by concern. "Honey," he started, "I never meant—"

"I suppose I am rather gullible," Honey interrupted, the stupid tears rushing to her eyes. "It must have been great fun for you. I should be honored to have provided you with an amusing anecdote to laugh about with Alex." She drew a quivering breath. "Do you know that I was even dumb enough to feel sorry for you? How absurd could I be to think that you could feel deeply about anything? Butterflies don't think or feel, they just flit on the surface of life and look pretty." Her voice rose bitterly. "No one expects them to be taken seriously or be anything but what they are.

I just made the mistake of forgetting that. I assure you it won't happen again."

She jumped to her feet and was several yards away before he caught up with her. He grabbed her by the shoulders and whirled her to face him. "I'm not a butterfly, damn it!" he said forcefully, giving her a little shake. "I may be a blind, stupid fool not to realize that I was hurting you by my teasing, but I'm not the callous bastard you think me. I'll match my sensitivity against yours any day. What the hell is wrong with not wanting to lay your emotions out in the open for everyone to see?"

"Nothing. Not as long as you're willing to admit that they exist," she spat back. "But you're not, are you? I know very well your paintings must be important to you, but you won't admit even to Alex that it's more than an amusing pastime. Why don't you face up to the fact that what you could give the world is very special, and stop hiding it as if it were something to be ashamed of?"

His face was as taut and stormy as hers. "What do you know about it?" he asked roughly, his blue eyes blazing. "Okay! So it's important to me. Maybe it's the single most important thing in my life. Does that satisfy you?"

"No!" she shouted. "Why the hell don't you have a show?"

"Because it *is* important, damn it," he said, with equal force. "Do you think I want to be known as just another celebrity artist? My work means something. I won't have it held up as a playboy's idle dabblings."

"But the critics won't do that," Honey protested. "They couldn't. All they'd have to do is to take one look and know that you're exceptional."

"Would they?" he drawled cynically. "I think we've established that you're a bit naive. Starving artists may be taken seriously, but not princes of the blood. I don't doubt that my work would sell, but I'd never know whether it sold because someone wanted a conversation piece by Lusty Lance to hang on the wall. Well, I'll be damned if I'll give it to them. I'd rather let the canvases pile up in a deserted warehouse."

There was such passion in his face at that moment that it took her breath away—passion and a painful bitterness that caused her to ache for him. "You're wrong," she whispered huskily. "So wrong. It wouldn't be like that."

"No, you're the one who's wrong," he said tersely. "I've seen it happen often enough. Believe me, I'd find the kind of success you're wishing on me a hell of a lot more frustrating than keeping my work strictly sub rosa for the rest of my life."

"But it's such a waste," she said, and suddenly the emotions that had crowded one upon another in the past few minutes took their inevitable toll, and two tears brimmed in her eyes and rolled slowly down her cheeks. "Such a criminal waste."

There was a curiously startled look on his face as he slowly lifted his hand to her wet cheek and gingerly traced the path of her tears. "For me?" he asked wonderingly. "I don't believe anyone's ever shed tears on my behalf before. I think I like it."

"Why would anyone cry for you?" she asked brokenly. "Have you ever shown anyone that there might be someone who was worth a few honest emotions, beneath that clown's mask you wear?"

"I've changed my mind. I don't like it," he said huskily. "Stop it, Honey. I can't stand what it's doing to me."

"Too bad," she said, the tears falling faster. "I can't say that I like it either. I don't want to cry for you. You don't deserve it."

"I know," he said, almost humbly, as he drew her into his arms and cuddled her comfortingly.

He pressed his lips to her temple. "But you can't take those tears back. You gave them to me and they're mine now. I'm going to keep them in a special place somewhere near my heart, and take them out when I feel particularly wicked or sad." He was rocking her gently. "I'll look at them and say to myself, 'See, you can't be all that bad, Lance, old boy. Honey cried for you.' "

"You fool," Honey sobbed, her arms sliding around to clutch at him fiercely. "Damn, you're such a crazy fool. Why am I letting you do this to me?"

His hand was stroking her hair now. "Because every Harlequin has to have a Columbine," he said softly. "And I think I've found mine at last. God, you feel right in my arms, love."

Her face was buried in the springy russet hair of his chest, and it felt deliciously rough against the smoothness of her cheek. He smelled of clean soap and salt and a slight muskiness that was potently virile, but oddly enough, for the first time in their relationship, she was not experiencing that almost overpowering physical magnetism. She felt only a magical sense of being protected and cosseted and an almost painfully poignant tenderness.

Lance tilted her head up, and the expression on his face was oddly stern. "Honey?" he asked gravely.

She shook her head bewilderedly. She wasn't entirely sure what he was asking of her, but she had an idea that it was more than she could yield in the turbulence of the moment. "Not yet, Lance. Please, not yet."

He regarded her thoughtfully for a moment, before nodding slowly. "I can wait a little longer," he whispered, "but it's getting more difficult all the time. Remember that, will you, Honey?"

She nodded, her expression as serious as his. "I'll remember."

"Good," he said, and bent to take her lips with infinite tenderness. "Lord, you're sweet to love."

So was he, Honey thought dreamily as he reluctantly released her. Strong and beautiful and wonderfully tender.

"Come on," he said gruffly, slipping an arm about her waist and turning her firmly toward the cottage. "My willpower is eroding rapidly. My parents may have had the bad taste to throw in a Lancelot with my other more sedate names, but I can assure you that I'm no knight in shining armor."

He looked very much like one to her at the moment. Patience and restraint weren't among the qualities for which Lance was noted, making his control all the more praiseworthy.

"Well, do you want to go up to the Folly for dinner?" he asked, arching an eyebrow mockingly. "I promise that I'll be the perfect escort, to make up for my bad manners, which you've so graciously forgiven."

Honey shook her head. "No," she said quietly. "You don't really want to go." She shot him a sidelong glance, her lips curving in an amused smile. "I think you want to get back to your studio, don't you?"

He frowned. "I'm not about to do that to you again," he said curtly, but she noticed he didn't deny it. "I intend to devote the entire evening to you. If you don't want to join Alex, we'll do something else. What would you like to do?"

He spoke as if there were all the choices in the world on this tiny island.

"Well, I'm having a hard time choosing between Pavarotti's concert and Baryshnikov's *Nutcracker*," she drawled wryly. "So I think I'll settle for a good book and an early night. Alex supplied me with a surfeit of the former, and I hardly think I'll be disturbed once you get back to your work, so I'll certainly get the latter."

"I told you—" he began impatiently.

"Yes, I know," she said soothingly. "But you should have learned by now that we peasants aren't accustomed to noblesse oblige." She smiled at him gently. "I want you to work, Lance."

"You're sure?" he asked, his face troubled.

"I'm sure," she said serenely. "I'll see what I can throw together for a meal before you disappear for the evening."

He was silent for a moment. "I don't suppose you'd want to come in and keep me company?" he suggested tentatively. "The couch is fairly comfortable, and the lighting is better than anywhere else in the cottage, if you're planning to read."

Her startled gaze flew to his face. "You don't mind people around when you're working?"

His shrug was oddly awkward. "I don't know," he said simply. "I've never let anyone into my studio before. I just think that I'd like to have you there with me. It may take some getting used to for both of us." His arm tightened on her waist. "Will you come, Honey?"

Her throat was suddenly so tight, she was having trouble swallowing, and she looked hurriedly away so that he couldn't see the mistiness in her eyes. "Yes, I'll come," she said softly.

Five

Who could imagine that watching a man in the esthetic pursuit of painting a picture could be such a sensual experience? Honey wondered dreamily. The soft, almost inaudible whish of the brush on the canvas, the quiet sounds as Lance shifted his stance or moved to reach for another tube—even the acerbic smell of turpentine and paint was ambiguously stimulating. Honey grimaced ruefully. She must really be far gone to find the smell of turpentine an aphrodisiac. Why not be honest and admit that it was the man himself whom she found so fascinating?

Her gaze ran lingeringly over the intentness of Lance's face as his eyes narrowed in concentration on the canvas sitting on the easel in front of him. She couldn't see the painting itself from where she was curled on the cream naugahyde couch across the room, but she could see Lance very well indeed.

He was rather like a painting himself, she thought. He was wearing the same faded jeans he had this afternoon, but he had donned an old blue chambray work shirt when he had gotten back to the cottage. Its sleeves were rolled up to the elbow, baring his tanned muscular forearms, and he'd left it carelessly unbuttoned almost to the waist. Honey could see the play of the sleek muscles of his shoulders as he moved, and the light blue of the shirt turned his eyes to deep sapphire.

Suddenly those sapphire eyes darted to where she sat with her book lying ignored on her lap, and a brilliant smile lit the bronze darkness of his face. "Okay?" he asked gently. "You're not bored?"

"I'm fine. This thriller Alex lent me is really absorbing," she lied shamelessly. She hadn't read a page in the hours that she'd been in the studio this evening. She'd been too enthralled with the infinitely more exciting mystery that was embodied in the form of Lance Rubinoff. "Would you like some more coffee?"

"Not now," he said absently, his attention once more on the canvas in front of him. "You'd better use that afghan. It's getting cooler, and your legs will get cold in those shorts."

Honey's lips quirked wryly as she remembered the lascivious glance she'd received from him when she'd appeared in these white shorts earlier in the evening. At the moment she could have had fence posts for legs, for all he cared. She obediently pulled the beige-and-rose crocheted afghan over her legs and gazed contentedly around her.

The studio, though much larger than her bedroom, was even more starkly furnished. Other than the couch she was resting on, there was only a large, paint-spattered work table jammed against the wall; it was cluttered with an assortment of paint and brushes. The easel was in the center of the room. There were canvases everywhere, some leaning against the wall beneath the bank of windows overlooking the beach, and others stacked carelessly in the corners. When Lance had opened the closet door to take down the afghan from the shelf, she had even seen several other completed canvases pushed randomly against the wall in a corner. She'd been tempted to protest Lance's deliberate offhandedness with those valuable paintings, but she wasn't about to disturb the felicity between them.

She'd felt a twinge of pain even as she'd prowled around the room gazing at the canvases he treated so carelessly. Each one was more brilliant than the last, and by the time she'd put the final canvas aside and made her way slowly to the couch, she was utterly drunk on the power and passion that leaped out of those paintings.

It was a real tragedy to keep these paintings hidden away where no one could enjoy them. There must be some way to convince Lance to exhibit his work, but at the moment she was unable to see it. She wasn't about to give up, however. For now it was enough to be here and watch the play of expressions on that strong, mobile face and let the crackling vitality that surrounded him like a visible aura flow into her. She scooted further down on the couch, resting her head on the cushion, and pulled the afghan up about her shoulders. She dropped the paperback on the floor. Lance probably wouldn't glance her way again for hours, so she needn't keep up the pretense of being interested in anything but the red-haired man across the room.

She was being carried, held in warm, strong arms, and her face was pressing against that lovely rough cushion that she recognized at once. She rubbed her cheek contentedly against him. "Lance?" she murmured sleepily.

"Shh," he whispered softly. "Go back to sleep, baby. I'm just taking you to bed. It's very late."

"Did you finish your painting?" she asked drowsily, snuggling closer to his vibrant warmth.

"Almost. I still have a bit of background to do."

She was gently deposited on a cushioned softness, and then the mattress sagged beside her as Lance sat down and calmly began to unbutton her orchid sun-top. "You shouldn't do that," she said sleepily, not opening her eyes. It was a token murmur rather than a protest. She felt it was somehow natural and fitting for Lance to be undressing her with those wonderfully gentle hands.

"You'll be more comfortable," he said, and his explanation seemed entirely logical. She heard his deep chuckle. "You needn't worry, Honey. I'm not about to try to seduce you tonight. I'm so exhausted that I can barely move." He had stripped off her top and was undoing the front clasp of her bra. "I just want to cuddle up to you and go to sleep. Okay?"

"Okay," she murmured. She could think of nothing more desirable than those warm secure arms holding her and closing out the darkness of the night.

The rest of her clothing was stripped from her, and he was gone for a few minutes. Then he was back on the bed, drawing the denim coverlet over both of them. He pulled her close and settled her head in the curve of his shoulder, her long white-gold hair splaying in a silky curtain over his chest. His warm naked skin felt hard and rough against her own soft curves as his arms held her close with the sexless affection of a little boy with his favorite teddy bear.

"Lord, this is nice," he said, already half asleep. "Isn't it great to be together like this, sweetheart?"

She nodded with equal contentment. Her arms tightened lovingly about him and she went peacefully to sleep.

* * *

The gentle tugging at her nipple sent a tiny thrill of heat through her, and she moved restlessly, trying to hide once more behind the veil of sleep, which had been pierced by sensation. Then the tugging increased in tempo and a warm strong hand enclosed her breast and began a kneading motion that completely ripped the veil aside.

She opened her eyes to the gray predawn hours of the morning and was unsurprised to see Lance's fiery red head at her breast. His tanned hand curled around its full whiteness appeared gypsy-dark in contrast.

"I thought you were exhausted," she said drowsily, her hand reaching down to stroke his hair.

He lifted his head with an impish grin. "I said I was tired, not dead, sweetheart. Even if I was, I'd probably have risen like Lazarus from the tomb at the sight that met my eyes when I opened them just now." His head bent, and his warm tongue gently stroked the nipple he'd already roused to button hardness. "It was dark in here when I undressed you, or I wouldn't have been able to nap even the little I did. My God, you're magnificent, love."

"Thank you," she said shyly, feeling the color mount to her cheeks.

"You're welcome," he said with equal politeness. There was a distinct twinkle in his blue eyes as he looked up again. "I love that grave-little-girl air you have sometimes. It's such a contrast to all this lush pulchritude that it blows my mind."

His hand resumed that slow, arousing kneading motion, and Honey felt a tingling in the pit of her stomach that was rapidly escalating into an aching need. "I don't think this is very wise," she said breathlessly as his teeth nibbled with erotic delicacy at the taut nipple.

"I do," he replied thickly. "I think it's the wisest thing I've done since I met you. I had to be crazy not to do it before. We both know we've been wanting it since the moment we met. Isn't that true, Honey?"

She nodded slowly. "Yes, I suppose it is," she said quietly. It was all so clear now that she'd accepted that simple truth. She had never wanted anyone in her life before this red-haired Scaramouche had appeared on her horizon, but she knew now that she must have realized even that first evening that they would eventually reach this point of no return.

He drew a long, deep breath and gave her a smile of such loving sweetness that she felt her throat tighten with emotion. "You won't regret it, love. I'll pleasure you, I promise."

"I know you will," she said tenderly. Everything that he was and did pleasured her. She knew now that he always would. "I hope I can please you, too."

"Good Lord, how could you help it?" His other hand reached up to cup her other breast. "Just looking at you is enough to make me lose control." One thumb raked the proud, hard peak that crested the voluptuous fullness of her breast, and a shiver of pure desire shot through her. His hand moved down to the softness of her belly and traced a delicate pattern on its silken smoothness. "You're like a lovely blank canvas just waiting for the first brushstroke to bring you to life." His lips moved swiftly down her midriff, dropping a trail of light kisses along the way. His teeth bit teasingly at the softness of her belly, and she inhaled sharply. "I want to paint you with the scarlet of passion." He gently parted her thighs. "I want to shade you with the gold of fulfillment." His hands were probing at the warm center of her being, and she made a sound that was half gasp at the incredible sensations that he was producing. He looked up and smiled with tender satisfaction. " And when you sleep in my arms afterward, I want you to be glowing with the dark rose of contentment." His hand moved with deft erotic expertise, shooting a jolt of hot, tingling pleasure to the heart of her. "Will you let me paint you with all the colors of loving, Honey?"

"Oh yes," she gasped. She felt as if she were already stroked with flames. "Yes, Lance, please."

He moved over her, parting her thighs and coming swiftly between them. Leaning down, he kissed her with a hot, lingering sweetness. "I don't think I can wait any longer, sweetheart," he muttered roughly, his chest moving raggedly. "It seems I've been waiting forever for you already."

"Then don't wait any longer," she whispered, her lips parting as she drew his mouth back to hers. His tongue entered into the moist sweetness, and he made a sound in the back of his throat as her tongue responded with a wild sensuality that she'd never felt before.

His hips thrust quickly forward, and her sudden cry was lost beneath his lips. He raised his head, his body stiffening in surprise. His face was a mask of shock as he looked down at her. "Honey?" he asked dazedly.

"It doesn't matter," she muttered feverishly, her hands clutching fiercely at his shoulders. The sensation was indescribable, she felt both gloriously, tantalizingly full and achingly incomplete. "Please don't stop."

"Oh, Lord, I don't think I can," he said thickly, his hips starting a rhythmic thrusting that sent an explosive heat rocketing through her. She writhed in an agony of molten need as he lifted her hips in his hands, drawing her closer to him with each movement.

The rainbow spectrum of hues that he'd promised her was all there as he moved with her, encouraging her with words of need and praise that he gasped in her ear in a litany of passionate longing. But he hadn't told her of the incredible sunburst of sensation that would result with the fusion of those colors.

When they were lying clutching each other dazedly in the exhaustion that was the aftermath of that multi-hued storm, she tucked her head into the hollow of his shoulder. Her hand resting below his heart drawing comfort from the strong, rapid beat that was gradually slowing. "You left out quite a bit, you know," she said dreamily. "You never mentioned the deep crimson of giving and this lovely lavender-mauve weariness."

His lips brushed her temple tenderly. "I discovered quite a few new shades myself," he said huskily, his hand stroking her hair gently. "Some of them I never even dreamed existed. You're quite an artist yourself, Honey Winston." His hand paused a moment in its stroking, and his voice was oddly troubled. "You shocked the hell out of me, you know."

"I know," she said wryly. "My friend Nancy assured me I was the last twenty-four-year-old virgin left on the face of the earth. I was a little afraid I would disappoint you." She raised her head to look up at him uncertainly. "Was I all right?"

His lips swooped down to kiss her with a gentleness that caused her throat to tighten with an aching tenderness. "Lord, you were fantastic, love," he said, his voice suspiciously husky. "I've never felt anything like that in my life. It was as if every part of you was holding me, loving me. I couldn't believe my luck."

"Neither could I," she said softly, her eyes twinkling impishly. "It's not every woman who's initiated into the intricacies of sex by such a notable practitioner as Lusty Lance. I should consider myself almost unique. I'm sure you don't usually waste that expertise on such unsophisticated quarry."

His brow wrinkled in a frown. "That's not amusing," he said curtly. "I told you that what we have is different. Now, be quiet and come here." He pressed her head back into the hollow of his shoulder, his arms tightening around her. "Did I ever tell you that I hate that Lusty Lance epithet?"

"No," she answered, nestling even closer. "Did I tell you that I think my own name is perfectly ghastly?"

"I believe you did mention something about it," he said, winding a lock of her hair around his finger. "I like it. It's as if I'm murmuring a love word every time I say it." His lips brushed lightly over her lids. "Honey sweet." His lips traveled to the lobe of her ear and nibbled delicately. "Honey soft." His lips moved to her mouth and his tongue entered to joust with her own in eager play. When their lips parted, he drew a shuddering breath. "Honey hot. I think I want to paint another picture."

Her eyes widened in surprise. "So soon?"

He chuckled. "Couldn't you tell by the number of canvases in my studio?" he asked softly. "I'm very prolific." One hand closed on her breast, his nail raking lightly over the nipple, sending a shiver of heat through her. "And I'm finding you a source of constant inspiration."

Honey found that she, too, was feeling more inspired by the moment, as his lips traveled down to her breast and his tongue flicked deliciously at the taut pink tip. "You're so damn beautiful, I want to *really* paint you, just as you are right now. Will you pose for me, Honey?"

She felt a sharp pain surge through her as she remembered what Alex had said about Lance's dislike of painting anyone with whom he was personally involved. Evidently she didn't fall into that category. Well, what could she expect? Lance had never pretended that he felt any lasting attachment for her. She must be satisfied with what he had to give.

"Why not?" she asked flippantly. "I can hardly complain about your making me notorious. You must have the most private collection of paintings in the entire world."

He started to say something, but she swiftly put her hand over his lips, silencing him. "On one condition."

He kissed her palm lingeringly before removing her hand from his lips. "And that is?"

Her hands reached up to draw his glossy, flamelike head back to her breast. "I find that I'm developing a few artistic tendencies myself," she said lightly. "I want to paint my own picture. Will you teach me how to do it?"

"Oh, yes, sweetheart." He chuckled, his blue eyes flickering. His teeth nibbled at one eager nipple. "First, you have to prepare the canvas."

And the lesson commenced.

It was late afternoon when she awoke, and the glowing rays of the sun were slanting through the window, softening the austerity of the room.

Honey stretched luxuriously, feeling delightfully lazy as she cast the denim coverlet aside. She felt a twinge of disappointment that Lance had left without waking her, but she firmly squashed the feeling. He was probably back in the studio again. She musn't expect to compete with the pull of that particular mistress, though she had every intention of making herself a worthy adversary of any other possible rivals.

She showered quickly and washed her hair, grumbling at her shortsightedness in not bringing a blow dryer. Exposed to the salt air, her long hair would need continual care and frequent washing. Oh, well, she would just have to go outside and hope the sun would dry it before nightfall.

She slipped on a pair of navy-blue tailored shorts and a pale-blue tailored blouse, tying the tails carelessly under her breasts. She didn't bother with shoes, and when she left the cottage, the sand was a delicious cushion beneath her bare feet. The tide was coming in, and the surf licked at her toes as she strolled briskly along the shore, her hands combing through her hair occasionally, while the soft, gentle wind obligingly dried it.

It was almost sunset, and Honey paused for a moment to gaze with breathless admiration at the scarlet and violet glory that was reflected mirror-like in the placid sea.

"It's a magnificent picture, but I like the ones we paint together more."

She whirled to face Lance, an eager smile lighting her face. "So do I," she said softly. "I think we get the colors better."

Bathed in the rosy sunset glow, his skin took on a golden patina, and his hair glowed like a flame above the sapphire eyes. He was barefoot, too, she noticed, and he hadn't bothered to tuck the tail of his white shirt into his jeans, nor to button it.

"I thought you'd gone back to the studio," she said.

He shook his head, his face surprisingly grave. "I went for a long walk. I had some thinking to do."

She moved closer. "I'm glad you haven't gone back to work yet," she murmured, smiling at him beguilingly. "I was wondering if I could seduce you into giving me another lesson."

"The key word being 'seduce,' of course," he said, a flame beginning to flicker in the depths of his eyes. "What a delightfully insatiable wench you've become, Honey. Any more practice and you'll be giving *me* lessons."

She took a step nearer him, until her breasts were pressing against the bare hardness of his chest. "You didn't object this afternoon," she observed with a grin.

"No, I didn't, did I?" he asked thickly. "I couldn't get enough of you. I was even tempted to wake you before I left and love you again."

"Why didn't you?" she asked, her arms sliding up his chest and around his neck, her fingers curling in the crisp hair at its nape. Her lips brushed his chin, and he inhaled sharply.

Then he was jerking her arms from around his neck and thrusting her forcefully away from him. "Damn it, Honey, stay away from me," he said sharply. "This is difficult enough for me."

She gazed up at him in hurt bewilderment. "What's the matter?" she asked huskily, her blue eyes sparkling with unshed tears. She'd thought he'd been joking before about her aggressiveness, but perhaps there had been an element of sincerity beneath the raillery. She backed slowly away from him, her lashes lowered to veil the pain that the thought brought. "You'll have to forgive me," she said brightly, smiling with an effort. "I'm a little new at this. You'll have to let me know what's bad form and what isn't."

"Oh, Lord, now I've hurt you," he groaned, running his hand through his hair in frustration. "It's not like that. I'm not rejecting you, damn it."

"It sounds remarkably like it," she said, still not looking at him. "But you needn't apologize, Lance, I understand perfectly."

He took an impulsive step forward, reaching out for her. Then he stopped abruptly, and his hands fell to his sides. "Honey, you're driving me crazy," he said in an exasperated tone. "You know that I can scarcely keep my hands off of you. I proved that this afternoon. You're the most warmly responsive woman I've ever known. I'd be the last one ever to discourage you from spreading a little of that warmth in my direction."

"Then what's wrong?" she asked, her violet eyes lifting in puzzlement to meet his own. "If you want me, and I want you . . ."

"It's not that simple," he said, scowling. "You were a virgin."

Her mouth fell open in surprise. "After today, I think it's a little late to worry about that," she said dryly. "It certainly didn't appear to bother you too much earlier."

"Look, I know I acted like a selfish bastard," he said, frowning. "I guess I went a little crazy. You go to my head, love." He threw out his arms in frustration. "I never dreamed you weren't experienced. I thought you'd be on the pill."

"The pill?" she asked dazedly. "Is that what this is all about? You're worried about my getting pregnant?" She suddenly started to laugh, her face alight with amusement.

His scowl grew darker. "I'm glad you're finding it so damn funny," he said indignantly. "We're on an island, remember? I could call the mainland to have something flown in, but Alex and others might find out. I thought that would embarrass you. I was foolishly trying to protect you."

She shook her head, her lips curved in a tender smile. "I'm the one who is supposed to be protecting you," she reminded him gently. "Don't worry, Lance. I'm not."

"That's because you're so naive," he said roughly. "You should be worried, damn it. Why the hell aren't you?"

Because the thought of a little redheaded Scaramouche with sapphire eyes filled her with an aching yearning. Because a part of him would be better than nothing at all. Because she would love this complicated, quicksilver boy-man all the days of her life.

She shrugged. "I don't know why you're so upset. There's no use worrying about something that may never happen." She grinned, her eyes twinkling. "We'll be here another few weeks, and I'll be darned if I'll live like a nun, now that I know what I'm missing." Then, as she saw the endearingly troubled expression on his face, she said gently, "I'm not fooling myself that this will be forever, Lance. Whatever happens, I won't hold you responsible. I waited twenty-four years for my first affair, and I fully expect to enjoy every minute of it."

"How very generous of you," he said, his lips tight, and for a moment she thought she saw a flicker of hurt in the depths of his eyes. "As ephemeral as you consider our affair to be, I still regard myself as being a little more than a ship that passes in the night. I think a portion of that decision rests with me."

"But you've already admitted that you have ambivalent feelings on that score," she said demurely, peering up at him through her lashes. She moistened her lips delicately with the tip of her tongue, knowing he was watching her compulsively. "I, however, am entirely determined and singleminded about the subject."

"Honey," he said warningly.

"I want to paint another picture, Lance," she said coaxingly, taking a step forward.

He took an involuntary step backward. "No, damn it. Not until I can take care of you."

"You always take care of me," she said softly, taking another step forward. "I've never felt so beautifully cosseted in my life as when I'm in your arms, Lance."

"God, I hoped you felt like that, Honey," he said

huskily. "You're so sweet to love that it takes my breath away. I wanted you to feel like the treasure that you are."

Her hands went to the buttons on her blouse and began slowly to unfasten them. "Treasures are always more precious when they're used," she said softly. "Did you ever see how ugly and tarnished silver becomes when it's left in the cabinet? Don't leave me on the shelf, Lance." She shrugged out of the blouse and dropped it carelessly on the sand.

Lance's eyes were fixed on her breasts as her hands went to the front closure of her bra. "Where's the woman who was too modest to wear a bikini?" he asked wryly, moistening his dry lips with the tip of his tongue.

"The sun's gone down now, and you did invite me to go skinny-dipping with you."

"Somehow I don't think that's what you have in mind," he said dryly.

She winked at him impishly. "Well, there are dips." She slipped out of the bra. "And then there are *dips.*"

He drew a deep, ragged breath. "God, you're beautiful," he said hoarsely, his eyes on the full mounds with their taut pink rosettes. "You're making it very hard for me, love."

"That's the purpose of the entire exercise," she said, her lips quirking. She took a step closer to him. "Now, don't you think it's time that I had another lesson in the subtle nuances of color coordination?"

"Don't do this, Honey," he grated out, his hands clenching into fists at his sides. "I'm trying to do what's right, for once in my life." His eyes were fastened on one pink tantalizing nipple, and unconsciously he licked his lips again. "I can't stand much more of this. If you don't get away from me, so help me, I'll rape you."

She took another step closer until her bare breasts were brushing against his warm chest. "So rape me; I'll help you," she said flippantly, her violet eyes dancing mischievously. She stood on her tiptoes and kissed him with loving sweetness. "Love me, Lance."

He made a sound that was almost a guttural groan of hunger, deep in his throat, and his arms crushed her to him. His tongue entered to stroke with a savage desire that took her breath away. He drew her down to the sand, so that they were kneeling face to face, while his hands moved feverishly over the smooth silken line of her back. "I hope you know what you're doing, Honey," he muttered, as he pressed burning kisses over her face and throat. "You've made damn sure that I don't."

She was sliding the shirt from his shoulders and down his arms. "I know," she said, pressing her lips to his shoulder. "I know very well what I'm doing."

He was breathing raggedly, and she could feel the rapid throb of his heart beneath her lips. "There's one thing you've got to promise me, Honey," he said hoarsely as he pushed her down in the sand, his hands working at the fastening of her navy shorts. "No abortion." His expression was pale and stern in the dim light. "Whatever happens, no abortion. Okay?"

She smiled up at him tenderly. It was entirely what she would have expected of someone as vividly alive as Lance. How much he had yet to learn about her and the love she felt for him. "Okay," she agreed softly, pulling him down into her embrace. "Whatever happens, love."

Six

The wind was tearing wildly at her hair and robbing her of breath as she and Lance ran the last few yards to the porch of the Folly. Lance didn't bother to knock, but threw open the door, bustled her into the foyer, and slammed the door behind them.

Honey was trying futilely to smooth her hair as she turned and gazed laughingly up at him. "You really know how to pick the time to accept a dinner invitation, Lance. That wind almost blew us away. I must look a complete mess."

"I like it," he said softly, his eyes running lingeringly over her tousled white-gold hair and equally windblown tailored cream slacks and chocolate silk blouse. "It makes you look very satisfyingly primitive," he added, smoothing his own rumpled hair. "Perhaps I should change the background in your painting. A Valkyrie should really have a storm setting to be really effective."

"Just so you don't insist on having me bare-breasted and wearing a horned helmet," Honey said dryly, making a face at him.

He shook his head ruefully. "I learned my lesson that first day I tried to paint you nude. I find you too much of a temptation in the buff, my proud beauty."

Her eyes twinkled teasingly. "I noticed you didn't get any work done that day. And I thought artists were supposed to regard their models in a purely objective light."

"Never purely," he said with a wicked grin. "Not when the model is you, Honey sweet. Objective? Perhaps in fifty years or so I might muster a little objectivity."

Honey inhaled sharply, feeling a flutter of delight deep in the heart of her. It was the first time in the two weeks they'd been on the island that he'd intimated that their affair was to be anything but fleeting. She didn't fool herself that Lance would make any lasting commitment to her.

The past weeks had been the happiest she'd ever known, and she felt she had grown closer to Lance Rubinoff than to anyone before in her life. Not only did they share a white-hot physical affinity that rocked them to their depths, but they'd found that they shared a gentle camaraderie that was amazing, considering the disparity in their upbringings. She was almost sure that Lance felt the golden ties that were being forged between them, but this was the first verbal indication he'd ever made that their idyll might extend beyond the confines of Londale's Folly.

Her face must have mirrored the glowing delight she was feeling, for his eyes were suddenly narrowed and intent, and he took an impulsive step toward her. "Honey," he said huskily, "let's go back to the cottage."

"Oh, no, you don't." Alex Ben Raschid's voice cut through the velvet sensual haze that was beginning to envelop them. Alex stood in the arched doorway of the living room. "I haven't been able to pry the two of you away from that seaside love nest since we arrived. I'm tired of my own company, damn it."

Honey could feel the hot color flood her cheeks, as she watched Ben Raschid stroll lazily toward them. Dressed in dark cords and a long-sleeved black shirt, no one could have looked more self-sufficient and less dependent than that sleek panther of a man.

Lance's expression was also plainly skeptical, as he took Honey's arm in a possessive clasp and turned to face Alex. "Nice to know we were missed," he said mockingly. "However, I don't seem to remember you pounding down our door. Admit it, Alex, you've been so busy wheeling and dealing that you didn't even remember that we were alive."

"I refuse to admit any such thing," Alex replied, his lips quirking. "I would never have committed the *faux pas* of interrupting love's young dream without a good reason. *I* don't have an artistic temperament to excuse my rudeness."

"No, just that Ben Raschid arrogance," Lance murmured silkily. "And you seem to have overcome your scruples enough to send a note down with an invitation that was the equivalent of a royal command."

"Sheer desperation," Alex said, making a face. "I may have been able to tolerate my own company, but I wasn't about to fight off the Teutonic Terror on my own. She's been calling, wanting to speak to you, for the past three evenings." He looked at his watch. "She said she'd be calling you tonight at seven-thirty our time. Knowing Bettina's Germanic efficiency, that leaves you exactly three minutes to gird your loins for battle."

Lance gave him a look of utter disgust. "My God, Alex, couldn't you have told her that I was in

Sedikhan? Clancy could have fobbed her off. Lord knows he's had enough practice."

Alex shook his head, a glint of amusement in his dark eyes. "She'd still track you down, with her usual bloodhound's persistence," he said. "It's a quality I rather admire. I thought she deserved at least to talk to you."

"Thanks," Lance said gloomily, running a distracted hand through the auburn hair that he'd so recently smoothed. "I'll do the same for you sometime."

"Teutonic Terror?" Honey asked, puzzled. "Who on earth are you talking about?"

"Baroness Bettina von Feltenstein," Lance replied absently, still scowling at Alex.

As if on cue, Justine appeared in the foyer. "Baroness von Feltenstein is on the phone for Prince Rubinoff," she announced quietly before disappearing once again toward the rear of the house.

Alex glanced at his watch. "She's thirty seconds early." His lips twitched. "Most reprehensible. Be sure to reprimand her, Lance." He gestured toward the door at the far end of the foyer. "You can take it in the library while I get Honey a drink."

Lance muttered a distinctly blue imprecation and strode quickly through the foyer, slamming the library door behind him.

Honey followed Alex to the bar at the far side of the room, slipped onto a yellow-cushioned barstool, and watched distractedly as Alex went behind the bar.

"Ginger ale?" he inquired as he took two glasses from beneath the bar and placed them on the polished teak counter.

"You have a good memory," she said. "Why is Lance so upset?" she persisted, watching as he poured his own brandy and replaced the crystal decanter beneath the bar.

"She's his parents' choice for a blushing bride,"

he explained. He came around the bar and half sat, half leaned on the stool next to her own. When he noticed Honey's look of surprise, he added quickly, "Not Lance's. He can barely stand the woman. She's a bit too aggressive for his taste. He just can't convince Bettina of that fact. She's been so brainwashed that she can't conceive why Lance doesn't want to marry her and have a multitude of splendidly bred Teutonic princelings."

"I see," Honey said slowly, looking down at her glass to mask the sudden jolt of pain she was feeling. "It must be very exasperating for him."

"I don't think you do see, Honey," he said quietly. "I've never known Lance to do anything he didn't want to do. He can't be bulldozed into a state marriage unless that's what he wants. I think you know Lance well enough to realize that's definitely not what he wants."

She looked up, and her eyes were bright with tears. "I haven't known Lance long enough to be that sure of him," she said quietly. "He's not the easiest person to understand. About ninety percent of Lance Rubinoff is beneath the surface."

"Well, if it's any comfort to you, I think you have a better chance at probing those depths than any other woman has had," Alex said gently. "The man is obviously crazy about you."

Honey felt a surge of hope. "It is a comfort to me," she said honestly, giving him a grateful smile. "Thank you for telling me, Alex."

"The woman is completely impossible!" Lance exclaimed explosively, striding into the room and heading immediately for the bar. "She's a ranting lunatic." He poured himself a double. "And she has the persistence of a bloody bulldog with a fresh bone!"

"I gather that you didn't convince her that you were quite happy with your single state?" Alex asked, arching a mocking brow.

"My God, when that woman begins quoting bloodlines, she makes me feel like a blasted stud!" Lance said disgustedly, downing half his drink in one swallow.

"Well, she can only judge by your past performance." Alex grinned. "The results may not be evident, but the inclination certainly was. Is she going to pay us a visit to try to further her cause?"

"Probably," Lance replied gloomily. "I did everything I could to discourage her, but it was like talking to a post."

Suddenly Honey couldn't take any more. Couldn't they talk about anything but that high-bred vamp? She slipped off the stool and wandered over to the French windows, where sheets of rain were pounding against the panes. "We're going to be drowned before we get back to the cottage," she said, with an effort at lightness. "This doesn't look like a pleasant little tropical shower."

"You won't be going back to the cottage tonight," Alex said calmly, and when she whirled to face him with a surprised exclamation, he gave a resigned sigh. "I forgot how primitive you are down at the cottage. You don't even have a radio, do you? You're right, this isn't just a shower. It's been officially labeled a tropical storm." His lips tightened grimly. "If it stays in the Gulf much longer, it will probably escalate to a full-fledged hurricane. At any rate, you won't have to worry about any surprise visits from Bettina for the next day or so."

"Thank God," Lance said emphatically, taking another drink. "I'm grateful for small favors."

"I sent Nate down to the cottage to pack your belongings and bring them up here," Alex said. "Until the storm passes, you'll have to remain as my guests. The cottage will be completely flooded in a few hours. I've told Justine to prepare a guest room."

"What about Lance's paintings?" Honey asked worriedly.

"They'll be quite safe," Alex said soothingly. "I told Nate to wrap them carefully in tarpaulin before trying to transport them."

Honey breathed a sigh of relief. She should have known that Alex would take every care. He valued Lance's work almost as much as she did.

"They should be in the library by now, if you want to examine them for possible damage," he continued, turning to Lance, as he finished his drink and set the empty glass on the bar.

Lance shook his head. "Nate's pretty careful. I'm sure they're all right," he said carelessly, finishing his own drink. "I'll check them after dinner."

"Perhaps you should take a look now," Honey urged, her brow creased in a frown. "You wouldn't want to chance having any of them ruined." She cast an uneasy glance at the rain pounding against the window. "There can't be much time left."

Lance's lips curved in a cynical smile. "I can always paint another one."

Honey expelled a deep breath of sheer frustration. "I won't even honor that idiocy with a reply," she said between her teeth. Then, unable to resist, she burst out, "You're not some hack painter, damn it. Everything you do is *important.*"

Alex gave a low whistle. "I think I detect the trace of a long-standing argument," he remarked, straightening. "If you'll excuse me, I believe I'll go to the library and make a number of completely unnecessary phone calls. Justine will let us know when dinner is ready."

"You needn't leave, Alex," Honey said tautly. "I know when I'm beating a dead horse. Where did you say the guest room is? I believe I'll go upstairs and freshen up."

"It's the first door on the left," Alex said promptly, settling back on the stool. "And if you're not going

to argue, I believe I'll stay and have another drink."
He cast an inquiring glance at his cousin. "Lance?"

"Why not?" Lance asked, his eyes fixed broodingly on Honey's back as she walked swiftly toward the door. "Lord, save me from obstinate
women."

That the charge was leveled at her as well as the
absent Teutonic Terror was more than clear, and
Honey felt a little stab of hurt along with her
annoyance and distress. She didn't answer, but
swept regally from the room and up the stairs.
There was very little she could do with her slightly
tousled appearance, but if she hadn't gotten out
of that room, there would have been the argument Alex had predicted.

Alex was right. Their argument was of long
standing, the only one to disturb the golden tran-
quility of their time together. Why couldn't the
man see that he needed that God-given talent
he'd been blessed with to be recognized? Such
great creativity couldn't be hidden away in a studio,
like the canvases that Lance had shoved carelessly away in the closet.

She stopped short on the top step. Oh, God,
surely Nate had gotten those paintings out of the
closet? Without thinking, she whirled and flew
back down the steps and through the foyer to the
library. Nate was careful, as Lance had said, but
he must have been in a tremendous hurry to get
all their belongings together and up to the Folly
before the deluge. What if he'd failed to check the
closet?

She burst into the library, paying no attention
this time to the portrait of Karim Ben Raschid,
which subtly made the room its own. The canvases
were stacked against the wall, carefully wrapped
in the waterproof tarpaulin. There were so many,
but were they all there? She hurriedly tore the
tarpaulin off the pictures, giving each one a cur-

sory glance. She had grown to know them all in the last weeks, as if they were beloved children. They were children, in a way. Lance's children, product of the genius he refused to acknowledge. Damn, why couldn't she remember which paintings had been in the closet? Perhaps Nate had brought them after all.

No, wait, where was the *Hidden Lagoon?* She remembered asking Lance how he'd gotten that curiously intimate effect, with the sheltering trees surrounding the mystic, tranquil waters. Frantically she went through the canvases again. Maybe she'd just overlooked it. Let it be here, please. It wasn't! Nate had missed it. And how many others that she couldn't recall at the moment? Lance's beautiful children.

No, damn it. She wouldn't let them be taken away by a stupid freak of nature!

Her movements were almost automatic as she swiftly spread out several tarpaulins on the floor and folded them carefully. She tucked the bulky bundle under her arm and left the library, running toward the front door. She had no time to get a coat or other rain gear. It would only protect her for a few minutes, anyway, in a torrential storm like this one.

She couldn't have been more right on that score. The rain hit her like a blow, and she was drenched to the skin in seconds. The wind was blowing water before it with such force that Honey had to struggle to keep her feet on the palm-bordered path down the hill to the beach.

The path was a muddy quagmire, as she half ran, half slid down the incline. The trip that should have taken her five minutes took her a full fifteen, and by the time she reached the beach, she was almost panicky. The storm was moving with such ominous swiftness. Would the cottage be flooded already when she reached it?

It was impossible to see the cottage until she was almost upon it, so blinding were the solid sheets of rain pounding at her. She stumbled over the front stoop and had to catch her balance by grabbing at the jamb of the front door, or she would have fallen to her knees. The stoop was already completely flooded, and water was running under the front door when she threw it open and staggered into the cottage.

She wasted scarcely a glance on the stripped living-dining area, but ran immediately to the studio. That, too, was stripped and bare. It was clear that Nate had salvaged all of the paintings he'd noticed, but when she threw open the door of the closet, Honey saw what she'd expected. Propped in a shadowy corner were three canvases. One was fairly small, but the other two were good-sized, and she immediately recognized one as the *Hidden Lagoon*. She gave a sigh of relief, and lifted the precious canvases carefully out of the closet, after meticulously checking the shelves to make sure she hadn't missed anything.

The water was washing under the door of the studio now, and Honey knew she didn't have much time. She quickly unfolded the tarpaulins. She'd purposely taken more than she'd thought she would need. Now, after her wild journey down the hill, she was glad of the extra protection. It would be ironic if, after all her trouble, the paintings were damaged on her way back to the Folly. Keeping a wary eye on the seawater that was rushing under the door in a constant tide now, she quickly wrapped each painting in a double thickness of tarpaulin and then tied them all together under the protection of a larger one. By the time she finished, a thin stream of water was washing around her kneeling figure, and she hurriedly picked up the paintings, hugging them to her breasts as she opened the studio door. The water gushed into the room with a little swoosh, and Honey could feel a thrill of sheer panic as she fought her way to the front door through the knee-deep water. If it was this bad in the cottage, what must it be like outside?

It was like jumping into the ocean itself when she stepped off the stoop. The pounding waves were more than waist deep, and it was impossible to keep the paintings entirely out of the salt water as she struggled to make her way toward the path, whose lower reaches were now invisible beneath the stormy surf. Her breath was coming in sharp, painful gasps as she finally tore herself from the deadly clinging waters, which threatened to suck her back into their embrace with each swirling pull of the pounding waves.

Honey staggered drunkenly to the side of the path and leaned against a tall palm, trying to get her breath. There was a sharp stitch in her side, and she felt almost dizzy with exhaustion as she clutched the bole of the tree with one arm and the paintings in the other. She'd never dreamed there was so much water in the world. For a while she couldn't determine what was sea and what wasn't, so thick was the blanket of rain that surrounded her.

The sea was again licking hungrily at her ankles, she noticed numbly. How high must she climb to escape its reach? She released her grip on the tree, tightened her arms around the paintings, and began to fight her way up the path. It couldn't be much farther, could it? It seemed as if she'd traveled miles already. She stumbled and fell to her knees in the mud of the trail, and for a moment she stayed there, too weary to move, gathering her resources for the next effort.

"Honey! My God, I could murder you!"

She raised her head slowly, not even surprised to see Lance standing on the path in front of her.

He was very wet, she thought numbly. His jeans were clinging to the strong line of his thighs like a second skin, the dark copper of his skin visible through the wet cotton of his shirt. She couldn't see his features through the dense curtain of rain, but his tone was enraged.

Great. That was all she needed at the moment, to have Lance furious with her. Well, she'd better face it standing up. She was starting to struggle to her feet, when Lance suddenly pulled her up, shaking her like a rag doll. That was just what she felt like, she thought dazedly. Her legs were certainly stuffed with cotton, for they gave way, and she felt herself falling. Then she was scooped up and held close to Lance's chest, while a string of obscenities issued from him in a strange, broken voice.

"Calm down, Lance," Alex's voice came out of the darkness somewhere over Lance's shoulder. "You're not making it any easier for her."

"I don't want to make it any easier for her. I could beat her. Just look at her, damn it!" Lance said harshly. "Take those blasted canvases from her and get rid of them, will you? She's got them in a death grip."

"No!" Honey gasped sharply, her arms tightening possessively on the paintings.

Alex was beside them now, and his voice was as gentle as Lance's had been harsh. "Let me have them, Honey. I'll take good care of them."

Yes, Alex would take good care of them, she thought tiredly. Her hands loosened, and the paintings were lifted from her clasp. Her arms felt oddly empty as they fell to her sides. "Yes, you take care of them, Alex," she said. "I'm so tired." She relaxed drowsily and then nestled closer in Lance's arms. There was an odd sound that was half growl and half sob beneath her ear, but she didn't hear it, as she fell peacefully asleep.

• • •

Honey's next conscious awareness was of being lowered into a tub of warm bubbly water that jolted her from sleep to a disgruntled wakefulness.

"Not more water," she protested disgustedly, opening sleepy eyes to glare indignantly at Lance. "I'm practically pruney now."

"Too bad!" he said, rolling up the sleeves of his wet cream shirt with one hand while he steadied her with the other. "You'll just have to bear with it. At the moment, you're so muddy, you look more like a tar baby than a Valkyrie. Now, be quiet while I get you cleaned up and into bed."

She opened her lips to reply, but they were immediately covered by a ruthless hand wielding a soapy washcloth, and she was forced to shut them abruptly. Lance's movements were far from gentle as he scrubbed her from head to toe, until she glowed pink and saucy as a baby. Then he washed her hair with equal impersonality and cool efficiency, his expression granite-hard and guarded. An expression that reminded her of Alex. Alex?

"The paintings!" she exclaimed, suddenly sitting upright in the tub. "Are they all right?"

"Alex said that would be the first thing you'd ask," he said, grabbing a bath sheet from the towel rack. "You'll be happy to know that they were in perfect condition when Alex unwrapped them." He stood up and lifted her out of the tub and wrapped her in the voluminous towel. "Which is a hell of a lot better than you. What in Hades happened to your knees?"

"My knees?" Honey asked vaguely. Looking down, she noticed with surprise that they were both badly bruised, and one had a ragged cut across the kneecap. "I must have done it when I fell in the mud." She frowned in puzzlement. "I don't remember its hurting when I did it."

"You were probably in shock," Lance said roughly, briskly rubbing her hair dry. "You're still not very coherent. Are you sure you didn't hit your head out there?"

She slowly shook her head, frowning at him crossly. "I'm perfectly coherent," she said resentfully, "though I don't know how you can judge. You haven't been letting me say a word."

"Silence is golden and, in your case, a good deal safer," Lance muttered between his teeth as he scooped her up and carried her into the adjoining bedroom. He sat her on the edge of the bed and left her for a moment to fetch the portable hair dryer from the dresser across the room. "It's a little late for you to turn verbose. Now, shut up while I get your hair dry. You'll be lucky if you come out of this without pneumonia."

She opened her lips to answer but she was interrupted again, this time by the shrill roar of the dryer, as Lance proceeded to dry her hair.

Honey sat obediently silent under the warm blast of air, but her temper was slowly burning. Lance acted as if she'd committed a major crime instead of merely trying to salvage a few paintings. She hadn't expected him to be grateful, but he didn't have to be so damned churlish. Even Alex had been more gentle with her than this red-haired bear of a man.

Lance clicked off the dryer and threw it carelessly on the lime-cushioned empress chair by the bed. "It's still a little damp, but it will have to do." He turned and strode toward the bathroom. "Get under the covers and keep warm until I get out of the shower." His hands were rapidly unbuttoning the sodden cream shirt. "But don't go to sleep—I still have to care for those knees."

Honey stood up, clutching the bath sheet firmly to keep it from slipping. "You needn't bother," she said coolly. "I'll attend to them myself. I'll be dressed for dinner by the time you get out of the shower."

"Dinner!" His laugh was a harsh bark as he pulled off the wet shirt and tossed it on the carpet. "We'll forget about dinner this evening. Thanks to your stupidity, I don't think any of us are in the mood for a congenial meal." He disappeared into the bathroom, slamming the door behind him.

Honey glared belligerently at the door before stalking angrily to the Korean wedding chest that served as a bureau in the corner of the room. So she was not only in Lance's bad books, but was to be sent to bed without any supper! She wasn't in the mood for a social dinner either, but she was hungry, damn it.

She snatched the first nightgown she saw in the drawer, and noticed with satisfaction that it was a shapeless, thigh-length cotton nightshirt with a fiendishly smiling Garfield the Cat on the breast. She certainly didn't want Lance to think she was trying to seduce him into a better humor. He was entirely in the wrong, and she would make sure that he was aware of that fact. Two minutes later she had folded back the lime-and-white bamboo-patterned spread on the bed and slipped between the sheets, plumping the pillow with furious energy and pulling the sheets up to her chin before settling down to wait grimly for Lance.

When he did stride back into the bedroom, with only a white towel draped about his hips, she felt a treacherous wavering of her resolve. Why did the man have to be so damn sexy? she wondered gloomily. He was all sleek copper muscle and virile grace as he moved toward her, and she felt a familiar stirring in her loins, which she tried to disregard. His face was still grimly set, she noticed sourly, and she girded herself for the battle to come.

"Did you take care of your knees?" he asked tersely as he sat down on the side of the bed.

"Of course I did," she lied defensively, her glance sliding guiltily away from him. She'd been so incensed by his arrogance and unjust anger that she'd completely forgotten. Her injuries weren't all that bad anyway.

"Fine!" he said curtly, ripping off the towel. He punched the button on the lamp on the bedside table, and the room was suddenly in darkness. She felt the mattress depress as he slid beneath the sheets and settled himself on his side of the bed. "Good night."

Good night? Was that all? How dare he be so cool and unconcerned, after the way he'd treated her? She was the injured party, and in more ways than physical, yet he was calmly going to sleep without giving her a chance to air her grievances. Could anything be more infuriating? Well, perhaps "calm" was the wrong word to use. Even across that icy expanse of bed, she could detect the tenseness of his muscles as he lay there, and a taut aura of leashed emotion was crackling about him like a live wire. It was clear that he was still angry with her and was letting her know it in no uncertain terms. Tonight was the first time since they'd become lovers that she wasn't sleeping in his arms. Not that it mattered to her if he was as remote and cold as the Himalayas, she assured herself. It was just that she had become used to that warm, loving embrace enfolding her, and she felt a little lonely without it. Suddenly there was a rumbling deep in her stomach. That did it! She'd had enough!

Throwing back the covers, she jumped out of bed and strode purposefully toward the louvered closet.

"Where the hell are you going?" Lance's surprised voice came out of the darkness behind her.

"I'm hungry," Honey said belligerently. "I may not be considered worthy of dinner, but you can't object if I go downstairs and raid the refrigerator. You may aspire to being a starving artist, but I'm just a pragmatic private investigator. I want something to eat!"

The light immediately flicked on behind her, and she riffled through the closet for a robe as Lance hissed an imprecation. She ignored him, pulling a white terry-cloth robe off a hanger and slamming the door behind her as she turned around.

"Garfield?"

"What?" she asked, frowning crossly at him. Then she followed his eyes down to the leering cat on her breast. "I like him," she said defensively. "He has character." She struggled into the terry-cloth robe. "And feelings! And that's more than some people I know."

"Garfield," he repeated in wonder. And suddenly he began to laugh. "My Lord, Garfield!"

She planted her hands on her hips and glared at him. It wasn't enough that this maddening man had been growling at her like a surly lion; now he actually had the gall to laugh at her!

Her fury only seemed to amuse him more, for he now dissolved in laughter as he gazed at her cross face and belligerent stance. "I fail to see what's so amusing," she said icily.

"I've never had a cat leer at me from the breast of a Valkyrie with such a royal bearing," he gasped, wiping his eyes on a fold of the sheet. "You'll forgive me if it struck me as funny."

"I'm not the one who's royal," she spat, her violet eyes flashing. "I'm just a poor humble serf. It's Your Highness who has the privilege of being rude and sulky and abusive and completely unreasonable!" She was practically sputtering by the time she finished, and was pacing restlessly back and forth. "And besides that, you're trying to starve me to death!"

"I'm sorry," he said, his blue eyes dancing. "I

can see that last sin outweighs all the others." His lips curved in a tender smile. "Come back to bed, Honey. I want to see if that pussycat knows how to purr as well as spit at me."

"If I did, I'd be tempted to do more than spit," she said through her teeth, turning and striding furiously toward the door.

Her hand had only closed around the knob when she felt herself being scooped up and carried kicking and struggling back to the bed. She was dropped on the counterpane, and he immediately followed her down, pinning her arms above her head and throwing a hard thigh over her flailing legs to hold her immobile. "Now," he said, smiling down at her furious face. "Purr for me, Honey."

It was too much after all she'd gone through tonight. Two tears suddenly brimmed and ran slowly down her face.

They had a galvanic effect on the man grinning impishly down at her. He stiffened as if she'd struck him, and his face looked almost frightened. "No!" he ordered sharply, "Don't do that to me. Stop it, do you hear?"

She didn't know what he meant, but there was seemingly no way she could stop the tears, now that they had started. "Nothing you could do would make me cry," she said fiercely. "I'm just angry."

"That's what I wanted, but you weren't supposed to cry," he said accusingly. His eyes were haunted as he looked down at her. "You musn't do that, damn it. You'll ruin everything."

She stared up at him in complete bewilderment. He was totally irrational. "I don't know what you're talking about," she said tremulously. "You're not making sense."

"Never mind!" he said huskily. "It's too late now anyway. I can feel myself breaking into a hundred pieces inside." She was released with dizzying suddenness, and his arms went around her in a bone-crushing embrace that almost squeezed the breath out of her. He rolled over, holding her in a clasp that was curiously sexless, for all its possessive strength. "Don't move. Don't say anything. Just let me hold you. Okay?"

"All right," she answered faintly. Her anger had vanished when she'd heard that first note of desperation in his voice. She couldn't have moved even if she'd wanted to, so convulsive was that iron grasp. "Lance?" she asked uncertainly. "Please tell me what's wrong."

"Everything would have been fine if you hadn't cried," he muttered throatily into her hair. "I could have held it off until you went to sleep."

"Held what off?" Honey asked bewilderedly. Then, incredibly, she thought she was beginning to understand. His body was shaking and trembling against her like that of a malaria victim. "My God, Lance, what's wrong? Are you sick?"

"I'm sick, all right," he growled with a short mirthless laugh. "I'm so scared, I feel like I'm going to fall apart. I've been frightened out of my mind since we first discovered you were gone tonight." His arms tightened. "Why the hell didn't you come to us instead of running off on your own? Do you know what kind of risk you ran going back to the cottage in a storm like that? You almost died, damn it. You had no right to take a chance like that over something as trivial as those lousy paintings."

"They're not lousy," she denied automatically. "They're as brilliant as your other work. I guess I didn't think about anything but saving the paintings, when I found they weren't with the others."

"Why the hell would you do something so incredibly stupid for a few daubs of paint on the canvas?" he asked throatily.

"They were part of you," she said simply. "I couldn't let them be destroyed." Her lips brushed back and forth caressingly on the tautness of his cheek. Her tone was gently teasing as she continued, "I was hired to guard you, remember? I'd have been remiss in my duty if I'd let anything happen to such an important part of your life."

"So you almost destroyed yourself instead," he said fiercely.

"I knew there wasn't much time." She was fighting to free herself from his embrace. It was terrible to feel so helpless when she wanted so desperately to hold him in her arms and comfort him. Then her arms were sliding around him and drawing him even closer with a fierce possessiveness.

"You were right there," he said bitterly. "Ten minutes later, and you wouldn't have stood a chance. I knew when we were racing down that hill after you that the odds were you'd already been swept away, that I might never see you again. I nearly went crazy," he whispered huskily. The words were muffled, but they held an odd note of wonder. "You cared that much about them?"

"I cared that much," she answered quietly. She was stroking his hair with an almost maternal tenderness. "Don't you think it's time to admit that you feel the same way about your work? You know it would have torn you apart to have anything happen to those paintings."

He raised his head, and she inhaled sharply as she saw the torment in his face and the blazing emotion in his sapphire eyes. "It wasn't worth risking you," he said fiercely. "Nothing's worth that. Promise you'll never do a thing like that again."

Honey felt a sudden surge of joy that was like the warmth of home fires burning bright. "I promise," she said thickly, blinking back the tears.

His head lowered slowly, until he was just a breath away. "I've never felt like that before," he said softly. "I've always been able to hide behind laughter and cynicism when anything has come too close to me. But it wouldn't work tonight, Honey." He kissed her with such lingering sweetness that she felt her throat ache with tenderness. "You've become too important to me. I don't think I could stand it if I lost you now." He buried his face once more in the thick silk of her hair. "Honey?"

"Yes?" she answered dreamily. Surely that last inarticulate murmur could be considered something of a commitment?

His words were oddly jerky. "If it means that much to you, I'll have a show." He heard her sharply indrawn breath, and went on quickly. "But you've got to promise to stay with me after we leave the island. I won't go through that phony charade alone." His voice was tinged with bitterness. "I know you look on this little island idyll as a purely temporary liaison, but if you want me to exhibit, you'll have to restrain your eagerness to get back to your sleuthing."

Where had he gotten the absurd idea that she was eager to leave him? She vaguely remembered making some comment that she didn't expect any permanence in their relationship but that had been to lessen *his* feeling of responsibility.

"But Lance—" she started, but he quickly raised his head and covered her lips with his own.

"No, you can't talk me out of it," he said when he lifted his head. "You'll have to stay and give me moral support or it's no go."

"Well, I suppose I do have a responsibility to the art world," she said liltingly, her lips curving in an impish grin. "I guess I could stick around and hold your hand until you see how right I am and how absurdly stupid you've been. Who's going to care a hundred years from now if you were a prince or a ditch digger, when those experts are gazing raptly at your paintings in the Louvre?"

"Who indeed?" Lance echoed, a reluctant smile

tugging at the corners of his lips. "We'll be lolling on adjoining clouds, and you'll look down and nudge me and say: 'See, I told you so.' "

"I hate people who say, I told you so," Honey said, making a face at him. "I'd never be so crass." Then her face sobered. "You won't be sorry, Lance."

"I'm glad one of us is so confident," he said wryly. "I guess only time will tell which one of us is right. I'll let Alex know that he can make arrangements with the Parke-Bernet Galleries. He's been after me for years. At least he'll be happy."

"Because he has the good sense to recognize genius when he sees it," Honey replied promptly. "And, like all good businessmen, he abhors a wasted talent."

"So do I," Lance said, his eyes twinkling. "Which is why I have no intention of wasting yours, sweetheart." His hand reached up to weigh her breast in his palm. "Are you sure you're hungry?" he asked wistfully.

"I'm sure," she said emphatically, despite the tiny responsive thrill she was feeling at his touch.

"I was afraid you were," he said morosely. "I guess we'd better go down and raid that refrigerator. It's obvious you're not going to let me seduce you until I satisfy the inner woman." He gave her a teasing kiss, his face alight with laughter. "And then, my love, I'm going to make sure that the inner woman satisfies me!"

Seven

The sun was shining brightly, and Honey felt as if she were glowing with a brilliance that could rival its warmth, as she skipped out on the terrace and took her place at the table.

Alex glanced up from the official-looking document he'd been examining with a scowl, and his expression relaxed into a warm smile that miraculously softened the hardness of his features. "Well, good morning. I take it that all is well with your world this fine day?" he drawled, throwing the paper carelessly on the breakfast table beside his plate. He reached for the coffee carafe and poured her coffee and refilled his own cup. "Where's Lance this morning?"

"Justine is taking some coffee up to that improvised studio you created for him," Honey said, taking a sip of her coffee. "He wanted to get to work changing the background of my portrait to a storm setting." She smiled mischievously at him. "He was most displeased with you for not having the cottage cleaned up by now so that we could move back down to the beach. He says the light is much better there."

"Ungrateful wretch," Alex said. "It's only been three days since the storm, and the cottage was a complete disaster. We don't have unlimited manpower on this island, you know. Nate's working as fast as he can."

"I know," Honey said tranquilly, reaching for a warm croissant and buttering it liberally. "And so does Lance, when he thinks about it. He's just impatient to get on with his work." She looked up, violet eyes dancing. "He has great respect for your drive and initiative and wishes you'd channel a little toward the cottage cleanup."

Alex shook his head wryly. "I suppose I'll have to phone the mainland and have some help flown out. I learned a long time ago that that red-haired demon refuses to give up when he wants something." One dark brow arched mockingly. "I guess you've discovered that too."

Honey felt the warm color surge to her cheeks. "Yes," she answered quietly, her eyes glowing softly. "I've found that out."

There was a curiously gentle flicker in the face of the man opposite her before it was masked by the usual guarded cynicism. "You may tell Lance that I'll be as glad to get rid of him as he will be to go," he said lightly. "It's not easy for a man of my proclivities to be odd man out in this garden of Eden the two of you have created for yourselves."

Honey's eyes flew up to meet his. "Have we made you feel that?" she asked, stricken. "Alex, I'm so sorry. How rude you must think us."

"Not rude, just crazy about each other," Alex said dryly. "I can't fault your manners." He pulled a face. "Though Lance could have been a little less blatantly content in front of a man in my celibate state. I'm not used to being an observer instead of a participant."

That was definitely an understatement, from what Lance had told her of Alex's marathon sexual activities. He was extremely highly sexed, and required a woman more often than most. Honey had been so involved with her own concerns that she had never questioned why Alex had voluntarily arranged his stay at Londale's Folly with no willing female to alleviate the abstinence of the past weeks. It must have been as difficult as he'd said, to watch Lance and her together.

"We've been very selfish and inconsiderate, haven't we, Alex? Will you forgive us?" Honey asked contritely.

"I will," he said with a mocking grin. "But only because my ordeal is finally at an end. I've imported some company for myself for a few days." He glanced casually at his watch. "In fact, the helicopter should be arriving any minute now."

"Company?" Honey asked, puzzled. Then she felt a chill of apprehension run through her. "The baroness?"

His brows lifted in surprise. "Bettina? Good heavens, no! The redhead from the Starburst."

Honey relaxed and grinned teasingly. "Oh yes, the inventive one who's really a Scandinavian blonde. Does she have a name?"

"Leona Martell," he supplied, rising to his feet. "Would you like to come down to the landing pad and meet her?"

"Why not?" she asked. She pushed back her chair and stood up. "Lance won't even miss me until this afternoon, when he finishes the background."

"Then I'll take advantage of your charming company while I may," Alex said, gesturing grandly for her to precede him.

Leona Martell was certainly as alluring as Alex

had said, Honey thought a little later as she watched him place his hands on the waist of the tiny but voluptuous redhead to swing her out of the helicopter to the pad. Redhead or not, she appeared to be as passionate as even the most demanding man might require, melting into Alex's arms and pulling his head down to kiss him lingeringly.

Alex was more than enthusiastic in returning the embrace, Honey observed with amusement. When he did lift his head to see her grinning at him, he pulled the redhead closer and winked impishly over the top of her head. Honey giggled irrepressibly, and Alex's smile widened as he turned the redhead around to introduce her.

"Honey, I'd like you to meet Leona Martell. Honey Winston, Leona," he said as he waved permission to the helicopter pilot to take off. "Leona is a law student at Rice University, Honey."

"How do you do, Miss Martell," Honey said politely, over the roar of the rotors as the pilot started the engine. If this gorgeous redhead was a law student, then she must be an extremely well-to-do one.. Those sky-blue slacks and ecru silk blouse practically screamed haute couture, and her rich red, curly hair had been styled and cut by a master.

The admiration was evidently mutual, for Honey's words were acknowledged with a distinctly vague pleasantry, while the redhead wistfully eyed Honey's long, silver blond hair. "My hair used to be almost that color," she said. "People used to stop and stare at me in the street."

"I'm sure they still do," Honey said politely. "You're a very beautiful woman, Miss Martell. Many men prefer redheads, no matter what they say in the song."

"I'll vouch for that," Alex said, carelessly touching a shimmering red curl at her nape.

To Honey's amazement, the remark was met by a bitterly resentful glance. It was so swift that it only flickered and then was gone, replaced by a dulcet sweetness. "Then that's all that's important, darling," Leona said softly. "I only recently had it done, and I suppose I'm not used to it yet. I've been trying to decide whether to keep it." She turned with a forced smile to Honey. "What do you think?" she asked brightly. "Would you dye that lovely hair, Miss Winston?"

Honey shook her head. "I'm afraid not," she said quietly. "But then, I couldn't afford to keep it as lovely as yours."

Alex's arm slid around the redhead's waist. "Let's go up to the house and persuade Justine to make us a fresh pot of coffee," he suggested softly, his dark gaze lingering intimately on her. He glanced up at Honey inquiringly. "Honey?"

She shook her head ruefully. She had an idea that Alex had more than coffee on his mind at the moment, and that she might find herself very much a third wheel. "I don't think so," she said. "I believe I'll go down to the cottage and see what progress Nate is making on the cleanup. I'll see you at lunch, perhaps."

"Perhaps," Alex echoed in a silken murmur that caused Honey to smother a grin as she waved cheerfully and set off down the path to the beach.

She had no intention of going down to the cottage and harrying poor Nate. It was very likely that Alex had been giving him a difficult enough time in the past few days. It was almost an hour later, when she was strolling barefoot in the cove, that she saw the ship. At first she thought it was a trick of the light. The dazzle of the sun on the water sometimes created strange mirages. Honey stopped and shaded her eyes curiously, expecting to see a cargo ship or tanker on its way to Houston's ship channel. Her brow creased in a puzzled frown. Surely that white dot on the horizon was too small to be either of those. It looked more like a small launch, and it didn't seem to be moving. It appeared to be rocking gently on the quiet waves as if it were at anchor. As if it were waiting. She tried to shake off the uneasiness that flooded her as she turned and began to walk slowly back toward the path that led to the Folly. How foolish to get upset over a launch that would probably be gone in an hour or two. It was more than likely just an innocent fishing party.

Yet it was an odd coincidence that the launch should anchor here, at the only cove that offered access to the island. A little too odd. Honey's stride quickened instinctively, keeping pace with her thoughts. That was the second out-of-the-ordinary occurrence today. First had been the arrival of Leona Martell, and now the launch waiting on the horizon. Waiting for what?

There couldn't be a connection, could there? Leona Martell had come at Alex's invitation. Still, something nagged at Honey. There was something not quite right about Leona Martell. Honey had been subconsciously aware of something amiss since she'd met her.

She skidded to a halt and inhaled sharply. Her hair! It was obvious that Leona Martell had liked being a blonde. Her expression had been frankly envious when she'd seen Honey's hair, and then there had been that strange resentful glance she had thrown at Alex. Why would a natural blonde who was very well satisfied with her coloring suddenly dye her hair red?

"Oh, my God!" Honey breathed, her eyes widening in horror. Then she was flying up the path to the Folly. She burst through the front door and took the steps to the second floor two at a time and then dashed down the corridor to the improvised studio where Lance was working.

He looked up vaguely as she burst into the room. "Lance," she said, trying to get breath enough to speak. "Alex told me once that almost everyone in your immediate circle knew of his passion for redheads, that it was practically a standing joke. Is that true?"

"What?" he asked absently, his gaze returning to the easel. "Yes, of course it's true."

"Oh, no!" she moaned frantically, and turned and raced from the room and down the corridor to Alex's room. How criminally stupid of her not to have made the connection at once. Since she'd come to the island, she had forgotten everything but Lance. She'd even been rocked by the blissful serenity of their relationship into forgetting her purpose for being here. She prayed that she'd remembered in time.

She burst into Alex's room and frantically scanned the apparently empty master suite, before she noticed the door ajar at the far end of the room. There was only the sound of running water, yet it was enough to send a chill through her. How terribly easy it would be to drown in a bathtub a man who was exposed and vulnerable. Had it happened already? She tore across the bedroom and threw open the door.

Alex was lying in the center of a huge, blue-veined marble sunken tub that could well have graced one of his ancestor's seraglios, and he looked up in stunned amazement as Honey bolted into the room.

Honey gave him a quick, relieved glance, her attention concentrated on the woman on top of him.

"No!" she cried sharply, and the redhead looked over her shoulder with the same shocked surprise Alex had shown. But she only had time for that one glance, before Honey jumped into the tub with them. She grabbed Leona quickly in a neck lock and jerked her away from Alex with one swift motion.

"Honey, for God's sake, stop it!" Alex shouted, struggling into a sitting position.

She paid no attention, for the redhead was struggling with surprising strength for one who appeared so fragile, and Honey needed all her expertise to subdue her. Who would have believed a nude body could be so slippery? It was like trying to handle a greased pig.

"Honey, so help me God, I'm going to murder you," Alex roared. "Let her go, damn it."

There was only one way to put an end to this. She spun the redhead around and stepped back a pace for leverage and then followed through with a right cross to the woman's jaw.

The redhead gave a guttural grunt, and her blue eyes slowly glazed over. Honey caught her as she started to slump, and heaved her out of the water onto the marble floor.

"Damn you, Honey," Alex groaned, covering his eyes with his hand. "Why the hell didn't you listen to me?"

"I can't talk right now, Alex," she said, levering herself out of the tub. "I've got to find something to tie her up with before she regains consciousness." She was gone before he could answer, but returned an instant later with a cord she'd appropriated from one of the drapes in the bedroom. She efficiently secured the woman's hands behind her back, then turned to Alex with a grin. "She must have a glass jaw; she's still out like a light."

Alex was gazing at the woman's unconscious form with dark, mournful eyes. "You shouldn't have done that, Honey," he said sadly.

"But you don't understand, Alex," Honey said briskly, reaching over to pick up a towel from the rack above the tub. She began to dry her legs.

Then, as an afterthought, she threw a towel modestly over the redhead's lax, naked body. "She wasn't what she seemed at all. I'm almost sure she's a part of the assassination plot against you and Lance."

"So am I," Alex said gloomily, his eyes still on the redhead. "I suspected it from the first night at the Starburst."

"You suspec—" Honey's lips fell open in surprise. "But why didn't you say anything? Why did you invite her to the Folly?"

"I told you I'd been taught never to trust anyone," he said, his moody glance shifting to Honey's shocked face. "She was a little too eager. When I discovered that she wasn't a real redhead, it was only logical to assume that she was the Judas goat staked out by the hunters." He shrugged, his brawny bronzed shoulders gleaming copper. Abruptly it sank home to Honey that he was totally nude. Thank heavens for those mounds of bubble bath! "I decided I'd rather shift the battleground to my own territory and see if I could lure them into my net."

"Then why did you tell me to leave her alone when I jumped into the tub?" Honey asked, perplexed.

His face darkened in a fierce scowl. "Because it's been two weeks, damn it," he growled. "Why the hell couldn't you have knocked her out *afterward*?"

Honey gazed at him blankly. "Afterward?" Suddenly she started to chuckle, and she sat down on the side of the tub and crossed her legs tailor fashion. Her face was alight with laughter, and her violet eyes danced with impish delight. "Oh, Lord, Alex, I'm sorry. I was afraid she was trying to drown you."

He gave her an indignant glance. "I assure you that no woman living would have tried to murder me at that particular moment."

"I'm sure you're right," she agreed solemnly, her lips quirking. "But surely she's no *great* loss. She wasn't a real redhead anyway."

"She was entirely adequate for the situation," Alex said dryly. "You owe me one, Honey."

"I owe you," she agreed lightly. "There must be a redhead somewhere in the world whom you can trust."

His lips twisted cynically. "I strongly doubt it. But you're the private investigator—you find her for me."

"I just might do that," Honey said thoughtfully.

"I imagine there's some perfectly logical explanation for this scenario," Lance said politely from the doorway. "Would either of you care to enlighten me?" He strolled lazily forward, interestedly eyeing the unconscious woman. "I suppose this is your lethal Delilah, Alex. Very pretty."

"You knew about her too?" Honey asked indignantly. "Why didn't someone tell me? How do you expect me to perform with any sort of efficiency if you both keep me in the dark?"

"You weren't *my* bodyguard, Honey," Alex said, leaning lazily back in the tub. "And Lance was more than satisfied with your performance, I'm sure."

"More than satisfied," Lance agreed solemnly, blue eyes twinkling.

"I guess you know about the launch as well," Honey said, crossly scowling at them both.

"Which one?" Alex asked, one brow arched inquiringly. "Mine or theirs?"

"Which one?" Honey sputtered. "The one in the cove. You mean there are two?"

Lance was squatting down beside Leona Martell now, and he opened her lid to examine judiciously one glassy eye. "Probably not anymore," he said absently. "Alex's men have more than likely dispatched the black hats with their usual efficiency."

He looked over at Alex with a frown. "She's really dead to the world, Alex. Did you have to hit her so hard?"

"Don't blame me," Alex disclaimed with a wry grin. "It was your beautiful Amazon, sitting there." He gave Honey an admiring glance. "Dear heaven, but she's got a fantastic right cross."

"Thank you," Honey said automatically, not really hearing them. "Alex's men?"

"Well, Karim's men, actually," Lance said, rising to his feet and strolling around to where Honey was sitting. "Sedikhan Petroleum has its own security force, and he's made sure that they're efficient and deadly. Do you think the old tiger would allow his precious grandson to wander over the face of the earth without making certain that he was well protected?"

"So that was why you refused a bodyguard," Honey said thoughtfully. Then her chin lifted indignantly. "You needed me like you needed a hole in the head!"

Lance kneeled down beside her. "I needed you," he said gently. "I needed you very much." He picked up her right hand and examined it with a frown. "You've bruised your knuckles." He brushed his lips tenderly over the darkening flesh. "You should have been more careful. You didn't have to hit her that hard."

Honey gazed at him with blank disbelief, torn between indignation, a desire to laugh, and that melting tenderness that was so much a part of her love for Lance now. "I'll remember that next time," she said dryly, a tiny smile tugging at her lips.

"I would have liked to see you in action," he said, turning her hand over to kiss the palm lingeringly. "It must have been beautiful. I was right to paint you as a Valkyrie."

"I hate to disturb you, but this bath water is

getting cold," Alex said patiently. "I'll give you one minute to get Honey out of here before I get out of this tub." He leered with mock lasciviousness. "Then she'll know what she's missing by settling for a red-haired Scaramouche like you."

Lance stood up and pulled Honey to her feet. "She'd better change out of those wet shorts anyway," he said solicitously. He cast a glance at the still-inert nude redhead. "What are you going to do with her?"

"Nothing, unfortunately," Alex said sadly, then gave Honey a glowering look as she giggled. "I suppose I'll radio the launch and have a dinghy sent ashore to pick her up. They'll all be flown back to Sedikhan to be tried."

They turned to leave, and there was an odd flicker of wistfulness in Alex's dark eyes as he watched Lance's arm slide around Honey's waist with loving familiarity.

"Honey!"

She looked over her shoulder at him inquiringly.

"Remember your promise."

She smiled at him serenely. "I'll remember," she said gently.

"What did you promise him?" Lance asked curiously as he shut the door of their room behind them.

"That's our secret," she tossed teasingly over her shoulder. She was riffling through the drawer of the Korean chest, and drew out a pair of white shorts. "You and Alex have kept enough from me." She frowned with annoyance. "I don't appreciate being treated like an outsider. I'm a qualified professional, damn it. Did it ever occur to you that I might be able to help? I'm not some weak, defenseless, clinging vine, you know."

"Oh, we know, all right," he drawled, his blue

eyes twinkling. "Alex is lost in admiration for your dazzling right cross. If I'm not careful, he'll probably try to recruit you for his security force."

"What will happen to that woman and her cohorts?" Honey asked, her face troubled. "I would have thought that they'd be turned over to the State Department rather than the sheik."

"It's better not to ask and better still not to probe," Lance said grimly "Justice can be swift and very ruthless in an absolute monarchy like Sedikhan. Alex is the only human being on the face of the earth whom Karim really cares about. It's not likely that anyone who threatened him would receive any mercy."

"Except you," Honey corrected softly. "He must care a good deal about you, to have been so generous."

Lance shrugged. "Maybe. It's hard to tell with a fierce old buzzard like Karim."

"Yet you're very fond of him," Honey said gently. "It's all there in the portrait you did of him."

"Just because you feel affection for someone is no sign it will be returned, Honey sweet," he said cynically. "I learned that a long time ago." For a moment there was a flicker of melancholy in the sapphire eyes, and then it was gone and he was padding catlike across the room toward her. "Would you like me to help you change?" he asked silkily.

She shook her head firmly. "You know very well where that would lead," she said, trying to frown severely. "And you have my painting to finish. Besides, I have to place a call to Mr. Davies and tell him the latest developments. This will put an end to my assignment for the State Department. You won't need me as your bodyguard now that the danger is past."

"Yes, I will," Lance argued softly as he kissed her lightly on the forehead. "I need you to guard my body from all kinds of dangers." He moved closer, so that her breasts were brushing tantalizingly against his chest. "The danger of cold." He kissed the corner of her lips. "The danger of loneliness." His lips moved to her ear, and he blew in it softly. "The danger of frustration." His arms went around her, burying his face in her hair. "The portrait will wait, Honey," he said huskily. "Show me how well you can guard me from all those things." His hands were at the fastening of the wet khaki shorts, and somehow she found that she had dropped the white shorts in her hand to the floor.

"I really should call Mr. Davies," she said a trifle breathlessly, for his hands were quickly unbuttoning her white blouse. "This isn't at all professional, Lance."

He unfastened her bra and pushed both the bra and blouse down her arms, until they too fell to the carpet. "Davies will wait, too," he said. "I've never made love to an Amazon," he added thickly. "Is it different from taking my Honey hot to bed?"

She had an idea that he was going to find out very soon. She could never hold out for long when Lance was really bent on seduction . . . not that much seduction was required. As usual, she was feeling as yielding as melting butter as his hands came up to cup her breasts in his warm, hard palms. With thumb and forefinger he plucked at the rosy eager tips until they were hard and thrusting and her breath was coming in little gasps. She closed her eyes, and her hands reached out to clutch him desperately by the shoulders to keep from being swept away into this hot vortex of sensation. "Lance, there are things that we have to discuss," she gasped. He bent his head and brushed his tongue over the nipple he'd aroused to such ardent readiness. "The situation has changed, and I have no valid reason for being here now."

"Nothing could be more valid than this," he said thickly. "Don't talk anymore, sweetheart. I want to love you. Can't you feel how I need you?"

She could indeed, and it filled her with excitement that was slowly turning her own hunger from a flickering flame to a white-hot fire. He was right. Now was not the time for speech, but for that magical ritual that seemed to grow in intensity and beauty every time it was performed.

Her eyes still closed, her hands went up to bury themselves in the thickness of his hair and bring him to her breasts once again. "Then, love me, Lance," she urged huskily, "love me."

Eight

"Lance, we've got to talk," Honey said, exasperation sharpening her voice. "You've been putting me off since yesterday morning. I won't stand for it any longer."

Lance finished buttoning his black shirt and looked up with an absent smile. "We'll talk tonight when I come to bed," he said evasively, tucking the shirt into his jeans. "I've got to work now." His eyes twinkled impishly. "I missed an entire day's work, thanks to your insatiable appetite for my virile body, and I've got to make up for it." His gaze moved over her lingeringly. "But you'd better pull that sheet up unless you want me to crawl back into bed and start all over again."

Honey automatically pulled up the sheet and tucked it under her arms, frowning crossly at him. He was being as evasive as a will-o'-the-wisp this morning, and he'd been no better yesterday. Every attempt at speaking seriously to him had been met by diversionary tactics worthy of a five-star general—provided that general had earned those stars in a bordello, she thought ruefully. She'd believed they'd explored every facet of physical love in the past weeks, but Lance had demonstrated last night that they'd just skimmed the surface. And she was wondering just how much of that had been genuine passion.

"*Now,*" she said quietly, a thread of steel in her voice. "Not later. Now, Lance."

He opened his lips to protest, then evidently changed his mind. He smiled at her beguilingly, strolled over to the bed, and sat down beside her. "All right, now," he agreed amiably, taking her hand in both of his. "I'm entirely at your disposal, sweet." He scooted a little closer and bent his head to nibble gently at the soft hollow beneath her collarbone.

Her other hand went automatically up around his neck to curl in the dark flaming hair at the nape of his neck. He was so beautiful, she thought dreamily, the somber black of his shirt only made him look more vibrantly alive than ever. The richness of that molten auburn cap, the sapphire of his eyes, the copper brown of his skin all took on a subtle drama in contrast. His hand reached out and gently tugged the sheet down to her waist, and his lips trailed soft, hot kisses down to the rise of her breasts.

"Lance," she said huskily, her hands tightening around his neck. Then, as he was bearing her back on the bed, she suddenly came to her senses. He was doing it again!

"No, damn it!" she cried, and pushed him away so forcefully that he almost fell off the bed. "No! No! No!" She wound the sheet around her firmly and slid over to the other side of the bed, where she knelt to glare at him belligerently. "We're going to talk!"

His expression was distinctly sulky as he said crossly, "I think you've made yourself clear. I don't know why it won't wait." He scowled. "Say what you have to say and get it over with."

She drew a quick, deep breath. "All right, I will," she said. "I can't stay here any longer. I have to get back to my office. My purpose for being here vanished yesterday, when the threat to your life was lifted."

"That's ridiculous!" he spat explosively. "There's no reason for you to leave. You like it here. We're fantastic together, in bed and out. Why in the hell would you want to go back to Houston? If that Martell woman hadn't been captured, you'd have been content to stay indefinitely."

"But we did catch her, and that's the entire point," Honey argued in exasperation. "I can't just drift along in some fantasy island paradise. I'm not made that way. I have a career and responsibilities."

"You promised to stay with me until after my show," he said stubbornly, his sapphire eyes blazing. "Your precious career can wait until then, can't it? Or isn't it worth it to you anymore?"

"Of course, it's worth it." She sighed wearily. "I fully intend to meet you in New York for the exhibit next month. I'm not trying to break off our affair, Lance. I'll be glad to fly to the island for weekends if you want me to, and perhaps you can come to see me if you're not too busy preparing for your exhibit. It's just that I think it's time to approach our relationship more realistically."

"Sounds charming," Lance said caustically. "Very cool and pragmatic and completely analytic. Exactly what I'd expect from a private investigator. Perhaps you could make up a schedule."

Cool and pragmatic? Every word she was uttering was creating a fresh wound, yet she knew that if she was to keep any part of Lance's respect, she first must respect herself. She'd known since the beginning of their affair that this moment would come.

"If it comes down to it, I just might do that," Honey said coolly. "And I see no harm in being pragmatic. You know as well as I that we can't go on like this forever. We've both got to return to our own lives sometime and go our separate ways."

"It doesn't have to be that way," Lance said haltingly, not looking at her.

"Yes, it does," Honey said softly, her face pale and strained. "I can't give up my work and independence any more than you can. I won't live the life of a mindless parasite even for you, Lance."

His lips twisted bitterly. "You're nothing if not eloquent. You make life with me sound as rewarding as going to the dentist for a root canal."

"Don't be stupid," Honey said impatiently. "You know I find you a very exciting lover. I think that I've made that more than clear. I still want to continue our affair. It just has to be on my terms."

"The hell it does!" Lance said roughly, his face stormy. He jumped to his feet, his eyes blazing down at her. "That cool, anemic little liaison you're describing may be enough for you, but I'll be damned if I'll put up with it. I want more, damn it. And by God, I'll have it!" He turned and strode angrily toward the door.

"Does that mean you want to put an end to our relationship entirely?" she called after him, trying, with that same coolness he'd condemned so passionately, to mask the sick dread she felt.

He turned at the door, his sapphire eyes gleaming like a finely honed blade in his white face. For a moment, the artist and lover she'd grown to know so well was gone and there was once again the shimmer of steel that lay just beneath the surface. "Hell, no," he said softly. "It means that I mean to have it all. I'm not letting you leave me, Honey. It will be a good deal easier on you if you make up your mind to that."

The door closed with a decisive click behind him.

Darn the man, why couldn't he see reason? Didn't he know how it was hurting her to maintain this cool composure when all she wanted to do was throw herself into his arms and do anything he wanted for the rest of her life? Didn't he realize what assuming the role of his mistress in public would do to her? She would grow to hate herself and, worse still, she would grow to hate Lance for what he'd made of her.

There must be some way of convincing him of the validity of her arguments, she thought gloomily, though at the moment she couldn't see it. But there was no question that she must continue to try. She didn't know if she could exist without having at least a small role in Lance's life, and the other option he'd given her was equally unpalatable. There must be a happy medium. She would just have to try again later, after he'd cooled down.

Perhaps she could discuss the problem with Alex and get him to intercede with Lance on her behalf. In the past weeks she'd developed an almost sisterly affection for Ben Raschid, and she knew that he liked her equally. Yes, she would see if Alex could get her viewpoint across to Lance.

With this aim in mind, she threw back the covers and strode swiftly to the bathroom. After brushing her teeth, a quick shower, and a vigorous brushing of her hair until it shone, she emerged twenty minutes later. A swift glance at the clock verified that if she hurried she could still catch Alex at the breakfast table on the terrace. She knew he liked to linger over coffee while he read his correspondence, before officially starting his day. She quickly donned a pair of white jeans, a loose boat-necked scarlet tunic top, and sandals, and ran out of the bedroom and down the stairs.

She might just as well have made a more leisurely toilette, for when she hurried out on the terrace, there was no sign of Alex. The table was set with the usual fastidious elegance, but only for two, and Justine was just setting the customary carafe of hot coffee on the table.

"Mr. Ben Raschid has already finished?" Honey asked disappointedly. She wouldn't dare beard Alex in the library once he'd actually started to work.

Justine shook her head. "He's flown to Houston for the day," she said cheerfully. "He left quite early, and asked me to give you a message." She straightened a bamboo placemat and continued. "He said he'd been on the phone to a Mr. Davies last night and that Mr. Davies was a little put out about the packages being forwarded to Sedikhan instead of to him. He decided to fly over to try to pacify him."

The "packages" being Leona Martell and her criminal accomplices, Honey thought in amusement. She could see how Davies would be a trifle upset at having his authority usurped, but she had no doubt Alex would be able to smooth his ruffled feathers. It didn't make her any happier, however, to have to delay her talk with Alex.

"Will he be coming back this evening?" she asked as she slipped into her accustomed place at the table.

Justine nodded and picked up the carafe to pour Honey's coffee. "Either tonight or early tomorrow morning. He said he was sure you and Prince Rubinoff could find something to do to amuse yourselves." The last sentence was stated impassively, but Honey could almost see the mocking gleam in Alex's dark eyes as he was giving the housekeeper the message. "Will Prince Rubinoff be joining you for breakfast?"

"No, I'm sure he's gone to the studio to work, Justine," Honey said quietly. "You might take him some coffee right now and sandwiches later for lunch. He'll probably be working all day."

Justine nodded again and quietly disappeared

into the house, leaving Honey sitting morosely, gazing blindly out at the stunningly lovely seascape view from the ⸌errace.

She finished her coffee and tried to eat a little but finally ended by pushing her plate away distastefully. Perhaps she'd go down to the beach and try to while away a few hours. It would be useless to try to read in such a tense state.

It was while she was striding down the path to the beach that she first heard the now-familiar throbbing sound of helicopter rotors, and she stopped in surprise. Her first thought was that it might be Alex returning, but she dismissed that idea as soon as it occurred to her. Alex couldn't have possibly completed his task and come back already.

She shaded her eyes and soon determined that it wasn't the orange helicopter that she'd become accustomed to seeing on the landing pad at the foot of the hill, but a brilliant blue-and-white one. Yet there was no question that its destination was the Folly. Her eyes narrowed curiously on the aircraft as it descended toward the landing pad like an ungainly butterfly. Then she accelerated her steps and strode hurriedly down the hill toward the pad.

When she arrived, it was to see a khaki-clad, gray-haired man, with "Sunbelt Helicopter Service" imprinted on the back of his shirt, assisting a dark-haired woman in a lovely melon pants suit out of the helicopter.

The woman looked up as Honey appeared beside them, and gave her an incisive glance. "Ach, no wonder," she boomed cheerfully. "You're even more attractive than your picture, Honey Winston." She smiled with sunny friendliness. "Permit me to introduce myself. I'm the Baroness Bettina von Feltenstein. Now, tell me, where are Alex and Lance hiding? They can't have been so cowardly as to **send** you out to face me alone."

Bettina von Feltenstein? This was the Teutonic Terror of Alex's description? This woman was so far removed from Honey's mental image that she could feel her lips drop open in surprise. Where was the sleek, beautiful vamp of her imaginings? There was nothing in the least sleek about the woman facing her. If her carriage had not been so graceful, her small, plump figure might even have been considered dumpy. And she certainly could not be termed beautiful, though her glowing complexion was really magnificent, and the large, luminous brown eyes behind the stylish tortoiseshell glasses were snapping with vitality.

"I'm not what you expected either," the baroness guessed shrewdly, her eyes narrowing on Honey's surprised face. "I wonder just what they told you about me." She shrugged and grinned with gamine charm, her brown eyes twinkling. "Nothing very complimentary, I'm sure."

"Nothing very much, Baroness," Honey recovered enough to say. "They only mentioned you in passing."

"Really? I'm disappointed that my phone calls had so little impact." She made a wry face. "But then, that's why I'm here. I hate telephones. It's so easy for people to be conveniently disconnected."

Honey smothered a smile and tried to reply with appropriate solemnity. "It certainly is. I'm sorry that you didn't let Alex know you were coming, however. He left for Houston this morning and may not be back until tomorrow."

"I doubt if he'd have changed his plans," the baroness said dryly. "In fact, he might have accelerated them. Alex and I aren't exactly soulmates. Lance is still here, of course." It was a statement, not a question.

Honey nodded, feeling a trifle bemused. It was impossible not to like the baroness, despite her blatant aggressiveness. "Yes, he's still here, but he's in his studio working. Would you like me to take you to him?"

"Not at the moment," the baroness said. "It's really you I came to see anyway." She turned to the helicopter pilot and instructed briskly, "You will wait here, yes? We will be back shortly." She didn't wait for the man's casual nod before turning back to Honey and slinging her large Gucci bag over her shoulder. "Now, where can we go so that we won't be disturbed?"

"I suppose we could go for a walk on the beach," Honey said slowly. She had heard the woman's name only in casual conversation, and she was sure Alex hadn't mentioned that she'd be coming to the island. Why would the baroness fly thousands of miles just to see her?

"That will be fine," Bettina von Feltenstein said. She looked down wryly at her exquisitely crafted high heels. "I guess I should have expected to run into this on an island." She calmly took off the shoes and slipped them into her voluminous shoulder bag. "It's fortunate that I always carry an extra pair of hose. These will be shredded to pieces by the time we get back." She gestured to Honey to precede her. "Lead on, Miss Winston. I'll try to keep up with those long, lovely legs of yours." Her lips turned down gloomily. "You would have to be tall as well as gorgeous."

Honey gave her a questioning glance before obediently leading the way down the palm-bordered path to the beach. The German woman didn't speak again until they reached the lower reaches of the hill and the trail widened enough for her to come alongside.

"You even carry yourself well," the baroness said moodily. "You'd be surprised at how many tall women have an absolutely atrocious posture. Do you know how many years I've studied ballet to get a slight edge over you sultry giantesses? Did you ever study ballet, Miss Winston?"

Honey shook her head, thinking of her very spartan upbringing in the orphanage. "I'm afraid not, Baroness," she replied gently.

"I suspected that," she said mournfully. "There's no justice in the world." She peered owlishly up at Honey through the thick lenses of her horn-rimmed glasses. "You're even younger than I am."

"Not very much," Honey said soothingly. How on earth had she been put in the position of comforting this small, strange rival for Lance's affections? "I'm twenty-four, Baroness."

"And I'm thirty-one," Bettina von Feltenstein said tersely. "I'm one year older than Lance. And call me Bettina; I will find it very hard to speak with frankness if we're formal." She added, "I will call you Honey. What an abominable name. Why do you not change it?"

She hadn't noticed that the baroness was shy about speaking her mind, Honey thought in amusement. "I agree with you, but it's not worth the bother," she said lightly. "How did you know I was here, Bar—Bettina?"

"Can we sit down?" Bettina asked abruptly, halting in her tracks. "This hot sand is most uncomfortable on my feet." Without waiting for Honey to agree, she plopped herself down on the sand in the shade of a palm tree. "I saw your picture in the newspaper and I thought it worthwhile to find out all I could about you," she said grimly. "Actually, the expression on Lance's face told me quite a bit."

"Newspaper?" Honey asked, dropping down beside her. Her brow creased in puzzlement. Then she remembered the photographer in the lobby of the hotel the night before they'd left. It seemed very far removed from her present existence. "They used that picture of Lance and me?"

The baroness opened her large shoulder bag and drew out a folded newspaper.

"They used it," she said curtly. "Complete with smutty innuendoes and juicy references to Lance's very disreputable past. Lance's parents were very displeased when they called me after they'd seen it."

"You know Lance's parents?" Honey asked absently as she spread out the newspaper. She glanced only briefly at her own shocked face as she stood in the curve of Lance's arm. It was the expression on Lance's face that caught her attention. He was looking down at her with desire and tenderness and a fierce protectiveness that filled her with a quiet joy.

"Our families have been very close since we were small children," Bettina said softly. "When Lance wasn't in Sedikhan, we were practically inseparable. Their Majesties have always approved of a match between us."

"So I understand," Honey said quietly, carefully refolding the newspaper and handing it back. "Yet the marriage has never come to pass."

"It will in time," Bettina said with complete confidence. "I'm a very determined woman, Honey. This marriage is not only desirable, but it's necessary for Lance."

"To keep the royal bloodlines pure and unpolluted?" Honey asked tartly, unconsciously moistening her lips. The absolute certainty that the woman exuded was making her uneasy despite the comforting message generated by Lance's expression in the newspaper photo.

"No, of course not," the baroness said. "I have a great respect for selective breeding, but there have been too many dynamic leaders born on the wrong side of the blanket for me to be a complete fanatic on the subject. I only use that argument with Lance because I can't tell him the truth."

"The truth?" Honey asked slowly.

"I love him," Bettina said simply, with utter sincerity. "I've loved him all my life. Everything I've studied and worked for since childhood has been to prepare me to be a fitting wife for him." Her face was earnest. "I'll be everything that he could ask for in a mate, Honey."

"Why are you telling me this?" Honey asked, looking away from that earnest little face to stare blindly out at the gentle roll of the surf. Suddenly she was no longer finding the situation amusing. It hurt to think of Lance in the intimacy of marriage with any woman. "Your relationship with Lance is none of my business."

"I don't usually go around confiding my most intimate feelings to strangers," Bettina said bluntly. "This is the first time I've felt it necessary to approach one of Lance's *petites amies*. After I saw that picture, I thought we'd better meet. I was frightened. I'd never seen Lance look at any woman like that before. I wanted to come to an understanding with you before a terrible mistake was made."

"Should I be honored that you consider me a threat?" Honey asked tightly. "I'm sorry if I can't see that we have anything to talk about. We obviously play two very different roles in Lance's life. There's no reason why the two should encroach upon each other."

"Ah, you realize that?" Bettina asked with a relieved sigh. "That is good. I was afraid that you might have hopes for a more permanent place in his affections. That is, of course, totally impossible."

Honey flinched at the sudden thrust of pain that struck her. "Of course," she said huskily.

The baroness's eyes were warmly sympathetic as she reached over and gave Honey's hand a bracing squeeze. "None of us can have everything," she said gently. "We must all compromise."

"And what have you given up, Baroness?" Honey asked sharply, blinking back the tears and turning to her with her chin lifted in defiance. "What do you intend to compromise?"

"I've given up the hope of ever having Lance look at me as he did at you in that newspaper photograph," she answered quietly, and the pain in her face mirrored that in Honey's. "I know that he'll never love me or desire me as he does you. I've had to accept that."

"How can you?" Honey broke out fiercely. "How can you possibly want a man who doesn't want you?"

"Because he'll learn to care for me," Bettina said serenely. "There are many ways of caring. If I cannot have his passion, I will earn his trust, his gratitude, even his affection." Her smile was bittersweet. "It's not everything, but it will be enough."

She would not feel sorry for the woman, Honey thought feverishly. This strange empathy that existed between them was far more dangerous than if the baroness had been openly antagonistic. How much more difficult it was to fight against a rival who loved Lance as much as she did.

"Is that what you came to tell me? That I have no real place in Lance's life?" Honey asked bitterly.

Bettina shook her head. "No, that isn't why I came," she said gently. "I came to tell you that there is room for both of us. I am a modern woman, and I have come to terms with the knowledge that you give Lance something that I can't." She shrugged wearily. "Glamour, sex, the love mystique—I don't know. Whatever it is, he doesn't see it in me. You'll have to supply it." She looked away. "I want you to know that as long as the two of you are discreet, I will ignore your relationship regardless of how long it continues."

"That's very generous of you," Honey said slowly,

and there was no sarcasm in her voice. In the baroness's place, she doubted very much if she could have made a similar offer.

"Not really," Bettina said throatily. "As I said, I made it my business to find out a great deal about you, Honey Winston. If you and Lance are lovers, it is because you have a genuine affection for him. That is essential." She looked up fiercely. "For, whatever happens, he must not be hurt. You understand that?"

"I understand," Honey said huskily. "I love him very much too, you know."

"I don't know," Bettina said quietly. "But I'm about to find out. How generous is your love, Honey?"

"I don't know what you mean."

"I want you to leave Lance," Bettina said, but then held up her hand at Honey's cry of protest. "Not permanently. Haven't I just told you that I don't expect that? Just until after Lance's exhibit in New York next month."

"You know about that?" Honey asked faintly.

"Alex told me on the phone the other evening," she said wryly. "I think he was trying to put me off by extending the hope that I'd see Lance in New York. I knew as soon as I heard about it that it might be the answer to all Lance's problems with his parents." She smiled sadly. "Do you know I've only seen that one portrait in the library? Do you know how envious I am that it is you who has seen all his work and persuaded him to show it?"

"What problems with his parents?" Honey asked curtly. This was getting more painful by the moment. "It's my understanding that they were never close."

"Lance has always wanted his parents' respect and admiration. This exhibit could give him that," Bettina said quietly. "I want to try to persuade them to attend the exhibit and encourage a reconciliation. There's only one difficulty."

"Me," Honey said huskily, her throat tight and aching with pain.

Bettina nodded. "If your liaison continues, it's bound to attract publicity." Her lips twisted ruefully. "Lance always does. Needless to say, we don't need to upset his parents while I'm trying to negotiate a truce." Her brown eyes were sober. "Do you love Lance enough to put his welfare above your own, Honey? It will be for only a little over a month, and then you can resume your relationship."

"You don't want me to see Lance at all?" Honey asked. And she'd thought becoming only a weekend lover was going to be difficult. She felt a shiver of loneliness run through her.

"You know that wouldn't be wise," Bettina said softly, her face sympathetic. "It would be impossible to keep your association quiet, after that newspaper story. If you're going to do something, do it right."

"I'm afraid I don't have your innate incisiveness," Honey said, her voice shaking despite her effort to steady it. "I don't know if I can do it."

"Of course you can," Bettina said briskly. "I'll make it as easy on you as I can. I'll fly you back to Houston this morning in the helicopter. Then I'll come back and explain everything to Lance. You won't even have to speak to him yourself. I think you would find that very difficult. Yes?"

"Impossible," Honey agreed miserably. "You have it all planned."

"My incisiveness is generally accompanied by my efficiency," Bettina said, her brown eyes twinkling. "You can phone him from Houston, if you feel it's necessary." She made a face. "I wouldn't recommend it. Very frustrating things, telephones."

Honey ran her hand distractedly through **her**

hair. "I don't know. It's all coming too fast. I've got to think."

"Of course you do," the baroness agreed promptly. "I have no intention of rushing you into a decision you'll regret later." She stood up and meticulously brushed the powdery sand from the melon pants suit. "I'll go back to the helicopter and wait for you there. You're a very loving, intelligent woman. I'm sure you'll make the right choice." She padded away, her plump figure indomitably majestic despite her stockinged feet and the little hops she occasionally gave to avoid the heat of the noonday sand.

Indomitable. That was the right word for her, Honey thought. She had swept boldly into her life, and suddenly everything was colored by the baroness's viewpoint. It was hard to ignore anyone as clear-thinking and fiercely loving as Bettina had proven to be. She had known Lance and his family for years, and that made her a far better judge than Honey as to what was best for Lance.

She frowned as the thought occurred to her that she would be making it ridiculously easy for a rival as strong as Bettina by removing herself from the picture for over a month. Was that what the baroness had in mind? Somehow she didn't think so. There had been too much sincerity in Bettina's face. Too much pain. Besides, if the relationship that existed between Lance and her would not withstand a month's separation, then it deserved to be severed. There were so many problems already surfacing in their affair that must be solved if they were to continue with any kind of harmony. Perhaps a month's hiatus would permit them time to think and see each other's point of view a little more clearly.

Why was she sitting here, when she knew her decision was really already made? She'd known when Bettina threw out the challenge to her love for Lance that she would have to pick up the gauntlet. She got to her feet and automatically dusted herself off as she set off toward the path that led to the landing pad.

Bettina was leaning against the helicopter, and she straightened slowly, her face tense as Honey appeared beside her.

"I'm going with you," Honey said curtly. "But it's got to be now. I don't want to see Lance before I go." Otherwise she would never have the courage to leave him. The pain was already shooting through her.

"Very wise," Bettina said, nodding. "You don't want to pack a bag?"

Honey shook her head. "Alex can have Justine pack my things and send them on to me. I don't want to go back to the house."

"Then we'll go," Bettina said briskly, opening the helicopter door. Following Honey into the aircraft, she gave the pilot a curt command and settled back into her seat. "Fasten your seatbelt," she ordered, adjusting her own.

Honey automatically obeyed, and they were soon spiraling into the heavens before leveling out and initiating a course eastward. She couldn't resist a look back at the emerald dot in the sapphire sea. It was a mistake, for she soon found the brilliant colors running together as the tears welled up in her eyes.

Bettina was watching her sympathetically. "You're doing the right thing, you know," she said gently. "That should help a little."

"Should it?" Honey said huskily. "Then there's something wrong. I don't think it does." She turned for one last look at Londale's Folly, but she was too late. It had already disappeared from view.

Nine

"Frankly, I think you're out of your mind," Nancy said bluntly, leaning back in her chair and regarding Honey, sitting in the visitor's chair by the desk. "You admit you're absolutely mad about the man, yet you're fading out of the picture for an entire month?" Her lips curved cynically. "Contrary to what you may have heard, absence does not make the heart grow fonder. Particularly when a man has as many women throwing themselves at him as your Prince Charming."

Honey flinched. That thought had been plaguing her ever since she had made the decision. It had been only a matter of hours, and she was already having doubts—not about the essential rightness of Bettina's arguments. Lance must have this chance for a reconciliation with his parents. Families were important, and who should know better than she, who had never had one? She wouldn't let Lance continue to be an emotional orphan, cut off from his parents and brother, not if there was any way that she could prevent it.

Yet she couldn't deny that it was frightening to face the ramifications of her actions. While Nancy's comment might have been tainted with the bitterness of her broken marriage, there was no question but that Honey was taking an enormous risk.

There had been no words of commitment spoken between them in all that golden halcyon period at the island. There had been words of passion. There had been laughter. There had been moments of tender exploration of the mind and emotions. That had seemed enough at the time. It was almost as if they'd both been afraid to disturb their magical Brigadoon with thoughts of the outside world. Once Lance was back in the reality of his own world, would that magic still hold?

"Then, I'd better find that out now, hadn't I?" Honey asked lightly, smiling with no little effort. "I know that I'm not going to change, and I don't think I'm equipped to handle a one-sided affair."

"You're not equipped to handle an affair, period. Why couldn't you have started out in the minor leagues and worked your way up to the big boys?" Nancy threw up her hands expressively. "Oh, no, your first affair has to be with Lusty Lance. Then you have to go and fall in love with him! Why couldn't you have chosen a nice, tame stockbroker or a used-car salesman?"

"I guess I just don't have your good taste," Honey said, her lips quirking despite the heaviness of her spirit. "I find I have a distinct partiality for princes."

"Thank goodness there aren't that many around," Nancy said gloomily. "For God's sake, stay away from Italy. I understand that they pop out from under every bush over there."

"I'll keep that in mind," Honey promised solemnly, her violet eyes twinkling. "What is the state of our finances?"

"Better than usual, thanks to Señora Gomez's

fee and the check we received last week from the State Department from Mr. Davies," Nancy replied. "Why?"

"I'm going away for a week or two," Honey said. "I just wanted to make sure that there was enough in the coffers to pay your salary and the bills until I get back."

"Am I allowed to ask where you're going?" Nancy asked caustically. "You're getting to be an absentee employer. The mailman will wonder if I'm just making you up, like that private detective on television."

"I don't think that would be a very good idea," Honey said quietly. "If you don't know where I am, you can't be coerced into telling anyone. The baroness has arranged for a place where I can stay for a bit, until Lance gets discouraged looking for me. I'll call you every few days to check in and make sure everything is running smoothly."

"Leaving me to fight off the ravening hordes." Nancy sighed. "You're probably right not to tell me where you're going. I could withstand bulldozing tactics, but if your Lance decides to use that notorious charm on me, I'd be sunk. I'd probably melt like an iceberg in Death Valley."

Honey couldn't have agreed more. Hadn't she found that charisma well-nigh irresistible from the moment they'd met? But she wouldn't think of that; it only made what she was doing that much harder. "I'm sure you'll survive," she said. "I'll call the day after tomorrow, when I've settled in."

Three hours later she'd finished packing her suitcases and was checking the tiny kitchen in her efficiency apartment to make sure that the utilities were turned off. There was nothing in the refrigerator to spoil, and there was nothing left to do but write a note to the manager of the apartment explaining her absence. She had just completed that when the phone rang.

"He just called, Honey," Nancy burst out as soon as she picked up the receiver. "I told him you'd already left town, but I don't think he believed me. I think you're probably going to have a visitor in the next hour or two."

"Do you know where he was calling from?" Honey asked, biting her lip worriedly. She knew very well that if she had to face Lance, her resolution, which was shaky at best, would vanish in the first strong breeze. And that seductive charm of Lance's could escalate to hurricane force when he chose. Which was the reason she'd opted not to face him in the first place.

"From the island," Nancy replied, to her intense relief. "But you can bet he won't be staying there."

"I'll be gone by the time he gets to Houston, then," Honey said. "Thanks for the warning, Nancy." She quietly replaced the receiver.

She hesitated a moment and then picked up the receiver and placed a call to the island, person-to-person to Alex Ben Raschid.

"Hello." Alex's voice was curt with impatience when he came on the line, and became even more so when she identified herself. "Damn it, Honey, do you know what hell you've raised? Why the devil did you leave the Folly without speaking to Lance first? He's been tearing around here like a madman ever since Bettina got back from practically kidnapping you."

"Is he still there, Alex?" Honey asked, when she could get a word in edgewise.

"He took off in the helicopter as soon as he finished talking to your secretary. For God's sake, how could you pull a stunt like this? When I got back to the island, I found Lance in a positive fury, the Teutonic Terror sobbing heartbrokenly, and you vanished from the face of the earth." Alex's voice was sharp with exasperation. "I'd just spent a whole bloody trying day convincing Davies that my grandfather wasn't going to take the entire assassination team out and behead them, and I come back to this!"

"I'm sorry, Alex," Honey said contritely. "I never meant to be a problem to you." Then she asked curiously, "Do they really behead people in Sedikhan?"

"Very rarely," Alex answered absently. "Honey, whatever possessed you to let Bettina bulldoze you into leaving? I thought you had more backbone than to let her intimidate you."

"It wasn't like that, Alex," Honey said. "It was my decision."

"You'll forgive me if I doubt that," Alex said dryly. "I'm familiar with Bettina's determination."

"So am I, now," Honey said ruefully. "But she wouldn't have been able to convince me to do something I wasn't willing to do. I'm not so easily swayed, Alex."

"I didn't think so until tonight," Alex said slowly. "Why did you do it, Honey? Lance was almost a raving lunatic. I've never seen him act like that before."

Honey ignored the question. "I want you to give him a message for me, Alex," Honey said quietly. "Will you please tell him I'll get in touch with him in six weeks' time? That is, if he still wants me to."

"If he still wan—" Alex echoed incredulously. "You're going to stretch this madness out for another six weeks? Good God, he'll tear Houston apart to find you."

"It won't do him any good. I'm leaving town tonight," she said gently. "Please just give him the message. Thank you for everything, Alex. You're a good friend."

There was a short silence. "You're making a mistake, Honey," Alex said quietly. "Lance isn't going to sit with folded hands, tamely waiting for you to get in touch with him." When she didn't answer, he continued with even greater deliberation. "And I hope I am your friend, Honey. I like you better than any woman I've ever known. But Lance is almost a brother to me. If it comes to a choice, then I'll have to side with him."

"I understand that," Honey replied. "But it won't come down to choices. I hope that I'll see you in six weeks, too. Good-bye, Alex."

"I rather think it will be a great deal sooner than that," Alex said softly. "Good-bye, Honey." The connection was broken with a decisive click.

Honey replaced the receiver, an uneasy frown wrinkling her brow. That last rejoinder had an oddly ominous overtone. Then she determinedly shrugged it off. It must be her imagination. Alex might be intimidating to his business rivals and political enemies, but he was her friend. It was foolish to be afraid.

Yet for some reason her final preparations for departure were even more hurried than was actually necessary. Fifteen minutes later she flicked out the lights, locked the door, and carried her suitcase down the wrought-iron stairs to her ancient blue Nova.

"I've saddled up Missy for you, Miss Winston," Hank called with a friendly grin that caused the sun creases to deepen about his keen gray eyes. "I hope that's all right."

"Missy will be fine, Hank," Honey answered with a smile. There hadn't really been any choice, Honey thought wryly as the stable-hand gave her a leg up into the saddle. Missy was as gentle as a rocking horse and the only animal in the entire remuda of horses on the Circle D Dude Ranch that she could manage to stay on. Horseback riding had definitely not been considered a necessary asset at the orphanage, and Honey had discovered as a beginner that she had little or no aptitude for equestrian pursuits. In the week she'd been here, she'd only managed to learn the bare rudiments, and wasn't at all sure that the aching muscles and decidedly tender derriere were worth the bother.

Yet she had to admit that these solitary morning rides did have their pleasant aspects. It was a relief not to have to maintain a sociable facade in front of the other guests, and she was so inept a rider that she had to concentrate to keep even Missy under control. It was virtually the only time she could shake the gloom and apathy that had beset her since she'd left the island.

Twenty minutes later she reined in at the little pine-shaded oblong lake, as was her custom, and slid gratefully from the saddle. She rubbed her jean-clad derriere ruefully, wondering if she'd ever learn not to bounce when that dratted horse decided to trot. After carefully putting the reins over the mare's head, as she'd been taught, she strolled down to the water's edge. This was her favorite spot on the entire ranch. Its quiet, serene beauty was a soothing balm to her troubled spirit, a balm that she dearly needed.

She leaned against the rough, gnarled bark of a pine and wearily closed her eyes, lifting her face in sensual contentment to the warm kiss of the sun. She supposed she should have been grateful to Bettina for arranging such luxurious accommodations at this isolated dude ranch, a short distance west of Houston. It was not the baroness's fault that she was a city girl and found all these trail rides and bucolic shenanigans a little wearing on the nerves. She'd be glad when she could go back to Houston and get to work again.

That might not be as soon as she hoped. When she'd called Nancy yesterday, it was to be told that

Lance had not abandoned his search for her and was driving Nancy crazy with phone calls and general harassment. Nancy had sounded frazzled and very cross. Evidently Lance was being quite unpleasant to the poor woman.

"Miss Winston?" the voice was deep, masculine, and very respectful.

Honey's lids flew open, to see two young men, dressed impeccably in dark business suits and discreetly patterned ties.

She hadn't heard them approach, yet they were standing only a few feet from her. They must have moved very quietly. "Yes, I'm Miss Winston," she answered.

"We've been looking for you, Miss Winston," the sandy-haired man said almost reproachfully. "We'd like you to come with us, please."

"Looking for me?" Honey asked, puzzled. "Are you from the ranch?" She knew before he shook his head that they were not. Those suits were far too expensive and cosmopolitan.

"No, ma'am, we're not," the dark-skinned man said gently. "We have our car parked about a quarter of a mile down the road. I wonder if we could persuade you to go with us now? We really do have to be on our way."

Honey shook her head as if to clear it. This was bizarre. "Why should I go anywhere with you? I don't even know you, and I certainly don't intend to get in any car with you."

"I'm sorry. We didn't introduce ourselves, did we?" the sandy-haired man asked with a frown. "I'm John Sax, and my friend, here, is Hassan Khalin. We're both employees of Alex Ben Raschid. We've been sent to fetch you."

"Fetch me?" Honey asked blankly. Employees of Alex Ben Raschid? Then she suddenly realized just exactly what manner of employees Alex had sent to find her. These soft-voiced young men must be members of that lethal security force Lance had mentioned. Now that she'd examined them more closely, she could detect that dangerous coiled tension beneath the smooth exterior that was the trademark of the professional. She stiffened and straightened slowly, her muscles tightening instinctively. "Then I'm afraid you've made a wasted journey," she said quietly, "for I have no intention of coming with you."

John Sax frowned in genuine concern. "Please don't take that attitude, Miss Winston," he pleaded, his blue eyes troubled. "You really must come with us. We have our orders."

She was tempted to tell them what they could do with their orders. How dare Alex do this to her? It was practically barbaric.

"Too bad," she said between her teeth. "Then you'll have to go back to your employer and tell him that I refuse to accommodate him. Good-bye, gentlemen."

"But we can't do that," Hassan Khalin protested. "We do have our instructions, as John said, Miss Winston. We must take you with us or be in quite a bit of trouble with Ben Raschid ourselves." He shook his head. "It's not very comfortable to be in that position, Miss Winston. Won't you change your mind?"

"No," Honey said emphatically, her face clouding. "If you want me to come with you, you'll have to use force."

The two men exchanged resigned glances. "We have a problem there as well, you see," John Sax admitted gloomily. "Ben Raschid said that he'd take us apart if we so much as disturbed a hair on your head. It's not the easiest assignment we've been given."

Well, at least Alex had had the courtesy to include that gracious little addition to his instructions. "You do have a problem," she said gently, her eyes narrowing. "For I don't intend to go peacefully, and that means not only a displaced coiffure but bruises and perhaps even cuts and scratches." She lifted a brow. "And while you're handling me with kid gloves, I can assure you that I'm not going to be equally kind. I'll be inflicting as much damage as I possibly can." Her gleaming smile had a touch of the tiger. "I think you'll be surprised at how much mayhem that constitutes, gentlemen."

"So we understand, Miss Winston," John Sax said with a gleam of genuine admiration in his bright blue eyes. "We were given an extensive dossier on you. Your credentials are very impressive, as was Ben Raschid's description of your prowess." He sighed. "Yes, the situation is very complicated."

"Then don't you think it would be better to give up and run back to your employer?" Honey suggested silkily. "Tell him that if he wants to speak to me, he can come and see me himself." And by that time, with any luck, she would be far away from the Circle D.

The same thought evidently had occurred to Sax, for he was shaking his head with a reproving grin. "You know we can't do that, Miss Winston," he said quietly. "Nice try, though."

"Then I don't know what you're going to do," Honey said flatly. "We seem to be at an impasse."

Khalin's face was gloomy. "We were afraid that just such a situation would occur, weren't we, John?"

His cohort nodded, an equally unhappy expression on his face. "We discussed the problem in some depth, and we could come to only one solution."

This was taking on all the nuances of a farce. It seemed impossible that she was standing here in this lovely sylvan setting talking so calmly to these soft-voiced, dangerous young men.

"And that is?" she asked warily.

She'd thought she was prepared, but when they moved toward her, it was with such deadly swiftness and smoothly coordinated timing that it caught her off guard. Khalin feinted to the left to distract her attention, and Sax followed through to her right. She only had time for a karate chop to Khalin's throat, which connected with a very satisfying thunk, before she felt a tiny sting on her arm, like the bite of a mosquito.

Then she was watching Khalin stumble to his knees with an out-of-sync deliberateness that was like slow motion. Everything was suddenly dimming, and she felt an instant of panic. Then she felt nothing at all.

Ten

When Honey awoke, she had that same heavy, distorted feeling, as if she were a swimmer fighting her way to the surface from the ocean's depths. Yet when she opened her eyes, it was with a sense of dreamy euphoria, rather than with the headache and nausea that she would have expected of a drug-induced unconsciousness.

Her gaze traveled around the room, and what she saw convinced her that she was still in a dream state. There couldn't be a room like this outside of a Turkish harem. She seemed to be reclining on a heap of tasseled white satin pillows. A gorgeous Persian carpet in delicate shades of pale blue and spring green on a cream background covered a polished parquet floor. There was even a copper brazier filled with glowing coals on the low teak table next to her that was giving off a heady, spicy fragrance. Incense? Yes, she was sure it was incense, she thought dreamily. It fit in perfectly with the rest of the fantasy.

She looked down at her own apparel and was

not at all surprised to find herself garbed in sheer chiffon amethyst harem pants, her silken stomach quite bare and the thrusting fullness of her breasts swathed in a matching pearl-trimmed top. What else would she be wearing in an Arabian Nights fantasy?

She turned on her side, waiting for the dream to fade and go away, and her gaze fell on a piece of folded notepaper on the table. She reached out a lazy hand and took it from the table, unfolding it with idle curiosity.

The words jumped out at her, shocking her into wakefulness.

Sorry, Honey. I did warn you.

Alex

Honey sat bolt upright on the silken cushions, her violet eyes blazing with fury. What kind of wild practical joke was this? The kidnapping was obviously Alex's doing, but this mad harem charade was completely at odds with everything she knew of him.

"Ah, you're awake at last."

Honey looked up, her heart leaping with joy and her face alight. It clouded swiftly as she gazed with rapidly returning fury at Lance, standing in the doorway. No one could argue about the dashing figure he made as he stood there, dressed in khaki riding pants tucked into mirror-bright black boots and a white shirt worn unbuttoned almost to the waist. My God, he was even wearing a white headdress!

Honey jumped off the cushions and struggled to her feet. "What the devil is going on here?" she shouted, facing him belligerently across the room.

Lance placed both hands on his hips, his face taking on a demonic leer. "Are you not woman enough to know?" he asked hoarsely.

"For God's sake, have you gone absolutely bananas?" Honey asked, running her hand through her hair distractedly. "They could put you away for a stunt like this. Have you completely lost touch with reality?"

Lance dropped the melodramatic pose, his face turning grim. "Hell, no," he said, his hands falling to his sides. "I just thought that you'd like to enjoy for one last time the pleasures of never-never land. Isn't that what you want from me? A romantic weekend affair with Lusty Lance, with no commitments or permanent ties? You couldn't wait to get off the island once your precious job was done, could you?" He tore the headdress off and threw it violently aside. "Well, the romantic fantasy's over. We're living in the real world now, Honey, and it's time you faced up to it. I'm not letting you run away again."

Honey's lips were slightly parted. "I didn't run away from the island," she protested. "I had a perfectly good reason for—"

"Bull!" Lance said succinctly, walking toward her with swift, pantherish strides. "Even you couldn't be so naive as to believe that story Bettina laid on you. Hell, yes, I was cut up, as a kid, when I couldn't seem to do anything right as far as my family was concerned; but, like all kids, I adjusted pretty damn quick. I'm certainly not pining for a reunion, as Bettina seems to think. No, that wasn't why you were so eager to leave. It was just an excuse. You were scared to death I was going to ask for something you weren't ready to give."

Was he right? Had she really been so eager to believe Bettina's interpretation of Lance's feelings because she was afraid of the eventual pain that would attend any long-term affair with him?

"I see you're not denying it," Lance said tightly. He stopped before her, his face taut and pale beneath his tan. "Well, I'm going to ask it of you anyway. I'm gambling that you care more for me than you do for that blasted career of yours. You're going to marry me, Honey."

"What!" Honey's eyes widened in stunned surprise.

"There's no use you arguing about it," Lance said roughly. "I'm not about to let you leave me again until the knot is well and truly tied." His hands grasped her shoulders, and he was looking down into her face with an intensity that made her breath catch in her throat. "Think about it, Honey," he urged persuasively. "Would you have risked your life saving those blasted paintings if I wasn't more to you than just your first lover? We've got everything going for us. Sex, companionship, love." Then, as she would have spoken, he held up his hand. "Yes, *love*, damn it! You do love me, even if you won't admit it. Would it be so much of a sacrifice to give up your work and marry me?"

"I can't do that," Honey said dazedly, feeling as if she were going mad. "My work? What about you? You're a prince, for heaven's sake."

"That's not my profession, that's an accident of birth," he said indignantly. "I'm an artist. You may be contemptuous of princes, but I know damn well you like my alter ego."

"I'm not contemptuous . . ." She trailed off helplessly. Then she tried again. "Royal princes don't marry orphanage brats like me. I don't even know who my father was." She shook her head. "I never expected you to want to marry me."

"Humility in a Valkyrie is definitely not becoming," Lance said with a flicker of amusement in his face. "Why shouldn't I want to marry you? You're the other half of me."

"I'm not humble," Honey said indignantly. "I know very well that any man would be lucky to marry a woman with my assets. I'm intelligent, hardworking, reasonably attractive, I have a fairly good sense of humor, I—"

Lance stopped her with his lips on hers, and when he lifted his head, he said tenderly, "You don't have to list your qualifications, love. You've already got the job." He shook his head ruefully. "That is, if you think you can put up with this slightly mad artist for the next fifty years or so. Lord knows why you would want to, after what you've been exposed to in the past few weeks. Attempted assassination, tropical storms, interfering baronesses, as well as my own blasted neglect and self-absorption. I can't even promise you that our future together won't be more of the same." His expression was grave and heart-catchingly tender. "I can only promise that you'll have all of my love for the rest of my days. Is that enough?"

"Oh, yes, that's enough," Honey answered, her throat aching with emotion. She buried her face in his shoulder. "Oh, Lance, I love you so much. I wasn't sure if I could bear it if it wasn't going to be forever for you, too."

"What a silly woman you are, Honey sweet," he said softly. "You were the one who was always talking about our affair as if it were going to end tomorrow. I always knew exactly what I wanted." He was stroking her hair with a gentle hand. "My Honey's head always on the next pillow and her hand in mine on every road I travel."

The words were as touchingly solemn as a wedding vow, and Honey drew a deep, quivering breath at the brilliant flame of happiness that exploded within her. "Your hand in mine on every road and byway," Honey repeated huskily, and that, too, was a promise. She looked up, her violet eyes star bright. "Forever."

Lance's face was so beautifully tender that Honey felt her heart melt with answering love for him. "It's crazy," she protested weakly. "For God's sake,

I'd be Princess Honey. Did you ever hear anything so ridiculous?"

"I like it," Lance said tenderly, his sapphire eyes twinkling. "And you'd be a honey of a princess."

She groaned, her lips twitching despite herself. "It's not funny, Lance. What would your parents say?"

He shrugged. "I couldn't care less what they say. My only real family is Alex and old Karim, and I can assure you that they'll not only approve, they'll applaud the match." Then, as her face remained troubled, he sighed resignedly. "If it will make you feel any better, once my parents realize that they have to accept it, I'm sure they'll move to put a good face on it. They'll probably even try to change your name." He raised a teasing eyebrow. "How would you like to be Princess Honorina?"

"That's even worse than the other," Honey said gloomily. "You wouldn't let them do that to me," Lance."

He shook his head. "I'll let you be anything you want to be, as long as it's with me," he said softly. "I can't bear being without you, Honey. This last week has been hell on earth."

"For me, too," Honey said huskily, looking up at him, her violet eyes swimming with tears. "Are you sure you won't regret this, Lance? I don't want you to make any sacrifices for my sake."

"You're the one who will be making the sacrifices," he said soberly. "As my wife, you'll have to give up your profession, for starters. It places you in much too vulnerable a position." His lips curved bitterly. "Assassination plots and kidnappings aren't all that unusual in our circles."

"Are you sure you're marrying me because you love me, and not because you need a live-in bodyguard?" Honey asked teasingly.

"I'm sure," Lance said thickly. "Oh, yes, sweetheart, I'm very sure." His lips brushed hers in a kiss of infinite sweetness, which deepened until they were both breathless, their hearts thudding erratically. "God, it's been so long since I held you like this. Do we have to talk anymore, love? I want to feel you hot around me."

She wanted that too, she thought breathlessly as his arms slid around her, his hands cupping the swell of her buttocks and bringing her urgently close to his own thrusting arousal. "Lance," she whispered lovingly, "I want—" She broke off as she felt the floor suddenly shake and vibrate beneath her feet. "Oh, my God, Lance. It's an earthquake!"

"What?" He looked down at her pale, frightened face, for a moment not comprehending anything but the hot need that was flooding him. "No, love. Much as I'd like to claim that my sexual prowess could make the earth shake for you, that is not an earthquake. We're on board Alex's yacht, and if I'm not mistaken, they've just started the engines."

He started to pull her back into his arms, but she put her hands on his chest, resisting him. "What are we doing on Alex's yacht?" She looked up at him indignantly. "You drugged me!"

"I did not," Lance denied. "I didn't know anything about it until they carried you aboard. I almost murdered Sax before Alex pulled me off him. All I told Alex was that I wanted you found and brought here." His lips tightened grimly. "He wasn't at all pleased either."

"That makes three of us," Honey said tartly. She gazed ruefully around the exotically decorated room. "I should have known as soon as I opened my eyes who was responsible for this." Then her eyes widened in alarm as she looked down at her chiffon-draped body. "And who put me into this harem outfit?"

Lance's eyes narrowed to smoldering intensity.

"Would I have let my men touch you, when I meant you for myself?" he hissed melodramatically.

"Oh, Lord, where are you getting those hokey lines?" Honey groaned.

"*The Sheik,* by E. M. Hull," Lance rattled off promptly. "I thought I'd do a little in-depth research to make it more authentic. I wanted a fitting swan song to my career as Lusty Lance." He smiled with gentle raillery. "Now that I'm marrying such an earnest young woman, I'll have to concentrate on being equally sober and industrious."

Honey shook her head in amusement. Lance sober? Never in a million years. He'd always be her wild, lovable Scaramouche, even if he lived to be as old as Methuselah.

"You didn't answer me," Honey persisted. "Why are we on Alex's yacht? Is Alex on board, too?"

Lance nodded. "Because Alex's captain is going to marry us once we get on the high seas," he explained calmly. "I'm not letting you out of my sight again until we're married. We'll have a more formal ceremony once we reach Sedikhan."

"Just like that?" Honey said, snapping her fingers. "What if I don't want to be married right here and now?"

For a moment his face was clouded with concern and there was a touch of uncertainty in his eyes. "You don't want to marry me now?"

"I didn't say that," Honey said softly. "I can't marry you fast enough to suit me. I just think it would be nice if you'd ask me instead of commanding me, Your Highness."

He took her hands in his, lifted them to his lips, and kissed the palms lingeringly, one after the other. "Will you marry me and be my love forever, Honey sweet?" he asked huskily, his expression grave and tender.

"Oh, yes," she whispered.

"Good," he said with satisfaction, his arms sliding around her. "Now that we've got that out of the way, let's get on with my seduction of your voluptuous person. Where were we?"

"You were quoting those campy lines from *The Sheik* to me," Honey said, making a face.

"Ahhh, yes," Lance said, his sapphire eyes flickering with mischief. "I have one more, which I saved for the *pièce de résistance.*"

"You do?" Honey asked warily.

He nodded, his face alight with love and the deviltry that was so much a part of him. " 'Must I be valet as well as lover?' " he quoted softly.

And her joyous laughter was smothered against his lips.

The Trustworthy Redhead

(Previously published as Loveswept #35)

One

"Here you are, lady," the cab driver said cheerfully, as he slapped the arm of the meter down and peered curiously out of the windshield at the brilliantly lit entrance to the mansion. "Seems they're having a party." He gave a low whistle as his gaze traveled over the cars parked in the courtyard. "This looks like a combined Rolls Royce-Mercedes car dealership. *Very* nice!"

Sabrina smiled, amused by the man's admiration for those purely mechanical toys. He seemed not even to notice the magnificence of the mansion itself. "Yes, very nice," she agreed, as she drew her white velvet cloak about her, adjusting the hood carefully to shadow her face. "And you're quite right that there's a party here. It's a birthday party."

He got out of the cab and opened her door. "A birthday party," he repeated thoughtfully, as he helped her out and then reached across the back seat to pull out a large, tarpaulin-covered canvas. "This is a pretty hefty present for a little thing like you to be carrying. Would you like me to take it inside for you?"

Sabrina shook her head. "I'm stronger than I look." She handed him the fare and accepted the painting in return. "If you'll just ring the doorbell for me?"

"Sure thing," he said. Suddenly his eyes widened in surprise. "Birthday party," he said, snapping his fingers as he made the connection. "Didn't I read about some fancy party in the newspaper this morning? It was for that billionaire oil sheik who's set Houston on its ear in the last few years."

Sabrina nodded calmly. "Alex Ben Raschid. It's his grandfather who's the sheik. He's only the heir apparent to the Sheikdom of Sedikhan."

"He may not run the country yet, but he sure must run everything else," the driver said wryly, as he punched the bell in the recessed entry to the doorway. "Sedikhan Petroleum seems to be buying up every industry in sight."

He cast a knowing glance at the young woman standing quietly at his side. Now he could understand his passenger's presence at what must be an elite party. The apartment complex where he'd picked her up, while respectable, was inexpensive, and Ben Raschid had a very rakish reputation where beautiful women were concerned. Even with her face shadowed by the hood of her cape, he could tell this one was exceptionally lovely. The door was suddenly opened by a white-jacketed manservant and the driver touched his cap in a parting salute. "Good night, Miss. Have a nice evening." He turned and strode swiftly back to his cab.

"You have an invitation?" the butler asked politely.

"No." Sabrina shook her head as she reached in the pocket of her cape, withdrew an envelope, and handed it to the butler. "I was told to give this to Mr. Clancy Donahue."

The butler nodded. "If you'll wait in the foyer, I'll see if I can locate him for you immediately. I believe I saw him step into the library just a moment ago." He glanced at the canvas in her hands. "May I take that from you?"

"No, thank you," Sabrina answered, her hands tightening protectively on the canvas. "I was told to deliver it only to Mr. Donahue."

The butler frowned uncertainly. "Then perhaps you'd better come with me," he said. "I'm sure it will be all right. Will you step this way?"

The elegant foyer was almost deserted, but as she passed the open doors of the ballroom she caught a brief glimpse of motion and color and heard the mellow strains of a live orchestra. Then the butler was knocking discreetly on a carved teak door opposite the ballroom. He preceded her into a large book-lined room, lit only by a single brass desk lamp on a massive executive desk which was the central focus of the room.

"You wanted to see me, Josef?" a gravelly voice demanded from a bar in one corner, and Sabrina's gaze flew to the shadowy alcove as a man came forward into the pool of light before the desk.

"This young lady has a parcel to deliver, Mr. Donahue," the servant said, handing him the note and silently withdrawing.

She would never have pictured Clancy Donahue as an executive assistant. The man looked more like a prizefighter than a businessman. The dark tuxedo he wore only served to emphasize the burly toughness of his tall, massive figure. His blunt features were granite hard beneath curly brown hair, heavily streaked with gray. He appeared to be in his early fifties and the look he directed at her confirmed her supposition. The wisdom of hard-lived years shone in the ice blue eyes that assessed her with a hint of suspicion.

Then he swiftly read the letter before looking up with a frown. "You know what is in this letter, I presume, Miss"—he glanced down at the letter again—"Miss Courtney. I see that it's been in your possession for almost six months."

Sabrina shook her head. "No, of course not," she said, faintly shocked.

"Seeing that it was a personal letter from Princess Rubinoff concerning you, I'd say you've exercised admirable restraint," Donahue said dryly. "Particularly since Honey failed to seal it. Not many women could be trusted to stifle their curiosity to that extent."

"She knew I wouldn't read it," Sabrina said, a thread of indignation in her voice. "I met Honey at a gallery exhibition of her husband's work six months ago and we became very good friends. She knew very well I wouldn't violate that friendship."

"As I said, admirable," Donahue repeated. "It's very brief and to the point. It merely states that Honey has arranged a little birthday surprise for Alex and I'm to help in facilitating the giving of the gift in whatever way you may require." He lifted an inquiring eyebrow at the canvas in her hands. "I take it that's the gift in question?"

"No, this is Prince Rubinoff's gift," Sabrina said softly. "Honey entrusted it to me at the same time she arranged for her own present." She set the canvas down on the floor, leaning it carefully against the desk. "I've had it at my apartment for the last six months and I admit that I'm rather glad to be rid of it. It must be very valuable. Prince Rubinoff is so enormously famous now."

"Well, then what *is* the present that I'm to facilitate?" Donahue asked impatiently.

"Me," Sabrina said simply, as she slipped the hood from her head to reveal the dark, flaming shimmer of her long red hair. "I'm from Novelty-grams Incorporated, Mr. Donahue. I specialize in bellygrams. Honey paid me quite generously to perform a dance for Mr. Ben Raschid's birthday celebration. That's her gift to him."

"A belly dancer?" Donahue muttered, momentarily shocked out of his cynical coolness, "Good Lord, a belly dancer! And a red-haired belly dancer at that." Suddenly he started to chuckle. "Are you sure it wasn't Lance who put you up to this?"

Sabrina shook her head, a smile tugging at the corners of her lips. "I scarcely saw Prince Rubinoff after I performed at the gallery exhibition. He was closeted away completing a portrait for almost the entire week of their stay. No, this is Honey's idea entirely." She continued gently, "You needn't worry, Mr. Donahue, the sheik's guests won't find anything offensive in my performance. I've been very well trained." Her green eyes twinkled. "I solemnly promise you that there will be no bumps and grinds."

"If it's Honey's show, I'm not worried about that," Donahue replied, his expression still amused. "I presume you're in full regalia. Am I to be permitted an advance preview?"

"Of course," Sabrina said serenely, opening the cloak to reveal her midnight blue, chiffon costume.

The costume showed off her lush golden tan, and the flaming silk of her hair against the dark blue of the chiffon seemed almost to issue a tactile invitation. The outfit consisted of a comparatively modest bikini with sheer chiffon panels that floated gracefully to her ankles. The panels parted when she danced and her midriff was bare. The bodice of her costume, while not shockingly low, displayed a generous amount of cleavage.

Donahue gave an admiring whistle. "Lovely, absolutely lovely," he said sincerely. "You're an exceptionally beautiful woman, Miss Courtney." There was a hint of mischief in his broad grin. "I think I can guarantee that you'll be Alex's favorite present at this particular birthday party. I can hardly wait to see his face when he catches sight of you. When do we get this show on the road?"

"At the intermission when the orchestra takes a break," Sabrina answered, pulling a tape cassette out of the pocket of her cape and handing it to him. "Honey wanted the performance to come as a complete surprise. If you'll just take care of starting my music on Mr. Ben Raschid's stereo tape player, I'll introduce myself."

"Right," Donahue said, checking his watch. "That should be in about ten minutes. You'd better wait here in the library until I come for you. I'll tell Josef to stand guard and be sure no one comes in to disturb you." His lips curved cynically. "Though I doubt that even your charms would tempt that pack of sycophants away from Alex." He strode toward the door with surprising grace for such a large man. "Lord, I can't wait until he sees you!" The door shut quietly behind him.

Sabrina shook her head ruefully. Donahue's reaction of impish delight was the usual one, and most of the time her clients arranged for her particular messagegram as a practical joke. But the joke was almost always good-natured and she hadn't run into any real problems due to the slightly sexual overtones of her performance. She was paid far better than the other performers at Noveltygrams who did the various singing telegrams and balloongrams, and God knew she needed every penny she could scrape together these days.

She picked up the painting and carried it over to a massive, brass-studded, black leather armchair. Placing the canvas carefully on the seat of the chair, she unwrapped the tarpaulin, but scrupulously avoided the mocking dark eyes of the man in the portrait. It was strange the effect that face had exerted on her since the moment she'd seen it in Honey's hotel suite. It had filled her with a nameless uneasiness which hadn't faded with familiarity. There was something about those smoldering dark eyes that seemed to know all the secrets in the universe and was not about to reveal a single one of them. Combined with the lean forcefulness of that bone structure and the passionately sensual curve to those finely cut lips, the image was very disturbing.

It was to be expected that Prince Rubinoff would produce a portrait of his cousin that was dynamically alive, and this one was undoubtedly brilliant. Dressed in dark pants and a simple white shirt, open at the throat, he was half sitting, half leaning on a gray stone balustrade, his dark hair lifting in the breeze. His lips were curved in a cynical little smile. Alex Ben Raschid had the bold, dangerous look of a marauding corsair!

Dangerous? How fanciful could she get? Ben Raschid could represent no possible threat to her. In less than an hour she would have completed her performance and be on her way. Ben Raschid might be regarded as an economic shark in his own territorial waters, but she'd soon be swimming serenely away and be home with David before he could possibly gobble her up.

Not that he would want to, she thought wryly. According to the columns, Ben Raschid had more women panting at his heels than he could handle. He'd hardly be diverted by a pretty little dancer like herself for more than a passing moment. It was natural that her imagination had been stirred by having that mocking, enigmatic face constantly before her for the last six months, but he had no real connection with her own struggles and triumphs. Yes, she'd be glad to have this episode over, so she could rid herself of both the picture and the fascination it engendered.

"Miss Courtney." She looked up, startled, at Donahue standing in the doorway. "It's intermission. The orchestra will be breaking for the next twenty minutes."

"I'm coming," she answered, as she slipped off her white ballet slippers and once again pulled the hood of her cape over her hair. "I'll wait at the entrance of the ballroom until I hear my music. If you'll please turn on my tape?"

"Delighted," he said with a grin, his blue eyes twinkling. "Believe me, the pleasure is all mine." He disappeared and she quickly left the library and crossed the gleaming, oak parquet floor to stand in the open doorway of the ballroom.

Sabrina's lips pursed in a silent whistle of admiration at the sheer magnificence of the enormous room. It seemed to sing with color and light. The polished inlaid floor gleamed; a huge amber and crystal chandelier flowered like a brilliant blossom from the center of the ceiling. Exquisitely gowned women were fluttering within its sparkling light like colorful butterflies while men in somber tuxedos were their elegant foils.

Sabrina stood patiently, waiting for her music to begin. Suddenly she had the sensation of being watched, and with a strange feeling of inevitability she slowly turned her head toward a cluster of people at the far end of the ballroom.

Her gaze met that of Alex Ben Raschid, and for a moment she was only conscious of those ebony eyes holding her own across the room. Then his eyes traveled lingeringly over her body that was still enveloped in the white velvet cloak until they rested, with amused curiosity, on one shapely bare foot.

He was well over six feet with a whipcord

strength that was shown to advantage in a beautifully tailored tuxedo. His portrait really hadn't done him justice, Sabrina thought dazedly. Ben Raschid stood out in this artificial atmosphere like a candle in the darkness—totally virile, totally alive, totally in command.

The familiar syncopation of her music throbbed through the loudspeakers and she shook her head as if to clear it. What was she doing gaping at the man like a bedazzled teenager when she had work to do? Even if she hadn't sincerely liked Honey and wanted her gift to be really special, she always took pride in her performance.

She took a deep breath before gliding gracefully to the center of the ballroom. The chatter of the guests and the clink of crystal hushed abruptly. She paused for dramatic effect, then pushed the hood back from her hair. "Good evening," she said softly. "I'm Sabrina Courtney. I've been sent with a birthday greeting for Alex Ben Raschid from Princess Rubinoff." Ignoring the sudden startled murmur from the guests, she slowly unbuttoned her cloak and let it fall from her shoulders to form a pool of white velvet at her feet. She was vaguely conscious that the murmuring became startled gasps, but the volume of her music had risen, and she began to dance.

She moved, turning, twisting, weaving graceful patterns that gradually built into a sinuous and sensual excitement. She'd chosen the most difficult dance in her repertoire, but it was also the most enthralling. Somewhere along the way she became one with the music, letting it carry her into the most ancient and passionate of rhythms. Nothing mattered but the dance and the throbbing sound. Then, as the wild music ended in a dramatic burst of chords, Sabrina fell to her knees in the traditional position of obeisance before Ben Raschid. There was a moment of silence and then a tremendous burst of applause from the guests.

Sabrina smiled triumphantly. They had liked her! She threw back her head, her flaming, waist-length mane a tousled glory, and her emerald eyes radiant. "Happy birthday, Alex Ben Raschid," she said breathlessly. "Priness Rubinoff sends her regards and a message. She said to tell you that she's kept her promise." Then, as her eyes met his, she flinched involuntarily and lowered her eyes hastily.

Ben Raschid's eyes were alive with barely controlled rage and something else that filled her with bewilderment and alarm. She leaped gracefully to her feet, and amidst the still applauding guests ran lightly to the door of the ballroom and into the hall.

She had reached the front door before she realized she had completely forgotten her cape and slippers. What on earth was wrong with her, she wondered crossly? Ben Raschid hadn't spoken even one word to her and she was in a perfect panic over that stormy, yet enigmatic look. Perhaps the man had indigestion, for heaven's sake!

"You were a complete triumph," Donahue announced behind her. "You should have seen the expression on Alex's face while he was watching you dance. I've never seen anything like it!"

Neither had she, she thought uneasily, as with a feeling of relief she turned around to face him. "I'm glad you enjoyed it, Mr. Donahue," she said quickly. "I really do have to leave now. I wonder if I could trouble you to get my cloak from the ballroom while I go to the library and get my slippers?"

"That won't be necessary," Alex Ben Raschid said as he entered the hall, her white velvet cloak draped over his arm. He put it over her shoulders, carefully lifting her hair so that it flowed down her back in fiery contrast to the snow white velvet. His action had an odd intimacy to it, and Sabrina felt a little tingle of shock that was out of all proportion to what should have been her reaction to a courteous gesture. "You go on back to the ballroom and enjoy yourself, Clancy. I'll take care of Miss Courtney."

"I'm sure you will," Donahue said obliquely, as he turned back to the door of the ballroom.

"No, really, I don't need any help," Sabrina protested, feeling once more that tiny shudder of panic at the thought of being alone with Ben Raschid. "Please go back to your guests. I'll just go to the library and phone for a taxi."

"And get your shoes," Ben Raschid added, his gaze lingering on her bare feet peeping from beneath the cloak. "It's really a shame to cover them. I've always thought feet were the ugliest portion of the human anatomy, but yours are quite lovely." He glanced up at Donahue, who'd paused at the door at Sabrina's words. "I think I can be trusted to find Cinderella's lost slippers, Clancy. But you might make yourself available in about forty-five minutes to drive her home."

Donahue nodded with an expression of mild surprise on his face and disappeared into the ballroom.

Forty-five minutes? "No one needs to drive me home, Mr. Ben Raschid," she said hurriedly. "I can take a taxi as I intended. I really think you should return to the party."

The man was completely ignoring her, his hand beneath her elbow propelling her swiftly to the library. He shut the door behind them with a decisive click.

He leaned against it, his eyes on her face. "I assure you that the party will wait," he said softly.

"Though I'm not sure at the moment if I can." His hand reached out and touched the curve of her cheek. "Your face is really exceptional, do you know that? Those slightly tilted green eyes, that delicate, fragile bone structure are fascinating as hell."

She moved away from his hand, not wanting him to know how disturbing she found it, and laughed lightly to reinforce that effect. "So I've been told. My rather exotic look was one reason why Joel hired me."

"Joel?" Ben Raschid asked, his dark eyes flickering. "Who the hell is Joel?"

"Joel Craigen, my boss," Sabrina said. "He owns Noveltygrams Incorporated. Did you think this was a one-shot fling on my part? I do this all the time."

"I don't believe I was thinking at all," he said slowly, his face darkening. "Not from the time I saw you standing in the doorway looking like a barefoot nun. Do you mean you dance for other men like that?"

Sabrina frowned in puzzlement. "Of course I do," she answered. "The bellygrams are very popular. I have at least one assignment a day, sometimes two or three. It's what I do for a living."

He uttered a brief, obscene expletive that caused her eyes to widen with shock. "That will have to change," he said grimly. "Why the hell don't you go out and get a respectable job?"

"Respectable!" The word was a cry of indignation. "I don't think any of your guests found anything objectionable about my performance."

"None of the men at least," he snapped. "They were eating you up with their eyes. That dance was supposed to arouse every man in the room to fever pitch. You can't argue with that."

"I don't have to argue anything at all," she said,

fuming. "Not to you. I'm sorry you didn't approve of Honey's gift, Mr. Ben Raschid, I'm sure she'll be very disappointed. But as for myself, I couldn't care less what you think!" She turned and marched over to the leather armchair where she'd stepped out of her shoes. "I think I'll say good night now. I'm sure you're eager to get back to your more respectable guests."

"Dammit, I didn't say *you* weren't respectable," he said, following her across the room, his face stormy. "It's your occupation we were talking about, and I have every intention of making sure you care what I think from now on. Why do redheads have to be so vol—" He broke off as his gaze fell to the portrait on the chair. "Where the hell did this come from?"

"I brought it with me," Sabrina said tersely, thrusting her feet into her ballet slippers. "It's your gift from Prince Rubinoff. I hope you like it better than you do his wife's."

"It's quite good," he said absently, as his gaze flicked back to Sabrina. "And Honey's present is also an enormous success. I couldn't be more pleased with her good taste. The wrapping is absolutely fantastic, and I can't wait to discover what's in the package."

"You've already received your gift," Sabrina snapped. "You seem to be under the misapprehension that the Princess contracted for more than just a dance for you." She moved toward the executive phone on the massive mahogany desk. "She bought my artistic services, not my body, for your delectation."

She reached out a hand to pick up the receiver but he stopped her by placing a swift hand over hers. "No," he said softly, a glimmer of steel beneath the satin of his voice. "I said that Clancy will take you home. I won't have you taking a taxi while you look like something out of an erotic dream. I'd take you myself if this party weren't more business than pleasure."

"You won't *let* me?"

"I won't let you," he repeated calmly. "Now, why don't you relax and humor me. It will save a good deal of wear and tear on your nerves. I'm not letting you out of here until I get you to answer a few questions. I'm curious why Honey sent you to me."

"But you know why she sent me," Sabrina answered, puzzled.

"Yes and no," he said absently, his eyes intent on her face. "I wonder if she really succeeded in her quest after all this time."

"Quest? I don't understand any of this."

"I know you don't, Sabrina," he said, smiling with a sudden warmth that was dazzling after the guarded somberness that had preceded it. "Don't worry about it. I'm going to make sure that everything will be quite clear to you very soon." He removed his hand. "Are you going to indulge my whim, pretty houri?"

"Do I have any choice?" Sabrina asked tartly. Her hand felt oddly lonely without the warmth of his covering it. Why was that, when his touch had so disturbed her? "Are you always this autocratic, Alex Ben Raschid?"

"So they tell me," he drawled mockingly. He leaned easily against the edge of the desk. "It will be practically painless, I promise you. Just give me all the details of your lurid past and I'll be more than happy."

"I doubt it," Sabrina said shortly. "My background isn't all that entertaining." Then, as he continued to wait patiently with that same enigmatic smile, she said resignedly, "I'm twenty-three years old. I was born and raised on a small ranch in the Rio Grande Valley not far from Corpus Christi. I'm an only child and both my parents died in an auto accident when I was sixteen. I attended the University of Houston for two years as an art major before I was forced to drop out and go to work. I'm self-supporting, hard-working, and independent." She cast him a glowering look. "And just as respectable as you, Mr. Ben Raschid."

"Alex," he prompted, with a grin. "And I'm sure you're a great deal more respectable. I've had a hell of a lot more years and opportunities to arrive at my present state of dissipation. This is my thirty-fifth birthday, you know."

She nodded impatiently, "Honey told me. Now that I've told you my entire life history, may I please leave?"

"I'm sure you've left out all the most interesting bits," Ben Raschid said dryly. "But I've always liked to make a few discoveries on my own. It makes a relationship that much more exciting."

"This is utterly absurd," Sabrina said, shaking her head in wonder. "How can I make you understand that I don't give a damn what you find exciting, or what you want?"

"I think that soon you'll care very much what I want," Ben Raschid said softly. "You see, I want you, Sabrina Courtney."

"This is crazy," she whispered, her green eyes widening with shock. "Thirty minutes ago you didn't even know I existed, and now you're propositioning me?"

"It's a bit of a shock to me, too." he said wryly. "I assure you my approach is generally a good deal more subtle." There was a flicker of anger in the depths of the coal black eyes. "You have an exceedingly odd effect on me, Sabrina, and I'm not at all sure I like it. This is the first time I've ever been caught off guard by my response to a woman."

"Should I apologize?" Sabrina asked caustically. Now that she'd recovered from her first shock at his words she was beginning to feel a rising anger at the sheer arrogance of the man.

Ben Raschid's brow rose. "Perhaps you should apologize at that," he drawled lazily. "I'm sure I'm not the first man your little performance has sent into a tailspin. You must be fully aware of your effect on the male libido." Suddenly the annoyance was gone, replaced by a dark intensity. His fingers reached out to trace the outline of her lips while she stared up at him in shocked amazement. "You have the most provocative mouth I've ever seen," he said huskily. "And your skin has the satin texture one sees only in very young children. I've never wanted to possess anything as much as I want you. You're going to belong to me in every way a woman can belong to a man."

Sabrina found it hard to breathe and she felt a tingling in the tips of her fingers. She shook her head to clear it of its strange lightness. "And what about what *I* want?" she asked, steadying her voice with an effort.

"I can make you want me," he said arrogantly. "Stay with me tonight, Sabrina. You won't regret it."

"Yes, I would," she said quietly. "I have no desire to be one of your conquests, Mr. Ben Raschid. I'm sure you can find someone else who will accommodate you. I don't want anything to do with you."

"And I want everything to do with you," he returned lightly. "But I can give you a little time." His hand reached out to stroke her cheek, seeming to take a sensual pleasure in its satin smoothness. "I'm not going to be able to wait very long," he whispered, his eyes flickering with that same hot intensity that had frightened her in the ballroom.

"You'll have to wait forever," she said tartly. "I don't intend to be one of your women. There's nothing about the position that appeals to me, even for the short time you usually keep your mistresses."

He smiled in genuine amusement. "I don't think you should count on anything but a very long-term lease. I don't believe I'll tire of you easily." His hand moved to her throat, not caressing, just resting lightly on the pulse point as if to detect the tumult of emotions cascading through her. "A very exclusive contract," he continued quietly. "No other men in your life or your bed while you belong to me."

What kind of woman did he think she was, she wondered wildly, caught in a bewildering maze of emotions. He was calmly giving her ultimatums and conditions, and completely ignoring her protests as if it were a foregone conclusion that she would give in to his demands.

His confidence was so complete that she wondered for an instant if her defenses could hold against this man's determined assault. But she knew they must. It would be like living in a silk cocoon whose strands would eventually strangle any independence or self-respect life might hold for her. She lifted her chin and looked up at him defiantly. "I'll have as many men as I like, but you won't be one of them, Alex Ben Raschid."

His hand tightened on her throat until it was not a caress but a threat, and his dark eyes blazed with anger. Then he slowly released her and stepped back. "I'd better send you home before I decide to keep you here," he said tightly. "I'd prefer to have you willing."

"Do you usually go in for slavery?"

One corner of his lips lifted in a flash of humor. "I couldn't have chosen anyone more suitably dressed for it," he said dryly. "No, my dear houri, I promised you time to get used to the idea but I'm beginning to regret my forbearance already. I think we'd better get you out of here." He opened the library door, and then, as she would have passed through it, he detained her momentarily by placing a hand on her arm. "It's only a reprieve, you know, Sabrina," he said softly.

She didn't answer as she sailed past him into the hall.

Donahue was standing by the ballroom door as if in anticipation, and at Ben Raschid's nod he smiled and came toward them, swallowing the last of his champagne and placing his glass on a passing waiter's tray.

"Take the young lady home, Clancy." Ben Raschid met his employee's eyes meaningfully. "And take good care of her."

Donahue nodded silently.

Ben Raschid turned to Sabrina. "I'll be in touch," he said softly, with an intimate smile.

Sabrina shrugged, feeling more courageous in the public atmosphere of the hallway. "Don't bother," she said coolly. "I plan to be very busy."

There was a choked sound from Donahue that might have been a chuckle, and she could almost feel the anger that emanated from Ben Raschid. "I'll be in touch," he repeated, this time menacingly. He turned and stalked back into the ballroom.

"My lady," Donahue said, with a mocking bow. "Your carriage awaits."

Two

Now that the evening was almost over, Sabrina felt numb with weariness. She leaned her head against the padded headrest of the luxurious Lincoln and closed her eyes. They had almost reached the apartment complex where she lived when Donahue spoke, as if unable to control his curiosity any longer. "Why did you try to make him angry?" he asked.

Sabrina's eyes flew open, and she made a face. "I didn't try," she said dryly. "It seems to come naturally."

Donahue shook his head. "People just don't talk to Alex Ben Raschid like that."

"Perhaps if they did, he wouldn't be so arrogant. Are you afraid of him, Mr. Donahue?" she asked tartly.

"Hell, no," he replied promptly. "We go back too far for that. I've known Alex since he was a teenager." There was an element of warning in his sideways glance. "But I can see why it might be wise for a pretty little thing like you to be a bit more cautious. Growing up as heir apparent to one of the richest oil sheikdoms in the world isn't likely to make any man shy and retiring. Even now he's one of the most powerful economic figures in the world. When his grandfather dies, he'll also be the absolute monarch of a country in his own right. It's only fair to warn you that Alex isn't hesitant about using that power."

Sabrina sighed tiredly. "Mr. Ben Raschid will have no problem with me; I won't get in his way. As a matter of fact, I'll stay just as far away from him as the Houston city limits permit!"

"Or Alex will permit," Donahue corrected wryly.

"In a day or two he'll forget I ever existed," Sabrina predicted confidently. "We don't belong to the same world."

"I wouldn't be too sure of that," Donahue said. "I've never known him to be so protective of a woman before. Usually he couldn't care less what his little playmates are up to as long as they're available when he wants them."

Donahue turned into the apartment complex and stopped in front of the building she indicated.

"Don't bother to get out," Sabrina said, with her hand on the door latch. "Thank you for bringing me home."

"Sit still, Miss Courtney." Donahue grinned. "I have my orders. Alex wants you delivered safely to your front door." He was around the car, gallantly helping her out with mocking panache and following her to the apartment door. He took her key when she withdrew it from the pocket of her cloak and unlocked the door. He said quietly, handing the key back, "Lock the door behind you."

"I will," Sabrina promised. "Thanks again, Mr. Donahue. You've been very kind."

"Sabrina, is that you?" Light suddenly flooded the apartment.

"Yes, David, I'll be there in just a minute," she called. Turning to Clancy Donahue she said hastily, "Good night."

"David," Donahue echoed thoughtfully, scanning the nameplate by the door. "David Bradford,

Sabrina Courtney." He gave a low whistle. "Alex may have more problems than he imagines."

"Please go," Sabrina whispered. David could be as curious as a chipmunk. He'd be out here any minute wanting to know who'd brought her home.

"Jealous, is he?" Donahue grinned. "Well, mum's the word. Good night, Sabrina." With a friendly wave of his hand he strode swiftly back to the car.

With a relieved sigh, she slipped inside and closed the door, locking it automatically behind her.

Angelina Santanella looked up from the horror movie she was watching with avid fascination. "You're later than usual, aren't you? David's been somewhat anxious."

"It's only a little after eleven," Sabrina answered, coming forward to perch on the arm of the heather tweed couch. "Where is he?"

"In the kitchen making himself a cup of hot chocolate," Angelina said, leaning forward to turn down the volume on the set. "I brought up a plate of coconut macaroons and they're practically all gone." She smiled broadly. "That boy surely does like his sweets."

"You spoil him, Angelina," Sabrina said, shaking her head reprovingly at the motherly-looking woman. The Santanellas occupied the apartment downstairs and their generosity was ample and open-hearted. "He's come to expect something from you every time you walk through the front door."

"*I* spoil him? That's the pot calling the kettle black. He washed his hair tonight and had me braid it for him in that heathen-looking pigtail he's so fond of." She frowned. "You know, you should make him cut his hair, Sabrina."

"He likes it," Sabrina said simply, "and it's no real bother."

The older woman shook her head, her face gentle.

"Nothing's a bother for you where that boy's concerned, is it? You've practically arranged your entire life around him."

"I love him," she said quietly. "He's closer than a real brother could ever be to me. And now he's my child as well."

"He does have parents of his own," Angelina reminded her, her dark eyes grave. "It's not right that you should have to shoulder the entire responsibility. It's too much, Sabrina."

"No it's not. You can't put limits on how much you give when you really care about someone. Jess and Sue do all they can. I'm the logical one to take care of David. He has to be near the drug rehabilitation center, and how could Jess and Sue possibly leave the ranch? It's not only their livelihood, it's where their roots are."

"They could help out financially a little more," Angelina persisted stubbornly. "You could get a safe, respectable job if you didn't have to worry about money all the time."

Respectable! It was the second time tonight she'd heard that word and she wasn't up to defending her job again at the moment. "His parents send what they can. The drought last year almost ruined them and they're just starting to recover. Besides it's *I* who owe them," Sabrina said simply. "They took me into their home without a second thought after my parents were killed. Jess and Sue owned the next property and David and I grew up like brother and sister. They certainly had no obligation to do all that for me!" She smiled cheerfully. "Besides, we get along very well. I make fairly good money at Noveltygrams and what David makes working for your husband pays his doctor bills."

"I know what Gino pays that boy and it's not enough to make a dent in that fancy psychiatrist's bill you get every month," Angelina said shrewdly. "You may be fooling the boy that he's helping out, but I keep the books." She sighed. "We'd like to pay David more but we just can't afford it. Maybe next year when the business is on its feet. David's worth three times what we're paying him. Gino says the boy has a green thumb."

Sabrina was well aware that Gino's Landscape Company was a fledgling enterprise. She was just grateful that Gino had found a place for David; it scarcely mattered that they could afford to pay him only a pittance. David genuinely loved working outside with his plants and flowers.

"How can we expect more from you and Gino?" she asked affectionately. "You've not only made a place for David in the company, but you're always cooking some delicacy for him. You even stay with him in the evening when I have to go out."

"He's no trouble," Angelina said gruffly. "He's such a good boy." There was a suspicious brightness in the liquid darkness of her eyes as she said hesitantly, "It's been so long. Is David ever going to be entirely well?"

"The doctors don't really know," Sabrina said huskily. "They don't have enough knowledge about the effect of so-called 'mind-expansion' drugs on the brain to really tell. He's come so far that I'm almost afraid to hope for more." She shivered. "When the ambulance took him to the hospital from the dorm that night, he was almost a vegetable." She stood up, and tried to smile brightly. "Well, you tell that 'good boy' when he finishes gobbling his cookies, that I'm in the shower, will you?" She shrugged off her cape and folded it over her arm. "Are you going to finish your movie before you leave?"

Angelina nodded as she leaned forward to turn up the volume on the set. "I think I will," she said, her expression already absorbed. "You know, I believe Dracula must really have been Italian. No one from Transylvania could be that sexy."

Twenty minutes later, Sabrina was showered, dressed in her faded green and white striped pajamas, and had slipped between the sheets of her twin bed. It had been a mad, bizarre evening and she felt totally drained.

How stupid to let the thought of Alex Ben Raschid upset her so. She had enough problems and responsibilities in her life without worrying about some wealthy playboy's arrogant threats. It was a matter of simple chemistry that had caused those violent reactions to zing between them. What else could it be? She was a young, healthy female with all the usual reactions to a man of Ben Raschid's potent appeal. As far as his own rather excessive attraction was concerned, it was probably the result of the unusual circumstances of their first meeting. According to the columns he was seldom without a woman in his bed, and it was obvious he wasn't used to resistance on the part of the opposite sex. Another pretty face was bound to come along at any moment and she'd be forgotten. Worrying about the man was ridiculous!

"Bree, can I sleep with you tonight?"

She looked up with a weary sigh, which she quickly smothered when she saw David's wistful expression as he stood hesitantly in the doorway. He was so beautiful in that navy Houston Astro T-shirt, she thought tenderly. His sapphire eyes were brilliant against his glowingly healthy tan, and the shining, white blond of his sunstreaked hair, pulled back in the shoulder-length braid Angelina abhorred, only enhanced his strong, classical bone structure.

"Did you watch that horror movie with Angelina?" Sabrina asked, trying to frown. "You know Dr. Swanson told you to stay away from that sort of thing."

He shook his head, a trace of indignation on his face. "I was reading some of Gino's horticulture magazines all evening." He smiled coaxingly. "I'm just lonely. You've been gone all evening, Bree."

She held out for a full two minutes before she melted as she usually did. "All right. Get on your pajamas and brush your teeth." She frowned. "But no talking to the wee hours. You have to get up early and go out on that job in Baytown tomorrow."

He was already turning away. "I won't," he promised eagerly. "I'll go get Miranda."

Which one was Miranda, Sabrina wondered in amusement, as she plumped up the pillow and propped herself up in bed.

Miranda proved to be an extremely wilted-looking daffodil in a natural clay pot. David put the plant carefully on the bedside table between the twin beds and sat down on the other bed with a contented smile. As usual he'd put on the bottoms of the blue cotton pajamas but his bronze, muscular chest with its golden mat of hair was bare. A child in a man's body.

"You don't mind if I leave a light on, do you?" he asked, his worried gaze on the daffodil. "Miranda needs all the light and sunshine we can give her."

And so did he, Sabrina thought, her throat suddenly tight and aching. During those first months when he'd started coming back from a near catatonic state, he'd been plagued by hideous nightmares which had almost ripped him apart. Even now he never slept without at least a night light burning. But she wouldn't think about that. It was over now, and David was so much better.

"Are you going to be able to save her?" she asked gently.

"I think so," David said. "She's responding more every day. All she needs is to know that someone cares what happens to her." His face was grave. "We do care, Miranda," he told the plant earnestly.

"Get into bed and cover up," Sabrina said over the lump in her throat. "Miranda knows you care."

He obediently slipped between the sheets but turned to face her, his deep blue eyes sparkling and wide-awake as ever. There was an almost bell-like radiance about him now, Sabrina thought. It was difficult to believe that he was a year older than she. The mind-expansion drugs, that had robbed him of so much, seemed to have stopped time for him, giving him a childlike simplicity and inner beauty that was poignantly touching.

His gaze was once more on his Miranda. "I think she does know we care now," he said contentedly. Then a tiny frown creased his forehead. "Flowers are so much easier than people, Bree."

"Are they, love?" Sabrina asked.

He nodded. "You can tell when someone is closing up and dying inside just by looking at them, but they won't let you help them. They won't let you near enough to tell them that you care." He bit his lip. "Or maybe I just don't know how. Did I know how before, Bree?" Lately he'd become aware of that time before, but he seemed to regard it almost as another incarnation.

Sabrina shook her head. "You were always too preoccupied to notice before," she answered.

His glance was startled. "But how could I miss it?" he asked incredulously. "It's right there."

"In many ways you see much more clearly now, David."

He shook his head wonderingly as his glance returned once more to his daffodil. There was a moment of silence and when David spoke again his voice was soft. "Bree, do you remember the movie *E.T.*?"

How could she help it, Sabrina thought ruefully. It was David's favorite movie and she had sat through it with him innumerable times. Something about that mythical tale of love and magic had struck an answering chord in the child that he was now.

"Yes, I remember."

"I was thinking," he said dreamily, "do you remember when E.T. touched those flowers and they blossomed and came to life? Wasn't that beautiful?"

"Yes, very beautiful."

His hand reached out and caressed one of Miranda's golden petals with a tender finger. "Wouldn't it be wonderful if we could just reach out to each other like that. Just one touch and we'd all bloom and unfold our petals in the sun. Wouldn't that be wonderful?"

"So wonderful," Sabrina murmured, blinking back tears.

He was still looking at the daffodil, his face absorbed. "Of course, it wouldn't be necessary all the time," he said gravely. "Some people blossom naturally all by themselves." His thoughtful gaze moved to Sabrina's face. "You did, Bree. You're like a poinsettia, all brilliant color and soft velvet petals." He smiled gently. "You're like velvet on the inside too. Sometimes I can feel that softness wrapping around me, keeping me safe and warm." He said simply, "It's nice, Bree."

Sabrina cleared her throat, smiling mistily. "I'm not sure I like you comparing me to such a fragile flower," she said lightly. "They seem to live such a short time."

David frowned. "They're quite strong, really,"

he said earnestly. "They go dormant, you know. They gather strength from the darkness and soon they bloom again."

Strength from the darkness. Yes, she'd discovered in these last two years that she had strength and determination to tap. Pray God, though, that darkness never returned.

"Well, I'm glad you recognize that I have a little stamina," she said briskly. "Now, what did you promise me about going to sleep right away?"

She scooted down in the bed, plumped her pillow, and closed her eyes decisively. She heard David's disappointed sigh and the sounds of him settling down in his own bed. She could hear his light breathing and the restless thrashing as he moved about. Then there was another long silence and she dared a surreptitious peek at him.

He was still wide-awake, his bright blue eyes intent once more on his yellow daffodil. As she watched, his finger reached out again to stroke Miranda's golden petals with loving delicacy. His soft murmur was a mere breath but it was enough to bring the tears to Sabrina's eyes.

"Wonderful."

Three

Sabrina fell to her knees in the obeisance that signaled the end of her performance and looked up at her red-faced client with a cheerful grin. "Congratulations on your promotion, Mr. Selkirk. I'm sure you'll make a fine vice-president."

There was a burst of good-natured laughter from the men at the table as well as scattered applause from the other luncheon patrons of the popular French restaurant. The flustered executive muttered something under his breath that might have been an acknowledgment, but he was too busy handling the jests from his business associates to really comprehend her words.

It was no more than she expected and she rose lightly to her feet and turned away with a friendly wave of her hand. She walked quickly to where Hector Ramirez was waiting at a table by the door. He picked up the portable tape recorder and handed her white velvet cloak to her. "I'll keep a careful watch on this tape, Sabrina, since it's the backup one. Never known you to leave your tape." When she glowered, he said quickly, "It went off pretty well, didn't it? The waiters were fairly cooperative this time. I didn't have to glower threateningly at more than two of them to keep them out of your way while you were performing."

It seldom took more than that ferocious scowl from a man of Hector's bulk to intimidate even the most confident individual. Which was the primary reason Joel had assigned the college student to accompany Sabrina on her jobs. In the gaudy red turban and white, flowing robe he resembled a picturesque harem guard.

"Can I drop you back at the office to pick up your motorcycle?" Sabrina offered, as she put on her ballet slippers.

Hector shook his head. "I've got a term paper to finish. I'll hop a bus to the library, and then hitch a ride with one of my fraternity brothers later and pick it up." He put his big hand solicitously under her elbow as they walked briskly from the restaurant to the parking lot. "As soon as I see you safely to that heap you call a car."

"My Volkswagen's a good deal safer than that cycle of yours," she said dryly. "At least it has four metal walls around it."

"You have no spirit of adventure," Hector scoffed. "You haven't lived until you—" He broke off suddenly with a low, admiring whistle. "Speaking of adventure, will you get a load of that Lamborghini? Driving one of those babies is what I'd call the ultimate experience."

These men and their passion for machinery, Sabrina thought with amusement. First the taxi driver last night and now Hector. She cast a casual glance in the direction he was indicating and suddenly all amusement was wiped from her face.

Alex Ben Raschid, in dark jeans and a black sport shirt, straightened slowly from the fender of the white Lamborghini, looking as supple and dangerous as a panther. The slanting rays of the afternoon sun touched his head, and his dark hair shone with peltlike luster.

"I've been waiting for you," he said curtly, opening the passenger door. "Get in."

"I beg your pardon," Sabrina said blankly. She'd felt a trifle bemused from the surprise of seeing him, but this command immediately caused her to bristle.

"I said, get in," he repeated, his expression grim. "Unless you want me to give everyone in the parking lot an even better show than the one you gave for those lecherous bastards inside."

Ramirez tensed, his eyes narrowed on Ben Raschid's stormy face. "You know this guy, Sabrina?"

"Slightly." Sabrina shrugged. "We met last night at the party in River Oaks. This is Alex Ben Raschid, Hector. Hector Ramirez is my co-worker, Mr. Ben Raschid."

"I knew I should have gone with you on that gig." Hector scowled. "This bozo give you any trouble, Sabrina?"

"You know Princess Rubinoff specified I handle the assignment by myself," Sabrina said, her gaze on Ben Raschid's furious expression. Something had put him in an awesomely bad temper and it was clear Hector's aggressive protectiveness was only serving to aggravate it. "He was no problem. I handled him."

He didn't like that either, Sabrina thought, her lips curving in slightly malicious amusement. Well, what could he expect when he was acting as if she were some little slave girl panting to amuse the great man.

"Get in the car, Sabrina," he said softly, and there was menace beneath the velvet. "Let's see how you manage to handle me today."

"She doesn't have to go anywhere with you," Ramirez said, his jaw jutting out belligerently. "Now, why don't you just buzz off, buster."

"Oh, she has to go with me all right," Ben Raschid said quietly. "That is, if she wants *you* to stay in one piece. It may be the only thing that will save you. At the moment I'm not even sure about that."

Sabrina started to smile at this outrageous threat but her amusement faltered and then faded entirely as her eyes met those of Ben Raschid. This was no playboy's idle boast. There was something coolly competent and extremely lethal about the man. She moved toward the open door of the Lamborghini almost involuntarily.

"It's not worth arguing about. Mr. Ben Raschid will take me home, Hector, and I'll pick up my car later. Will you call Angelina for me and ask her to look in on David if I'm a little late?"

Hector frowned. "You're sure, Sabrina?"

"I'm sure," she said, giving him a reassuring smile as she got in the sports car. "Don't worry, everything will be fine." She cast Ben Raschid a poisonous glance. "The gentleman isn't quite the uncivilized savage he appears."

"Don't bet on it," Ben Raschid snapped, slamming the door and striding around to the driver's seat. A moment later they were roaring out of the parking lot while Hector gazed after them with a troubled expression on his face.

"Your David appears to be very complacent," Ben Raschid said harshly. "I was under the impression that he wouldn't take kindly to your seeing other men. Or does this Angelina offer him her own brand of comfort when you decide to amuse yourself? I understand *ménages à trois* are becoming increasingly popular these days."

Sabrina had forgotten Donahue's misinterpretation of the relationship between David and herself, but evidently he'd given a full report to Ben Raschid. "That's really none of your business," she said sarcastically. "But I'm afraid I've not reached quite your level of sophistication. I find a one-on-one relationship much more desirable."

"I'm glad to hear it," Ben Raschid said, "because that's what I have in mind for you. So you can just resign yourself to giving this Bradford his walking papers. I've never wanted a woman this way before, and you're not getting away from me." He smiled with lazy sensuality. "I promise that once I get you into my bed, you won't want to."

"The great lover," Sabrina scoffed, to hide the breathlessness that flooded her at the thought of Ben Raschid touching her.

"Exactly," he said coolly. "You won't be disappointed. I think you'll find I have enough experience to make you forget your roommate."

The biting acid of his last remark revealed a bitterness that pleased Sabrina. He evidently didn't like the idea of another man receiving favors that were denied him, and she felt a perverse thrill at disconcerting the arrogant Alex Ben Raschid. Her intention of telling him the truth of her relationship was discarded. Once he was convinced that she wouldn't have an affair with him, her deception wouldn't matter. Besides, she had an uneasy feeling she might need all the barricades she could erect between them.

"David loves me," she said truthfully.

"Love is a word for children," Alex said. "I'll teach you more interesting emotions, Sabrina."

"Like lust?"

Ben Raschid smiled intimately, his eyes lingering on her lips. "I had that in mind for lesson one," he admitted.

"I prefer the old-fashioned concepts, like love, affection, and loyalty. I wouldn't be a very good pupil," she said tartly.

"An interesting paradox," Alex said, his lips curving mockingly. "Old-fashioned ideals and a swing-ing lifestyle. Don't you have trouble reconciling the two?"

"Not at all," she answered coolly. "And now that you understand that our views are incompatible, don't you think you'd better drive me back to pick up my car?"

"Without trying to change your mind?" He shook his head. "I don't give up that easily. You're going to have dinner with me. I intend to show you what a harmless, uncomplicated man I really am."

Sabrina eyed him skeptically. He was about as harmless as a live electric wire and as uncompli-cated as a master computer. She noticed that they'd now turned onto the Gulf Freeway and were headed rapidly east toward the Gulf of Mexico. "May I ask where you're taking me?" she asked suspiciously. "You do realize that you've practi-cally kidnapped me? Don't you ever ask instead of take, Mr. Ben Raschid?"

"Alex," he corrected impatiently. "And you'll find I can ask as politely as the next man." He gave her a sly, sideways glance and suddenly a mischie-vous grin lit the darkness of his face. "If I'm sure the answer will be yes."

Sabrina shook her head, a reluctant smile tug-ging at the corners of her mouth. "Where are we going?" she persisted.

"Galveston," he answered. "I thought that since neither of us is dressed for dinner, we'd have a picnic on the beach."

"I wouldn't have thought that would be your scene," she said flippantly. "It seems a bit primi-tive for a sophisticated man of the world."

The glance that he gave her was as intimate as a kiss. His eyes ran over her face and then her body as if he wanted to memorize them. "You persist in underestimating me, Sabrina," he said softly. "I'm very adaptable. You'll find that I can be very primitive."

Sudden color flooded her face and her breath caught in her throat. What on earth was the matter with her? One smoky glance from those dark, guarded eyes and she was trembling like a schoolgirl. Her glance slid quickly away from his. "How did you know where to find me?" she asked, moistening her lips nervously.

"I had Clancy call Noveltygrams and track you down," he answered. He frowned fiercely. "You really do perform that glorified hootchy-kootchy two and three times a day. I couldn't believe it when I walked into that restaurant and saw you dancing for those drooling old goats." His hands tightened on the steering wheel until the knuckles showed white. "It made me sick to my stomach. I had to get out of there or I'd have yanked you out of the place by that gorgeous red hair."

"You could have tried," Sabrina said tartly, her eyes flashing. "My dance is *not* a hootchy-kootchy, and I'd have thought that anyone from a mideastern country such as Sedikhan would appreciate that fact."

"All right, it's a beautiful dance." He glared at her moodily. "And you're so damn beautiful doing it that it makes me ache just watching you. That doesn't mean it's not as provocative as hell. You can't deny that every man in the room was only thinking of one thing while you were moving those hips like some blasted fertility goddess."

"Not everyone has his mind in the bedroom constantly the way you do," Sabrina defended. "It was a joke, for heaven's sake. Those men were just having a good time."

"Well, from now on they can have it without panting after you as if you were a bitch in heat," he said tersely. "I'm not about to let you keep on putting me through this hell."

Her mouth fell open in stunned surprise. The sheer unadulterated nerve of the man! "You have absolutely nothing to say about either my professional or private life," she said icily. "I'll thank you to remember that fact."

The look he threw her was compounded equally of anger and exasperation. Then he drew a deep breath. "Look, I have no intention of quarreling with you. That's not what I had in mind when I was lying awake all night thinking about you. You caught me off guard in the library last night and I knew damn well that I was saying and doing all the wrong things. You needn't be afraid I'm going to throw you down and rape you. I don't operate that way."

He wouldn't need to, not with his virile solar power that could melt all resistance like hot wax. "Then you'll turn the car around and take me back?" she asked.

He scowled. "I didn't say that. Why can't you just relax and try to enjoy yourself. Who knows—by the time the evening is over you might discover I'm not such a bastard after all."

"Do I have a choice?"

"None," he replied. "So we might as well declare a truce." He raised a mocking brow. "Okay?"

"Okay." She sighed, resigned. As he'd said she had little choice, and in a few hours she would be safely back in her apartment. It was a limited commitment at best.

"Good," Alex said. He turned left at Stewart Beach and proceeded away from the crowded bathing area until they came to a deserted stretch of sand a few miles down the road. Then he switched off the engine and turned to face Sabrina. His eyes traveled over her again with the same smoldering intimacy that had been there before. "Now what were you saying back at the restaurant about the way you handled me?"

Sabrina backed against the car door, her green eyes startled as she realized how very isolated they were on this barren stretch of beach. Alex's eyes suddenly gleamed with mischief as he opened his door and got out. He stretched lazily, the movement pulling his dark shirt taut over his lithe muscles.

"Get out, Sabrina," he ordered dryly. "The only appetite I'm about to satisfy at the moment is for the food in the hamper in the trunk."

She got out of the car hurriedly, feeling foolish about having risen to the bait so easily. She helped him spread a beach blanket and tablecloth, and then set out the veritable feast the basket containing: Fried chicken, potato salad, bread, fresh strawberries, and a bottle of red wine.

"Primitive?" She raised an eyebrow quizzically.

He grinned. "I like to live well. Who said picnics have to be hot dogs and marshmallows?"

"Who, indeed," Sabrina said wryly, biting into a crisp piece of chicken.

The silence between them was strangely compatible as they sat cross-legged on the blanket, eating the delicious food with only an occasional remark. Perhaps it was the serenity evoked by the soft sea breeze that induced the lazy euphoria, or the sound of the surf, or the sun setting in a blaze of color. Alex filled their wine glasses and they sat quietly watching the last traces of scarlet fade from the sky, their reflection turning the clouds the delicate pink of cotton candy.

Sabrina leaned back on one elbow with a sigh of contentment. "Will you answer a rather personal question?" she asked hesitantly, thinking dreamily how the fading light hollowed his cheekbones and highlighted that sensual mouth, rather like an El Greco painting. "There's something I've been curious about for the past six months. It's driving me crazy."

His lips twisted mockingly. "We wouldn't want that. There's only one way I want to drive you insane and it's not with curiosity. Ask away."

"The message that Honey told me to give you after my dance. What was the promise that she said she'd kept?"

"You," he said simply, and then began to chuckle at her blank look of surprise. "It's a long story and much too involved to go into at the moment. To put it as briefly as possible, I've always had a passion for redheads and a few years ago Honey made me a pledge. I'd just had an encounter with a very unprincipled redhead, and Honey promised someday she'd find me a redhead I could trust."

"And that's supposed to be me?" Sabrina asked dazedly.

Alex nodded. "You must have made a very deep impression on Honey. Clancy said you became good friends that week they were here in Houston."

Sabrina's lips curved in a reminiscent smile. "We had an instant rapport, and by the time they had to leave we were almost as close as sisters. I'm glad she thought I was worthy of trust."

"Honey is exceptionally naïve. She trusts everyone until they prove her wrong."

"Then you must never have disappointed her," Sabrina said quietly. "She's very fond of you, you know."

His brows lifted in surprise. "You discussed me?"

"Not really. I can only remember one thing she actually said about you in that entire week."

"And that was?"

"Honey said, 'If I were blind and Alex took my hand, I'd trust him to lead me through hell.' "

For a moment there was blank surprise on that closed, usually cynical-looking face. Then to Sabrina's amazement a surge of color flooded his bronze cheeks and his dark eyes were suddenly naked and vulnerable. He hurriedly glanced away and his voice was curiously husky when he spoke. "As I said, Honey's incredibly naïve, but she's right in this instance. I'd do a hell of a lot for her. And there aren't many people in this world worthy of affection."

"What a very cynical thing to say! And how completely untrue. The world is full of people who deserve all the affection we can give them. Surely you must have found that. What about your parents? Aren't you close to them?"

"Not exactly." The words were oddly stilted. "I haven't seen very much of them since I was a small child."

Sabrina's eyes widened in surprise. "I don't understand." Surely even if Alex came from a broken home, he would be close to one of his parents. "Are they divorced?"

"No, they're still together." He laughed shortly. "Of course, that might be due to my grandfather's distaste for divorce. They wouldn't have wanted to give up what they'd gained by selling me to him."

"*Selling you?*"

"My parents find Sedikhan a trifle barbaric compared to the more civilized pleasures of the Riviera." Alex's tone was mocking, but his expression was bitter. "When I was eight, they signed over complete custody of me to my grandfather in return for a villa in Cannes and a very generous lifetime income."

"And they told you what they'd done?" Sabrina asked, appalled.

He shook his head. "My grandfather showed me the contract," he said. His eyes flicked from the rolling surf to her horrified face and for an instant there was something hurt and lost in the depths of them. Then it was gone, masked by a fierce defensiveness. "I'm glad he did it. It was better that I realized at once I couldn't rely on them just because they were my parents. I would have found out later anyway. The parasites of the world always reveal themselves eventually. Sometimes you just have to wait a little longer for the clever ones to show their true colors."

"My God, you were only eight years old," Sabrina said faintly, feeling a little sick to her stomach. "Surely he might have waited until you were older." Could anyone blame Alex for his lack of trust in his fellow man with the kind of upbringing those few poignant sentences had revealed?

"Why should he have?" Alex asked simply. "My grandfather's a great one for calling a spade a spade. He didn't do it to hurt me. I think he genuinely cares for me in his own way. He just wanted to protect me from any possibility of my parents using me later."

"And did they try to use you later?" she asked gently, hoping against hope he'd answer in the negative.

"Of course," he said with a curiously bittersweet smile. "I told you, parasites always react according to their natures. I was fortunate that my grandfather had prepared me for it."

"Yes, very fortunate," Sabrina said huskily, her throat tight with tears as she thought of that vulnerable little boy taught so early about pain and disillusion.

"I didn't need them anyway," he said defiantly. "I had my cousin, Lance, and my grandfather. I didn't need anyone else."

"No, I can see that," Sabrina said lightly, glancing hurriedly away so that he wouldn't see the sudden mist of tears in her eyes. "You wouldn't need anyone but them."

Alex shook his head impatiently. "My God, why am I telling you all this? I don't think I've even given my charming parents a thought in the last five years and you have me spilling out my entire past history. It all happened a long time ago. None of it matters now."

But it did matter. Sabrina had caught a glimpse of another Alex Ben Raschid entirely in the past few minutes, an Alex capable of loyalty and affection and as vulnerable to hurt as any other man. She'd been unbearably moved by that brief insight, and found herself wanting to reach out and hold him close as she did David after one of his nightmares.

"Just because your parents hurt you doesn't mean that no one else can be trusted, Alex," she said gently.

"They didn't hurt me," he denied fiercely, and already the mockery was beginning to mask that instant of vulnerability. "And of course *you* can be trusted, Sabrina. Honey would never have sent you if you couldn't, would she?"

"No, she wouldn't," Sabrina agreed quietly. Why did the sudden raising of that barrier of mockery cause this aching pain in her breast?

Alex's expression darkened moodily. "She apparently didn't delve too deeply into your personal life. I don't know how the hell she expected me to trust you when you're already playing house with another man." His resentful eyes traveled over her scantily clad form in the midnight blue harem outfit. "Not to mention the kick you seem to get out of giving every man in Houston his quota of cheap thrills."

It seemed the truce had definitely come to an end. Sabrina carefully put her wine glass down on the sand and said quietly. "I don't have to take that from you. I think it's time you drove me home."

Alex muttered a very explicit curse. "Why do I always say the wrong things to you?" he asked in exasperation. "At this point I should be wooing you gently. Why does everything have to be different with you?"

"We're obviously incompatible. That's what I've been trying to tell you. Not only are our lifestyles as far apart as the poles but we have different attitudes and commitments."

"Commitment." He repeated the word as if it left a nasty taste in his mouth. "You consider that you have some type of commitment to this David of yours?"

Her eyes met his directly. "Yes," she said candidly. "There's no question of my commitment to David." A look of wonder in sapphire eyes, a tender finger stroking velvet petals. David.

"Commitments can be broken," he said tightly, his dark eyes smoldering. "It seems I'll just have to convince you how desirable it would be to make that break. Honey can be fooled like any other woman. I probably can't trust you any more than I can anyone else." His expression darkened broodingly. "But who the hell cares?"

Then suddenly he was pushing her down on the blanket, leaning over her, a hand on each side of her face but not touching, his body heat tantalizing her. She felt as though his dark eyes were hypnotizing her, holding her in a web of golden languor. Then his lips were covering hers—not roughly, but with infinitely gentle butterfly kisses that teased until her mouth instinctively shaped itself to take more. She could feel the shudder that shook him as she arched against the warmth of his body, slipping her arms slowly over his shoulders and around his neck to bury her fingers in his hair.

Then his tongue was teasing her lips provocatively, tracing the pouting line erotically. "Open your mouth," he said hoarsely. "Let me love you, Sabrina."

She shook her head dazedly, her senses swimming from his experienced lovemaking, but he took the gesture of bewilderment for negation. "Don't say no, Sabrina." He framed her cheeks with his hands. "You won't be sorry. It will be good for you." Then his lips were hard on hers, not coaxing, but taking now, parting her lips almost savagely to deepen the kiss excitingly. He groaned deep in his throat and suddenly the body he had withheld from her was joined to hers in a breathless embrace.

Alex's arms chained her to his muscular form, rolling her over so they lay side by side on the blanket. His lips probed hers in hot, drugging kisses that left her aware of nothing but a nameless hunger. His mouth moved from hers to bite gently on the sensitive cord of her neck, then down to the fullness of her breasts, lingering on the golden flesh of her cleavage before his hands moved slowly to unfasten the chiffon top. Instinctively her hands rose to stop him. It was all happening too fast. Alex's eyes were glazed with passion as they glanced up impatiently to meet her own. He took her lips again, slowly, sensuously, sending her into a world of erotic sensation. She could feel the muscles of his thighs go taut as his hands cupped her breasts, teasing the peaks through the thin material. She gasped, the muscles of her stomach tensing, her breasts swelling at the stimulation that was causing a fluid melting in every limb.

"You're beautiful, do you know that?" he muttered, his lips parting from hers briefly, only to dip down to taste again and again the honey of her lips in hot, scorching kisses. "When you were dancing, all I could think of was getting you alone so I could have all that beauty to myself. I want to see you, every lovely inch of you." His gaze still holding hers, his hands moved deliberately to the front fastening of the midriff.

Sabrina didn't try to stop him this time. She knew with a rush of primitive pride that she wanted him to look at her and find her desirable. He carefully parted the flimsy chiffon barrier and gazed down at her, his eyes dark and intent. He was absolutely still for a moment, before he made a low sound of mindless hunger and lowered his lips to caress the taut, rosy peaks. She arched convulsively as his hands cupped her naked breasts that his burning mouth was caressing.

She gave a little cry that was half protest, half plea. "No, please, Alex." She was on fire, yet feeding on the flame, writhing captive of a response she'd never experienced. Pleading with him to stop, knowing that if he did she would hate him for withdrawing this exquisite torment of the senses.

With easy strength he rolled over until she was on top of him, their bodies fitting together with unbelievable intimacy. His lips covered hers in a long, hot joining while one hand held her hips glued to his thrusting body, and the other caressed her naked back. As their lips parted, he buried his mouth in the hollow of her throat. "God, I'm aching for you. I've been in a fever for you, Sabrina. You've got to belong to me."

She couldn't answer. What had seemed impossible a few hours ago was now happening. She lowered her lips to his with a sense of inevitability, a moth to the flame he'd fired so skillfully. She kissed him with a sweet responsiveness that may have lacked Alex's experience but evidently was more than satisfying, to judge by the shudder that wracked his body.

His arms tightened around her convulsively for a moment, then with a muttered imprecation he rolled over abruptly and tore himself away from her. She lay where he had left her, staring at him in hurt bewilderment. Her body suddenly chilled when separated from his warmth.

He sat a few feet away, his arms clasping his knees, his body rigid. He fumbled in his shirt pocket for a slender brown cigarette, lighting it with a shaking hand and inhaling deeply. He glanced at her. "Please cover up," he said, his eyes fixed compulsively on her bare breasts. "I'm trying my damndest to keep my hands off you."

Sabrina's hands flew to the front of her midriff, his sarcasm making her feel suddenly cheap. She sat up, fighting tears, fumbling at the fastening of the chiffon top.

"Wait." He was kneeling beside her. With urgent hands he parted the midriff and gazed for a long moment. Then, lowering his head, he kissed each taut peak lingeringly. "I didn't mean to be so sharp, sweetheart. It's just that I'm aching for you."

Sabrina drew a shaky breath, leaning toward him yearningly.

He drew back slowly. "You're so damn lovely," he said roughly. He pulled the top closed reluctantly, fastening it slowly. Then he took her in his arms as carefully as if she were a beloved child and rocked her soothingly. "And so very much *mine.* I've never felt so close to anyone in my entire life. It scares the hell out of me, love."

She buried her face in his shoulder, her arms slipping around his waist very naturally. She'd been subjected to so many tumultuous and bewildering emotions with him that she gratefully accepted the comfort he was extending. "You don't want to make love to me any more?" she asked wonderingly. It seemed impossible that he could stop so abruptly when she was still aching and throbbing for more.

He laughed shortly, his hands stroking her silky hair gently. "Oh yes, I want to make love to you. I came within an inch of taking you on this damn blanket."

"Then, why . . ." Her voice trailed off as some fugitive feeling of shame overtook her. Was she so lost in his sensual web that she would plead for him to make love to her? The thought sent a shock of distaste through her, dispelling the euphoric mood generated by the wine and his sexual expertise. She stiffened in his arms and tried to draw back, but at the first signs of withdrawal he bound her tighter to him with instinctive possessiveness.

"I've got an idea we're going to be something special together," he said thickly. "I didn't want to start our relationship like some sex-starved adolescent at a drive-in movie. When I get you into bed, I may not let you out for a week, so we'd better be comfortable."

He kissed her quickly and then reluctantly let her go. He bent to bundle the blanket and hamper into a careless pile, then stowed them in the trunk of the car. In a matter of minutes they were traveling the streets of Galveston. Alex didn't speak until they'd left the outskirts of the port city and were speeding down the Gulf Freeway toward Houston.

"You're coming home with me tonight," he told her quietly. "I'll take you back to your place to pick up your clothes. You won't have to bring much, just enough to last until I can buy you others."

"I can't do that!" Sabrina cried, shocked out of the dazed bemusement his lovemaking had woven about her.

Alex's mouth hardened ruthlessly. "If you think I'm going to let you spend another night with that lover of yours, you're mistaken," he said, his hands tightening on the steering wheel until his knuckles whitened. "I'm going to own you completely, Sabrina, and if anyone so much as touches you, I'll destroy him."

There was an implacable sincerity in his voice. Sabrina shivered uncontrollably at the picture his words evoked. She knew she could never live the life he'd planned for her even to repeat the exquisite sensual pleasure he'd shown her. After the freedom she'd known all her life, the role of a rich man's possession would stifle her. Even if there hadn't been her responsibility toward David, the situation would have been impossible.

"For how long?" she asked bitterly. "Until the next curvy body catches your eye?"

"Do you want me to say forever?" he asked. "I don't believe in forever." He reached over and caressed her thigh. "Will it satisfy you to know that I can't imagine anyone else in my bed? And that this is the first time in my life I've felt that way?"

She pulled her leg away from his touch, liking it far too much. "It wouldn't work," Sabrina said shakily. "You'd soon get bored with me. I'm not terribly brilliant or fabulously talented. I'm probably not even the prettiest girl you've known."

"No, you're not," he said coolly. "You're intelligent, but no Einstein, and I've known many women who were more classically beautiful." He grinned mischievously. "I'll have to judge your other 'talents' later." Then he sobered. "I won't be bored with you, Sabrina. You fit me. I enjoy your spirit and independence, and you have a bright, clear-thinking mind."

"So it's my brain that attracts you?" she scoffed.

"No," he admitted, "that's only a plus." His dark eyes ran over her lingeringly. "There's a sexual chemistry between us that's stronger than any I've ever known. I find you infinitely desirable. You can turn me on more by tilting your head or wrinkling that aristocratic little nose than any other woman can by doing a striptease. I want you to know that I've never kept a woman before. I'm not saying there haven't been plenty of women. I'm no celibate. I take what's offered, but I've never wanted the responsibility of a permanent mistress. I've always found it easy enough to satisfy my physical needs without the demands of that type of relationship."

"Then why start now?" Sabrina asked coldly, imagining with a twinge of hot anger the many women who'd appeased those needs.

"Trust a woman to misunderstand," he growled. "I'm trying to tell you that I think of you differently. For the first time in my life I want a woman totally dependent on me. I want to buy your clothes, pay your bills. I want everything you have to come from me."

"That's pretty chauvinistic, isn't it?" she asked caustically. "I'm a person in my own right, not some kind of robot programmed for your pleasure."

"I don't want a robot, Sabrina. I want a warm, responsive woman in my arms."

They'd arrived at the apartment complex and Alex drove unerringly to her apartment area and parked smoothly. She didn't remind him about her car. She only wanted the security of home now. After switching off the engine, he turned to her. He pulled her close and buried his face in her hair. "God, you're good to hold. I've been wanting to touch you since we left the beach." His mouth covered hers urgently, as if he were starved for the taste of her. Sabrina melted against him, forgetting everything but the potent magic he stirred in her. "I needed that," he groaned hoarsely, when their lips finally parted. "I can't take much more of this." He pushed her away, and ran his hand through his hair. "I'll give you forty-five minutes. If you're not down here by that time, I'm coming up to get you."

She gazed up at him, tears misting her emerald eyes. Her gaze lingered yearningly on the bold, cynical features she probably wouldn't see again after tonight. She'd do all she could to further that aim, out of sheer self-preservation. Alex had reached out and touched her, and not only on a physical level. That other, more ephemeral, closeness could be infinitely more dangerous to her. "You really expect me to do it, don't you?" she asked wonderingly. "Disrupt my life, give up my friends, turn myself into some sort of plaything for your gratification."

"Don't be a fool, Sabrina," he said, frowning. "I could have taken you on that beach tonight and you wouldn't have done a thing to stop me. You want me as much as I want you. Do you think I can't feel it when you're in my arms?"

"No, I must be pretty obvious," she said simply. "I don't have your breadth of experience, and I can't hide, or connive, or mask my feelings. I wanted you to make love to me and I couldn't have stopped as you did. If you hadn't stopped, perhaps I'd be committed to you in a way that would make you uncomfortable."

She backed away from him, pressing against the door as he reached for her. "No, don't touch me!" She shook her head desperately. "You did stop, so we're both saved. Believe me, I don't want to feel any sort of commitment to a man like you. It would destroy me. There's no room for you in my life. Stay out of it, Alex!"

"You're not going back to him," he said harshly, his dark eyes blazing. "You belong to me!"

Sabrina wrenched her arm away and jumped out of the car. She turned, her breasts heaving, her flaming hair wild about her pale face. "I belong to myself! I won't be owned or pampered or made into something I'm not. I won't be your mistress, Alex." She turned and stalked away.

His voice followed her with soft intensity. "You will, Sabrina, I promise you. You will."

Angelina was sitting on the couch in front of the television set but she looked up with a sigh of relief as Sabrina came into the apartment. She leaned forward to flick off the set. "I'm glad you're home," she said, her plump face concerned. "When Hector phoned, he was yammering something about Lamborghinis and over-sexed bozos. I couldn't make heads or tails out of it." Her gaze narrowed on Sabrina's flushed face and suspiciously bright eyes. "Are you all right?"

"I'm fine," Sabrina said throatily, shrugging out of her cape. "David wasn't worried, was he?"

"I just told him you were working late." She stood up and straightened her flowered overblouse. "He's downstairs in our apartment with Gino. They're going to watch that National Geographic special together. I'll send him up to you when it's over."

"Has he had his dinner?"

"Of course he's had his dinner," Angelina said indignantly. "Would I let the boy starve while I had enough lasagna to feed an army?"

"Sorry, I wasn't thinking," Sabrina said, smiling with an effort. "I should have known you'd take good care of him for me. You always do."

"I should think so," Angelina sniffed, as she crossed to the front door. She paused and her face was suddenly serious. "You know that we're always glad to have David at any time, Sabrina. He'll always be safe with us. You can't go on devoting your entire life to him as you've been doing for the past two years. You haven't even had a date since David came out of the hospital." She frowned sternly. "If you want to see this young man again, you do it."

"I won't be seeing him again. There's no way it could work out for us." She smiled sadly. "Besides, he's not the type of man you'd approve of my becoming involved with, Angelina. His intentions are definitely not honorable."

"Neither were my Gino's." She grinned impishly. "For that matter neither were mine." She turned to leave and then suddenly whirled back to face Sabrina. "I forgot to tell you. David's father called this evening while you were out."

"Jess?" Sabrina asked worriedly. "Was he calling from the ranch?" Jess called every Saturday evening with clocklike precision to speak with David. Any deviation from this norm made her definitely uneasy.

Angelina nodded. "He asked you to return his call when you came in."

As the door closed behind Angelina, Sabrina was already moving across the room toward the phone on the end table.

Jess Bradford's deep voice answered at once.

"Jess, this is Sabrina. Is Sue all right?"

"She's fine, Bree," Jess shot back. "I knew you'd jump to conclusions when I called. The doctor says she's doing better than she has for quite a while." There was a long pause. "But she doesn't think she's up to coming to the rodeo this weekend. I thought I'd give you some warning so you could prepare David."

"Oh, Jess, he's going to be so disappointed," Sabrina wailed. "He's worked so hard to get back his old skills. We've been going down to the stable every Saturday for the past seven months. Can't you get her to change her mind?"

"I don't even want to try, Bree," Jess said simply. "I can't risk her losing ground now that she's on her way back. I almost lost both of them when David was hospitalized."

"I know, Jess," Sabrina said, her voice gentle. In many ways, Jess's ordeal had been the worst—Sue's nervous breakdown when she was unable to accept David's problem had literally torn him apart.

"It's not that she doesn't want to see him," Jess went on wearily. "She's begun to talk about him again. Nothing much, just a remark now and then. But at least it's a start."

"Yes, it's a start," Sabrina agreed softly. David had been born when Sue was in her early forties and she'd almost given up hope of having a child. David had seemed a miracle to her, and the bond between them had been one of the strongest and most loving Sabrina had ever known. Yet it hadn't been strong enough for Sue to bear David's tragedy. The only way she'd been able to survive her pain was to close herself away from all thought of David. She hadn't even been permitted to see him since he'd left the hospital.

"I don't think this would be the time for her to see him anyway," Jess said, a thread of anxiety in his voice. "What if he gets hurt in the rodeo while she's there? Are you sure Swanson okayed his entering the competition? The doctor won't even let him drive a car!"

"There are different skills involved," she answered

patiently. "The reason David isn't allowed to drive is the monotony factor. The doctor thinks he might lose concentration and have an accident. It's very difficult not to pay attention when you're on the back of a bucking bronco. You know that David can do anything with horses, Jess."

"I know he *could*," Jess said pointedly. "He's not the same person, Bree. You know that better than anyone."

"That doesn't mean we have to write off everything he was before," she argued passionately. "He can do this, Jess. And by God, I want him to have his chance!"

"Okay, simmer down, Bree," Jess said. "I know you wouldn't let him ride if you thought there was any chance it was unsafe. I was just concerned."

"So am I, Jess," she whispered, closing her eyes. She'd been frightened out of her wits since the moment David had told her he wanted to enter the competition. "But he really wants this. He's been riding in the Houston Rodeo since he was sixteen. We can't keep him in a cocoon forever. He's got to begin to live again."

"I know you're right," Jess said wearily. "It's just so blasted difficult to accept. I guess I just want to take care of him."

"You'll be here on Saturday, then?" Sabrina asked.

"You're damn right," he said gruffly. "Tell him I'll be there with bells on. Juan Mendoza is lending me his box at the Astrodome so we'll practically be in David's lap when he takes home the prize money."

"I'm so glad, Jess," Sabrina said huskily. "He needs all the support we can give him."

"Until Saturday, Bree." He broke the connection with a soft click.

Yes, until Saturday. She replaced the receiver wearily and walked toward her bedroom. This was what was important and real in her life. Not that mad, sensual magic she'd experienced on the beach tonight and certainly not Alex Ben Raschid. That being the case, it made no sense that she was suffering this sudden, aching loneliness. Absolutely no sense at all.

Four

"I told you he could do it, Jess!" Sabrina said jubilantly, her face alight with a fierce pride. She threw herself into his arms, and hugged him ecstatically. "Wasn't he wonderful! Third place! Did you see his face?"

"I was too busy looking at yours," Jess said dryly, unwinding her arms from around his neck. "For a moment there I wasn't sure which one of you had won the prize." Despite his joking words there was a suspicious moisture in Jess's eyes as his gaze tried to search out David's figure in the pens at the far end of the huge arena.

"Oh, it was his prize," she said softly, her emerald eyes glowing like stars. "It was his victory all the way." She sat down on the padded seat in the box and sighed contentedly. Third place! Her glance moved absently around the opaque, domed auditorium, scarcely noticing the gaily dressed western audience in attendance at the Houston Rodeo. She was too filled with exhilaration generated by David's triumph to be conscious of anything else. "Weren't you proud of him, Jess?"

Jess Bradford sat down beside her. "Very proud," he said quietly, taking her hand in his. "As proud as I am of you, Bree. You've worked miracles since he left the hospital two years ago. I don't know what Sue and I would have done if you hadn't been there for him." Jess's gray eyes darkened with pain. "God, it's such a waste. He was so brilliant. Why would he want to experiment with drugs, anyway?"

"Why does anyone?" Sabrina asked soberly. "Curiosity, perhaps. David always wanted to try everything, do everything. If he'd been lucky, he might have satisfied his curiosity and got off scot-free." Her face was taut with pain. "He wasn't lucky. The acid that pusher sold him was very dangerous stuff."

"I wish I could get my hands on that bastard," Jess said grimly. "I'd tear him apart."

"David doesn't even remember him," Sabrina said. Her clasp tightened on Bradford's work-roughened hand. "And I try not to myself. It's over, Jess. All we can do is pick up the pieces."

Jess's rugged face was creased in a frown, his gray eyes brooding. Then his expression brightened slightly. "I didn't tell you, Bree. Sue and I had a long talk last night. She wants you to bring David home for a visit."

"But you said—"

"She believes that it's time," Jess interrupted. "She thinks she can take it now." His face was grave. "I hope to hell she's right."

"So do I," Sabrina said, biting her lip worriedly. "If she's not, it could hurt them both terribly."

"That's why I want you to come with him. You've become the center of his life now, Bree." His gaze was serious. "He may need you. Can you come right away?"

How could she not come when he put it like that? Yet it undoubtedly presented problems. They needed the money she earned at Noveltygrams far too much for her to run the risk of being replaced, as she surely would be if she just blithely took off without clearing it with Joel.

"I'll have to see if I can make arrangements," she said, running her hand distractedly through her hair. "When are you going back to the ranch?"

"Tonight," he said. "I don't want to leave Sue alone too long." He leaned forward and kissed Sabrina gently on the forehead. "Don't worry about it, honey. If you can't work things out, we'll just have to postpone it."

"I'll call you Monday and let you know," Sabrina promised. She looked up and leaned forward eagerly as a blare of trumpets announced the starting of the grand parade. The finale was a colorful parade of all the rodeo participants, led by the country-western superstar who was this year's lead attraction. She applauded enthusiastically at the stirring spectacle, her eyes searching the column of riders. "Do you see David?"

Then she spotted him near the end of the parade. He was dressed in black jeans and a brilliant blue satin shirt, his golden braid gleaming under the lights. He was an almost barbarically handsome figure on his black stallion as he lifted his head, his eyes searching the stands. When he saw them, his face lit with such joy that she caught her breath. He took off his black Stetson and waved it jubilantly at her.

Sabrina waved back, her throat tight and aching with tears. She saw the eagerness on his face as he suddenly gathered the reins, his gaze still fixed on her face. Sabrina suddenly knew what he was going to do. "Oh, no," she whispered. "He wouldn't, would he?"

"He would," Jess said, his lips twitching in amusement.

He did.

He left his position in the parade, cut across

the vast arena in front of the outraged superstar and his entourage, and reined in before their box.

"Hi, Bree," he said happily, his face alight with pride. At a signal, his horse bowed low before Sabrina. "Good trick, isn't it? I wanted it to be a surprise. Every time you had to work and Gino took me to the stables in your place, I practiced it." He looked around in surprise at the applause of the crowd, then grinned delightedly and waved his hat in acknowledgment. He turned back, his expression hopeful. "Did you like it, Bree?"

Sabrina could feel the color stain her cheeks as the eyes of the entire audience turned to their box. Yet all she could say to David was, "I loved it. It's a wonderful trick."

David's pleased smile was rainbow brilliant. He edged the horse closer, then stood in the saddle balancing for a moment before vaulting lightly over the rail into the box.

Oh Lord, what next?

"Did you know that there's an amusement park right next door, Bree?" he asked excitedly, not even noticing the crowd's renewed applause. His face was eager. "Could we go over there after the rodeo?"

Yes, she knew about the amusement park and so had he formerly. How many times had they run over to the park with their friends after a rodeo? "I don't see why not, love," she said lightly, over the lump in her throat. "I want to see if you can ride those merry-go-round horses as well as you did that bronco." She turned, "Jess?"

"It's all right with me," Jess said quietly. "I'll meet you down at the pens and help you curry your horse and stable him temporarily. Bree can meet us at the front entrance."

His face alight with excitement, David nodded and turned back to the rail.

"David."

Sabrina impulsively moved forward. To hell with their amused audience. She kissed him gently on the cheek. "I'm so proud of you."

"I'm glad," he said simply, but his smile could have lit all of Houston. Then he vaulted over the rail and onto the black horse and was riding back to his position in the parade.

"I'll see you in about twenty minutes, Bree," Jess drawled, as he left the box. She nodded absently, her gaze on that proud, glowing figure on the glossy black stallion.

The huge crowd started moving up the stairs of the stadium as the last of the parade left the arena. Sabrina had gathered her belongings from the box and joined the slow crawl to the exits when a firm hand pulled her out of the aisle into the now vacant bleachers.

"Hello again, Miss Courtney," Clancy Donahue said cordially.

His massive figure looked much more at ease in Tony Lama boots, Levi's, and a blue chambray shirt than it had in the tuxedo, and his breezy grin was just as warm.

"You look right at home with all these cowboys, Mr. Donahue," Sabrina said. "Are you here with your family?"

He shook his head. "I've always been a loner," he answered. "I've been too busy batting around the world raising hell to acquire any dependents. Alex and Lance are as close as I've ever come to a family."

"Yes, I remember you mentioned knowing Alex as a boy," Sabrina said. "Was that in Sedikhan?"

"Yep, I was bossing one of old Karim's oil rigs when he was scouting around for someone to take over the job of tutoring the boys."

"Tutoring?" Sabrina's eyes widened in surprise.

A rough diamond like Donahue seemed a bizarre choice of tutor for a boy destined to be one of the wealthiest and most powerful men in the world.

"It came as a shock to me, too," Donahue said dryly. "But the old man knew what he wanted. When he called me into his office, he had a dossier on me that dated back to the time I was in diapers. He knew Alex would have to be tough as steel to survive and keep what was his. Sedikhan isn't exactly the most civilized country, even these days. My job was to make sure he was smarter, and a hell of a lot more lethal, than the wolves who would try to gobble him up."

"And did you succeed?"

Donahue's grin was just as genial but there was a glint in those cool blue eyes like sunlight on a bared sword. "What do you think?" he asked softly.

Sabrina shivered as she remembered the sudden chill she'd known in the parking lot three days ago when Ben Raschid had confronted Hector Ramirez. "I think perhaps you did your job very well, indeed."

"So do I, Miss Courtney," Donahue said with satisfaction. He made a face. "Sometimes I think I did too good a job. A little cynicism goes with the territory, but Alex has problems trusting anyone these days. It's turning him into an exceptionally lonely man."

"It doesn't appear to bother him very much," Sabrina said skeptically. "And according to the gossip columns he has more than enough willing companions."

"Women?" Donahue shook his head. "Alex doesn't have any use for women except in the most basic sense." His eyes narrowed thoughtfully on her face. "At least he didn't until now."

"Me?" She shook her head. "I assure you that

Alex views me in exactly the same light as he does other women."

"Somehow I don't think so, or I wouldn't be here right now, Miss Courtney." He paused. "I have a message for you."

"I gather this meeting isn't accidental."

"Well, in a way it is. Alex didn't know you were here until he spotted you on closed-circuit television."

"Alex is here?" She felt a rush of panic.

Clancy Donahue gestured across the arena. "Sedikhan Oil has a corporate box, and Alex is entertaining a few guests." He raised his eyebrows puckishly. "A mideastern head of state, the mayor, and a few movie stars." He shot her a sidelong glance to judge the effect of his words.

"How nice for him," she said flatly, only half hearing him, wondering wildly how she could escape without seeing Alex.

"He wants you to join us, Sabrina," Donahue said quietly.

"No!" The word burst out with the force of a pistol shot. Then, gaining more control of herself, she lowered her voice. "Please convey my thanks to Alex, but I have other plans."

All the laughter left Donahue's face. "You don't want to defy him this time, Sabrina. He's not in a very good mood. In fact, that's quite an understatement. I hope I never see him as angry as when he saw you kiss that cowboy."

"He saw me kiss David?" she asked faintly.

"Fifty thousand people saw you kiss him," Donahue amended dryly. "But Alex was the only one who broke the stem of his champagne glass when he watched your touching little scene. He got quite a nasty cut, too."

"Perhaps he had too much to drink," she said

coolly. "I'm sure my actions couldn't have such a violent effect on Alex."

"It's none of my business what's been happening between you two, but don't underestimate your effect on Alex. He's been perfect hell to work with the past week and I'd bet the responsibility lies on that little red head of yours," Donahue said grimly. "I also know what I saw in his face upstairs. He said two words to me—'Get her!'—and I knew I'd better not slip up on this little assignment." He smiled coaxingly. "So how about it, Sabrina? You wouldn't want to get me in trouble with Alex would you? Why don't you come along like a good girl?"

"Does he pay you extra for acting as a pimp?"

She thought for a moment that he just might hit her. But he drew a deep breath and the smooth control was back. He said coldly, "I'm not bringing you to his bed, Miss Courtney. Alex wouldn't thank me for that. He likes to stage his own seductions in his own time. I'm just a messenger inviting you to a very respectable party.

That half the society women in Houston would give their eyeteeth to attend," he added ironically.

Sabrina felt a twinge of remorse that her temper had led her into such a harsh condemnation. She couldn't help liking Clancy Donahue and it was true he was doing nothing shameful in carrying out Ben Raschid's orders.

She turned toward him, her eyes glistening with tears. "I'm sorry," she said in a low voice, "that was terribly bitchy of me."

"You're damn right it was," he said grimly, then smiled reluctantly. "But not entirely unjustified. My duties don't usually include standing in for Alex. He would have come after you himself if he weren't tied up with a rather temperamental oil sheik. Mahoud wouldn't understand being deserted for a lowly woman." Then, noticing her tear-brightened eyes, he touched her cheek gently with one finger. "Damn, you're just a baby!" he said abruptly. "Do you want some good advice? Run like hell, kid."

"You're not being a very loyal employee, are you?" Sabrina asked, liking him more every moment.

He said lightly, "I have a hunch you're a great deal more vulnerable than the ladies who inhabit Alex's world. He's pretty potent stuff. He could hurt you badly."

"I know." Her expression was nakedly revealing.

Donahue smiled almost tenderly. "It appears my warning comes a little late."

"I'll get over it," she said determinedly.

"I hope so, Sabrina," he said skeptically, his blue eyes kind. "In the meantime I'd get as far away from Houston as I could. Alex isn't going to let you go easily. Not now."

Sabrina laughed shakily. "This isn't some feudal kingdom; this is one of the most modern cities in the world, and I'm not leaving my home and my friends just because you think Alex may decide to practice some form of sexual harassment. That would be ridiculous." She broke away from him, then turned back abruptly. "I'm not running away," she said softly, "but thank you for your concern. You're a nice person, Clancy Donahue."

"I like you, too, Sabrina, but you're making a mistake." He shrugged. "Now, what do I tell Alex?"

"I don't suppose you could tell him you missed me in the crowd?" she asked hopefully.

Donahue shook his head. "He's probably watching us right now on closed-circuit television."

She shivered at the thought, imagining Alex's eyes on her. It was almost as if he were right here beside them. She lifted her chin defiantly. "Then you can tell him I had a previous engagement," she said, starting up the now deserted stairs. She smiled recklessly. "Tell him I regret refusing his gracious invitation, but I have a date with a carousel."

"Hi, Jean," Sabrina called cheerfully as she entered the modest offices of Noveltygrams Incorporated on Monday morning.

Jean Roberts, Joel's receptionist, looked up with a sunny smile. "Hi, Sabrina. What brings you in? Going to hit the boss for a raise?"

Sabrina shook her head, her ponytail bouncing saucily. "Nope, I wanted a few days off to go visit friends. Will you tell Joel I'm here?"

Jean nodded and picked up the phone, speaking into it briefly. "He says to go right in."

Sabrina nodded, then waved gaily before opening the door to the inner office.

Joel Craigen leaned back in his chair and said genially, "You're looking great, Sabrina." He waved to a chair in front of his desk. "Sit down and tell me what I can do for you."

She perched on the edge of the chair. "I was just wondering, could I have a little time off, Joel?" she asked hesitantly. When he didn't respond immediately, she continued, "If it's inconvenient right now, of course I'll forget about it."

Joel was toying with a pencil, not looking at her. "We might work something out."

"That's great! I'll only be gone for a few days, Joel."

He dropped his pencil on the desk and rubbed hard at his thick neck. "Well, actually, Sabrina, I've been trying to reach you for the last half hour. I wanted to have a little talk with you. The truth is, I've decided to discontinue the bellygrams."

"Discontinue?" she asked blankly. "But they're one of the most popular grams on your list! Jean told me last week there were lots of bookings. You'd have to cancel them!"

"Then I'll cancel them," he said flatly. "The bellygrams are out."

Sabrina shook her head dazedly. It didn't make sense. Why would he cancel one of his most lucrative acts? She smiled uneasily. "Well, if they're out, they're out. Can you fit me into one of the other acts?"

Joel shuffled papers on his desk. "Uh, we're pretty well staffed right now, Sabrina. You know how it is." He looked up at last to meet her disappointed gaze. "Oh, hell!" he exploded in disgust, tossing the papers aside and running his fingers through his thinning hair. "Dammit, Sabrina, this is bull," he said roughly. "You're fired. I can't use you any more. Not now, not ever."

"But why?" she asked, stunned. "I'm good. You know I'm good, and I've always been very reliable. I don't deserve this. What did I do wrong?"

"I wish I knew," he said wearily. "But you sure made someone mad as hell."

"What on earth do you mean? Did one of my clients complain?"

"Not directly. All I know is I got a phone call this morning from Jim Hudson, head of the legal department of Sedikhan Petroleum."

"Sedikhan Petroleum!" Sabrina gasped.

Joel gave her a keen glance. "You know something about this, Sabrina?"

"I may," she answered grimly, her fists clenching involuntarily. "What did they want?"

Craigen took out a cigar and lit it before leaning back again in his chair. He quoted briefly, "Sabrina Courtney is not to perform in any capacity. She is to be terminated immediately, or any required action will be taken against Noveltygrams."

"That's ridiculous," Sabrina said furiously, "What could they possibly do to you?"

"Plenty," Joel said tersely, "For starters, Alex Ben Raschid sits on the board of the bank that's considering my expansion loan. I'm strictly small potatoes, Sabrina. Sedikhan Petroleum could force me out of business in two months' time if they decided to exert a little muscle."

"There must be laws to prevent a company from doing that," Sabrina protested hotly. "Who is Alex Ben Raschid, some kind of dictator? I just can't believe you're giving in to him!"

"Do you think I like having them lean on me?" he asked harshly. "I'd like to tell them to go to hell, but this business means a lot to me. I've worked damn hard and invested every cent I could lay my hands on. There's no way I'm going to let it go down the drain. It may not be fair, but you're expendable, Sabrina," he finished bluntly.

The surge of rage that shook her prevented her from speaking for a moment. How dare Alex do this to her! The supreme arrogance of the action took her breath away. How vicious to take away a person's livelihood just to avenge a blow to his self-esteem. Somehow she hadn't believed him capable of such pettiness, and her disillusionment added fuel to her anger.

Mistaking her silence for despondency, Joel said with gruff sympathy, "I know you need the job, kid, and I'll give you a damn good reference." He began to toy with the pencil again, obviously wishing this interview were over. "Maybe if you can smooth over your differences with Ben Raschid we could work something out."

She leaped to her feet, her eyes blazing. "You expect me to go to him on my knees, begging for my job back?" she gritted, leaning forward and putting both hands on the desk. "I may be naïve, but I still believe that no one should give up his self-respect for money. I don't want to work for you any more, Joel." She drew a deep breath, trying to control herself. "I'm going to see Alex Ben Raschid all right but only to tell him what a grade-A bastard he is!"

She turned and stormed out of the office, past the startled receptionist, to the ancient red Volkswagen parked at the curb.

Five

The Sedikhan Petroleum Building was known to everyone in Houston. A towering skyscraper, it seemed to be composed entirely of reflecting glass and was a miracle of modern architecture. When it had officially opened a year before, the Sunday Supplement had carried a four-page pictorial story on it. Sabrina, however, didn't even notice the much-touted exterior as she pulled into the parking lot. She walked determinedly into the lobby, and after locating the executive offices in the directory, entered the elevator and pushed the button for the top floor. Ordinarily the plush luxury of the building would have intimidated her, but now the affluent surroundings only reminded her of the arrogance of the man she was going to see. That someone with such wealth could be so ruthless, so callous, only added fuel to her anger.

When the elevator door opened, she strode into the lushly carpeted foyer like a young Amazon going into battle. The outer office was occupied by a sleek brunette at a mahogany desk. She looked up with a dazzling smile that rapidly faded as she took in the sight of Sabrina in her faded Levi's and white oxford cloth shirt. "May I help you, please?" she asked.

"I'd like to see Alex Ben Raschid. I'm Sabrina Courtney."

The brunette smiled tolerantly. "I'm afraid Mr. Ben Raschid is a very busy man. He never sees anyone without an appointment. Do you have an appointment?"

"I do not have an appointment, but I'm going to see Alex Ben Raschid *now*." The last word was said with such intensity that it caused even the confident receptionist to waver.

"I'll ring his private secretary, Miss Courtney," she said coolly, picking up the receiver, "but I don't think it will do any good. Mr. Ben Raschid never sees anyone unless they're expected."

"Oh, I'm expected," Sabrina said grimly. "I'll lay odds that Alex is expecting me."

The brunette looked puzzled as she spoke into the phone. She listened for a moment, her expression changing to one of shock, then she said briskly, "Right away, Miss Johnson," and replaced the telephone. "You're to go right in, Miss Courtney," she said to Sabrina. "Mr. Ben Raschid left orders that he would be available to you at any time."

"How kind of him," Sabrina said bitterly, only the surface meaning of the double entendre reaching the receptionist, to judge by the look on her face.

"It's the door on the left and straight to the end of the hall," she said, her glossy smile once more in place.

The door at the end of the hall opened to a luxurious office done in beige and orange, and the desk this time was occupied by a dark-haired woman in her middle thirties with an air of computerlike efficiency.

The secretary didn't even raise an eyebrow at Sabrina's appearance but said coolly, "I'm Velma

Johnson, Miss Courtney. I'm sorry you were kept waiting." She waved a perfectly manicured hand at a brown tweed couch. "Won't you sit down, and I'll order you some coffee. Mr. Ben Raschid is in conference with two department heads, but he should be through shortly.

Sabrina strode past her to the single door on the wall behind her desk. Turning the knob, she said emphatically, "Miss Johnson, I don't care if he's in conference with the King of Siam. I'm seeing him!"

The two older men seated in front of the large, teak executive desk looked up, startled at the intrusion. Sabrina ignored them as she walked across the wide expanse of plush, hunter green carpet, her whole attention fixed on the man behind the desk.

Alex Ben Raschid was dressed for business in a charcoal gray suit and vest, his white shirt contrasting sharply with his dark hair and golden tan. He was studying some papers in front of him as she walked in but looked up abruptly when one of the men broke off in the middle of a sentence. His ebony glance raked over her boldly, and a slow, mocking smile lit his face.

Velma Johnson, hurrying in behind her, broke in apologetically, "I'm sorry, Mr. Ben Raschid, I told her you were busy."

He rose to his feet in one lithe movement and came around the desk, "It's all right, Velma," he said coolly. "Sabrina is sometimes a little impatient, aren't you, darling?" He put an arm around her waist affectionately, but Sabrina could detect the steely strength beneath the casual embrace. "I suppose I should be flattered."

Flattered! "Alex, you are—"

"Yes, darling, I know," he interrupted smoothly. He turned to the two men. "If you'll excuse me, we'll continue this meeting at another time." As they began putting their papers into their brief-cases, he turned to Velma Johnson. "See that I'm not disturbed until Miss Courtney leaves."

Sabrina caught a knowing exchange of glances between the two department heads and bit her lip in frustration. When the door finally closed be-hind them, she was positively seething. "I don't know what you think you accomplished by that little charade," she exploded, breaking away from Alex.

He seemed content to let her go, now that there was no longer an audience. He seated himself on the corner of the desk and crossed his arms, watch-ing with all evidence of enjoyment the rage that illuminated her face. "I merely wanted to put a good façade on the situation," he drawled smoothly. "I wouldn't want you to be embarrassed the next time you meet the gentlemen."

"As I don't intend to see either man again, I don't see that your argument is valid," she said icily.

"You didn't like them?" he asked, raising a brow. "They're quite nice, but of course we'll avoid them if you've taken a dislike to them."

Sabrina mentally counted to ten before answer-ing. "I don't even know them. But if they have anything to do with you, I wouldn't touch them with a ten-foot pole!"

"That's good, Sabrina, I wouldn't want any other man closer than that to you," he said softly.

"Will you stop talking inanities?" she asked furiously. "You know why I'm here. How could you do such an unspeakable thing? No, don't tell me. I'm sure it comes quite easily to such an insufferable egotist." She was pacing up and down the room as she spoke but stopped in front of him. "Did it ever occur to you here in your ivory tower that some people *need* to work for their living?"

There was a flicker of anger in the dark eyes that watched her, and a muscle jerked in his cheek. "I think when you get to know me better, Sabrina, you'll find I work quite hard. What's more, I provide jobs for thousands of employees."

"Is that what makes you think you can play God?" she asked scornfully, tossing her head.

He muttered a low oath. "Believe me, I'm leaning closer to Mephistopheles at the moment. You'd try the patience of a saint. Don't go too far, Sabrina." His tone was soft, but ominous. "You're no doubt ranting about the action I was forced into taking this morning."

"Forced?" she spat, her green eyes darkening to almost emerald with anger. "Who could have forced the great Alex Ben Raschid to get me fired?"

"Why, you did, Sabrina," he said mockingly. "If you'd agreed to come and live with me, none of this would have been necessary. If you'd come to the party yesterday, I would have offered you a job at Sedikhan Petroleum then."

"And just what would my duties have been?" she grated.

"Anything you like. Secretarial, sales, whatever suits you. I told you I'd let you set the pace"—he paused—"at least for a while." He stood up and moved slowly toward her and she backed away involuntarily. "The offer is still open, Sabrina," he said caressingly. "I wouldn't take away one job without providing another in its place—at double your present salary."

"And that's supposed to make it all right?" she asked incredulously." "How would you know I'd like your job? For your information, I was quite happy with the one I had. I don't want your darn, stuffy job!"

The flicker in his dark eyes leaped into flame as Alex's hands clamped on her upper arms. "You may enjoy flaunting that luscious body before strange men, but you'll have to give up your teasing little games. I find I'm curiously possessive of you, Sabrina." He pulled her closer so that the last words were muttered into her hair.

The magic of his sexual magnetism was pulling at her even as the words repelled. She could feel the erratic pounding of his heart and the heat of his body through his clothing. She reached up to push him away, but his hands slid down her arms to her wrists, pulling them behind her back and arching her body to fit his. His muscles were taut, his arousal shockingly obvious.

"See what you do to me?" he whispered huskily, his tongue exploring her ear. With little kisses he followed the line of her cheek until he reached her lips, and his mouth covered hers. He groaned, his tongue invading with an intimacy that caught at her breath. She made a sound between a moan and a sob. Too late she realized she should never have come here. His lovemaking was causing her to doubt even her reason for approaching him. Had it really been rage or had that been an excuse to once more come shivering to warm herself at this flame of physical pleasure?

He'd released her arms to pull her hips still closer to his in even greater intimacy. Free, she didn't push him away, instead she slipped her arms under his coat to press herself closer to him. He gave a husky laugh and swept her off her feet, then carried her to the massive executive chair behind the desk, where he cradled her on his knees possessively.

"Why do I feel this tenderness whenever I hold you in my arms?" he asked, his lips moving to caress the lobe of her ear. "Even when I'm wanting you so much I ache with it, I want to treat you as if you were Dresden china." His lips moved to the pulse point under her chin. "I knew you'd be angry that I'd pulled strings to get you fired, sweetheart, but I had to do it." His lips moved down to the hollow of her throat. "I couldn't take it. You can see that, can't you? Forgive me, Sabrina. I promise I'll make it up to you, love."

Perhaps it was those words, "Forgive me,"—so alien to Alex, she knew—but she was lost and felt only the need to give whatever he asked of her. Then he was kissing her again. His swift hands dispensed with the buttons of her shirt and the front fastening of her bra, freeing her breasts to his palms. She gasped as his fingers caressed and teased. When he looked down, a flush mottled his cheeks and his eyes glazed with desire. "Do you know, you have the most perfect breasts I've ever seen," he whispered. "They were meant to be loved." He lowered his lips to take one eager nipple in his mouth and she shuddered with the incredible sensation he evoked with his lips and tongue. Suddenly her hands were working at the buttons of his vest and shirt.

"Alex, accounting has finished—" Clancy Donahue broke off abruptly.

One moment she was cradled on Alex's lap, his lips at her breast, the next she was crushed to his chest, her head buried in his shoulder, his arms wrapped around her protectively.

"Damn you, Clancy," Alex's voice rumbled angrily beneath her ear. "I told Velma we weren't to be disturbed. What the hell do you mean breaking in here?"

"Damn! I'm sorry, Alex." Donahue's voice *definitely* sounded sorry. "Velma wasn't at her desk, and I knew you wanted this report." There was the sound of a hasty withdrawal and the closing of a door.

Alex's arms loosened their viselike hold as he put her a little away from him. "Now, where were we?" he murmured huskily.

But the moment of shock and embarrassment at Donahue's intrusion had flooded Sabrina with cold reason. She felt a sickness in the pit of her stomach at her own abysmal weakness. If Donahue hadn't come in, she would have yielded anything Alex demanded. She shook her head dazedly and pushed herself off his lap, her hands fumbling at the buttons of her shirt. Surprisingly, he let her go after one keen look at her face.

"I was afraid Clancy had blown it," he said, his lips curving in a wry smile as he watched her move away. She noted dully that he didn't bother to button the waistcoat her eager fingers had unfastened; perhaps he wanted to remind her of his power over her. It was quite an effective ploy, she thought miserably, shame darkening her face. There was no way she could deny she'd not only been submissive, but eager. How could she have been such a fool? Her shaking hands lifted to refasten the ponytail Alex had loosened, the movement pulling her shirt tight over her breasts. She looked up at the sound of his sharply indrawn breath.

"Don't be provocative, Sabrina. I'm within an inch of taking you right here and now. And we both know you wouldn't be unwilling very long, don't we?"

His question pierced her armor with fatal accuracy. Suddenly the tears that had been threatening rolled down her cheeks as she stared at him with the helplessness of a hurt fawn.

"Damn!" he swore softly. He was across the office and she was in his arms again. His embrace was almost sexless, a warm, protective enfolding only meant to comfort, not entice, as he held her for a long, peaceful moment. "Easy, sweetheart. Damn it, don't you know what that does to me? I think I'm back in cool control again and then you do something like that and it blows everything sky high." He drew a deep, shuddering breath. "I feel like I'm melting inside. God, I've never known anything like this in my life."

How many facets were there to his character, Sabrina wondered? He changed like a chameleon from one moment to the next. With a sigh she moved away from him. "I'm quite all right now," she said with fragile dignity.

His mouth twisted. "I wish I could say the same." He ran his fingers through his dark hair. "I don't usually find myself acting big brother to a woman I want to bed, nor do I generally seduce women in my office."

The faint note of accusation in his voice caused her to raise her chin in indignation. "I suppose that's my fault, too," she said. "I forced you to make love to me!"

"In a manner of speaking. You're a very desirable woman and your promiscuous behavior is an open invitation to any man."

"Promiscuous! How can you call my behavior promiscuous? I've done everything in my power to discourage you!"

His lips twisted cynically, and there was leaping anger in his dark eyes. "I appear to be excluded from your amorous propensities," he said harshly. "It's enough to give one an inferiority complex when you appear to be so overly generous with your favors with everyone else. Doesn't your lover object to your other men?"

"My lover?" Sabrina asked blankly.

"That young fool of a cowboy you kissed in front

of half of Houston," he said bitterly, "And who was the older man you were so intimate with in the box? Another lover?"

"Why not?" she said sarcastically, her voice rising. "If I'm a *femme fatale*, why not another man? Why not *ten* other men?"

He reached out and shook her. "Damn you, was that your lover?"

"Of course he's my lover," she said, almost hysterically. "They're all my lovers!"

"You bitch," he gritted, his hands tightening on her shoulders.

She felt a feverish excitement that ignored the danger inherent in taunting him. The pain and humiliation he'd inflicted on her were crying out to be revenged. "I told you I'd take as many lovers as I liked," she said wildly. "And there's nothing you can do about it."

Alex took a deep breath and suddenly the cool businessman was back, the dark eyes masked but emanating such power and menace that she would rather have faced the unleashed violence of the moment before. He released her very carefully and stepped back, buttoning his jacket and smoothing his hair casually. "I can do a great deal about it. I was prepared to be patient, but you've made me angry, Sabrina. I'm not waiting any longer. You'd better run along now," he said dismissingly, as he moved behind the desk. "I have an appointment in a few minutes."

She moved to the door dazedly, suddenly wishing she'd not lost her temper and taunted him. Alex Ben Raschid in this mood was a very dangerous man.

As she turned the knob of the door, he spoke behind her. "Oh, Sabrina," he said softly, almost absently, "beginning now, you're mine. I don't really care whether you acknowledge it or not, but if you let any other man so much as hold your hand, I promise you that you'll regret it."

The chill of steel sheathed in warm velvet . . . that's how his voice sounded, she realized, a shiver racing up her spine. She closed the door quietly behind her.

"How long are we going to stay here, Bree?" David asked hesitantly, a troubled frown creasing his forehead. He leaned against the trunk of a cottonwood tree and tipped his Stetson farther back on his head.

"Hold still, love," Sabrina commanded absently, her charcoal pencil moving rapidly across the sketch pad. "We've only been here for a little over a week." She glanced up with swift concern. "I thought you were having a wonderful time."

"I just think it's time for us to leave," David said haltingly.

Sabrina slowly closed the sketch pad and put it on the grass beside her. "Why, David?"

His sapphire gaze was fixed thoughtfully on the lacy pattern of the leaves above his head. "I just think it's time," he said huskily.

Something was definitely troubling him, and Sabrina had a good idea what it was. She'd been conscious of the strain since the moment they'd arrived. It would have been too much to hope that David wouldn't be even more aware than she. "Is it your father?" she probed gently.

"No." He smiled wistfully. "It's been fun being with Dad and working the ranch together like we did before." He was silent for a long moment. "It's Mother, Bree."

"She loves you very much, David."

"I know," he said. "I know she does. But I'm hurting her." His eyes fastened gravely on Sabrina's face. "Sometimes I can almost feel her pain and that hurts me, too. Why am I hurting her, Bree?"

"It's very complicated, love," Sabrina said throatily, looking away from him evasively. "Perhaps it only needs time to make it right."

"I don't think so," he said, biting his lip. "When she looks at me, it's as if she's searching for something and not finding it." His face clouded. "I try to be there for her, Bree, and sometimes for a moment or two I think I really am." He shrugged helplessly. "But then it slips away."

What could she say? She'd seen that expression on Sue's face and knew what David meant. How could she tell him it was the son who'd perhaps vanished forever his mother was searching for? His mother had been wrong in thinking she was ready to accept this stranger-child, and after a week Sabrina had doubts she would ever make the adjustment. It had been a mistake coming back to the ranch even for a visit.

"We'll only be staying a few more days," she said. She stood up and dusted off her jeans. "Will you be glad to get back to Gino and Angelina and all your flowers?"

He brightened immediately. "Yes." Then he frowned. "I hope Miranda's okay."

"Gino wouldn't let anything happen to any of your plants." Sabrina said comfortingly. She picked up her pencil and sketch pad. "Come on, lazybones. We've got to get back to the ranch. We're supposed to go to that party at Juan Mendoza's this evening."

David got obediently to his feet. "Do I have to go, Bree?" he sighed, as he trailed behind her to the tree where the horses were tied.

"Your parents don't ask much of us," Sabrina said. "Juan Mendoza is a very important man in the Cattleman's Association and the biggest rancher in the valley. I don't think Jess wants to offend him."

"Okay," David said absently, lifting his head to look at the rapidly darkening sky to the east. "It looks like we're going to get a real gullywasher."

"That's good isn't it, after that drought all last summer?"

He was still frowning uneasily at the rapidly building thunderheads. "Maybe," he answered. "Dad says the drought caused erosion along the river, and we've been getting an awful lot of rain lately. The river is almost over the banks now."

He gave her a leg up, then mounted himself and rode swiftly up the hill. Sabrina followed more slowly and paused for a moment on the rise. The wind swept through the cottonwoods. It stirred the tall grasses and caused an uneasy shiver in the mare she was riding. She patted the horse's neck, murmuring soothingly while she took in the sight of the lowering sky and a flash of lightning in the distance. Storms had always excited her, she felt a strange exhilaration that was close to the primitive.

With a kick she sent the mare racing after David's chestnut, tearing over the ground, passing David with a low laugh. "I'll see you at the house," she shouted, and the distance was covered in a matter of minutes. She reined in at the stable, competently unsaddled the mare, and put out feed and water. Then she ran up the porch steps and into the house.

Sue Bradford came hurrying into the hall from the general direction of the kitchen, a worried frown on her face. Tall, brown-haired and slim, she had always possessed a youthful vitality and cheerful enthusiasm. It was painfully disconcerting to see the expression of haunted sadness that had aged her so drastically in the past two years.

"I'm glad you're back," she said. "Jess just left for the south basin bordering the river. He wants David to join him as soon as possible. They're predicting a storm that will cause the river to crest and very likely flood the basin. The herd will have to be moved."

Sabrina turned at once toward the door. "David's probably at the stable by now. I'll go after him and we'll both ride out right away."

Sue was shaking her head. "Jess said to only send David. He has Pete Donaldson and Jake Montieth helping out. Thank God for neighbors you can count on in times like these." Her lips curved wryly. "Believe it or not, Jess wants you to go on to Mendoza's party. He's afraid of offending the great man if one of us doesn't attend."

"Jess wants me to go to a *party* when we may lose the south herd?" Sabrina asked incredulously.

Sue shrugged. "Don't ask me to fathom that man's thinking," she said dryly. "I've only had thirty-four years to work on it."

Sabrina shook her head. "It's crazy. Are you supposed to go the party and fiddle while Rome burns, too?"

Sue shook her head. "He knows better than to try to bulldoze me into leaving." Then she smiled comfortingly. "The situation isn't as bad as all that, Bree. Shifting the herd shouldn't take more than a few hours. I only want to be here to make sure they have dry clothes and hot food waiting when they straggle in like drowned rats."

"Then let me do that, Sue," Sabrina said stubbornly. "I don't even know Señor Mendoza very well."

The older woman reached out to shake her arm reprovingly. "Now stop arguing and do what you're told, Bree," she scolded with an affectionate grin. "You've got your assignment and I've got mine. All you have to do is make an appearance, present our apologies, and socialize for an hour or so. Now run along and get dressed while I go send David out to the basin." She turned and strode briskly out the screen door.

Sabrina grimaced ruefully as she mounted the stairs to the second floor. There was nothing she could do but accede to their requests, but she wasn't going to stay at Mendoza's party longer than absolutely necessary. It just might be the fastest duty appearance on record.

When she'd showered and washed her hair, she studied the clothes in her closet critically. She hadn't brought much with her, but there was one that might do, a sleeveless peach jersey sheath with a bateau neck that was deceptively modest in front but slashed to the waist in back. The warm peach shade showed off her tan and accented the flame of her loose, gleaming hair. She slipped into bone high-heeled sandals, and used a minimum of makeup—peach lip gloss, a touch of mascara, a brush of powder. Glancing casually into the full-length mirror, she decided that she would do. The Mendozas wouldn't be concerned with the appearance of such an unimportant guest anyway.

When she came downstairs, Sue was standing in the hall with an umbrella in her hand and a raincoat over her arm. "You're going to need these," she said briskly, and as if on cue there came a low rumble of thunder. "It's been pouring for the past fifteen minutes."

Sabrina slipped on the raincoat and belted it around her slim middle. "You're sure you want me to do this?"

"I'm sure," Sue said firmly, as she handed Sabrina the umbrella. "The keys are in the station wagon. You'd better not chance taking your

Volkswagen in weather like this. Tell Consuela Mendoza I'll call her tomorrow." Then she added with a frown, "Be careful crossing the river. The county supervisors have been going to replace that bridge with an elevated one for the past five years, but they've never gotten around to it."

Sabrina nodded. "Don't worry, I'll watch it." She hesitated, drawing a deep breath. "Sue, I've been meaning to tell you. David and I will be leaving soon. I have to find work and he shouldn't be away from Dr. Swanson for too long."

For a moment there was a flicker of unmistakable relief on Sue Bradford's face; seeing it, Sabrina's heart ached. Then it was gone and Sue was saying quietly, "Perhaps you're right. We'll talk about it later, Bree."

"Right." Sabrina turned away to keep Sue from seeing the suspicious mistiness in her eyes. "We'll talk about it later. I just thought you should know."

She ran to where the station wagon was parked, and in a few minutes she was driving through the storm. The wind whipped against the car in sheets; the windshield wipers were useless. Sabrina tensed with strain as she maneuvered the car almost blindly along the county road that crossed the Concho River.

As she approached the river the visibility improved and the rain slowed to just a steady downpour. It was only while she was actually crossing the bridge that Sabrina felt any real misgivings. The river was not yet out of its banks but it was dangerously close, and the engorged waters were already even with the floor of the bridge. Then she was across the span and was able to relax for the remaining ten-mile drive to the Mendoza ranch.

Her eyes widened as she drove into the flagstone courtyard and took in the fountain and the imposing bulk of the white stucco Spanish mansion. The gracious hacienda was as remote from the homey comfort of the Bradford ranch as it was possible to get.

At the front entrance the car door was opened immediately by a young, white-clad Mexican servant carrying a large black umbrella. Then she was shepherded into the brilliantly lit entrance alcove and the doors were ceremoniously opened by another smiling servant, who divested her of her rainwear and escorted her to her host.

Señor Mendoza shook Sabrina's hand warmly. "It is such a pleasure for my wife and me to welcome you to our home," he said cordially. A small, plump man, he was dressed faultlessly in a dark, tailored business suit and gray silk tie. He looked more like a Wall Street banker than a prosperous rancher, Sabrina thought. The woman beside him, equally cosmopolitan, was thin with high, elegant cheekbones and silver wings in her stylishly coiffed dark hair. Her black dress had the understated elegance of an original.

"Jess and Sue send their apologies, Señor Mendoza," Sabrina said politely. "They were unable to come due to an emergency at the ranch."

Mendoza nodded understandingly. "The storm, yes? I hope it's nothing serious."

She shook her head. "Merely a precaution. Jess felt the south-basin herd should be shifted. He and David are doing it now."

"A sound move," Mendoza agreed. "I'm desolate that my friend Jess was unable to be here, but we feel fortunate he was able to send such a lovely deputy."

Señora Mendoza's cool hand, held out in gracious greeting, didn't convey the same sense of welcome, Sabrina thought, though her murmured acknowledgment was cordial enough.

"Come let me introduce you to our other guests."

Señor Mendoza took Sabrina's arm and ushered her into a dimly lit lounge, elegantly decorated in various shades of blue.

There were perhaps fifty people clustered around the room. Soft music came over a stereo system, and a waiter with a tray of drinks circled unobtrusively. For the next fifteen minutes Mendoza acted the conscientious host, introducing her with scrupulous courtesy to his obviously affluent, elegantly dressed guests.

The center of the lounge had been cleared for dancing and Sabrina found no lack of partners as the evening progressed. She especially enjoyed the attentions of Jaime Mendoza, a dark, solemn young man in his early twenties, whom the Señor had introduced with some pride as his only son. Sabrina found Jaime as courteous and charming as his father, if a little lacking in humor, and rather boyishly entranced by her red hair. She was beginning to wonder if she'd stayed long enough to fulfill the duty Sue had imposed, when there was a sudden stir at the door. She glanced casually in that direction, but as there were several people blocking the way she couldn't determine the cause of the disturbance.

She turned her wandering attention back to Jaime, with whom she'd been dancing, but his attention had also been distracted. "My father's guest of honor has finally arrived," he announced. "His private jet was delayed by the storm."

"Really," Sabrina replied disinterestedly. The arrival of another of Señor Mendoza's business associates was hardly earthshaking.

But the new arrival seemed to hold a fascination for Jaime. "He is a very important man. My father was flattered when he requested advice on purchasing commercial property in this area."

Sabrina nodded politely. "I'm sure your father's advice would be invaluable to any businessman."

"That is true," Jaime agreed seriously. "He's considered quite shrewd."

Sabrina hid a smile. Ah-h, the self-importance of the young.

"Pardon me, Señor Mendoza, I believe your father would like to speak to you." The low drawl stopped her breath and froze her blood. She stopped dancing so suddenly that Jaime looked down at her in surprise.

He turned to the man standing beside them. "Mr. Ben Raschid!" he exclaimed, smiling ingratiatingly, though obviously at a loss as to why so illustrious a guest would deliver a message ordinarily sent by a servant.

Alex Ben Raschid nodded in acknowledgment, and with one smooth movement pulled Sabrina out of the young man's arms and into his own. "You wouldn't want to leave the lady alone in the middle of the dance floor," he said, smiling wickedly. Jaime stood looking at them for a moment, only daring the slightest expression of suspicion to touch his features before turning and going in search of his father.

Alex propelled Sabrina's stiff body around the dance floor. The low voices of the other guests, the clink of glasses, the music, all seemed to exist outside her frame of reference. Her body moved mechanically in time with his; her mind was numb.

As if angry at her lack of response, Alex's arms tightened around her waist and she was pulled so close to him she could feel every line of his taut, masculine body as they moved to the music. His face was buried in her hair and she could feel his warm breath in her ear. "You've caused me a great deal of trouble, you know," he murmured, his hand rubbing sensuous circles in the small of her back.

She drew a deep, shuddering breath. "I assume this is not a coincidence."

"Hardly," he said, sounding quite amused.

"How did you know where to find me?" She threw back her head to look into his face.

"You were in the Mendoza box at the rodeo. I discovered from your friend Angelina that you and your lover had left town. She refused to tell me any more than that. The rest was a matter of probing and maneuvering."

"At which, I haven't a doubt, you're a past master."

"Yes," he said coolly, "I am."

"Then your investigation—excuse me, your 'probing,' as you put it—must have brought to light the fact that Jess Bradford isn't one of my lovers! I'm sorry to prove your assessment of my character wrong in this case. I'm sure it must have been a big disappointment to you."

"Jess Bradford may not be on your list," he growled, "but his son is evidently retaining his place in your affections." His hand tightened on her waist. "Are you still sleeping with him?"

"You bastard," Sabrina said deliberately. "I'm here because I want to be here, and it's no business of yours what I do." Her lips twisted. "Though I must admit you made it easier to come to a decision. I suddenly found I had a good deal of free time on my hands, thanks to your intervention."

"You know I would have given you a job," he said roughly. "You didn't have to run away with that damned cowboy." His dark eyes narrowed as he took in the angry emerald of her eyes, the defiant tilt of her chin. "But you weren't running away *with* him, were you, Sabrina?" he asked slowly. "You were running away *from* me. I frightened you in the office that day."

"No!" she snapped. He must never know that the real source of her fear of him was the power he held over her emotions. He had weapons enough in the battle being waged between them. She would not provide him with additional ammunition.

"I think 'yes,' " he said consideringly, his gaze raking her face, weighing the quivering lips and the uncertainty that lay behind the defiance in her eyes. "I meant to frighten you," he said. "Not enough to make you run away, just enough to keep you out of anyone else's bed until I'd gotten you into mine. You reacted a bit more strongly than I'd gauged."

"Why should I be frightened of you?" she asked shakily, her brave façade crumbling under the driving force of his personality. "I'm my own person. I have my own thoughts and my own goals. I run my life to suit myself, Alex Ben Raschid."

He smiled at her and she caught her breath. There was no mockery in the smile. It was as if, perceiving the victory to be his, he'd discarded all antagonism. It was a tender smile, enfolding her in its glowing warmth. Her eyes widened with surprise as they met his, and something passed between them that was at once as strong as an electric current and as delicate as a gossamer thread. Neither desire nor anger, that ephemeral touching, it was a rapport she could see was as disturbing to Alex as it was to her.

He pushed her head down against his shoulder and they moved silently to the music. She closed her eyes helplessly against the tide of heat that seemed to fill her every limb with a languor and sweetness that was unbelievably right. His hand was buried in her hair and he stroked it sensuously.

"Do you know why you should be afraid of me?" he asked huskily. "I'll tell you. I want you so much that I want to absorb you into myself. I want to be so close to you that there's no Sabrina Courtney any more, just an extension of Alex Ben Raschid. I want your thoughts, your emotions, and your body." She felt a shudder run through him. "Oh, yes, I want that body of yours," he said raggedly. "I haven't been able to think of anything else for the last two weeks. I keep seeing your hair spread out on that damn blanket and feeling your body move under mine." He felt the quiver that ran through her at his evocative words, and his lips brushed the silken skin at her temple, savoring the pulsebeat with the tip of his tongue. "I hate you for what you're doing to me. I can't get the scent and feel of you out of my mind. Would you like to know how many women I've taken to bed since you ran away?"

She would have pulled away from him, but he defeated her with merciless strength. "No, damn you, don't stiffen up on me. It's you I wanted, not them. A few of them were quite accomplished," he said roughly, "and God knows I wanted to get you out of my system. I thought they would erase this crazy hunger I have for you, but they didn't. After I'd finished with them, I still wanted you just as much. More. And toward the end it made me sick to touch them. I was like a damn eunuch."

The pain that his word evoked was incredible in its intensity. The thought of Alex in bed with another woman, making love to her, enjoying her accomplished caresses, their bodies wrapped together in a passionate embrace. Alex making another woman feel this dark magic that made her a helpless captive in his arms.

"Please. Let me go," she begged, trying to twist away, her eyes tormented. She felt if she stayed in his arms one more second she'd die of the agony he'd inflicted with such callous disregard.

"You haven't been listening, Sabrina," he said grimly. "Do you think I've told you all this to hurt you? We may both be damned before it's over, but I *can't* let you go!"

"Hurt me? You could never hurt me!" she denied wildly. "You have to care about someone to be hurt by them. You mean nothing to me, Alex Ben Raschid. You could have a hundred women and I wouldn't care!"

With a desperate wrench she broke away, and ignoring the curious stares of the other dancers stalked blindly from the room. She wanted only to get away from him, from the words that had torn the protective bandage from emotions now throbbing and raw as new wounds.

She ran down the hall, opened a door, and slipped inside. There were no lights on; she could see only the vague outlines of table and chairs in a formal dining room. She leaned against the closed door, welcoming the anonymity of the darkness as would an animal in pain. Her breath came in little, sobbing gasps as she let the realization roll over her. Oh God, she loved him!

She felt sick. She'd gone through so many emotions in the last few minutes she felt as though she were in shock. How had it happened? She'd fought so hard not to care for him. She'd told herself it was only physical, that he'd merely caught her imagination as any attractive man might have done. She'd tried to erase the memory of the tenderness that had surged through her that afternoon on the beach when he'd revealed his background. How she'd shuddered at the treatment of him by his parents! How soft and weak she'd gone when she'd glimpsed the great vulnerability hidden behind that tough façade. She'd tried to ignore those flashes of wry humor that appeared so unexpectedly. And she'd been scrupulously careful not to think about those rare moments when he'd enfolded her in that gentle, protective cloak of affection. She'd blocked it out, ignored it, rejected it with everything that was in her, but at the thought of him with another woman the truth had struck her with the force of a blow. She'd felt as angry and betrayed as if they'd been married a dozen years.

Her lips twisted bitterly in the darkness, the tears ran helplessly down her cheeks. Marriage? Permanence would have no place in Alex Ben Raschid's scheme of things. He wanted her now, but how long would it be after he possessed her before his passion faded and he went back to those other women he'd spoken of so callously? He'd never mentioned love, only raging hunger, possessiveness, blind and overwhelming desire. He admitted to obsession, but not love.

Lord, how stupid could she get? As if she didn't have enough problems in her life she had to fall in love with a man as dominant and demanding as Alex. Even if she accepted the little he had to give her, he would claim every particle of her emotional and physical response for the time they would be together. How could she possibly grant him that when there was David to think about?

She wiped her eyes childishly with the back of her hand. It was too late to stop herself from loving Alex, but she must find some way to keep him from twisting her life so she'd never be able to straighten it out again.

She shivered as she remembered how difficult it had been to resist his sexual expertise when she'd thought what she was feeling was only physical attraction. How much harder it would be now that she'd admitted to herself he could be the most important part of her life. One thing was certain, Alex's mere physical presence would quell any resistance she could make. For she would be fighting not only him, but herself. Her love for him would be as formidable an ally as he could wish, for she wanted desperately to belong to him in all ways.

She reached a shaking hand to her temple, which was beginning to ache fiercely. She was so broken and confused that she couldn't seem to think straight. She certainly couldn't risk seeing Alex until she could defend herself against him. She would have to leave at once before she saw him again.

As she reentered the living room, she was immediately approached by Señor Mendoza. "Sabrina," he said, "I have been looking for you."

Her smile was strained as she said, "I wasn't feeling very well and I wanted to get some air. I thought it might help my head, but I'm afraid it hasn't. I'll have to go home."

The sympathy in Mendoza's dark eyes deepened as he took in the paleness of her cheeks. "It's true, you don't look well at all," he said, "but you're not to go home tonight. That is why we were searching for you. Jess called and said he was worried about the bridge supports. He would prefer that you not try to cross the bridge in the dark tonight. I naturally told him we would be happy to have you as our guest. My wife will show you to a guest room."

"I'm staying here tonight?" she repeated dazedly.

"It will be our pleasure," he assured her. "But why don't you sit down. I will get you a drink." He disappeared into the crowd.

She stood there, frozen, her eyes automatically searching the guests until she spied the figure she was looking for. Alex stood in a corner, unaware of her, absently looking down at his drink, while the man talking to him was eagerly explaining something to him. Her gaze went lovingly over the tall, virile strength of him while a tenderness filled her that was frightening in its intensity. Stay in the same house with Alex tonight? The intimacy of the mere idea was wildly appealing.

Suddenly he looked up and their eyes met across the room. Her breath caught in her throat. He put down his drink on a nearby table, left the man he was talking to as if the poor fellow didn't exist. The moment she realized he was coming toward her, she became panic stricken. She couldn't face him. Not now. She turned and ran from the room, down the hall, and out the front door.

Six

The rain was falling steadily, and the young servant was still on duty outside with his big, black umbrella. She brushed him aside and ran out to the far end of the courtyard where the station wagon was parked. She was wet through in seconds but she didn't even feel the cold. Her only thought was flight. She jumped into the driver's seat, turned on the ignition, and in a moment she was driving out of the courtyard and onto the access road as the boy in the vestibule stared bewilderedly after her.

The panic goading her gradually abated as she continued to drive. This had been a crazy thing to do, driving off into the night like some soap-opera heroine. Driving the car made her feel more in control, though, and slowly the ability to think logically returned. Where was she going? She couldn't drive around in the rain all night. She certainly couldn't return to the Mendoza house. She'd left her purse and belongings when she'd panicked, so she couldn't drive into town and stay at a hotel. There was only one course of action: to try the bridge. She'd drive to the approach and stop and take a look at it. If it appeared safe, she'd go for it. If not, she'd have to resign herself to parking somewhere along the road and spending the night in the station wagon.

The pounding of the pain in her head seemed to keep tempo with the rain on the roof. As she drove the rain dwindled to a fine drizzle, and now that visibility was improved her foot pressed harder and harder on the accelerator; the car flew along the country road. The back of her neck was rigid with tension as she crested the last hill and started down the other side, her eyes straining to make out the dim outlines of the bridge in the darkness.

She didn't notice the water until the station wagon's wheels hit it with such violence that muddy water sprayed in all directions, completely obscuring the windshield! For one terrible moment she thought she might overshoot and drive straight into the icy waters of the river. But the engine cut off abruptly, and she hurriedly rolled down the glass and stuck her head out the window. She was surrounded by water almost up to the car door handles.

The Concho had obviously overflowed the basin at the bottom of the hill, and her car had landed right in the middle of the flooded road. She leaned her head on the steering wheel in sheer frustration. She was stuck, she realized dismally. There was no possibility of backing the station wagon out. The engine was no doubt thoroughly flooded.

She could see the muddy, yellow water begin to trickle in a thin stream under the door; it would be only a matter of minutes before the interior of the car was flooded.

She gave a resigned sigh as she realized there was only one thing to do. She'd have to abandon the car and climb back up the hill on foot. Once she reached the upper slopes, she'd be safe from the rising water, and only have to worry about finding shelter or stopping a passing motorist.

Neither prospect was very promising, she thought gloomily. She was miles from the nearest inhabited ranch house and this particular road led only to the bridge and the few ranches beyond.

She slipped off her flimsy high heels and threw them on the back seat. She rolled down the window as far as it would go, then wriggled feet first through the narrow opening. She gave a little gasp as she immediately sank into the cold, muddy water which swirled around her waist. She took a few tentative steps away from the car; it was hard going. Mud sucked at her stocking feet. She slogged ahead with determination, spurred on by thoughts of the poisonous water moccasins inhabiting the river banks, and she was out of the water and mounting the lower reaches of the hill in double-quick time. Chilled and reeling from the ordeal, she could at least be grateful that the falling rain was washing away the filthy scum of the river water.

As she approached the top of the hill, she suddenly saw the beam of headlights coming fast up the other side. Without thinking of anything but preventing the driver from coming to the same fate she had, she ran to the middle of the road, waving her arms urgently. "Stop! You've got to stop."

As the car crested the hill, she realized it was traveling too fast to halt before it reached her. She stood paralyzed in the beam of the oncoming headlights knowing the car would hit her but unable to move.

The driver also must have realized the hopelessness of attempting to stop because he turned the wheel violently to the right. Miraculously only the left fender brushed her, throwing her to the ground. The car plowed into the shallow ditch at the side of the road. She struggled to her feet, racing to the wrecked car and whimpering over and over to herself, "Oh please let him be all right. Please, don't let him be hurt." Then with a surge of relief she realized the driver's door was opening. "Oh, thank God," she gasped, as she reached the car.

"You'd do well to pray. I'm on the verge of murdering you, Sabrina," Alex said grimly, getting out. His face was pale with emotion and there was a small cut at his hairline that was bleeding profusely.

She wasn't even surprised. It seemed a logical extension of this nightmare evening for this to be Alex. "I thought I'd killed you," she said numbly, conscious of a sudden weakness in her knees.

"You damn near did, and yourself, too, you crazy woman," he snapped. "What kind of trick did you think you were pulling, standing in the middle of the road trying to flag someone down on a night like this?" He grabbed her shoulders. "I almost killed *you*!"

She collapsed against him, sobbing, burrowing against him as if he were the only security she would ever know. He stood still, holding her softness to him securely, but she could tell by the unyielding tightness of his hard, muscular body that he was still shaken and angry.

"It was the flooding," she gasped between sobs. "The valley is flooded at the bottom of the hill. I was trying to warn you."

"So you almost killed us both," he said dryly. "Not the brightest solution."

"I'm sorry," she whispered miserably, burrowing closer to his warmth. "You're right. It was a stupid thing to do."

He was perfectly still for a long moment and when he spoke there was a note of surprise in his voice. "You must be in worse shape than I thought," he said. "I've never heard you so docile. Let me take a look at you." He pushed her away and surveyed her critically for a moment, taking in the bare feet, the sodden clothes clinging to her shivering body, her hair plastered to her head and hanging in lank strands about her pale face. He swore softly and fluently as he took off his suit jacket and wrapped it around her. "You little fool, you're half drowned."

The jacket was warm from his body and she hugged it to herself gratefully. Then she noticed guiltily that the rain was wetting him almost as thoroughly as it had her and he was hurt and bleeding as well. She started to take off the jacket and hand it back to him.

"Keep it on," he ordered. "You'll be damn lucky if you don't get pneumonia as it is." He knelt and peered under the car for a moment, then straightened and said disgustedly, "The back axle is broken. I thought I heard it give when I hit the ditch."

"You can't drive it?" she asked.

"Not likely," he said, grimacing. "And we certainly can't stay here. We need warmth and shelter." He reached into the car, turned off the lights, and then slammed the door. "This is your territory, is there a ranch or a cabin nearby?"

Sabrina shook her head. "The Mendoza Ranch is closest and that's almost ten miles, and the Bradford spread is across the bridge."

"A barn? A cave? Think!"

"There's a vacant ranch house about a half mile from here," she said slowly. "The Circle C."

"Which way?" he asked.

She pointed wordlessly, and he took her arm and set off briskly, half carrying her along. By the time they'd reached the turnoff to the ranch, she was breathless but the exercise had warmed her considerably.

"Not very imposing," Alex commented, as they reached the front porch of the cedar ranch house, which was at the top of a rise overlooking the highway. "But at least we'll be dry. We'll have to break in if we can't find an open window."

"That won't be necessary," Sabrina said calmly. She reached under the window sill of the left front window, withdrew a magnetic key box, and extracted the front door key. She opened the door and turned to meet his questioning stare. "I used to live here," she said simply. "When my parents died, Jess Bradford bought the property, but he had no use for the house itself. It's been deserted for a number of years."

"You're full of surprises," Alex said, following her into the hall.

The dark house looked terribly desolate, Sabrina thought sadly, looking around. All the furnishings and mementos that had made the place dear to her were stored under covers in the Bradfords' barn. Only unwanted pieces too dilapidated to be of any real use were left—a couch in the living room, a broken chair in the kitchen. The old drapes had also been left at the windows, as they hadn't fit the windows of the apartment in Houston. Everything was covered with a thick layer of dust.

Alex fumbled in his pocket for his lighter. The small flame helped him appraise their surroundings. He disappeared into the room to the left of the hall. "There's a fireplace in here," he called briskly. "If we can make a fire, we can at least dry off." He was taking charge again as he always would, his vitality bringing the dead house back to life.

"There should be some wood in the wood box in the cellar," Sabrina offered quietly, watching as he strode from room to room, reconnoitering the situation for assets and liabilities so he could grasp and control it.

"You supply our every need," he said lightly. "I don't suppose there is anything you could change into upstairs?" She shook her head silently. "Too bad," he said, and striding to the living room he ripped the drapes from the window and tossed them to her. "Get out of those wet clothes. All of them," he ordered. "I'll get that wood and start a fire."

She stared at the cream and chocolate-striped drapes in her hand and smiled, recalling a similar scene from *Gone With the Wind*. Well, she wasn't Scarlett O'Hara, she thought wryly, and she didn't even have a needle and thread, so there would be no fabulous gown created from these drapes!

She shed her wet clothes hurriedly and, wrapping one of the panels around her body sarong-like, belted it at the waist with one of the ties. She wrinkled her nose in distaste at the musty smell as she tossed the other panel around her shoulders like a shawl.

Alex entered the room carrying a load of wood, and without a glance at her deposited it near the fireplace and set about building a fire. Soon it was blazing brightly and he took the time then to wipe the wound on his forehead. Now that it was no longer bleeding, it appeared to be only a small cut, she noticed with relief.

He looked her over and his mouth went up at the corners. "Very fetching."

"Well, you're no Rhett Butler either," she said crossly, knowing she looked a sight.

He grinned at the reference. "Well, frankly, my dear, I don't give a damn," he mimicked in a fair Gable imitation.

She chuckled.

"Come over here," he commanded, putting some additional kindling on the blaze. She obediently crossed to him and stood with her hands out, basking in the warmth of the fire.

"Not too close," he warned. "There's no screen." He rose lithely and, crossing to the dilapidated, dark brown couch against the wall, he stripped it of the four large seat cushions and tossed them in front of the fireplace.

"Your hair is still wet," he said, frowning accusingly as she settled down in front of the blaze.

"It will dry," she said contentedly, soaking up the heat from the fire like a contented kitten.

He stood up and left the room, coming back with two pieces of cloth that she recognized as the kitchen curtains. She chuckled. "What would you have done if we'd taken all the curtains with us?"

"I'd have managed," he said confidently, and she knew it was true. He would always manage to wrest whatever he wanted from the world. He was that kind of man. He knelt beside her. "Bend over."

She obeyed and he briskly toweled her hair, not stopping until it was almost dry. Sitting a little away from her on the cushion, he started to dry his own hair. "You grew up here?" he asked, his dark gaze on her face.

She nodded, staring into the fire dreamily. "I was born and raised in this house," she said softly. "Then, when my parents died, I moved in with the Bradfords and later to Houston when I went away to college. But I always wanted to come back. I'm not really a city girl."

"You seem to have acclimated remarkably well."

She knew he was referring to her supposed affair with David, but decided to ignore it. As if he, too, were reluctant to enter a discordant note in the harmony of the moment, Alex went on to other subjects. They talked for a long time, with an amazingly easy intimacy, and when a silence finally did lapse, it was deliciously comfortable.

"Why have you fought me, Sabrina?" he asked suddenly. "I can give you almost anything in the world. What do you want?"

She looked at him, his dark, tousled hair, the white shirt open to the waist revealing the strong, corded muscles and the springy pelt of virile, dark hair on his chest. You. Only you, she thought.

She drew her knees up and rested her chin on them, gazing dreamily into the fire. "I guess I want what my parents had," she said softly. "I want to build a good life. I want roots and an affection that will only get stronger as the years pass."

"Your parents must have been unusual people," he said quietly.

"No, they were really very ordinary people. They just loved each other," she said huskily.

They were both lost in their own thoughts and there was a long silence in the room. The only sound was the crackle of the burning logs and the light rhythm of their breathing.

"Sabrina?"

Her eyes flew to his, startled out of her meditation. And what she saw there caused her to draw a sharp, shallow breath.

"You know you're going to belong to me tonight," he stated simply.

She had known for some time, she thought calmly. There was only one fitting conclusion to this intimacy of their time together. "Yes," she whispered, lost in the darkness of his eyes. "I know that, Alex."

"Come here," he said, holding out his hand, and she obeyed him wordlessly. She knelt facing him, not touching him, just looking into his eyes and waiting. Her hair was a wild, flaming areole around her face, her eyes deep emerald in the flickering light, and her lips parted in unknowing anticipation. His gaze lingered over every feature like a caress.

He reached out slowly and pushed the improvised shawl away from her shoulders. His eyes fixed with intent absorption on the satin of her shoulders as his hands closed on them almost gingerly and he brought her carefully, surely into his arms.

"Alex," she said huskily, her eyes suddenly shadowed with doubt. "It's not just because of that passion you mentioned you had for redheads, is it? You don't have to pretend you care for me, but I'd like to know I mean more to you than that." Her lips were trembling as she tried to smile. "I always have hated to be just one of a crowd."

One large hand reached out slowly to wrap itself in her long, silky tresses. "God, no, love," he said thickly. "I've never felt anything like this before in my life." His eyes were ebony stains in the bronze tautness of his face and his expression was oddly grave. "I've been thinking quite a bit lately about those redheads in my past. I remember reading a poem once about 'the mystic memory of things to come.'" His hand was combing gently through her hair in a deliciously soothing motion. "I've had a crazy notion since I met you that maybe there is such a thing. Perhaps I was searching for my own sweet redhead among that faceless throng." A tender smile curved his lips. "You certainly took your time about appearing on the scene, sweetheart. I'd almost given up."

Sabrina felt her throat tighten achingly and for a moment she didn't think she could speak. She'd expected a mocking reassurance, not this moving gift he'd given her with such simple eloquence.

"That sounds remarkably romantic for a man who believes love is a word for children," she said shakily.

"It's all your fault," he said, tilting her head to look into her eyes. "I never wanted to feel like this about any woman. Since the moment I saw you, I've been trying to convince myself that it was just lust I felt for you." He touched the softness of her lips with a finger so gentle that she had a fleeting memory of David and his golden Miranda. "God knows, I feel enough of that, but there's more, too. I want to *cherish* you." He shook his head helplessly. "Lord, that's an old-fashioned word, but it's the only one that fits. I want to care for you. I want to wrap you in all the gauze of tenderness and all the velvet of gentleness that still exists in this harsh world of ours. I can't bear to think of you in pain or need." He took a deep breath. "Will you let me cherish you, Sabrina?"

"Oh, yes," she said huskily, feeling a surge of love and delight that made her dizzy. "I want that, Alex."

He slowly pushed her down on the cushions and his hands were shaking a little as he undid the tie at her waist and carefully opened the cream and brown folds, spreading them on the cushion like silken butterfly wings. He groaned as he stared down at the graceful curves and shadows revealed to him in the flickering firelight. "You're all flame and snow and a sweet, burning grace."

Unable to wait any longer, he left her for a moment to rapidly strip off the rest of his own clothing and rejoined her, pressing her deep into the cushions, their bodies flesh to flesh so that she could feel his bold arousal. How much more graceful and beautiful was his hard muscular beauty than her own soft curves, she thought dreamily. She hadn't realized until now that broad, supple shoulders tapered to a slim middle and tight, muscular buttocks could have this almost singing symmetry.

He slowly lowered his lips with a deliberateness that caused her to hold her breath in anticipation. Then his warm tongue flicked out to caress one taut nipple and she stiffened with unbearable tension. She could feel her breasts swell and harden beneath that teasing tongue as if on command. Alex's hands closed around the fullness of those burgeoning mounds, weighing them in his palms, while his lips suckled lightly at the sensitive nipples. She made a little whimpering sound deep in her throat and he glanced up with a flicker of satisfaction. "That's right, darling," he said hoarsely. "Burn for me. Tell me how much you want me."

But she couldn't tell him. It was all too much. She could only make those little cries of desire and entreaty as his teeth pulled gently at the taut, pink rosette while his hands began a rhythmic kneading motion that was incredibly erotic. Her hands reached out blindly, running over the smooth, brawny copper of his shoulders to encircle his neck and pull him closer to her breasts.

She felt him shudder against her. "Touch me," he ordered raggedly. "I love to feel your hands on me. Do you know how often I've lain in bed and thought about your hands caressing me, loving me." His own hand reached up to take one of her hands from his shoulder. He brought it to his lips, his tongue stroking her palm. She shivered, her breath catching in her throat. She hadn't known that soft, vulnerable hollow could possibly generate this tingling awareness in every nerve in her body. Then, his dark eyes gazing compulsively into hers, he carried her hand to that taut hardness of his belly, holding it firmly against his warmth. "Touch me," he urged again.

She wanted to touch him. The hard flesh of his stomach had an almost magnetic attraction for her. The light springy dusting of hair beneath her palm felt delightfully abrasive as her hand moved over him curiously. His body was so different from her own, she thought absently. So hard where she was soft, so rough where she was smooth, so aggressive where she was pliant. Almost without thinking her hand curled about that warm aggression, holding him with loving tenderness.

She dimly heard Alex inhale sharply and his body bucked convulsively. She glanced up swiftly in concern. "Did I hurt you?" she asked.

"Oh, I'm hurting all right," he gasped, his lips curving wryly. "But for heaven's sake don't stop!"

Her hand tightened around him and he bucked again, his eyes closing while a shudder went through every muscle of his body. "Maybe you'd better stop after all," he said hoarsely. "I can't take much more of this." He opened his eyes and they were glazed and intent. "And I want to touch you, too, love." He reached down and gently removed her hand from him. "Lord, I feel cold and lonely without you," he whispered, taking a deep breath. "I can't wait to have your sweet warmth chaining me to you." He swiftly parted her legs and slipped a hand between them, the tips of his fingers moving in light, rhythmic patterns on the inside of her thighs, until she could feel the center of her being tighten and convulse in tempo with that tantalizing touch. She was writhing beneath his manipulations, her breath coming in little gasps, and she instinctively tried to close her thighs to capture and hold those maddening hands that were giving her only enough to drive her out of her mind.

"No, little flame," he said softly, looking up at her face, his own expression beautifully sensual. "Don't close me out." His fingers moved intricately and she suddenly cried out, her body arching in that age-old offering of woman, as an incredible sensation shot through her. "God, you're responsive." His hand moved again. "And so fantastically tight. I can't wait even a moment more for you. Are you ready for me, love?"

Was she ready for him? She felt as if she were going up like a skyrocket with every word he was speaking, with every motion of those magical, tormenting fingers.

He didn't wait for an answer, but gently widened the opening of her thighs and leaned forward to kiss her lingeringly on the mouth, his tongue entering to explore the moist interior with a hunger that took her breath, and caused her own tongue to seek his with an equal urgency.

Then he was surging forward and her cry of surprise and pain was smothered against his lips. He lifted his head, his expression dazed. "So tight," he murmured. His eyes widened incredulously. "My God . . ." he breathed, his gaze flying to her face.

Why was he waiting, she wondered wildly. The pain had only lasted for an instant and now this feeling of being beautifully, fantastically full of him was absolutely mind-blowing. But as much as she had of him, she wanted more.

"Alex, please," she gasped. "I *need* you."

There was an expression of almost pained pleasure on his face. "Dear Lord, and I need you," he choked. "I'm burning up, sweetheart." Then he was moving, in a driving rhythm that succeeded in satisfying that need while creating a feverishly molten new one.

She had the sensation that she was falling off

the edge of the world into a dazzling place of sheer, tactile pleasure. His hot words breathed in her ear were almost as arousing as his driving body, urging her to move with him, telling her how much her breasts pleased him, how exciting he found the way she clung to him.

Then the tension was mounting toward the final explosion of sensation, and she instinctively arched to meet each forceful thrust with an eagerness that caused Alex to close his eyes in an agony of pleasure. How beautiful he was with that expression of blind sensuality on his face, she thought dazedly. It filled her with an almost primitive satisfaction that it was the enjoyment of *her* body that brought him this exquisite torment. That every movement of her hips, every touch of her hands could cause this strong man to gasp and shudder with the need that was tearing them both apart.

Her legs tightened around him, her hands curving around his hips to cup the hard, sculptured line of his buttocks in her palms. He felt so *good*. Then she was pulling him toward her, matching his rhythm with one of her own.

Alex's eyes flicked open and he was gazing down at her, his dark eyes glazed. "God, little flame," he gasped, the bronze muscles of his chest heaving with the force of his breathing. She could see the pulse in his throat racing like a triphammer. "It's too good. It can't be real."

But it was real, gloriously, excitingly real. And when the tension snapped and they were tossed headlong into the final storm of feeling that was like no other, that was real, too. There was nothing less dreamlike on the face of the earth than the man above her who cried out in hoarse, almost guttural satisfaction, and clutched her to him while the whole world exploded around her and left her clinging to him like a child in the darkness.

She was vaguely conscious, in that moment of dazed euphoria, of Alex shifting positions to lie beside her on the cushions, enfolding her in the shelter of his arms and pushing her head into the hollow of his shoulder. She could feel the thunder of his heart beneath her ear and the light dew of perspiration on the dark golden skin that was her pillow. Her tongue darted out in lazy curiosity to taste the brawny smoothness of his shoulder. It was warm and slightly salty, and somehow deliciously exciting even in this moment of complete repletion.

Evidently Alex also found it exciting, for the thunder accelerated beneath her ear and he drew a deep breath that was more of a shudder. "God, don't do that, love," he gasped, his arms tightening around her. "Give me a couple of minutes to recover before you try any experiments that might lead down that particular road."

"I was just curious," Sabrina said dreamily, nestling her head back and forth on his shoulder like a kitten on a favorite satin cushion. "I wanted to know how you taste."

She could feel his chuckle reverberating beneath her ear, and his hand was gently stroking the silky hair at her temple. "And did you enjoy it, little flame?"

"Oh yes, very much," she said softly. Then she lifted her head to look into his face with bright, curious eyes. "Do you taste like that all over?"

He stared at her for a moment in blank surprise and then started to laugh, shaking his head in rueful amusement. "I haven't the slightest idea, but I'd be delighted for you to find out for yourself." He held up a hand. "In a few minutes, that is."

Sabrina frowned. "Am I being too aggressive,

Alex?" she asked uncertainly, her green eyes darkening to a troubled emerald as she gazed down at him.

"Lord no, sweetheart," Alex said huskily, his hand combing through the silky length of her hair with an almost sensual pleasure. "It's just that you're such a surprise to me that you've caught me off guard. I've never had the experience of wanting a woman again almost the instant I've left her. It's shaken me up a little." He pulled her lips down to meet his own in a long, soft kiss of dizzying sweetness. "There's not a thing in the world wrong with you, little flame," he said thickly when their lips parted. "There couldn't be anything more perfect than what we've just had together."

"I didn't think so," she said lightly, trying to hide how his words had moved her. "But it's always nice to have one's opinion confirmed by a man of your experience."

"Experience," Alex repeated slowly, his body stiffening against her own. His expression darkened grimly as he gazed up into her bewildered face. "I'd forgotten about that." With a swift movement he shifted her aside and was rolling off the cushions away from her. He snatched up the silky drapery he'd removed so eagerly such a short time before and tossed it to her. "Cover up," he said tersely. "We have some talking to do."

"Talking?" Sabrina asked warily.

She gazed down at the cream silk on her lap for a moment before she slowly shook out the folds and wrapped the length around her like a cloak. His words as well as his sudden rejection had shocked her out of the dazzling physical euphoria she'd been feeling only seconds before. She lifted a shaking hand to brush a lock of hair away from her face and moistened her lips nervously. She supposed she should be grateful that Alex had brought the real world back into focus for her, but instead she felt only an aching sense of loss.

Her gaze ran lingeringly over him as he sat naked in the firelight, a discreet distance from her own position on the cushion. He'd made no effort to veil his own nudity, she noticed with a tiny thread of resentment. He lit one of his slender brown cigarettes and inhaled deeply, his eyes determinedly fixed on the blazing logs as he drew up his knees and locked his arms loosely around them.

"Don't you think you owe me an explanation?" Alex asked finally, darting her a glance as stormy as black lightning. He took another pull on the cigarette. "Is that cowboy you live with gay?"

"What?" Sabrina said blankly, then swift color pinked her cheeks. This was zooming back to reality with a vengeance. She straightened slowly and drew the drapery about her almost defensively. "No, I don't think I owe you an explanation," she said with equal sharpness. "If you're referring to the fact that I was a virgin, it's no one's business but my own."

"The hell it's not," Alex said roughly, turning to face her and tossing his half-smoked cigarette into the flames. "I regard it as very much my business. It's not every day I make love to a woman I've been given to understand has been living with a man for over two years and find she's green as grass."

"I'm sorry to disappoint you," Sabrina said tartly. "Perhaps your next seduction will live up to your expectations."

"Don't be ridiculous," he said impatiently. "You know very well I nearly went crazy loving you. We were completely fantastic together." He frowned. "It's just that I've run into something that I don't understand at all." His lips tightened. "I don't like not understanding even the tiniest thing about you, Sabrina. It makes me damned nervous. Now what the hell is Bradford to you?"

She smiled sadly. "I told you before, Alex," she said quietly. "I have a commitment to him. I think that's really all you have to know."

"And I told you, you'd have to forget about it." His voice was sharp as a glittering scalpel. "The bond between you can't be all that strong if he was able to keep his hands off you while he was living in the same apartment." His lips twisted. "Two years! I wouldn't have lasted two minutes in the same circumstances! He doesn't have any leaning toward the priesthood by any chance?"

"No," she said wearily. "You don't understand, Alex, and at the moment I don't feel in the mood to make explanations. David is part of my life and there's no reason why you should be allowed to dissect that particular aspect of my existence just because we shared a rather unique physical experience." She drew a deep, steadying breath. "We both know what happened tonight has no real bearing on our everyday lives. We each have our own paths to walk and tomorrow this probably won't even seem real."

"But, it *was* real, damn it," he said moodily, "and I don't agree tonight is an isolated episode out of time. What we had just now, we can have again, and a hell of a lot more. You're crazy if you think this physical chemistry between us is commonplace attraction."

"I don't deny that it's more than that," Sabrina said huskily, glancing away from the burnished copper beauty of his naked figure by the fire. God, this was painful. Each phrase she spoke was tearing at her raw emotions like the flick of a whip. She'd known it would be a mistake to commit her body to Alex in this ultimate physical surrender. Why else had she panicked and run away? Well, the time for running was over. "All I'm saying is that it isn't enough. Sex is all very well and good, and it may be sufficient for the type of relationship you have in mind"—she drew a deep, shaky breath—"but I need more than that, and I don't believe you're capable of giving it."

"I can give you anything in this whole damn world," Alex said roughly. "I told you that before. Name it."

She shook her head, her long lashes lowered to mask her pain. "Will you give me your trust, Alex Ben Raschid?" she asked softly. "Not just for a day or a week, but forever? Will you give me your laughter and your friendship as well as your passion?" She tried to smile. "You see, the price *is* too high for you. And it would be too high for me as well if I found you couldn't meet it after I'd committed myself."

There was a moment of tension-fraught silence. "I'd try," Alex said gruffly, and her gaze flew back to him in surprise. "We've already established that I haven't an overabundance of faith in the human race, but, by God, I'd give it my best shot. As for the other, how can I promise you friendship when all I want to do is come back over there and have you wrap those lovely golden legs around me and bring me home to you." He ignored the little gasp she gave and continued tersely, "Friendship has to grow and you're not willing to give me the time for that growth." His expression was oddly stern. "I don't think you're long on trust yourself, Sabrina."

"Perhaps not," she agreed quietly. "Your actions since the night we first met haven't been calculated to inspire me with that particular emotion. You frightened me." Her eyes met his with a directness that was like a challenge. "But don't think you'll be able to accomplish that feat again, Alex.

I've been acting as insipid and wishy-washy as a mid-Victorian virgin and I assure you it's not my nature to be so meek. Like you, I was caught off guard. I'm usually not so easily intimidated."

There was a flicker of tenderness in the darkness of his eyes and a thread of pride in his voice as he said lightly, "If that's a warning, little flame, then I'm the one that will probably be intimidated. If you're going to display more independence and defiance than you have to date, I'll have my work cut out for me just keeping you from dominating *me*."

Sabrina could feel a reluctant smile tugging at her lips, despite the gravity of the moment. The idea of Alex being dominated by anyone, much less her, was laughable. "I don't think we need worry about that," she said.

"I'm not so sure," he said, frowning. "Now that you have this hold on me, I may have a hell of a lot to worry about."

"Hold?" she asked, her eyes widening in surprise.

His expression had darkened moodily. "I thought I was obsessed by you before, but it's nothing to what I feel now that I've had you. Desire can be a very powerful whip to hold over a man. I don't appreciate your having that kind of power over me."

Sabrina could feel her mouth drop open in surprise before it snapped shut and she glared at him with angry impatience. "For heaven's sake, Alex, could anything illustrate how far we are apart than that asinine remark? I have no intention of wielding any emotional whips and I certainly don't want any so-called power over you. Why don't you just admit there's no possibility of your ever being able to trust me? It would be a great deal less painful for both of us."

"The hell it would!" His dark eyes flickered

angrily. "Okay, so I backslid a little. I said I'd try, not that it would be easy. For God's sake, give me a chance. I told you we need time. *I* need time, blast it!"

"How much time?" Sabrina asked wearily, feeling the aching pain surge through her now that her anger and indignation were ebbing away. "I'm afraid I'm not willing to give you a great deal, Alex. You could hurt me too badly in the interim."

"You may not want to wield the whip but you have quite a natural talent for snapping it, Sabrina," he said dryly. "Will you give me four days to convince you that what we have is worth keeping? It's not as long as I'd like but I think I can make it do."

"Four days," she repeated softly, gazing at him with a yearning tenderness she found impossible to conceal. She had little hope that the time he asked would yield any lasting resolution to their problems. Yet she desperately wanted to wrest those four precious days for herself. Would it be too much to ask for that time with Alex before she once more resumed her responsibilities?

His raking glance read and deciphered that softening, and he moved with swift aggressiveness to take advantage. "Four days," he said coaxingly, his voice like dark velvet over the words. "Give me four days and I promise you'll never want to leave me again, Sabrina. I won't even mention that damn cowboy during the entire time. It'll be just you and me starting out fresh and new. You can teach me to trust, and I'll teach you what that lovely body of yours was meant for."

His glance was a scorching brand as it went over her with lingering thoroughness. Sabrina could feel her breasts swell beneath the cloth she was clutching around her, until the sensitive nipples rubbed with erotic abrasiveness against the material. She felt a hot, melting ache begin to throb in her loins and she shook her head in instinctive rejection as she realized how her body's need was interfering with what should be a coolly logical decision.

Alex evidently mistook her confusion for a negative decision, for his face hardened. "Don't turn me down, Sabrina," he warned with soft menace. "I'm not asking much, but I *will* have those four days!"

"Threats, Alex?" she asked quietly.

"I'm not above using threats if they will get me what I want," he said, his lips tightening. "I don't fool myself that personal threats would have any influence on you, but you're still very vulnerable. There are people out there in your world whom you care about."

He didn't have to say any more. There was that lethal menace about him that Donahue had honed to razor sharpness. "Not a very pleasant way to start a relationship," she said sadly.

"Do you think I wanted to threaten you?" he asked huskily, and, incredibly, there was a flicker of pain in his face. "Don't you know that I want to give you what you need from me? But, damn it, you've got to give me the opportunity to do it!"

"It seems I have little choice," she said. Then she shook her head impatiently. "I'm not being altogether honest, Alex," she said quietly. "I won't pretend to be a victim when I'm nothing of the sort. I would have given you those four days anyway, but you didn't give me the chance, did you?"

"That's very generous of you," he said slowly, and there was no trace of sarcasm in his voice. "Will you be equally honest and admit it's what you want, too?"

"Yes, I'll admit it's what I want," she said faintly.

His eyes were narrowed on her with a hot intimacy that was causing her heart to accelerate and her chest to tighten with emotion. Her tongue ran over her lower lip nervously. "I want *you*, Alex."

Suddenly he was beside her on the cushion. "Then take me, Sabrina," he urged huskily. "Do you know that little pink tongue has darted out and teased the hell out of me at least three times during the past few minutes? I don't think you were even aware of it. My God, what a waste when I'm crazy to have you do that to me." He leaned forward so that their lips were almost brushing. "Give me your tongue, little flame."

Her lips parted and her tongue slowly caressed the full warm curve of his lower lip, before licking hungrily at the corners of his firm mouth like the flame he had called her.

Then Alex's tongue was darting out to touch her own in a hundred glancing kisses that were like an erotic minuet. She felt as if she were on fire, every inch of flesh on her body exquisitely sensitive, even though as yet only their tongues were touching.

Alex's hands were on her shoulders and he was brushing the drapery impatiently aside. One gentle hand was closing around her breast while the other reached between her thighs in a bold assault that robbed her of breath. There was something she had wanted to ask him, but for a moment she couldn't remember what it was through the sensual haze that was enveloping them. Then he was pushing her gently onto her back on the cushions and coming over her with an aroused urgency that caused her to give a little gasp of surprised pleasure.

"Alex," she asked breathlessly. "The four days. Where are we going to spend them?"

"At the moment I'm not at all sure if we'll ever

get away from in front of this fireplace," he muttered thickly, as his lips lowered to nibble teasingly at one engorged nipple. "Let's talk about it later, little flame. Now I want to see you burn for me again."

She was already burning for him, she thought feverishly. He was right, there would be time to talk later. This was the only thing of importance in the universe at the moment. She pulled him down eagerly into her embrace.

Seven

Alex was up before she awoke and had flagged down a Mexican farm worker in an ancient rusty pickup. How he convinced the old man not only to wait until he had brought her from the ranch house, but also to drive them to the Corpus Christi Airport, she could only guess.

He had ignored all her protests against going to the airport in her disheveled condition, that she must contact the Bradfords and Señor Mendoza and let them know she was all right, that she couldn't just fly off blindly to some unknown destination.

"You can call the Bradfords from the airport," he said arrogantly, dispensing with her objections one by one. "Clancy Donahue will contact Mendoza. He's waiting at the Corpus Christi Airport with the Lear jet. You can get everything you need to last you for a few days at the airport shops." He smiled with a teasing intimacy that brought hot color to her cheeks and a boneless melting to her limbs. "You won't need very much. After last night, I may not let you wear a stitch for the entire time I have you in my power, woman."

"That may prove a little embarrassing unless you intend to spend the next few days at a nudist colony," Sabrina said dryly.

He shook his head. "Not a nudist colony," he said, an impish grin lighting the darkness of his face. "Though the idea has definite possibilities." He cocked his head as if pretending to consider. "No, I'd be much too jealous to share your charms with a bunch of gawking strangers. We'll just have to settle for Londale's Folly."

"Londale's Folly?" Sabrina asked blankly.

"It's a private island owned by Sedikhan Petroleum, in the gulf about eighty miles south of Houston," he said briefly. "*Very* private. I have a house there." There was a hint of grimness in the glance he shot her. "I'm not taking any chances of your changing your mind about allotting me my full time with you. You'd find it a bit difficult swimming back to Houston from the Folly."

"Your faith in my word is touching," Sabrina said, with an ironic smile.

"That's what you're supposed to teach me, remember?" he asked lightly.

The pickup was permitted immediate entry by the security officer at the high, wire gate to the field, and chugged directly to the Lear jet at the far end of the tarmac. The pilot, Don Whitehead, opened the door to admit them and didn't bat an eye at Sabrina's rumpled clothing and bare feet when Alex introduced her. Well, why should he, Sabrina thought, knowing a twinge of the green-eyed monster. Piloting a man with Ben Raschid's penchant for lovely bedmates must have accustomed him to seeing a good many women in strange states of dress.

"What's the matter now?" Alex asked impatiently, noticing the tiny frown creasing her forehead after the pilot had retired to the cockpit.

"Nothing," she said quickly. She glanced around the interior of the jet. "This is really quite lovely, Alex."

The furnishings of the plane were sumptuous. The chairs and couch were upholstered in rich cocoa and gold tweed, the walls paneled in mahogany. There was not only a bar at the far end of the cabin but even a tiny kitchen.

Alex pointed to a cream extension telephone resting on a built-in mahogany desk. "You can do your telephoning from here while I go to the terminal and do some shopping for you, then I'll get Clancy working on the arrangements. I'll send catering over to stock the kitchen. Do you have any preferences?"

"Just a sandwich," she said absently, her mind on the difficult call she was about to make.

He nodded briskly. "There's a restroom and shower adjoining the kitchen area if you want to use it. I'll use the VIP facilities at the main terminal." He turned and strode out the door and down the portable metal steps.

Sabrina stared at the phone, biting her lip worriedly, and then reached for the receiver. What the devil was she going to say to Jess and Sue? "Sorry I didn't come home last night, but I was being ravished by a dashing sheik who is whisking me off to his lair for a few more days of dalliance?" Well, she'd come up with something. She drew a deep breath and rapidly punched the Bradford number.

The task turned out to be much easier than she'd expected. It was Jess who picked up the receiver and, after expressing relief at her safety, he listened quietly to her halting explanation that she was going away for a few days.

"I can't say it comes as a surprise, Bree," he said slowly. "The phone lines have been on the fritz since last night, but Juan Mendoza finally got through early this morning. He was a little concerned, to say the least, when both you and this Ben Raschid disappeared without a word. He felt a bit responsible that he'd been manipulated by Ben Raschid into staging the cocktail party. I take it you and Ben Raschid are . . . friends?" The last word was uttered with embarrassed gruffness. "You're sure this is what you want to do?"

"I'm sure," Sabrina said softly. "Tell David I'll be back on Monday and we'll return to Houston the day after." She paused. "Sue did tell you we'd be leaving?"

"She told me," Jess said with a terseness that covered a thread of pain. "It looks like you're still carrying the ball, Bree. It's no wonder you want to run away for a while. God knows we don't have any right to ask what we do of you." He drew a deep, shaky breath. "But I do ask it of you. I have no choice. You will be coming back, won't you, Bree?"

"I'll be back Monday," she repeated gently, her throat aching at the almost pleading note in his voice. "And you're not asking anything of me that I wouldn't do anyway. I made my choice a long time ago, Jess. I love David and there's no way I could desert him now."

"You couldn't say we'd shown it in the last two years, but Sue and I feel you're as much our child as David, Bree," Jess continued bitterly. "We've taken a hell of a lot from you, haven't we? You probably wouldn't be forced to go on this little illicit jaunt with a man like Ben Raschid if you were at liberty to form a more lasting relationship. But what man would be willing to accept the responsibility of a problem like David?"

Sabrina felt a dart of pain so piercing that it took her breath away. She had subconsciously acknowledged a long time ago the truth that Jess stated so frankly, but it had taken on new and poignant meaning since Alex had catapulted into her life. "David's *my* problem," she said shakily. "It wouldn't be fair to ask anyone else to share it." Then she rushed on, her tone firming to deliberate lightness. "Don't worry about it, Jess, it will be years before I'm ready to settle down. By that time we'll probably have David completely well again."

"Maybe," Jess said skeptically. "Bree, are you sure—"

"Look, I've got to hang up now, Jess," Sabrina interrupted, trying to stall off any more of his troubled probing. Though well meant, it was getting a little more painful than she could take at the moment. "Give Sue and David my love. I'll see you Monday."

She replaced the receiver quickly and drew a deep, steadying breath. It was done. Though Jess's words had unintentionally hurt her it was undoubtedly better that she face the reality they encompassed. These four days were all she could expect to have with Alex and she must make the most of them. She would live each day with a zest and joyousness that would make every one a bright jewel to treasure forever. She could do it. If she could gather strength from the darkness, how much more could she garner from the sunlight of this time with Alex?

She rose to her feet and strode to the shower at the rear of the plane.

She was blow-drying her hair with the portable dryer she'd found in a small, compact cabinet under the basin when she heard Alex roaring her name.

"Damn it, where the hell are you, Sabrina?"

She shut off the dryer and frowned in puzzlement. Now what had put him in such a temper?

She tightened the white bath towel around her, tucking the ends beneath her arms.

"Sabrina!"

She slapped the dryer down on the vanity. "I'm coming!" she called, her voice sharp with exasperation. She strode swiftly from the bathroom, her hair flying wildly about her in a flaming, silky cloud. "What's all the urgency?"

Alex halted in mid-stride, a flicker of relief crossing his face before it darkened crossly. "Why didn't you answer before I shouted myself hoarse?" he said roughly, carelessly tossing the armful of packages and the tan pigskin suitcase he was carrying on the seat of a beige contour chair. "And why the hell are you parading around in just a towel? How did you know I was alone?" His lips tightened. "Not that you probably would have minded," he muttered.

"I didn't hear you, I was blow-drying my hair," Sabrina snapped. "And I wouldn't have been parading out here in a towel if you hadn't been bellowing like an angry moose. I thought at the very least the plane must be on fire." She marched over to the chair. "Now if you'll excuse me, I'd like to get dressed. Naturally a shameless slut like me wouldn't feel shyness or modesty, but I am a little chilly."

"Damn, I didn't say you were a slut," he said hoarsely. Then he was behind her, his arms sliding around her and bringing her back against his hard, taut strength. "Why do you put words in my mouth?"

"Close enough," she said, trying desperately to keep her body stiff and unyielding in his arms. The thin terrycloth barrier of the towel might just as well not have been there. She could feel every corded muscle of his hips and thighs against her own rounded softness, and his arms felt beautifully right cradling her so protectively. "And I don't have to put words in your mouth when you do such a superb job of expressing yourself without my help." She tried to wriggle away from him but his arms tightened possessively.

"No," he said sharply, and she could feel his chest move against her back as he took a deep breath. "Don't move, sweetheart. Just let me hold you. Okay?" Then his lips were at her throat, nuzzling aside the silky tresses until they were pressed against the pulse just under her chin. "God, I'm sorry," he muttered thickly. "I know I shouldn't have blown up like that with you. It was just that I was scared half out of my mind. When you didn't answer, I went into a panic."

"Panic?"

"I thought you'd left me," Alex said simply. "I thought your cowboy had talked you into going back to him and you'd cut and run." His next words were muffled against her throat. "Lord, I hate being this vulnerable. It tears me apart."

Sabrina knew a flutter of melting tenderness that had nothing in common with the hot sensuality she'd been aware of only a moment before. She relaxed against him in helpless compliance with the emotional response his words generated. "You're not alone in this, you know," she said huskily. "I can't say that I like what's happened to me either. But I'm not flailing out at you for no reason."

"That's because you're a warm, sweet woman," he said huskily, his lips moving up to her earlobe and nibbling at it gently. "My woman." His tongue darted teasingly into her ear. "Tell me you're my woman, Sabrina?"

"Chauvinist," she charged a trifle breathlessly. She could feel his body hardening against her own and she had a fleeting memory of his powerful, naked body crouched over hers, his supple shoulders gleaming copper in the firelight. She felt a curious weakness in her knees. She shot him a teasing glance from beneath her lashes. "Why don't you tell me you're my man, instead?"

"Why not?" he said mockingly, his hands sliding up to cup the fullness of her breasts through the towel. "I wouldn't think of offending your liberated sensibilities, Sabrina. Particularly when it appears to be nothing less than the truth." His thumbs were lazily stroking her nipples through the rough terry material. "I *am* your man, little flame." She gasped as he increased the abrasive friction that was causing the taut peaks of her breasts to harden yearningly. "Every muscle in my body, every talent I possess, every bit of experience I've acquired over the years are completely at your disposal." His hands slowly pushed the towel down to her waist and thumb and forefinger were gently plucking at the nipples he'd already aroused to such excruciating sensitivity. "Tell me what you want, love," he urged softly, his warm breath stirring the hair at her temples. "Tell your man how he can please you."

One hand left her breast to wander down to the apex of her thighs, and he began a lazy, circular, rubbing motion through the towel. She shivered as she felt a hot wave of unadulterated desire rock her. "Do you like that, sweetheart? Do you know how much I like to touch you there? You're so soft and sweet." His hand increased its stroking tempo until she was arching instinctively against it, her eyes closing against the tide of pleasure he was causing to break over her. "So hot."

"Alex." His name was almost a gasp on her lips and suddenly she couldn't take any more. She turned in his arms and her trembling fingers were at the buttons of his shirt. "Damn you, Alex. Liberated, hell! You know you're driving me crazy."

There was a flicker of mischief in the darkness of his eyes, despite the pulse she could see leaping in his throat, signaling his own arousal. "Well, I didn't actually *know*," he drawled, smiling. "I admit I did have a strong hunch, though." He raised an eyebrow quizzically as she pulled his shirt out of his pants and parted the material, baring his muscular chest with its springy pelt of dark hair. "Does that mean you don't want to be liberated any more?" He pulled a face. "Pity. I was just beginning to enjoy my submissive role."

Submissive? Sabrina gave a very unladylike snort of disbelief. She should have known better than to try to play games with Alex. He had too much experience on his side, and that inborn arrogance was a little too strong to allow him to yield anyone a total victory. Or was it?

"You like aggressive women, then?" she asked sweetly, her eyes narrowed thoughtfully on his face. "I'll have to see if I can't accommodate you." She leaned forward and deliberately rubbed her naked breasts against the hard muscles of his chest. The mockery was abruptly wiped from his face. "Do you like that, sweetheart?" she asked with dulcet sweetness, parodying his own seductive whisper. "Do you know how much I like to touch you there?" She bent her head and her tongue darted out to caress one hard male nipple. He groaned this time and his hips gave a spasmodic jerk forward. She looked up into his eyes and crooned soulfully, "You're *so* hot."

For a moment he gazed down at her in blank disbelief. Then suddenly he was chuckling. He threw back his head and laughed with such robust enjoyment that it was her turn to stare at him blankly.

His arms went around her and he gave her a warm, affectionate hug that was almost avuncular. "Oh Lord, Sabrina, there's no one like you," he said, still chuckling. He pressed her head to his chest, rocking her back and forth like a proud parent with his favorite child. "Just when I think I've gotten the best of you, you do something like this. It'll be a wonder if I have the least bit of ego left by the time these four days are over."

"I don't think you have to worry too much about that," Sabrina said dryly. "I haven't exactly noticed you've turned into a shrinking violet since I came on the scene." But her arms slipped around his waist beneath his shirt and she brushed a light kiss on the warm flesh cushioning her cheek. God, she loved him so much. How could you help but love a man who could subdue his pride, and laugh at himself, without losing one particle of the essence that made him all strong, virile male?

There was a sound somewhere between a snort and a cough behind her. Sabrina stiffened and made an instinctive movement to turn and face the new arrival on the scene, an action instantly quelled by Alex's arms tightening about her protectively. It was a good thing he had, she realized an instant later, embarrassed color flooding her face. Naked to the waist, with only a flimsy towel draping her hips, she was scarcely presentable.

"Shall I go out and come in again?" Clancy Donahue asked politely.

"You have abominable timing, Clancy." Alex sighed resignedly over her head to Donahue standing at the door. He carefully folded the edge of his shirt around Sabrina's naked back, affording her a little more covering. "Do you intend to make a habit of this?"

"You're obviously not going to give me the opportunity." Donahue's voice was laden with displeasure. "I made those arrangements you ordered. You know what a damn fool you're being, don't you?"

"Not now, Clancy," Alex said impatiently. "Go on up to the cockpit and give Sabrina a chance to get dressed. You're embarrassing her."

There was a disgruntled murmur behind her and then the soft click of the cockpit door. She raised her head from Alex's chest, her cheeks still flaming. "I don't think you need to worry about my appearing draped only in a towel any more," she said ruefully. "That was the second time I've been embarrassed to death by Clancy's arrival."

Swift concern darkened his face. "I wanted you to be discreet, not ashamed." His hands left her back to cup her face in his palms. "You shouldn't ever be ashamed of that lovely body, little flame," he said softly. "You're all glowing satin color and singing grace." He kissed her with a tenderness that caused her to catch her breath. "If I sometimes get uptight about you displaying all that magic to anyone else, it's just because I'm a jealous bastard and like to guard my own. Okay?"

"Okay," she answered throatily. She smiled shakily. "Now I think I'd better put some clothes on, don't you? Clancy must think I'm trying to establish going topless as the current fashion."

He released her reluctantly and stepped back, watching as she pulled the towel up to cover her breasts and tightened it around her. "It's not a half-bad idea," he said wistfully, his eyes on her cleavage. Then he pulled his gaze forcibly away and grinned mockingly. "And Clancy would never hint you'd ever do anything that wasn't entirely right and proper. He's a great fan of yours." His lips tightened grimly. "He's a little too enthusiastic in his support of you at times. Did you know he tried to talk me out of coming to Corpus Christi to get you once I'd located you? It's the first time since I was a kid that I was tempted to take a swing at him. What the hell did he think I was going to do to you?"

"Probably exactly what you did," Sabrina said, her lips curving in amusement. She felt a warm surge of affection for the gruff Texan. "He knows you very well, Alex." She turned briskly back to the chair and started to gather up the packages. "How much time do I have to get dressed before we take off?"

"About fifteen minutes," he said absently, still frowning. He watched her broodingly as she turned back toward the bathroom. "How did I know you were a virgin?" he said defensively, looking like a sulky little boy.

"Would it have made any difference?" she asked over her shoulder as she crossed the cabin. Why was he so upset by Donahue's championing of her? It seemed completely out of character in someone as ruthlessly single-minded as Alex.

His lips curved in a reluctant smile. "Probably not," he admitted sheepishly. "I wanted you too much to give a damn about anything!" His expression became oddly grave. "I guess I just resent the fact that Clancy felt he had to protect you from me. I want to be the one to protect you from anything that could hurt you."

"Cherish?" Sabrina asked softly, as she paused at the door and gazed at him across the cabin.

"Cherish," he echoed. There was a touch of uncertainty in the depths of his eyes and lines of tension about his mouth. "I didn't just take a lush little redhead I had a yen for to bed last night, Sabrina. I think you know that despite what Clancy thinks. Are you sorry you let me love you?"

How could she be sorry? It had been the most

wildly beautiful experience of her entire life. Whatever was to come afterward, that fact was incontestable. Her emerald eyes were glowing with tenderness as she said huskily, "You've got to get rid of these chauvinistic misconceptions if we're ever to understand each other, Alex. I didn't *let* you love me, I demanded it. I wouldn't think of accepting such a passive role. Keep that in mind in the future." The door closed softly behind her.

In fifteen minutes she was dressed in the cream Halston pants suit with its chic tunic top and graceful, cowl neck. The matching medium-heel sandals were not only fashionable but marvelously comfortable. For that matter everything fit splendidly, she thought with satisfaction. Alex had been almost uncannily accurate in his guesses regarding her sizes. Then she felt a swift surge of heat flood her entire body at the memory of the events of the previous night. It wasn't all that amazing when she came to think about it. In those feverishly passionate hours before they had finally fallen into an exhausted slumber, he must have weighed and measured every inch of her, not only with his eyes but with those talented hands and those lips that had practically driven her out of her mind.

There was still a flush of color on her cheeks as she returned to the cabin and found it unoccupied except for Clancy Donahue, sprawled lazily in an easy chair, leafing through a magazine. He rose easily to his feet, his brows raised and his lips pursed in an appreciative whistle as his gaze ran over her.

"Very nice," he said lightly, his blue eyes twinkling. "I found the other outfit a bit more aesthetically pleasing, but a man can't have everything." Then as her blush deepened to a color rivaling her hair, he added more soberly, "Sorry about that. I promised Alex I wouldn't say anything to embarrass you, but he should have known I wouldn't be able to resist. This unruly tongue of mine has been landing me in trouble since I was a lad. Speaking of exotic outfits, I have something that belongs to you." He reached into the pocket of his tweed sports jacket, pulled out a cassette tape, and held it out to her. "You forgot this the night of Alex's birthday party. I suppose I could have mailed it to you but I had an idea I'd be seeing you again very soon anyway." His eyes twinkled. "I just didn't think I'd be seeing so *much* of you."

"Thank you," she said quickly, taking the tape. She sat down in the chair next to his. "Where is Alex?"

Donahue nodded in the direction of the cockpit. "He decided to take over the controls himself since it's only a forty-minute flight to Houston International. You'll be changing to the helicopter there. Londale's Folly doesn't have a landing strip. He usually prefers to have Don take over on longer flights so he can rest or work as the mood takes him." He smiled. "Of course it could be that he decided discretion was the better part of valor, with a lovely thing like you sharing the cabin. I got the distinct impression he wasn't up to exercising much more restraint where you were concerned, and he practically burned my ears off for the embarrassment I'd already caused you."

"I'm sorry. That was quite unfair," she murmured. "It wasn't your fault I was embarrassed."

"I totally agree! But that didn't stop Alex from blistering me with that poison tongue of his. Sometimes I rue the day I taught him my rather uniquely explicit vocabulary." He scowled. "I only wish he'd picked up a grain or two of common sense along with it."

"I gather you're a trifle displeased with him," she said idly, as she fastened her seat belt. "I seem to remember your calling Alex a fool. That's hardly the action of the poor, downtrodden employee you're picturing yourself to be."

Donahue's face darkened grimly. "He is a fool," he repeated stubbornly. "He knows better than to take chances in his position. It's the first time I've ever known him to take a risk for no good reason." He glared at her resentfully. "I'd say it's carrying your desire for privacy a little too far, risking Alex's life just to spare yourself a little publicity, Sabrina."

"Risking Alex's life?" Sabrina's eyes were wide with surprise and questioning. "I don't have any idea what you're talking about, Clancy."

He studied her for a long moment before the skepticism slowly faded from his face. "I should have known it was all Alex's idea," he said gruffly. "Forget I mentioned it, kid."

"Forget you mentioned it?" Sabrina said, staring at him incredulously. "You've just accused me of putting Alex's life in danger and now you want me to forget it?"

"It would be a hell of a lot more comfortable for me if you would," he said gloomily. "Alex is going to tear a strip off me for even bringing it up."

"Clancy, will you stop this waffling and tell me what you meant?" Sabrina was practically seething with frustration. "Why is Alex's life in danger?"

"I didn't say his life was actually in danger," he said defensively, "just that he was stupid to take the chance." Then, as she drew a long, exasperated breath he continued reluctantly, "Alex has given orders that for the next four days you're to be totally alone on Londale's Folly. He doesn't want any of his security force even to set foot on the island. He had me send the housekeeper and handyman to the mainland for your stay there."

He scowled in disgust. "Did you ever hear anything so crazy in your life?"

Sabrina could feel the tension flow out of her like the air from a pricked balloon. My God, what a tempest in a teapot. He'd frightened her half to death. "Is that all?" she asked, with a profound sigh of relief. "Clancy Donahue, if you ever do that to me again, it's you whose life will be in danger!"

"Is that all?" Donahue echoed grimly. "I assure you that it's quite enough! Would it interest you to know that there have been three attempts on Alex's life since he came of age? And four kidnapping attempts? Why do you think he maintains a security force that rivals the U.S. Secret Service?"

"I didn't know he did," Sabrina said faintly. She suddenly felt icy cold. "Why would anyone want to kill Alex?"

"Oh, for heaven's sake, Sabrina! Because he's Alex Ben Raschid, of course," Donahue said wearily. "You can't wield that much power without stepping on a few toes along the way. Not to mention his position as the next ruler of Sedikhan. Old Karim has been ill lately and it's just a matter of time until Alex takes total control there as well. It's only logical that any group hoping to topple Alex's family from power would pick a time like now to do it. If anything, security should be tightened, not eliminated entirely as Alex is doing, on the island."

"I see," Sabrina said slowly. She moistened her suddenly dry lips. "Then of course that's what you'll have to do. I have no objection to security men on the island. I'm sure Alex will change his mind when you tell him how urgent you feel the arguments are for their being there."

"Fat chance," Donahue said ruefully. "Alex

doesn't do anything he doesn't want to and it's obvious he wants to keep you very much to himself." Then, as his keen eyes raked over her pale, strained face, he reached out and covered her hand, giving it a firm, reassuring squeeze. "Don't worry, hon, I'll find a way of protecting him, even if it means anchoring the yacht offshore and ringing the Folly with a small flotilla!"

She bit her lip. "You're sure?" She felt a surge of almost fierce protectiveness, along with chilling panic, at the thought of Alex in danger. Nothing could happen to Alex. She wouldn't let it. It was ironic that both David and Alex, whom she loved in such different ways, should be able to inspire this same maternal ferocity.

"I'm very sure," he said comfortingly. "And don't forget, in the general run of events Alex is more than capable of taking care of himself. I made damn sure of that."

"That's right, you did," Sabrina answered, the tight coil of fear loosening a trifle. "Thank God for that!" She gave him a grateful smile. "And thank *you* for keeping him safe all these years, Clancy."

His blunt face was gentle as he gazed at her searchingly for a long moment. "So the running is all over."

"Yes, the running is over," she answered simply. "I never should have bolted in the first place. I told you it wasn't my way."

"I hope it works out for you, kid," Clancy said softly, his blue eyes kind.

There was a mellow ping and the seat-belt light glowed over the cockpit door. It was followed immediately by the whine of the jet engines. Donahue hurriedly fastened his seat belt and checked Sabrina's before settling back in his chair.

"We have forty minutes," he said, a curious

smile on his face. "I think that should be just about enough time for me to tell you about a fascinating place I have a hunch you'll be visiting soon. It's a country that's half space-age technology and half Arabian-nights fairy tale. It's a land called Sedikhan and the first time I saw it I said to myself . . ."

Eight

"This is your room," Alex said briskly, throwing open the door and preceding Sabrina into a guest room with lush, deep, sea-blue carpet. He crossed to the double bed in the center of the room and tossed onto the aqua satin spread the small suitcase containing the clothes he'd purchased at the airport. "I'm just down the hall in the master suite." He cast a glance at the gold watch on his wrist. "It's only a little after four. Would you like to go for a walk and explore the island a bit before we scrounge in the kitchen for something for dinner?"

"What?" she asked, bewildered. *Her* room? She'd assumed they'd be sharing a room. Alex certainly hadn't impressed her as the type of man who'd be content to occupy his own bed and visit her when the mood struck him. He was much too possessive. "Oh, yes, that would be very nice," she agreed politely.

"Fine," he said tersely, not looking at her as he turned and strode quickly to the door as if eager to escape. "Suppose I meet you downstairs in fifteen minutes then?" The door closed behind him.

She stared blankly at the door for a long moment before she moved slowly toward the bed, opened the pigskin suitcase, and pulled out a pair of white shorts and a yellow cotton suntop. What on earth was the matter? Alex had acted so cold and had practically run out the door.

Now that she thought about it, he'd been curiously remote and stilted from the moment they'd changed aircraft at Houston. She really hadn't noticed it at the time, assuming he was just absorbed in the mechanics of flying the helicopter. Then, too, she'd been excited at her first glimpse of this lovely, tropical island and the enchanting hillside villa built entirely of gleaming gray stone. But there was no doubt in her mind now that something was definitely wrong. Alex's cool rejection of her had been far from subtle.

As she automatically stripped off the cream pants suit and dressed in the shorts and suntop, her mind gnawed at his strange behavior. It just didn't make sense. She couldn't believe Alex could change so radically from the passionate lover of this morning. She scoffed at the very notion that the thrill of the chase was over and he could have lost interest. She thrust her feet into white strappy sandals. Alex's mood was totally incomprehensible.

Her expression must have reflected her uncertainty and dismay when she came down the stairs, for Alex's face darkened in an impatient frown as he stood in the foyer watching her. "You're looking at me as if I were Bluebeard incarnate," he said roughly. His glance went over the snug white shorts and low-cut blouse moodily. "And you haven't got on enough clothes."

Sabrina's mouth fell open and for an instant she could only gape at him. "It must be almost ninety degrees outside, and if you'll recall, you're the one who chose my entire wardrobe for our stay on the island." She crossed her arms over her chest and glared at him belligerently. "Which, I might add, seems to be comprised principally of very scanty shorts and tops and a bikini that would make a Bourbon Street stripper blush."

"I know," he said gloomily. "I chose them before I decided . . ." His voice trailed off. "Oh hell, I guess you'll have to wear them." He grabbed her elbow and hustled her hurriedly toward the front door. "Come on, I'll show you around the island."

If she'd had any thoughts of a leisurely amble around this tropical paradise, she would have been rudely disillusioned. Alex behaved as if he were in training for the Boston Marathon as he bustled her out of the house and down the palm-bordered path to the beach. He gave her a brief and concise history of the island, lending it all the color of a stock report. The only time he allowed her to stop was to examine the exterior of the small, stone cottage in the cove, which, he told her, Honey and Lance Rubinoff occupied when they visited the island. Even then he flatly refused to allow her to enter the cottage, and the marathon was on again.

By the time they returned to the house, Sabrina's cheeks were flushed, not only by the sun and their rapid pace but in angry exasperation. There was no possible excuse for Alex to behave so churlishly. When he showed every indication of continuing his sterile, guidebook tour in the house, starting with the terrace, she decided she'd had enough.

She skidded to an abrupt stop and jerked her elbow away from his firm hold. "Okay, Alex, I've had it!" She marched to the gray stone balustrade bordering the flagstone terrace and levered herself so that she was sitting on the wide ledge. She planted her hands firmly on her hips. "I'll be damned if I'll stand you treating me as if I were some kind of plague victim. If you've changed your mind about wanting me here, you only have to say so. I don't need any demonstration like the one you've just put me through."

"I don't know what you're talking about," he said, frowning like a sulky little boy. "You said you wanted to see the island."

"Don't play dense, Alex," Sabrina gritted between clenched teeth. "We both know you've been acting very peculiarly since we arrived on the island."

"Maybe a little," he admitted moodily. "Give me a little time and I'll get a handle on it."

"Alex, we only have four days," she protested impatiently. "What in the world is wrong with you?"

He was across the terrace in four swift strides. "Damn it, this is what's wrong!" He grabbed her hand and brought it to his steel-hard arousal and held it there. "I want you. I'm aching like hell and it's promising to be a permanent state of affairs where you're concerned."

An instant of shock was quickly superseded by relief that made her almost weak with reaction. Good Lord, was that all? Her hand gently moved over the warm hard length of him. "I don't see anything wrong there," she said softly, her other hand moving to the buttons of her suntop. "Why didn't you tell me? I think we can take care of that problem fairly easily."

He closed his eyes, his hips thrusting forward against her hand and his lean face taut with an almost pained delight. "Sabrina, don't do that," he choked hoarsely. "You're killing me."

If it was killing him, it was with pleasure, Sabrina thought tenderly, noticing the color suffuse the bronze darkness of his cheeks. He was so beautiful like this, with a look on his face that was so strong, yet oddly vulnerable. Her hand moved in a more aggressive caress and he gave a groan, quickly followed by a shudder through his entire body. "Sabrina!"

Then he was jerking desperately away from her, his eyes flicking open. He hurriedly drew back from her as if she really did have the plague. "No, damn it!" he said emphatically. "I'm not going to do it. Stay away from me, Sabrina!" His dark gaze was drawn compulsively to her breasts which were almost entirely revealed by the half-buttoned suntop. "And cover up!"

"You seem to be saying that to me quite a lot," Sabrina said bewilderedly, her hands automatically drawing the blouse closed. "At this rate, you're going to give me a complex."

"And you're going to drive me stark, staring insane," Alex said, drawing a deep breath. "I'm definitely not made for the celibate life."

"Celibate?" Sabrina asked dazedly. "Who's asking you to be celibate? What about all those lovely things you were going to teach me?"

"I changed my mind," he said tersely, and then, as her eyes widened in disbelief, he continued quickly, "only for the next couple of days." His lips twisted wryly. "I don't think I can hold out any longer than that."

"Why would you want to hold out at all?" she asked blankly. "There can't be any question in your mind about my willingness on that score."

There was a glint of warm tenderness in Alex's eyes. "No, I've no doubt about you, love. You're the most beautifully responsive woman I've ever known."

"Then why?"

"It's *because* we're so damn good together," he said simply. "Like I said, I seem to be in a permanent state of arousal whenever I so much as have a fleeting thought about you. The minute I take you to bed, there's every possibility we'd spend the rest of the time together making love." He shook his head, his lips tightening. "Pleasurable as that might be for both of us, at the end of four days you'd get out of that bed and walk away. The only things I'd have taught you about me and about yourself would be purely physical. I can't afford that, Sabrina."

"So it's celibacy for both of us?" She chuckled, her eyes dancing. Alex's struggle to keep himself from taking her most definitely had a funny side. Then her smile faded, to be replaced with a poignant tenderness. No, it wasn't funny at all. It was sweet and tender and a little sad.

"Until we establish those other levels of communication you said were so important to you," he said sternly. "And no amount of seduction on your part is going to change my mind."

"I told you this morning you weren't alone in this," she said gently, her face glowing with a loving tenderness that caused the man watching her to inhale sharply. "Why won't you believe me? Instead of treating me as if I were an enemy out to undermine you, why couldn't you just discuss it with me? You know, I believe your reasoning seems quite sound."

His dark eyes flickered warily. "You do?"

"I do," she answered softly. Much as she hated the thought of any postponement of her physical relations with Alex, there was something very appealing in the idea. She would learn all she could of this multidimensional man, whose personality seemed to be gradually capturing every corner of her heart.

"And if you'd told me the problem, I would have helped," she added. "That's what caring is all about. Don't you know that?"

"I haven't had much experience in that area,"

Alex answered, his gaze intent on her face. "Perhaps you can teach me that, too."

"Perhaps."

If example could teach him, then Alex should prove a very good student, she thought mistily. Sometimes the love she felt for him seemed to be literally radiating out from her, like a glowing sun.

She slipped from the balustrade to the flagstone terrace, her hands swiftly buttoning her blouse. "Now, if we're to start off this platonic friendship properly, it would be a good idea if I got out of these clothes. Where did you say your bedroom was? Oh yes, just down the hall from mine."

"My bedroom?" he asked blankly.

She chuckled. "Don't worry, Alex, I'm not about to force myself into your bed. I just thought I'd raid your closet and try to find something to wear that was a little less revealing than these clothes." She crossed the few feet separating them and gave him a light, loving kiss on the lips. "You see, there's no way I'd ever want you aching or uncomfortable even if it's with desire for me." She kissed him again. "And that's caring, too!" She turned and walked swiftly toward the French doors that led to the lounge.

"Sabrina."

She turned at the door, her eyes inquiring.

"Do you play chess?" Alex's expression was so beautifully tender that at first she couldn't pull her gaze away from it to comprehend his words.

Then she frowned in puzzlement. "Not very well. I don't really have the sort of logical mind it requires. Checkers are more my game. Why?"

"I just thought we should have something to occupy us for the next two days," he said, smiling. "Checkers it is, then." As she turned once more to the door his voice was a husky murmur behind her. "Thank you, Sabrina."

"For what?" she asked over her shoulder.

"For caring, love, for caring."

"Alex, just one more," Sabrina pleaded. "I haven't got any shells with this lovely lavender pink. One more won't hurt."

"That's what you said about the sand dollar," Alex said, trying to frown sternly at her. "You must have gathered at least two hundred shells this afternoon. Why do you have to have that one?"

"But this one has such a beautiful—"

He held up his hand. "Okay, okay." He untied their makeshift knapsack and gestured resignedly. "Throw it in with the rest. I must be getting soft. Not only do I let you take the shirt off my back to carry your loot, but I find myself conned by a red-haired brat who has all the appeal of Huckleberry Finn."

"Huckleberry Finn was very appealing," Sabrina protested, placing the shell in the knapsack and watching contentedly as Alex once more knotted the ends. "He's my favorite Mark Twain character. He had such a spirit of adventure." She made a face as she looked down at her less-than-elegant apparel, comprised of a pair of Alex's jeans she'd rolled up to her knees to wade in the surf, and a blue shirt whose tails were flapping about her thighs. "I can see your point though." She sighed ruefully. "I think I may have gone overboard on toning down my sex appeal. You'd have to be a child molester to see anything attractive about me at the moment."

He straightened and slung the bundle over his shoulder, his muscles rippling like burnished copper in the late afternoon sunlight. "Oh, I don't know," he drawled, his dark eyes twinkling. He reached out and gave her ponytail a teasing little tug. "You definitely have something you didn't have when we arrived at the island day before yesterday."

"I do?" Sabrina asked warily. She'd discovered that at times Alex could exhibit an almost puckish sense of humor. "And what is that?"

"Three freckles across the bridge of your nose," he said, touching one with the tip of his finger. "And a better knowledge of the game of checkers."

"*I* was the one who was conned," Sabrina sputtered indignantly. "You didn't tell me you were a damn expert at the game. And then you had the nerve to play me for kitchen duty. Is that any way to treat a guest?"

"I can't cook," Alex said logically, lacing his fingers through hers and automatically shortening his stride as they turned back toward the path that led uphill to the villa. "It was better for both of us that you take over in that department. Besides, I consider I'm being very generous to help you with the washing-up when that was included in the wager."

"Very generous," Sabrina said ironically. She darted him a curious glance. "Where did you learn to play checkers anyway?"

"Clancy."

"I should have known." She sighed resignedly. "No wonder you win all the time. Clancy would make sure there wasn't a chance of your not coming out on top in any passage at arms." Her gaze raked the horizon. "Is he really out there somewhere? I haven't seen any sign of the yacht all the time we've been here."

"Knowing Clancy, you can be sure of it," Alex said dryly. "He's as worry prone as a hypochondriac in a leper colony." His expression darkened grimly. "And the reason you haven't seen the yacht is that he knows I'd have his hide if you did. I'll be damned if I'll have him frightening you off."

"I'm glad he's out there," Sabrina said soberly, her hand tightening involuntarily in his. "I wish you'd let him stay at the cottage. I don't like you to take chances, Alex."

"There's very little risk," he said carelessly. "As I said, Clancy just likes to fuss." He raised an eyebrow as he glanced down at her troubled face. "But I'm glad you're concerned. It shows I'm making progress. Maybe my monklike abstinence is being rewarded, after all." He made a face. "I certainly hope so. I'm finding the path of virtue strewn with thorns despite the fact that I'm trodding it with Huckleberry Finn."

She stopped and turned to face him, her expression grave. "Has it been bad for you, Alex?" she asked, a tiny frown knitting her forehead. "I thought you were enjoying yourself." She could feel the foolish tears misting her eyes and blinked them away determinedly. "I've loved every minute of it."

"And so have I," Alex said gently, then noticing the liquid emerald of her eyes gazing up at him uncertainly, he muttered an extremely blue imprecation. "Now I've hurt you!" he said impatiently, running his fingers through his hair. "Why do redheads have to be so emotional?"

"Don't generalize," Sabrina said, her lips trembling. "I'm not one of your harem of redheads. I'm me, Sabrina Courtney."

"A very emotional Sabrina Courtney," Alex said gruffly. "But you're right, I should be the last one to complain. You can't be too emotional to suit me, sweetheart."

"Make up your mind, Alex," Sabrina said, trying

to free her hand from his grip. "You're being contradictory!"

"Because, as usual, I seem to have put my foot in my mouth," Alex said ruefully. "I suppose I should be used to it now with you. It's been that way ever since the moment we met." He took her arm and propelled her toward a palm-shaded hillock several yards away. "Come on, we're going to talk. I'm not about to let a misunderstanding rear its ugly head at this stage of the game."

When they reached the palm trees, he dropped the bundle to the ground. Placing both hands on her arms, he pushed her gently to her knees. "Sit down," he said, "this may take quite a while." He sank to his knees facing her and settled back on his heels. "Now, be still and let me try to explain myself, okay?"

"Okay," Sabrina replied, gazing blindly over his shoulder at the gentle roll of the surf.

"Look at me, please," he asked, before cradling her face in his hands. "Stay with me, Sabrina. This is the first time since we came to the Folly that you've gone away from me somewhere I can't follow. Come back to me, sweetheart." His hard face softened with a luminous tenderness. "I'm lonely for you."

"Are you, Alex?" she asked uncertainly. The world had narrowed to his dark intent face so close to her own. "I wasn't sure."

"Then be sure," he said softly, his fingers moving upward to caress the delicate skin of her temples with mesmerizing gentleness. "When I suggested this little platonic hiatus, I fully expected it to be hell on earth. I thought I'd be roasting on hot coals the entire time. Shall I tell you what I found instead?"

She nodded slowly, her eyes fixed almost hypnotically on his dark ones that seemed to encompass all that was loving and caring in the world.

"I found a companion I'd want beside me if we were stranded on this island for the next hundred years. I found a woman who is half pixie, half tomboy, and still manages to be all woman." His voice was so low it was almost a whisper but it rang with a sincerity that caused her throat to tighten painfully. "I found the other half of me. Sometimes I feel as if we're so close I could read your mind." He shook his head, his lips curving in a rueful smile. "It would probably be better if you could read mine. It would prevent a good many misunderstandings."

"You're not the easiest man in the world to understand, Alex," she said huskily. "The first time I saw your portrait I thought you looked like a man who knew more secrets than the Sphinx."

"Do you think I don't know how I shut people away from me?" he asked quietly. "But I haven't closed myself away from you, Sabrina. The gates were rusty and creaky with disuse, but I've held them open and let you take a look. I don't think you've seen any dark secrets to send you running away in panic."

She shook her head. "No, the man I've seen hasn't frightened me, Alex," she said softly. "I like him very much."

She liked him far too much. There had been moments in the last two days when she'd felt she'd made a terrible mistake in allowing this time of exploration and discovery between them. Her body might someday forget the witchery they knew together, but how was her mind to make a similar adjustment, now that she'd discovered the man behind the mask? The wry humor that was always just beneath that enigmatic surface, and the gossamer gentleness that could emerge so unexpectedly from the tough shell he'd built around himself. The other half of him. Yes, she'd felt that ephemeral bond and known it was gaining strength with each passing moment. When their stay on the island was over, would she find it too hard to break?

"Good, I'm glad you like me," he said gruffly. "Remember that. There's going to come a time when I'll remind you that you found something besides my virile young body fascinating." He frowned with mock sternness. "So, from now on, don't get any crazy ideas just because I drop the casual, lustful remark." He sighed. "I'm sorry, love. I appreciate the effort, but you could be wrapped in sackcloth and ashes and I'd still want you." He kissed her lightly on the tip of her nose. "But that doesn't mean I don't like having my Huckleberry Finn around." There was suddenly a glint of mischief in the darkness of his eyes. "Especially as young Huck owes me kitchen duty again tonight, and I haven't had anything to eat since breakfast."

"Philistine," Sabrina accused, jumping to her feet. The moment was so charged with emotion she felt a swift rush of relief that Alex had chosen to lighten it. They had been much too close to words that mustn't be spoken. "If you promise to wash all my shells for me, I just might oblige, despite the way you hustled me."

He retrieved the knapsack and weighed it consideringly. "No deal," he said, standing up and slinging it over his shoulder. "It would take me the better part of the evening and I have other plans for tonight."

"Plans?" Sabrina asked, as he took her hand and their steps once more turned toward the path.

"I said I could last two days," he reminded her quietly. "And I think I accomplished what I set out to do. You can't deny we know each other better now than some couples who have been married for years."

Sabrina felt a little tingle of heat surge through her and she unconsciously licked her lips in anticipation. She knew she'd been eagerly waiting this decision, though she hadn't admitted it even to herself. They'd made the attempt to dampen down the explosive sexuality that was ever present between them, still the undercurrents had been unmistakable. Now the waiting was almost over. She'd be in Alex's arms tonight.

"No, I can't deny we know each other better," she agreed softly, casting him a sideways glance redolent with mischief. "But I'll be darned if I'll play both roles you seem to require of me, Alex Ben Raschid. If you want a mistress in your bed tonight, the kitchen slave has to go!"

When they reached the house, Alex proceeded directly to the suite to shower and change while Sabrina continued on to the small utility room adjoining the modern kitchen. She'd put a load of clothes in the dryer before they'd started out on their walk this afternoon, and she wanted to fold and return them to Alex's room before she went to her own room to change. Since she'd been sharing Alex's wardrobe for the past two days, it had been necessary to wash clothes frequently.

A happy smile tugged at the corners of her mouth as she folded the jeans and shirts when she took them out of the dryer. It would be good to get back into clothes that made her look a bit more alluring than the ones she had on now. Wearing his may have been both practical and discreet, but it had chafed at her pride to know she wasn't at her best with Alex. Heavens, it was natural for a woman to want to be beautiful for the man she loved.

She was mentally going over the neglected wardrobe in her closet as she gathered up the neat pile of clothes. There was a silky polyester blouse in a nile green shade that might look rather good with her eyes. She climbed the stairs and strode briskly down the hall to the master suite at the end of the corridor.

Alex didn't answer her perfunctory knock and, when she opened the door, the sound of the shower running in the adjoining bathroom supplied the reason. She crossed to a teak bureau against the far wall and cast an admiring, proprietal glance around the large, lovely room.

Like the rest of the decor of the house, it had a vaguely tropical atmosphere, with a thick shag carpet in a variegated blue green, the exact shade of the sea she'd been playing in a short time ago. One wall was entirely comprised of a sliding, louvered closet in a rich, polished teak, and there was an elegant empress chair beside the king-sized bed.

After the first glance at that massive bed she carefully avoided looking at it. There were too many hours to get through before she could afford to visualize Alex making love to her there.

She briskly opened the top drawer of the teak bureau and put in two pairs of jeans. Now had Alex taken these T-shirts from the second or third drawer? The second, she decided, and pulled open the drawer.

The pale blue nightgown was so sheer that it was a mere drift of cobweb chiffon, and for a moment she just stared at it with a queer sense of shock. Then she reached out with a careful hand to lift the beautiful thing from the drawer. Judging by the size, the owner must be an exceptionally voluptuous woman, she thought numbly. The nightgown fell from her fingers in a pool of color and she couldn't take her eyes off it. It exerted the same deadly fascination as a lovely coral snake and she felt as if she'd been stung with a poison that was just as nerve paralyzing.

Oh God, why did it hurt so much to know that Alex had made love to another woman in this very room, in that bed? Everyone who could read a newspaper knew Alex changed mistresses with a rapidity that was positively dizzying. Why wouldn't he bring one of them to this island? And why couldn't she accept it like a mature, sophisticated woman instead of feeling like a betrayed child?

The pain was almost comparable to the agony she'd known at the Mendoza party, when he'd spoken with such callous ruthlessness of the women he'd taken. Yet that reality seemed to be of another world. It didn't belong on this island with the man who'd carried her shells over his shoulder and teased her about her freckles. The very closeness they'd attained in the last two days made the intrusion seem even more foreign. He was hers, damn it!

"Moving in?" Alex asked casually. He was leaning indolently against the doorjamb of the bathroom. "I thoroughly approve. We'll be much more comfortable in here than in your room." He leered with mock lasciviousness. "I can't wait to show you the sunken bathtub. It's almost as large as one of the guest rooms."

She must have been staring at that nightgown longer than she'd realized, she thought absently. Alex was dressed in close-fitting khakis that intimately molded the strong, muscular line of his thighs. The sleeves of his dark brown sport shirt were rolled up casually to the elbow, revealing his bronze forearms. He'd even had time to neatly comb his hair that was still damp from the shower.

He came to her and dropped a light kiss on the

nape of her neck. Sabrina was vaguely aware of the clean fragrance of soap and a light woodsy cologne. He reached around her and with a disapproving frown picked up the blue chiffon gown from the open drawer. "I don't remember choosing this for you." He dropped it back into the drawer. "It must have been temporary insanity. There's no way I'm going to let even that little bit of mist come between us tonight." His arms slid around her and he drew her back against the warm length of his body.

"You did include a nightgown in the wardrobe you gave me," she said tightly, "but this isn't it. I've never seen this one before."

"No?" His lips moved up to nibble at her ear. "Then it must be Honey's, she wears that shade of blue quite a bit."

"I thought you said Honey and Lance always used the cottage when they were here," Sabrina said coolly, her body stiff and unresponsive in his arms.

She could feel his muscles tauten against her like those of an animal sensing danger. "They usually do," he said warily, stepping back and turning her around to face him. "Except when there's a bad storm. Then the cottage becomes flooded and they have to vacate." His eyes were narrowed on her face.

"How unfortunate," Sabrina said caustically. "And they use *your* suite when they're driven here as orphans of the storm?"

"If I'm not on the island. Lance likes that bathtub," he answered absently. His hand tightened on her arms and his face was growing grimmer by the second. "What the hell difference does it make?"

It shouldn't make any difference. Why was she pushing like this? Why couldn't she just leave it alone? It was as if something was goading her to strike out at him.

"No difference," she said tartly. "I'd just feel more comfortable if you remembered who occupied your bed the last time you were here. It doesn't promise well for the future, does it?"

"I thought we'd settled all that," he said, giving her a little shake. "Why are you doing this, Sabrina?"

There was a tightness about his face and a smoldering anger in his eyes that she hadn't seen there for a long time. "It was a shock, I suppose," she said brittlely. "I wasn't expecting to run into this particular skeleton in your closet." She was speaking rapidly, almost feverishly. "Or should I say bureau? You must give me a tour and let me know what to avoid. I wouldn't want you to think I was invading your privacy."

"You can tear the damn house apart looking for traces of my lurid past for all I care," he said roughly, and the smolder had definitely burst into flame. "Damn it, I don't know who that nightgown belongs to if it's not Honey's! I don't remember having another woman here on the island, but what difference does it make if I did? I can't wipe out the past and I've no intention of apologizing for anything that happened before you came on the scene."

"I'm not asking you to apologize," she said, smiling brightly, her face stiff and frozen. "I've just decided I need a little more time to think about all this."

Oh Lord, why was she saying this? Ten minutes ago she'd wanted nothing more in the world than to be in Alex's arms. Why couldn't she forget the faceless woman who'd worn that little bit of nothing?

"Well, you're not going to get it," Alex said angrily.

"This is crazy, Sabrina. Since the moment we met you've been telling me what a cynical bastard I am, and how you can't involve yourself with me because I don't have the capacity to trust. Well, I've been beating my brains out trying to give you what you want from me. Good Lord, I haven't even *mentioned* that cowboy you're so committed to since that night at the ranch!" He shook her harder. "Do you have any conception of how difficult that's been for me? But I've met your damn test, and there's no way you're backing away from me now."

"I'm not backing a—"

"The hell you're not," he interrupted. "Do you think I couldn't feel you pulling away from me every time I mentioned anything resembling permanency in our relationship? I tried to ignore it, and told myself that as soon as you were sure of me all that hesitancy would go away. I've done everything I could think of to show you what you mean to me. What else do you want from me?"

"Is it too much to ask you to give me a little more time?" Sabrina asked desperately, trying to shake off his hold.

"You bet it's too much," he said tersely. "Because it's not jealousy, and it's surely not any reluctance to go to bed with me that's causing you to act this way. You're frightened, Sabrina."

"Why should I be frightened?" she asked, moistening her lips nervously. "I told you I was through being intimidated by you, Alex."

"You *are* scared," he said slowly, his eyes narrowing on her face. "Why the hell didn't I realize it before? It's *you* who doesn't trust what we've found together. I realized a long time ago it was strong enough to take anything life could throw at us, but you still have your doubts." He drew a deep breath. "I'm throwing the same challenge back at you, Sabrina. Trust me. And I'm raising the pot. Love me. For as God is my witness, I love *you*." His hands dropped from her shoulders and he stepped back. "Think about it." As he turned away from her, his face was harsher than she'd ever seen it. "I'm going down to the terrace, but I'll be damned if I'll wait long before I come after you." The door closed behind him with a firmness that was almost a slam.

Sabrina stared blankly at the door, as stunned and bewildered as if he'd slapped her. Could it be true? She dropped into the empress chair, gazing unseeingly before her. Alex's words had affected her deeply; it could well be he'd uncovered a truth she'd hidden even from herself. She sat until the golden rays of the late afternoon sun had faded to the melancholy lavender of twilight, her mind feverishly replaying her actions since she'd met him.

Good Lord, how cowardly could a person be. She'd always thought she'd have the courage and strength to face anything, but she hadn't even passed the first test after she'd realized her love for Alex. First she'd run away, and then after they'd made love and he was edging her too close to a commitment, she'd shifted the burden completely on his shoulders, skirting her own personal apprehensions. He was right. She'd been afraid to trust him, afraid to tell him about David and her responsibility that might last a lifetime. And today when she'd subconsciously realized it was really love Alex felt for her, she'd tried to push him away again with that idiotic fit of jealousy.

How could she have been so blind—even to let Alex subdue his pride and be the first one to say the words that put a label on this magical bond between them. Love. What a beautiful word, and how harsh he had sounded saying it. She was at fault there as well, but she could at least make this right.

She rose suddenly to her feet and started determinedly for the door. She was through running away. She'd given so generously to David of her faith and her love but she'd been positively miserly with those gifts with Alex. Well, it was time for a change and she knew just how she was going to signal that change to him.

Nine

Forty minutes later she'd finished showering and brushing her hair until it was a shimmering, fiery veil about her shoulders. Then she set about removing the evidence of those three freckles Alex had commented upon. The pixie would have to go, it was glamour she wanted tonight. After another ten minutes with mascara, eye shadow, and a touch of lip gloss, it was glamour she had.

Now for something to wear. The nightgown that Alex had chosen in Corpus Christi would be just right for her purpose. Its ivory satin sheen was not only complimentary to her figure and coloring, but though cut in the deceptively clinging style of the thirties it was really quite full. She'd need every bit of that fullness. She cast a last, critical glance at the mirror and nodded with satisfaction. She'd never looked more alluring in her life.

Then she was snatching the cassette tape Clancy had returned to her and hastening out of the bedroom and down the stairs. She stopped only long enough to grab Alex's portable cassette player from the library before hurrying toward the French doors that led to the terrace. She paused there for a moment and drew a deep breath, aware suddenly of butterflies in her stomach. Strange—she'd never been nervous before a performance in her entire career. But then no performance had ever been as important as this one.

She slowly opened the door and stood there silently for a moment. Alex was standing with his back to her at the balustrade, looking out at the wine dark sea, and the full moon lent an almost daylight clarity to the scene. The warm gentle breeze was lifting the dark silk of his hair, and it stirred a fugitive memory. Why hadn't she realized before that Lance Rubinoff's portrait of Alex had been painted on this terrace? But perhaps it hadn't been meant for her to know until now. At the moment it was easy to believe in a fate that would bring them full circle, from the portrait that was her first contact with Alex to this final confrontation.

She put the cassette player down on the glass breakfast table and though it made only a tiny scraping sound it was enough to cause Alex to whirl on her, with a wariness that filled her with remorse. There was a crackling tension she could feel across the space between them. What had he been thinking while he'd waited for her to come down?

Whatever it was, she couldn't read it in the shadowed tautness of his face as he gazed at her for a moment that seemed to last forever. Then he gave a long, deep sigh that was almost a shudder. "Where's Huckleberry Finn?" he asked huskily.

"I sent him on vacation." She smiled with loving tenderness. "You know how he likes to go adventuring. I told him I'd keep you company. I don't think you'll mind the substitution."

"Somehow I don't think I will either," he said thickly, his gaze flickering over her hungrily. "Why don't you come over here and let me find out?"

"Soon," she promised lightly. "But first I have something to give you. It's in the nature of a farewell performance." Her finger touched the button on the tape recorder and the terrace was suddenly alive with the throbbing syncopation of sensuous music. With a movement as graceful as the lifting of swallow's wings, her arms rose above her head.

It was a poignantly beautiful dance at the beginning, moving as a stately ballet. She improvised as she went along, wanting to give him something as exquisitely meaningful as the love she felt for him. Then, as the tempo accelerated, she exploded into a passionate, sensual litany of desire. She was vaguely aware of Alex's tense figure as she whirled and gyrated. Her shimmering hair whipped about her sinuous body like a flame.

For the man watching her, the dance seemed to go on for an eternity and each minute the desire for that flame of a woman was mounting to an almost unbearable pitch. Then when he thought that he could stand no more the music came to an end with a triumphant crash of cymbals, and Sabrina was kneeling before him in traditional obeisance.

Her breasts were heaving and her emerald eyes shining like stars as she looked up at him. "I have a present for you, Alex Ben Raschid," she said softly. "All my love. All my trust. Forever." Then, before he could answer, she was on her feet and running down the terrace steps to the path leading to the beach.

"Sabrina!"

Only a laugh answered him as she fled, all moonlight satin and flame, racing down the hill as if on wings. She didn't look back but she knew Alex was following and she laughed again. She was so filled with excitement and a heady euphoria, she felt as if at any moment she would leave the ground and fly away. Her bare feet skimmed over soft, cushioning sand still warm from the sun, until she reached the palm-shaded hillock where they'd stopped that afternoon.

It seemed a lifetime ago, she thought as she turned and waited for Alex. He was only a few yards behind and in an instant she was in his arms, his lips covering her face with hot, scorching kisses. His chest was heaving from the chase, but the little breath he had he gave to her, as their lips clung with a passion that was painfully intense.

"No," She broke away from him and hurriedly backed away. "Not that way."

"Sabrina." Alex drew a deep, shuddering breath, and his hands clenched at his sides. "My God, I can't take much more. *Any* way, damn it!"

He looked so taut and strained that for an instant she was tempted to fly back into his arms. But no, she wanted more for him than that.

"I want it to be right," she said gently, and slowly reached up to slide the satin straps of her gown from her shoulders. She let the bodice fall to her waist, feeling the warm breeze caress the swollen tautness of her breasts. Then with painstaking deliberation she slowly slid the gown over her hips, and let it fall in a shimmering ivory pool to the sand. "The performance isn't over yet, Alex."

She flowed toward him, her naked flesh shining in the moonlight like the satin gown she'd just discarded. She stopped before him and her hands reached out. He stood there, his body tense, scarcely breathing as she unbuttoned his shirt with steady hands. Strange they should be steady when she was quivering so inside.

"I don't suppose you'd let me help you," Alex rasped, as she pushed the shirt from his shoulders and down over his arms.

She shook her head, her hair caressing his bare

chest. "No." She brushed a kiss in the hollow of his shoulder. "I want to do everything for you." Her hands were at his belt and unfastening his pants, while her lips traced a multitude of light, teasing kisses across his chest and the springy dark pelt that narrowed to a fine line at his waist. Her lips traced that line while she impatiently pushed his khakis and briefs over his hips, falling to her knees to complete the task. Then he was tearing off his shoes and socks so that he was as naked as the woman kneeling before him.

"You know, of course, that you're driving me crazy," he said hoarsely. "Chinese water torture is mild compared to this." He jerked suddenly as her tongue seared an extremely sensitive area. "Sabrina!"

Then she was on her feet, her arms sliding over his shoulders to curl in the silky hair at his nape. "Well, you did once promise I could taste you all over," she whispered mischievously. "Aren't you a man of your word?"

"Later," he groaned, as his arms went around her, his hands cupping her buttocks and lifting her against his iron-hard arousal. "Much later. I can't exist another minute without being inside you, love."

As he lifted her higher her legs instinctively curled around his hips, and then with a frantic adjustment he plunged home, reaching his goal with a savage explosiveness that took her breath away.

"Alex!" Her arms tightened around his neck and her head fell to his shoulder. The sensation was unbelievable. For a moment she felt joined to a runaway comet, splitting the universe as it ran its fiery circuit. Then Alex was moving and the universe was being reborn with a power and velocity that made her gasp. She didn't remember when he sank to his knees in the sand. She was too dazzled by the physical and emotional responses he was wringing from her with each bold thrust and tactile manipulation of her body.

"Lord, little flame, I can't stand it," Alex gasped. "I've never known anything like this in my life. The whole world is exploding!"

Then the world did explode, but neither of them cared when there was a galaxy of pleasure to be gathered from each rapturous movement, each lingering kiss, every stroking caress whose denouement was as beautiful as the climax before it.

Then they lay sated and dreamily euphoric in each other's arms, joined in a union as blissfully peaceful as the other had been tempestuous.

"Alex?"

"Hmmm?"

"Did you like my performance?"

She could hear his deep chuckle beneath her ear as his hand gently stroked the hair at her temple. "Your solo was absolutely superb but it was our duet that really blew my mind. I can't wait for the encore."

"Alex?"

"Hmmm?"

"I hate to mention it, but this sand is tickling my back," Sabrina said, shifting her shoulders to find a more comfortable position.

"I can see right now what a shrew of a wife you're going to be." Alex sighed, a smile on his lips as he looked down at her. "What other woman would have the nerve to complain after I'd given her my very best."

"Was that your best, Alex?" Sabrina asked, her eyes twinkling. "I was hoping that practice would make perfect."

"And now you're insulting my expertise," he said in mock indignation. There was a sudden mischievous glint in his eyes. "Well let's just see if it was, shall we?" His hands moved down to cup her buttocks, and, holding her securely chained to his body, he suddenly rolled over so that she was on top of him.

"Alex, what are you doing?" Sabrina gasped, as he leisurely reached up to cup her breasts in his hands, his thumbs teasing her nipples into taut prominence.

"Enjoying myself," he answered promptly. "You were so involved with teasing *me* before that you didn't let me play with *you*." He lifted his head to capture one engorged nipple in his lips and nibbled at it with tongue and teeth. "Have I ever told you how much I love your breasts?"

"I believe you have mentioned it," she choked. Who would have thought, after that first wild, exhilarating culmination, that she could want him again so soon. She felt a sudden bold stirring within her and her eyes widened in amazement. "Alex?"

"Why are you so surprised?" He chuckled. "You should be aware of the effect you have on me by this time." He sat up suddenly and swiftly lifted her legs and wrapped them around his hips. "I think you're right, this sand is a little uncomfortable. Hang on tight. I don't want to lose you, love."

She clutched desperately at his shoulders and her legs clamped automatically around him as he got to his feet. "Alex, I don't understand what—" She broke off, unable to speak, while incredible pounding sensations surged through her as he ran with her down the short stretch of beach to the rolling surf.

Then, as Alex waded forcefully into the sea, she was deluged by a complexity of sensations that made her light-headed: The first shocking chill of the water against her warm flesh, the silky flow of currents around them, and the hot friction of their bodies as Alex started to *move*.

Later, she couldn't have said how long that wild, heated union lasted in those moonlit waters, but she was so weary when Alex carried her back to the beach that she could scarcely lift her head. She was vaguely aware of being set gently down on the sand, then he was putting her arms into the sleeves of his brown cotton shirt.

"Where are we going?" she asked drowsily, as he scooped her up in his arms and started rapidly across the sand.

"Back to the house," he answered, brushing her temple with a gentle kiss. "I don't want you to get a chill. Just relax and let me do everything for a change."

She wasn't about to argue, when it seemed too much trouble to wriggle even a finger. She snuggled closer to him, his heartbeat a reassuring metronome beneath her ear. "You don't have any clothes on," she observed. "Won't you be cold?"

"With you in my arms?" he asked mockingly. "No way, little flame."

"That's very complimentary, if not precisely accurate." She chuckled. "This time I'm *sure* I've had your best."

"Are you?" There was a glint of mischief in his eyes as he looked down at her. "You shouldn't ever be that positive of anything without in-depth research. Look what I had to contend with in that sea tonight. Currents, water temperature, not to mention keeping both of us from drowning." He cocked his head as if considering. "No, upon reflection, I'd say I operate much more effectively in a bathtub. Shall we try it when we get back to the house?"

"Later, perhaps," she answered lazily. "I don't think I could move a muscle at the moment."

"Would you like to make a small wager?" he asked, and then as her eyes widened in disbelief, he shook his head. "Sorry, love. I can't seem to get enough of you. You're right, we'll go to bed and I'll let you rest."

"You don't have to give in so easily," she pouted in mock disappointment. "I thought you'd at least put up a fight." Then her expression became grave. "I need to talk to you, Alex. There's something I have to tell you."

"Not tonight," he said softly, his arms tightening around her. "We have the next fifty years or so to talk. You said everything that was important on the terrace. Love. Trust. Forever. Nothing else really matters, does it?"

"No, I guess it doesn't," Sabrina said huskily, nestling still closer to his dear, hard warmth. "Nothing else is really important but that."

She didn't realize until later what sound pierced the veil of her exhausted slumber, but suddenly she was wide-awake and sitting bolt upright in the king-sized bed. Her heart raced as if she'd been running. "Alex, did you—"

Alex! The pillow still retained the impression of his head but the covers on his side of the bed looked as if they'd been hurriedly tossed aside. She felt a chill of panic run through her and drew a deep, steadying breath. He was probably in the bathroom. Nothing was wrong, she assured herself. But the bathroom door was still open the way he had flung it when he'd carried her to bed from that outrageously sybaritic tub, and the bathroom was dark. And somehow she didn't think he would have left her for any but the most urgent of reasons. Those last moments before they'd fallen asleep had been so poignantly tender. . . . Damn it, where was he?

She was out of bed and across the room with a speed that reflected the frightening answer that had just occurred to her. Four kidnap attempts, Clancy had said. Her hands searched frantically through the closet until she found Alex's white terrycloth robe. Oh, God, and three assassination attempts! Why hadn't she insisted on the security men being quartered on the island? She shrugged herself into the robe and was tying the belt as she reached the door. She was probably crazy—and Alex would be downstairs safe and sound. Oh, God, let that be true!

Her bare feet skimmed down the hall and at the head of the stairs she gave a sigh of relief. The foyer was brightly lit, and so was the living room opening off it. Of course Alex was all right, how idiotic to imagine he could be snatched away in the middle of the night without her even being aware of it.

"Alex, why didn't you wake me?" she called, as she reached the bottom of the stairs. "Do you know how frigh—"

She broke off as Clancy Donahue, dressed in worn jeans and a disreputable navy sweatshirt, strode out of the living room into the foyer. His expression was set and grim. Sabrina's breath stopped in her breast. "Clancy, what are you doing here? Where's Alex?"

"At the moment I'm fixing myself a drink," he said gruffly. "Come on, I think I'd better fix you one, too." Then, at her horrified gasp, he said quickly. "Alex is fine. I didn't mean to frighten you."

"Well, you did," Sabrina said indignantly. "First you pump me full of warnings and forebodings, then Alex disappears, and you tell me I'm going to need a drink. How do you expect me to react?"

"I said I was sorry," Clancy said defensively, taking her elbow and propelling her into the living room. "I've never claimed diplomacy is my strong point. I spoke without thinking, I guess I'm a little upset."

"Upset?" Sabrina asked in exasperation. "Clancy, where *is* Alex?"

"On his way to Sedikhan," Clancy answered tersely.

Sabrina could feel the blood drain from her face. "Sedikhan?" she asked haltingly.

Clancy hurriedly pushed her down on a yellow, cushioned bar stool. "I thought you might need that drink," he said, picking up the snifter of brandy he'd poured for himself and thrusting it at her. "Now don't go jumping to conclusions. He had to go, damn it."

"In the middle of the night?" Sabrina asked blankly. "Without any warning?" She set the brandy down on the bar without tasting it. "Without telling me?"

"That was supposed to be my job," Clancy replied gloomily. "And I'm not doing it very well, am I?" He scowled. "I don't know why he couldn't have done it himself. He said you were tired and he didn't want to wake you. Yet the blasted copter barely gets off the ground and you're down here asking me quesions."

The helicopter. It must have been the helicopter taking off that had awakened her, she thought dazedly. "Why did he have to return to Sedikhan?"

"His grandfather," Clancy answered. "The doctors think Karim may have suffered a heart attack. They don't know how serious his condition is yet, but apparently it's grave enough for them to send for Alex." He picked up the brandy snifter she'd refused and took a sip. "I received a radiogram aboard the yacht a couple of hours ago and came by launch to give Alex the word."

"I see," she said slowly. "I'm sorry to hear that. Alex is very fond of his grandfather, isn't he?"

Donahue nodded. "They're as close as two exceptionally strong personalities can be," he replied. "They care for each other, but for the most part find it more comfortable to be half a world apart." His lips curved wryly. "I wouldn't be too concerned if I were you. Karim's a tough old bird. He'll probably live to be a hundred."

A sudden thought occurred to her. "Why didn't you go with him?" she said, frowning accusingly at him. "You said Alex's enemies would find a situation like this tailor-made, yet you let him go off alone."

"He's not alone," Clancy said sulkily. "He'll have half the security force of Sedikhan at his disposal once he steps off the plane."

"I still think you should have—"

"So do I, damn it!" he interrupted. He crashed the snifter down on the bar. "Do you think I like the idea of letting him go off without me? He's never before turned down my help in a tight spot." He glowered at her. "Until now. I have orders to stay here and look after you."

Sabrina's mouth fell open. "Me?" she said, her eyes widening. "Why should you take care of me? Alex is the one in danger."

"That's what I tried to tell him," Clancy growled. "He wouldn't listen to me. He said he wouldn't take the chance of leaving you alone and unprotected on the island. So I'm stuck here playing bodyguard to you until Alex comes back."

"And when will that be?" she asked.

He shrugged. "Who knows? It depends on how ill Karim turns out to be. A week or two perhaps."

She shook her head. "I can't stay here that long. I promised I'd be back at the Bradfords' on Monday."

"Call them and tell them you've been delayed," he said promptly. "Alex gave me orders you weren't to leave the island until he could come back to you."

"Orders?" Sabrina bristled, her eyes narrowing. "I don't like orders, as Alex is very well aware. You can't keep me on the island if I don't want to be here, Clancy."

"Look, Alex didn't have the time to observe all the courtesies, Sabrina," Clancy said impatiently. "His grandfather may be dying, remember?"

Sabrina felt a surge of remorse. He was right. It wasn't fair of her to be annoyed with Alex when he'd undoubtedly been worried and distracted. And his arrogance was too ingrained for him to change overnight. There would probably be many compromises for them both to make in the future. But it didn't change the fact that she'd made a promise to David.

"I can understand why he was upset," she said gently. "But I've got to keep my promise, Clancy." She stood up and tightened her robe. "I'm going upstairs to get dressed now. Will you take me back to Houston?"

"Alex will have my head if I do," Clancy said gloomily. His face was troubled as he continued awkwardly, "Maybe it's none of my business, but I'm going to have my say anyway. Don't go back to that cowboy just because you're upset with Alex for leaving you like this. I think that was what Alex was worried about when he ordered me to keep you here. He doesn't want to lose you."

"He isn't going to lose me," she said softly. "And when he's had time to think about it he's going to know that."

"Not if you go back to the Bradford ranch," Clancy said flatly. "He's jealous as hell of that guy you've been living with." He frowned. "Don't do it, kid. Alex really cares for you. I think he would have taken you with him to Sedikhan if it hadn't been safer for you here." Clancy glanced away. "I had to go up to your bedroom to wake Alex, you know." His gaze shifted back to her and though there was a flush on his cheeks, his eyes were suspiciously bright. "You needn't blush like that," he said gruffly. "What I saw in that bed was nothing to be embarrassed about. The two of you are beautiful together, and Alex's face, when he was looking down at you, was beautiful, too." He scowled. "Don't you dare tell him I said that, he'll think I'm going soft. But it *was* beautiful, damn it, as if he were all lit up inside."

"I won't tell him," Sabrina promised huskily. "But I can't stay here either, Clancy." She smiled reassuringly. "Don't worry, it's going to be all right. There aren't going to be any more misunderstandings from now on. We've gotten past that point."

He cast her a distinctly skeptical glance. "Maybe *you* have, but I'm not at all sure about Alex." He sighed resignedly. "I'm not going to talk you out of it, am I?"

She shook her head. "No, I have to leave," she said quietly. Then her emerald eyes glinted teasingly. "Besides, with me safely tucked away at the ranch, you can join Alex in Sedikhan. You know that's what you want to do anyway."

"That's right, I could," Clancy said, brightening. He made a face. "Not that Alex won't make my life hell on earth when he finds out I've let you go back to Bradford. What the hell am I going to say to him?"

"You're going to give him a message from me,"

she said serenely. "Tell him I'll be waiting for him to come to me."

"That's all?" Clancy asked, surprised.

She was already striding swiftly toward the door. She paused in the doorway and a gentle smile lit her face. "Not quite," she said softly. "Three more words. Love. Trust. Forever."

Then she turned and left the room.

Ten

"Bree, why wouldn't you speak to that man on the telephone this morning?" David asked, a troubled frown creasing his forehead. "Dad says he was calling all the way from London."

"Alex?" Sabrina looked up from her weeding to smile at him. "I just thought it best. Did you think I was being rude, love?"

David shook his head. "I knew you must have a good reason," he said slowly. He carefully plucked a weed that was encroaching on a young slip. "I'd just never heard you refuse to speak to anyone before, and then you told Dad to tell him you'd expect to see him this evening. It confused me. Don't you like him, Bree?"

"Yes, I like him very much," Sabrina said softly. "And I think you will, too." She moved a few inches to pull at another weed. "I just thought it would be simpler if he came to the ranch to talk to me."

"I thought you must like him a lot to go away on a trip with him," David said gravely, wiping his hands absently on the knees of his faded Levi's as he sat back on his heels. "And then when you came back you told me we were going to wait a few weeks before leaving the ranch." David's expression was puzzled. "Is this what we've been waiting for, Bree?"

"Yes, this is what we've been waiting for, David," she said quietly. "Have you minded staying here these extra weeks?"

"No, I didn't mind. It gave me a chance to put in this flower garden for Mother. Now all she'll have to do is nurture and guard it after I leave."

"I'm sure the garden will make her very happy," Sabrina said gently. It had been impossible not to notice the aura of strain about Sue in the last two weeks, but David had seemed oddly serene and happy. Perhaps working with his beloved plants had helped assuage the pain and bewilderment of his mother's rejection. "You never told me what you planted in her garden, love." Sabrina motioned with her trowel to the bushes bordering the house. "Besides the roses, of course."

"I tried to plan it," he said eagerly. "This row is red chrysanthemums, I've planted pinks over there, and white myrtle by the screen door."

"It sounds lovely," Sabrina said. "And what's underneath the kitchen window? I noticed you spent hours landscaping that particular spot."

His gaze followed hers to the brick-bordered alcove and he smiled gently. "I've planted blue forget-me-nots and rosemary there, Bree."

The smile faded from Sabrina's face. Forget-me-nots. And everyone knew rosemary meant remembrance. David certainly did. She remembered the night he'd excitedly brought up that old horticulture magazine of Gino's to show her the chart with all the flower meanings on it.

"Why rosemary, David?" she asked quietly.

"So she'll remember me," he said simply. "I thought about it a long time, Bree. I know we probably won't be coming back here again. Isn't that right?"

What could she say to him? "Probably not, David."

"I didn't think so," he said, and for a moment there was a poignant wistfulness in his eyes. "That's why I planted the garden." He bit his lip. "Do you remember what I said about me not really being there for her, Bree?"

"Yes, I remember, love."

"Well, I figured this was one way I could be there." His forehead knotted in concentration. "And it won't hurt her to look at my flowers and think of me, will it?"

"No, I think it will make her very happy," Sabrina said huskily, her eyes brimming with tears. "What do all the other flowers mean?"

"Love," he said simply. "They all mean love. That's all I really wanted to say."

A garden of love and remembrance. Could there ever be a more beautiful gift? David had overcome his own pain and found a way to ease his mother's unhappiness. The quiet serenity she'd seen in him these past two weeks had been hard won.

She drew a deep, steadying breath and lowered her eyes. She wouldn't weaken him with her tears. "Will you show Alex your garden when he gets here this evening?" she asked lightly.

"If you want me to," he said. "Does he like flowers, Bree?"

"I don't imagine he knows much about them," she admitted cheerfully. "But I'm sure he would enjoy hearing about Miranda and your plants in Houston as well."

"Okay," he said eagerly, his face brightening. "Maybe I'll take him down to the stable to see my horse. Does he ride?"

"I don't even know," she said with a grin. "Why don't you ask him?"

"I will." His face once more darkened in a worried frown. "Are you sure he'll like me? I want him to."

"He'll like you," she assured him gently. Then, as he continued to frown, she added gravely, "Do you remember what you told me a few weeks ago, about how wonderful it would be if all we had to do was reach out and touch to make one another bloom?"

He nodded slowly.

"Well, Alex is one of those who will bloom if you touch him, David. On the outside he's all closed up and guarded, but when he unfolds his petals, he's beautiful." She smiled, her expression serene. "Now if you'll excuse me, I'll leave you to do the rest of this weeding on your own. I'd like to be on my way before it gets dark."

"You're not going to be here?" David asked, surprised.

She shook her head. "I'm going to the Circle C," she said quietly. "I want you to get to know each other and I think it will be easier if you're alone. Will you tell Alex I'll be waiting there for him?"

David nodded. "He won't be angry, will he?"

"Perhaps a little," she said calmly. "But he won't be when he understands."

"If you say so," he said absently. "Look, Bree." His finger gently touched one green sprig. "We bury them in the earth and yet they fight their way to the sun. It's a miracle. Who could believe something so beautiful could come out of the darkness."

"I believe it," she said, her gaze on the gentle wonder radiating from his face. She turned leaving David to continue to nurture his garden of love.

When Sabrina parked the Volkswagen in front of the ranch house it was already sunset. There wasn't much left to do, thank heaven. She'd come over earlier in the week and swept and scrubbed the room until it sparkled. Now she went directly from the dim hallway into the living room, and lit the logs she'd carefully laid in the fireplace. Soon there was a crackling blaze.

Then she set about lighting the candles. It took her a long time, for she'd garnered every empty wine and soda bottle she could find at the Bradfords', wrapped them in glittering silver foil, and mounted a white candle in each one. There wasn't much she could do to make this large, empty room look festive, but she wanted Alex to know as soon as he came in that she regarded his homecoming as a celebration. When she finished arranging the candles, she gave a contented sigh. Their dancing shadows played on the walls, and they lit the darkness like a birthday cake. Yes, Alex would know she was celebrating.

She moved to the fireplace and dropped down on the cushions she'd carefully covered with a crisp, cotton sheet. She kicked off her sandals and tucked her blouse into the waist of her jeans. She'd deliberately dressed as casually as possible but hadn't been able to resist wearing this simple, white poet's blouse with its extravagantly full sleeves that buttoned at the wrist. It gave her the romantic air of a corsair and exactly matched her mood tonight. Crossing her legs tailor fashion, she settled herself patiently to wait.

The candles were almost half burned and she'd had to twice restoke the fire before she heard the car pull up outside. Then there was the sound of swift, firm footsteps on the porch, the front door was thrown violently open, and she felt her breath stop and her heart turn over. God, she had missed him! It seemed more like a year than two weeks since that night on the island.

Then he was there, lighting the room with a vitality brighter than her candles. His close-fitting black jeans hugged the strong line of his thighs and the sleeves of his black sports shirt were rolled carelessly to the elbow. His dark silky hair was rumpled and there was a grim frown on his face.

He halted in surprise, his gaze wandering about the room. When he finally zeroed in on Sabrina, an amused smile replaced his frown. "You never cease to amaze me, Sabrina," he said, shaking his head ruefully. "I come tearing in here fully prepared to shake the living daylights out of you and you meet me with this! How the hell am I supposed to stay angry with you?"

"You're not," she said softly, her eyes running lovingly over his face. He looked tired. His skin was stretched taut, throwing his cheekbones into bold prominence, and around his mouth were deep lines of tension. "Why were you angry with me?" she asked.

"Why do you think?" He scowled. "You disobeyed my orders and left the island. You refused to take any of my telephone calls, and let me go through hell wondering why you'd returned to Bradford. You knew I couldn't leave Sedikhan until my grandfather was well enough to assume control again. Yet you let me simmer for two agonizing weeks."

"I'm glad your grandfather is better," she said quietly. "I read in the newspaper that he's almost completely recovered now. There were some rumors he might be thinking of abdicating in your favor."

His lips twisted derisively. "Not very likely. As long as he can stand on his own two feet, he's not about to give up even a smidgeon of the power he wields." Alex shrugged. "Which suits me just fine. There's more than enough for the two of us." He paused. "I told him about you."

"You did?" Her eyes widened in surprise.

He nodded. "Hell, I couldn't hide the fact that I

was chomping at the bit to get back to you." He smiled wryly. "He pumped Clancy of all he knew about you and then tackled me. He doesn't approve of the way I've handled our entire affair, incidentally."

"How unfortunate," she said, her lips curving in amusement at the idea of Alex forced to sit tamely while his grandfather gave him advice to the lovelorn.

"He thinks I should have had you kidnapped and then kept you in a lovenest somewhere until I'd gotten you pregnant." Alex spoke solemnly, but with a glint of mischief in the depths of his night dark eyes. "I have to admit that the idea appealed to me." His expression darkened. "Particularly when you let me go through that entire time without a word."

"I sent you word," she reminded him gently. "In fact, I sent you three of them. Remember?"

"I remember," he growled. "It was the only thing I had to hang on to for two blasted weeks. You expected a lot from me, Sabrina. I'm still amateur status at this trust business. I very nearly sent one of my men to bring you to me."

"But you didn't," she said quietly. "That's pretty impressive going for an amateur."

He came to her now. "I'm glad you appreciate my progress," he said, grimacing ruefully. "But you knew how jealous I was of Bradford."

"Yes, I knew that," she said quietly, as he sat on the cushion facing her. "But it was a difficult situation to explain." She unconsciously tensed. "You've talked to David?"

"Yes," he said absently. His hand reached out to touch the collar of her poet's blouse. "I like this. When I walked in the door, I didn't know if I'd find my Huckleberry Finn or a flame in white satin. Instead I find a court page from another century.

I never know what to expect from you." He moved his hand to stroke her cheek with mesmerizing gentleness.

"I talked to Bradford and his wife and I'm sure they told me everything you wanted them to," Alex went on quietly. "And then I had a long talk with your David. We discussed his garden and Gino and Angelina. He told me about a daffodil named Miranda and his best friend, Bree, who was like a beautiful poinsettia."

"He told you that?"

Alex nodded, his lips tightening grimly. "He was a hell of a lot more confiding than his precious Bree. Why couldn't you have just told me about him? Did you think I was such an insensitive bastard that I wouldn't see how special he is?"

"I was frightened," she said simply. "I'd never loved anyone the way I loved you, and I suppose I was subconsciously afraid you'd reject David." Her gaze was direct. "You do realize that it's a package deal, Alex? There's no way I can desert David now."

"I'd be a fool not to realize that after meeting the boy," he said gruffly. He stroked the silky hair at her temple. "You couldn't desert anyone you cared about."

"And you know it may be for the rest of our lives?"

"I realize that." His hand dropped to her shoulder and he met her eyes with a gravity and tenderness that caused her throat to tighten achingly. "I love you. You're the other half of me, remember? I could no sooner reject someone who was important to you than I could cut off my right arm. I want to shoulder all your burdens if you'll let me, love." He frowned, his eyes narrowed thoughtfully. "The first thing we'll do is round up the best damn doctors in the world and work at getting him well."

She should have expected that from Alex, Sabrina thought tenderly. He'd never be content until he'd exhausted every possibility. "He may never be any better," she said quietly. "The doctors just don't know, Alex."

"Well, they will before I'm finished," he said arrogantly. "And one of them had better find a way to help him." Then, as she chuckled irrepressibly, he grinned a bit sheepishly. "Sorry. I just can't bear the thought of the waste of a human being like David."

"And if the doctors can't help?" she asked.

His face softened and his dark eyes glowed with the tenderness that had made Clancy call him beautiful. "Then I'll set about creating him the most exquisite garden on the face of the earth," he said gently. "And we'll let him plant it with love. Then we'll nurture it and protect it all the days of our lives. Enough?"

"Enough," she said huskily, blinking rapidly. "I'm sorry. I think I'm going to cry."

"No, you're not," he said firmly, taking her in his arms and cradling her with poignant gentleness. "I won't have it."

She laughed throatily, tightening her arms about him. "I think you've stayed a little too long in Sedikhan," she said teasingly. "You're obviously going to be unbearably autocratic until I get you straightened out again." He felt so good. His lean sinewy warmth, the scent of soap and that woodsy cologne, the hard vital *feel* of him.

His lips brushed the pulse point just under her chin. "God, it seems like a century," he said thickly. "I'd lie in bed and think about that last night we had together and I thought I'd go up in flames. I was sure I'd have you in bed five minutes after I walked through this door."

"Then you're considerably behind schedule," she said softly, pressing her lips to the hollow of his cheek. "Please feel free to call on me any time to help you put it right."

"Don't worry, I have every intention of doing just that," he said, running his hands on her back in an exquisitely gentle caress that was both soothing and arousing. "But I've discovered something absolutely astounding."

"You have?"

He nodded and pushed her away to gaze down at her tenderly. "As much as I'm aching to love you and have you respond in that wild, sweet way, I want to wait a little longer." His lips lowered to hers. "I want to sit before the fire with you and hold you in my arms. I want to stroke that shining red hair and hear you laugh. Then I want to talk about commitment and love and growing old together. Would that be all right with you, little flame?"

She couldn't speak over the lump in her throat but her emerald eyes were glowing with a radiance that was answer enough. He kissed her once again and then tucked her head into the hollow of his shoulder, his strong arm encircling her with loving protectiveness.

They were silent and content for several long, peaceful moments, and then, slowly, they began to speak, while a hundred candles blazed in joyous celebration around them.

**His love for her is madness.
Her love for him is sin.**

Sunshine
and
Shadow

by Sharon and Tom Curtis

COULD THEIR EXPLOSIVE LOVE BRIDGE
THE CHASM BETWEEN TWO
IMPOSSIBLY DIFFERENT WORLDS?

e thought there were no surprises left in the world ... but
e sudden appearance of young Amish widow Susan Peachey
as astonishing—and just the shock cynical Alan Wilde needed.
e was a woman from another time, innocent, yet wise in
ays he scarcely understood.

resistibly, Susan and Alan were drawn together to explore
eir wildly exotic differences. And soon they would discover
mething far greater—a rich emotional bond that transcended
th of their worlds and linked them heart-to-heart ... until
eir need for each other became so overwhelming that there
as no turning back. But would Susan have to sacrifice all she
erished for the uncertain joy of their forbidden love?

ook for full details on how to win an authentic Amish quilt
splaying the traditional 'Sunshine and Shadow' pattern in
pies of SUNSHINE AND SHADOW or on displays at partici-
ating stores. No purchase necessary. Void where prohibited
law. Sweepstakes ends December 15, 1986."

ook for SUNSHINE AND SHADOW in your bookstore or use
is coupon for ordering:

Heirs to a great dynasty, the Delaney brothers were united by blood, united by devotion to their rugged land . . . and known far and wide as

THE SHAMROCK TRINITY

Bantam's bestselling LOVESWEPT romance line built its reputation on quality and innovation. Now, a remarkable and uniqu event in romance publishing comes from the same source: TH SHAMROCK TRINITY, three daringly original novels written three of the most successful women's romance writers today. K Hooper, Iris Johansen, and Fayrene Preston have created a tr of books that are dynamite love stories bursting with stron fascinating male and female characters, deeply sensual love scene the humor for which LOVESWEPT is famous, and a delicious fresh approach to romance writing.

THE SHAMROCK TRINITY—Burke, York, an Rafe: Powerful men . . . rakes and charmers . . they needed only love to make their lives complet

RAFE, THE MAVERICK by Kay Hooper

Rafe Delaney was a heartbreaker whose ebony eyes held laughin devils and whose lilting voice could charm any lady—or a horse—until a stallion named Diablo left him in the dust. It too Maggie O'Riley to work her magic on the impossible horse . and on his bold owner. Maggie's grace and strength made Ra yearn to share the raw beauty of his land with her, to teach h the exquisite pleasure of yielding to the heat inside her. Magg was stirred by Rafe's passion, but would his reputation and h ambition keep their kindred spirits apart?

LOVESWEPT

YORK, THE RENEGADE by Iris Johansen

Some men were made to fight dragons, Sierra Smith thought when she first met York Delaney. The rebel brother had roamed the world for years before calling the rough mining town of Hell's Bluff home. Now, the spirited young woman who'd penetrated this renegade's paradise had awakened a savage and tender possessiveness in York: something he never expected to find in himself. Sierra had known loneliness and isolation too—enough to realize that York's restlessness had only to do with finding a place to belong. Could she convince him that love was such a place, that the refuge he'd always sought was in her arms?

BURKE, THE KINGPIN by Fayrene Preston

Cara Winston appeared as a fantasy, racing on horseback to catch the day's last light—her silver hair glistening, her dress the color of the Arizona sunset . . . and Burke Delaney wanted her. She was on his horse, on his land: she would have to belong to him too. But Cara was quicksilver, impossible to hold, a wild creature whose scent was midnight flowers and sweet grass. Burke had always taken what he wanted, by willing it or fighting for it; Cara cherished her freedom and refused to believe his love would last. Could he make her see he'd captured her to have and hold forever?

THE SHAMROCK TRINITY

On sale October 15, 1986
wherever Bantam LOVESWEPT Romances are sold

Only in a lost world could she discover passion's true treasures . . .

Fiery Obsession

by Lynne Blackman

Innocent and lovely Sloan Hyland's dreams of sensual passion—and fears that they will never come true—are all she knows . . . until her uncle Dean, a powerful New York art dealer, takes her with him on a feverish journey in search of a priceless artifact. Deep in the steamy Mexican jungle, Sloan meets Dominick, the daring, enigmatic leader of the expedition . . . the keeper of Sloan's dreams and captor of her unspoken desires. As the promise of golden riches lures them ever deeper into the exotic, shadowy paradise, Sloan's mind and body are overwhelmed by a secret, heated obsession—a fiery dream that will explode into reality on sacred tribal grounds, where rituals of love and the mysteries of the ancients flourish as if time did not exist.

Fiery Obsession

Look for it at your bookstore or use this coupon for ordering:

Heiress to one of the world's great fortunes, a temptation no man could resist— she was drawn into a lush and frenzied world of grandeur . . .

MIRELLA: intelligent, passionate, and voluptuous. She seeks the ultimate in pleasure and lasting love.

RASHID: playboy, hedonist, master of eroticism. Behind his suave charm lies the threat of betrayal.

ADAM: dedicated archeologist, a man of vast sensual power. From his marble palace in exotic Istanbul he dreams of taking Mirella in the

Soft Warm Rain

As they explore the limits of luxury and pleasure, they will experience delights beyond their wildest fantasies. And before their bodies are sated, they will lose their hearts.

Look for it at your bookstore or use this coupon for ordering: